Cry Of The Whippoorwill

Fred J. Bognar

ISBN: 0615898149
ISBN-13: 9780615898148

Dedication

This amazing work of art is dedicated to our Aunt Mary in memory of her beloved husband, our dear Uncle Fifi. Her pure spirit, spunkiness, and generous heart are the reasons this work was created so many years ago. This book, as a culmination of her love and support to her late husband, is a testament to the humor and kindness with which she and Uncle Fifi lived. We hope it serves as a reminder to her of how much they are both loved.

Acknowledgments

When I inherited this book, it was in its most raw form—loose pages in a stack, created on an antique typewriter. When I read the original manuscript, I was surprised at how inspired I was by the story, the writing, and the characters. It was entertaining, heartwarming, and an all-around page-turner, and I felt an overwhelming pull to do something with it.

Because Aunt Mary loved and supported my Uncle Fifi so dearly, and because his life and passions were so monumental to my life, I was inspired to find a way to finish this manuscript and have it published for her, giving her the gift of this story as close to its original form as possible. But, seeing as how I'm not particularly fond of writing epic narrative stories, I sought the professional guidance of Round Table Companies. The support I've received, from start to finish, enabled me to see the best version of my Uncle Fifi's legacy between these pages. As such, I'd like to thank Katie Gutierrez, the executive editor for this project, for her overseeing of the book at every stage, and I would also like to thank Lizzie Vance, whose eyes touched every last page of this book several times in an effort to make it shine. Lizzie also helped write the ending of the book, and I imagine it turns out just as Uncle Fifi would have wanted it to.

I'd like to thank my mom, as well, for the time she's spent reading and re-reading this book (and for the effort of keeping this gift a surprise!). Both, my mom and husband have been unending reserves of support for me during this process, and I could not have done it without you.

Most importantly, I would like to acknowledge my dear Aunt Mary. Thank you for your love, laughter, kindness, excitement, and passion for life, and for the way you stood by and adored Uncle Fifi throughout your entire lives together. You are an inspiration to me in so many ways. I love you dearly, and I hope you enjoy receiving this book as much as I've enjoyed giving it.

With all my love,

Heather

I

The sun sank slowly into the West, casting shadows along the Big Horn River like no painter's brush could describe. The high mountain peaks, the green of the forest, the tall pines, all in contrast with the colorful skies created by the setting sun. A herd of buffalo edged their way toward the cool waters of the river. Thirsty, tired, perhaps hungry, and how well they knew, the ever hunted.

With the coming of nightfall, many other creatures in the wilds would soon appear along the waters' edge to quench their thirst, some on the prowl for food during the course of the night and others soon to retreat. A squirrel came out of a hole high up in one of the tall pines and was about to scamper down when suddenly it dove back in. It appeared at the entrance again for another look, this time making no attempt to come down but instead kept staring at a solitary figure lying on the ground nearly concealed by the heavy branches of the tree.

He appeared to be in his early thirties. A pleasing face to look at, tanned by the sun and hardened by the winds. One that could manage an easy grin or a smile, and if the occasion should arise, an expressionless face, casting off a cold stare that had many a men hoping to talk their way over to the bar for a fast drink. His buck-skin attire, including moccasins, a six shooter in a case strapped to his right side and a knife strapped to his left, placed him in the category of an Indian scout. At the moment, his mission was far from his mind as he gazed out over the gorgeous valley from beneath the pine boughs. His thoughts were of a cabin, a wife, and maybe children; for this surely was the ideal spot.

Even Lance Winsor was entitled to a dream once in a while, he said to himself with a sigh, and suddenly his grin vanished as the far-away cry of the whippoorwill echoed faintly in his ears. He listened to it again. His many years on the frontier had given him vast knowledge through the many experiences he had encountered. One of them being sounds created by the wild creatures and duplicated by humans at various times for whatever purpose. To Lance that cry was not the original; it could mean but one thing— Indians— far out in advance, scouting for the tribe using the bird call to elude detection. There is no question about it. The Indians are following the river and heading west. *Are they really giving up to the great white father's demands or will they go in just so far, merge all the tribes and make a stand against the on rushing progress of the white man's nation?* Lance wondered but briefly, for he well knew the code of the red man.

Cautiously he shifted his position so that he could observe more keenly and at the same time froze as three braves on horseback appeared at the bend of the river. They rode on, slowly glancing about for signs that may give away the presence of an intruder, anyone that may have been in the vicinity recently. Suddenly, it occurred to Lance that the scouting being done by the braves was a bit too out in the open and his thoughts concerning the matter were soon cut short by a sharp crow call three times in succession about a hundred yards distant.

Lance summed up the situation: there was no time to waste now, and scouts were along the river bank; then again, scouts were also higher up along the right and left wings of the river. Trapped, he shuddered at the thought, but then again there were many tight spots before. Steeling a glance toward the river he noticed that the three riders had stopped. Could the change in birdcalls mean that he has been detected, or perhaps be a signal for something else? There was only one thing to do now: lay still and wait.

He was swiftly planning an escape should a chance prevail. His hand slid toward his gun, loosening it slightly while his other hand took a tight grip around the handle of the ten-inch blade. A twig snapped. The noise of the breaking branch making his heart skip a few beats. The tempo of breathing kept pace with the pounding of the pulse. The noise was close, but he could see no one. If only he knew how many there were. Another twig napped. His eyes strained but still no one. Blades of grass and weeds bent under heavy knees. Small branches and bushes shook slightly, by no means made by the soothing touch of the south wind.

It came as no surprise, Lance summed up the occurrence. Two. He could see now the movement of the brush and placed the number of invaders at two. Crawling on hands and knees toward his hideout meant but one thing, his presence was known. He wondered just where he could have made a slip. Covering his tracks with the greatest of skill and yet, here they were, the red devils.

He was ready, come what may. Two to one, at the moment, was not bad odds. Lance got up on his knees and was about to get into position to throw his knife at the first red skin within distance and use the gun on the other when all of a sudden a bloodcurdling scream in back of him changed all plans. He whipped around in time to take the full impact of a snarling savage who pounced down upon him welding a razor edge tomahawk that near missed Lance's ear taking along some of the skin and imbedding its self deep in the back of the tall pine tree. They were both fast getting on their feet. The death struggle was short; the savage tripped, falling into a clump of bushes with Lance on top. To brace himself for the shock due to the fall, Lance eased up on the knife hand which he very quickly took advantage of and thrust the blade through the Indian's neck. At the same instant another tomahawk failed to find its mark as it flew by the head of the Indian fighter. Lance spun around and tugged franticly for his gun to blast the other tomahawk thrower but to his amazement the savage let out a death cry, his face wrinkled in pain, staggered forward a few yards, he fell on his face. Embedded deep in the small of his back was a knife.

Puzzled by the turn of events, Lance cautiously got up trying to spot the third member of the party and he did, his eyes falling upon a pair of feet protruding out from behind a boulder. Taking a closer look he noticed a gaping hole in the neck. Another one for the happy hunting grounds. That there was someone else around was obvious. Lance looked around wildly and was about to call out when he was cut short by a voice that said, "It's safer to hunt buffalo, fella."

Appearing from behind a clump of bushes was a buckskin-clad figure, lean, about five feet ten, a few inches shorter than Lance and perhaps a few years younger. Indian scout like himself, but the many he had come in contact with were never more welcome than the one now coming toward him with an amusing grin. "Blade Turley is the name, came out some time ago from Penna." He offered his hand after switching a bloodstained knife he held from right to left. Lance, still bewildered by the fast shuffle that took place within the last few minutes, finally managed a smile and grasped the outstretched hand. Filled with gratitude and relief, he shook it warmly and said, "Winsor. Lance Winsor is mine."

Before another word was uttered, a screaming arrow whizzed by, taking along the tail of a raccoon cap that hung off the belt of Blade Turley.

Both men dove for cover. Lance cursed under his breath for not being more cautious; he knew there were more of them down in the valley, and yet his thoughts ended there as Turley whispered, "Make your way up to that heavy oak and attract his attention and I'll try to get him from behind that boulder." And with a half smile he added, "After all, it was my tail that he parted from my raccoon cap. By the way, if there should be more than one, cut in on the party." With that last bit of humor, he edged his way slowly toward the rock.

Lance, crawling cautiously, was about halfway up to his post when another arrow tore in to the brush just above him. He stopped moving and hugged the ground ever so close. A minute passed, two, five. He decided on his next move. Spring up fast and dive behind the fallen tree not more than five feet away. A chance he had to take, he couldn't just lay there. Slowly he began to brace himself, every muscle in his body tense. With every slight move he expected an arrow to come crashing at him. Just a little higher and then, he froze, listening. He heard footsteps treading softly over the dry leaves and twigs. They grew fainter. Then it ceased completely. Lance relaxed but for a moment. Turley's voice cut the rest short. "Winsor, let's breeze out of here."

Lance suddenly came to life. He got up on his feet and dashed over towards Turley, who now was on top of the boulder trying to spot the Indian who was headed toward the river. "A few more yards and I would have had him," said Turley, "but as he kept edging his way up, he spotted one of the dead braves and took off like a half crazed fox out of a brier patch."

"There are more of them down in the valley," said Lance. "I caught sight of them just before we got jumped on up here. They were scouting the valley pretty tight and it sure looks to me like they wanted no strangers around. There's something beside buffalo meat cooking in the pot."

"You know," cut in Turley, "if it wasn't for me, they probably would have missed you. They were much farther down but came up to this level after getting a glimpse of me. I came upon a horse tied to a tree up over the ridge and decided to have a look, and ran into the pair. They gave chase and I headed in this direction climbing toward the top at the same time. When that Indian jumped you I turned and took a fast look back and at the same instant saw the other two swiftly get up on their feet and head in that direction. While you fought to keep your scalp from being hung up on some braves display belt, I caught a glimpse of you and dashed down to join the knife throwing contest."

"I don't know where that third brave came from," said Lance. "Near got me, but I'm sure glad that you are the curious type. Thanks for the help. I see now why they call you Blade."

Turley grinned, and at the same time walked over to one of the dead braves and yanked out the knife. Wiping it off on a clump of moss, he slid it back into the sheath of which he carried two, plus a long barreled six-gun. Facing Lance he asked, "What's the next move Winsor? I've got a little time to kill; if it's all right with you I'll tag along."

"You've just talked yourself into a sleepless night and maybe more trouble," said Lance. "I have yet to find out a few things I was sent out here to get. After dark I'm going down in to the valley and do a bit of scouting. Right now lets take care of the horses."

The sun sank slowly into the west. The evening shadows crept over their paths as they climbed toward the top of the ridge. The mystifying silence of the great forest aided Lance in his thoughts concerning the strange events that took place within the past hour. He saw nothing of the main tribes that were supposed to cross the river and penetrate deep within the Big Horn country.

The U.S. government and the Sioux nations, under a new treaty, agreed to the terms. The government was in need of the territory that was to have been vacated by the Sioux. In order to maintain peace and prevention of interference of the nation's progress, the tribes were to go into the new territory where they wouldn't be hampered by the young but progressive nation.

The last thought drew a sigh. Lance went back to the earlier days when the white man first came into the country. There were wars, massacres, and treaties then, too. As the white man progressed inland, the Indian was pushed further west. The red man became tired, discontented and his hatred for the whites grew. They battled every inch of the way. Lance knew well that the Big Horn country was a temporary home for the tribes and as well an old story to the red man. Sooner or later there would be another advance, resentment, more battles. Massacres and ambushes in between. Lance thought about the valley again. Maybe he would quit scouting and settle down. The idea appealed to him, trapping and hunting, panning gold and who knew, perhaps a few head of cattle or a ranch. As he got to the top of the ridge he sat down, took out his tobacco and started to roll a cigarette.

Turley, who was still a few yards away, stopped and took another look down the mountainside. Observing nothing suspicious, he climbed to the top and sat down beside Lance, who offered him the bag of tobacco.

"Thanks, this sure ought to taste good. It's been quite a spell since I've tasted good tobacco; been smoking dried oak leaves of lately."

Turley rolled his, put it to his lips and lit it. He inhaled deeply, blew out the smoke slowly, and with a frown appearing on his face asked, "What brand might this be?"

"Dried maple leaf," said Lance and that drew a chuckle from the other.

"I should have known."

"Well, lets get over to the horses before it gets too dark," said Lance. "We'll have something to eat and settle down for a couple of hours before going down to the river."

"That suits me fine and you can tell me this situation. Haven't told me much of anything yet," said Turley.

"Didn't want to scare you off," said Lance in amusement.

Turley grinned but said nothing.

They stamped their cigarettes into the soft earth and went toward the horses. Suddenly they both stopped dead in their tracks, listening to the noise they heard. Like lightening, their three blades flashed from their sheaths and just as fast, the men were in a crouching position, ready for action. A big deer then startled the men as it tore through the brush where it was in hiding when they came upon it. Lance let out a little sigh. He turned around and was about to say something to Turley when he remarked, "Forward, Mr. Winsor, you've got protection" and laughed softly. Lance smiled and started off again but was still cautious of the two knives that Turley held ready for action. *Sure is a knife fighter that fellow,* he thought. *Wonder how many Indians met the business end of those blades*? His thoughts on the matter soon ended as the outline of the horses came into view. An hour later the men lay sprawled out in a well-concealed cove, chewing on dried beef and raw potatoes. Lance went over his earlier thoughts with Turley bringing him up to date with the present situation.

"Who are you working under," asked Turley?

"General Custard at Fort Laramie. I left there about a week ago."

"You have a Texas saddle on your horse if I remember correctly; been wondering what you are doing up here in Sioux country." Turley let out with a soft laugh and said, "I've been scouting for the military down at Fort Worth for the past few years and sudden like, I quit. Felt that I had enough of the frontier. Hankering to get over to St. Louie for a spell. They tell me that it is quite a town now, dance halls, beautiful girls and plenty of good old eastern whisky."

"You're sure headed in the wrong direction," cut in Lance. "How come you got off the trail?"

"Well, I've got a little personal business to attend to, that is if I'm lucky enough to get the chance, and it involves quite a bit of gold which could be used right well in Kansas City."

"Don't tell me that you are turning prospector," chuckled Lance. Before Turley could continue, both men bolted up as a screech owl let out with a weird scream that seemed to split the silence of the night into a million pieces.

The owl sensing the presence of others now flew off into the night. The horses, too, were startled by the nocturnal bird and shuffled about uneasily. Lance walked over and patted them on the mane. He talked to them gently while his eyes pierced the darkness suspiciously.

Turley broke the tension and Lance was well aware that the Pennsylvanian wore a broad grin as he offered a suggestion: "Your chance of living to a ripe old age is far greater in St. Louis than it is out here. Come on over and sit down. Maybe I could convince you to go along."

"Now I'll tell you something," said Lance, "your chances were a lot better getting to St. Louie from where you first started then it is going to be from here" and he continued amusingly, "I have a strong feeling that you are going to be my guest for a while. I hadn't noticed a pick and shovel that you might have brought up with you so I take it that you're not going to dig for the gold you mentioned. Tell me the rest of the story you started a while ago."

The conversation was amusing, drawing a few chuckles, a few smiles now and then. Not too often on the wild frontier will one have the opportunity to enjoy pleasant company and conversation. "Well," said Turley, "getting the loot won't be easy and I'm sure going to need a lot of luck."

"A little while back a Sioux chief and a small band of braves entered an Apache Village."

"What," exclaimed Lance? "Are you sure it was Sioux?"

"Positive," cut in Turley, "that a Sioux appeared in an Apache village seemed kind of odd to us too. The scout reporting the incident said that on questioning some of the tribe, he found out that the visiting chief was from up in the Big Horn country. Maybe you know him. It was Crazy Horse." Lance whipped around facing Turley and grabbed him by the arm. "I knew that would interest you," put in Turley.

"Did you find out why he was there?" Lance half shouted.

"Take it easy, Winsor, or we'll have visitors if there are any prowling around."

With that, Lance let go of Turley's arm, who in turn was giving it a massage after the vice-like grip, and settled back at the same time muttering to himself, "Crazy Horse in Apache Country, this will be bad news back at the fort."

"Want to hear the rest?"

"Sorry," said Lance apologetically. "That sort of shocked me, go on."

"He came down to invite the Apache chief to an all-out council that was going to be attended by the chiefs of major tribes, however, we were unable to learn where or when it was going to be held. During his short stay, Crazy Horse kept a vigilant eye on the chief's daughter. I guess she made his head spin, for he made an attempt to take her back with him as his squaw. The Sioux got quite a setback down there. He was told bluntly by the old chief that the meeting wasn't going to be attended by him nor did he have any desire to let his daughter go with him. With that the Sioux left the village. What took place next is still a bit hazy since we couldn't get all the details.

"Several weeks later the Apache chief, four of his braves, and his daughter were ambushed. The braves died on the spot, the chief badly wounded, and the girl was carried off. The chief was able to tell what happened when a search party found them but he died on the way back to the village. There were four in the ambushing party. Three of them were known to us at the fort as trappers but were suspected gun smugglers and the other, an Indian brave, who the old chief recognized as one of the party that visited the village with Crazy Horse. So, we gathered the facts and came to this conclusion. The Sioux chief on the way back North, ran into the trappers, who probably offered a deal on guns at the same time showing their colors. That these men could be bought at a price was a possibility. There is no question that the chief had revenge on his mind and grasped this opportunity to offer a fabulous·price in return for the Apache girl. The brave was left with the trappers to guide them up to the Big Horn if the venture was successful.

Well, it was shortly after the Apache villagers offered any man's weight in gold for the safe return of the girl."

At this, Lance whistled softly and said, "Turley, I sort of feel, that St. Louis has quite a wait, before you walk up main street dragging along your bag of gold, partner, you'd better off digging for the stuff with a pick and shovel."

"Yes, I know this isn't going to be easy, didn't plan on coming up this far but they had quite a start on me. Picked up their trail and first spotted them along the headwaters of the Arkansas River about three days later. I tried twice to cut in but they were much too alert to pounce on so then I decided to wait for another opportunity. As the days went by I began to grow impatient. There wasn't too much time left before they would reach their destination. On checking the roughly sketched map, that was given to me at the fort by one of the old timers, I observed that the source of the Big Horn river was only a short time away and decided to move in on their camp after nightfall.

"That night I crept up to their camp inch by inch, cautious as a mountain goat, before making a leap. Got within hearing distance and what I heard delayed my attack temporarily. One of the trappers asked the Indian how much farther they had to go. Two days to the river then one day up along the waters. During the short discussion I gathered that the party would make the trip to the river then would make camp. From there the Indian was to go alone to contact the chief and on their return, make the trade. I decided then to make my final attempt at the river because they would be down one man and my chances may be a little better. After traveling hard and with very little sleep, I figured that I was one full day ahead of them. They should be along the river here somewhere late tomorrow afternoon."

"Maybe things aren't going to turn out like you planned," said Lance. "I believe that the Indian lied when he told the trappers that there was one day to go after reaching the river. As you well know, there are other red skins here already and adding to your grief, they are Sioux."

"Yes, I know." replied Turley, "that is why I want to go along with you tonight." With a faraway look in his eyes he added, "Things don't look too good."

"Well, if there is a chance you can count on me for help," said Lance, "you helped me out of a rough spot."

Turley's eyes brightened. "Partner, I'll cut you in on the gold, two can spend more in St. Louie, and you will get to see the most beautiful Indian girl that ever roamed these parts."

The way Turley phrased that last remark drew a chuckle from Lance and he said amusingly, "Are you sure it's not the girl you are after for reasons other than the gold? After all, there are many white men with Indian wives. Tell me about her, I guess that you've seen her before."

"Seen her twice before at the village while patrolling with the military and I tell you again, some looker for an Indian girl and before you cut me short again," went on Turley, "it's roulette wheels and dance hall girls for me, plus the fact that I'm not the marrying kind."

"All right, all right," said Lance, "you've got me convinced. It's St. Louie for you." Lance, laughing softly, got to his feet. "Are you ready? It's about time we get going down to the river, maybe we can join the Indians for supper."

"I rather we didn't," put in Turley. "It would probably be our last." He walked over toward Lance, who drew up another notch in the belt that held firmly his knife and gun. "I'm ready, Captain. Lead the way."

Cautiously, they made their way down the side of the mountain. Every now and then they would stop to listen. With the exception of heavy breathing, the dead of night was silent. Nothing stirred! Nothing moved! Even the cool breeze that usually roamed the area had gone elsewhere to play. Lance wondered, as he moved slowly forward, where the main tribes were at the moment.

Back at the fort, Lance was assigned this area to check on the tribes' movements. It was in this vicinity that they were to cross the river and penetrate deep into the Big Horn country. But, till now, he came in contact with only a few members of the tribe. Stopping suddenly, he whispered over his shoulder to Turley, who was a short distance behind him. "I can see the river. Let's move on up to the bank. The other side of the river should be about the spot where I first saw the three braves on horseback."

The slow moving water gleamed, under the brilliant rays of the moonlight. Both men laid near the rivers edge, their eyes scanting the other side for any sign that may betray the presence of others. Turley dipped his hand into the cool water and brought it to his lips in the cup of his hand. Muttering to himself, he whispered, "Almost as good as eastern whiskey."

Lance cast a glance at Turley and grinned, saying, "If we ever get back to the fort, I'll see that you get your share of the stuff."

Turning, Lance was about to get on his feet, when a faint howling sound, that seemed to be coming from far up the river, reached his ears. "Did you hear that?" he asked Turley.

"Yea, sounds like a lobo wolf."

"Maybe, maybe not," said Lance, who now wore a serious expression.

"We've found nothing here, so a trip in that direction is the next move. Turley, you don't have to go along –"

Turley cut him short, "Don't say it. You bribed me with that whiskey you mentioned a little while back. To the wolves' den, Captain, you have company."

A slow smile crept up to a wide grin as Lance got to his feet once more and headed toward the unknown destination. They eased through the tall pines, silently, ever alert. Every once in a while, they would hear the howl, stop, listen, then go on. With each passing mile, it became louder, their piercing eyes observing nothing suspicious. Another hour went by, then another. Finally, Lance went over to a thicket and dropped down. Turley followed suit, remarking, "I was beginning to wonder whether or not you were trying to set an endurance record. That was quite a stretch."

"Curiosity, among other things, kept me pushing," replied Lance. "Have you noticed that for the past hour or so, the howling ceased?"

"Yea, I did. However, I don't think we passed the wolves den yet."

"No," said Lance, "but we should be close and have those knives ready just in case your wolves den turns out to be an Indian camp."

In a short time they were on their way again. Advancing about a half mile, Lance decided to wade through the river to the other side. He was about to tell Turley his change of approach, when suddenly, both men dropped to the ground, as a howl once more echoed through the valley. "That, my friend, is an Indian. He is guarding," said Turley. Another howl from a little farther above cut Lance short. They were tense and listening. Then everything went quiet again.

Lance broke the silence by whispering. "They're guarding a camp. Got to find out how big it is. If it's the main tribe that is supposed to move west, then our mission is completed here and we'll head back for a little shut eye."

"And if it isn't, what then?" asked Turley.

"Then I would say that it is a small band waiting for your prize, the Apache girl. In that case they got wind of it somehow. Let's move in a little closer and see if we can spot the camp."

They crawled along, hugging the ground. A hundred yards from where they began, Lance stopped moving. "What's the matter?" asked Turley.

"There's a campfire up ahead," replied Lance. "Let's move on in a little closer and have a look."

A few minutes later, they were on their knees, looking out over a clump of bushes. Near the fire sat eight braves and four chiefs. The chiefs were wearing full headdresses. The dying embers cast flickering shadows across their stone-like faces. One of the chiefs was doing the talking, slowly motioning with his hand every now and then. Lance spoke the dialect and strained his ears, but the chief talked in low tones which seemed to vanish with each new word he uttered.

Gazing in other directions, Lance noticed the outlines of many horses and tepees, and a general indication of mass movement. He put his hand on the Turley's shoulder, who was lost in thought, and said, "These are the main tribes, all right. Our business is done here. Let's ease out and head back to the cove."

Lance was about to move back but Turley's question stopped him momentarily.

"Which one of those was crazy horse?"

"I don't know," replied Lance. "We were too far away to . . . "

The whispering conversation suddenly ended. They could hear soft, slow footsteps and the crunching of dried leaves and twigs. The two scouts turned and pierced the darkness behind them. Outlines of a brave came into view, another, and then another. There was no time for plans and they didn't dare to move. Knives out in readiness, they just huddled there, waiting. The first brave turned and headed in another direction. Lance hoped the others would follow, but that thought was short lived. They didn't, and soon would be close enough to feel one anothers' breath. Like a flash, Lance threw his knife. It tore into the braves' stomach, who let out an agonizing yell. The quiet night suddenly came to life. Lance pounced upon the brave and retrieved his knife, at the same time drawing his gun and firing it point blank at a screaming savage, who fell dead across his lap. Another gun barked, and the outline of Turley appeared. Lance was up on his feet. "Turley, over here." Reinforcements were coming from camp. Arrows screamed past them in the darkness. "This way, keep close to me, let's go."

They crashed through the brush at full speed, a minute later through a small clearing and headed down toward the river. Pursued from the rear, Lance planned to swim across the river and informed Turley on the run. As they rushed out of the thicket and were about to slide down the bank into the water, they stopped abruptly.

Blazing arrows whizzed by, three canoe loads of savages following the hunted, added to their grief. Back into the woods they scampered. An arrow tore through Lances buckskin coat causing quite a tear. It dangled there for a moment. Conscious of the fact, he grabbed the weapon and snapped it in half, discarding the pieces as he rushed along. A few minutes later, Lance headed towards the mountain and started the climb.

Turley was never more than a few yards behind him. About halfway up, they stopped to gather their wits. Tired and breathing heavily, both braced themselves against a tree. "I think we left them behind a little," puffed Lance. Turley didn't say anything but nodded in agreement, panting twice as hard. "Look over there," Lance pointed a finger toward the moonlit river. They observed the outlines of the three canoes being paddled back up the stream.

"Giving up the chase, I hope," said Turley.

"Listen," cut in Lance. Their ears picked up that old familiar sound of moccasin feet on leaves. "They're coming this way, not much noise, could be only one of them. Now look," went on Lance, "you go on ahead about fifteen feet and conceal yourself behind one of those trees. If he's alone, I'll try to get him and muffle his outcry. Then we'll high tail it out of here before the others can find out what happened should there be any more around. If something goes wrong and we have to get away fast, head down toward the river."

Turley, crouching low, made his way over to a tall pine and ducked behind it. Lance stood behind another, ready, waiting. Not a sound, nothing moved, the silence was deadly. His friend's advance was noticed, this he assumed. Whoever it was coming toward them stopped, but not for long as the slight swishing of the branches indicated that the attempt forward was being continued. Lance stiffened slightly as he caught sight of the pursuer and frowned a bit when the other turned and headed in an upwardly direction. Hoping that the brave would walk away from them was short lived. Upon reaching a deer path, he turned again and continued the approach. Now it was up to Turley to do the job, for the latter was up at that level.

Lance turned slightly and stole a glance toward his friend in hiding. He strained his eyes but saw nothing. His head snapped back as he heard the low call of a night owl. That the nocturnal bird was being imitated by the Indian was an old story to the scouts. The brave had stopped and stood motionless about fifteen feet directly up above Lance who peered at him from behind the tree. The latter was planning his next move, and it had to be fast. Another low owl call. Those calls were signals to the others. Nothing worked out according to plan. Once again, no time to waste. He looked over his target, the outline was quite clear, in another instant his knife flashed in the moonlight as it sailed through the short clearing, and the third call died on the red skin's lips, as the blade sunk deep into his side.

Lance was already on his way to retrieve the knife at the same time alerting Turley. He pulled out the blade and jammed it into his sheath. Let's go.

They lost no time in getting away, once again pursued by the alerted braves. Down the mountainside, ripping, tearing in their haste to get away. Once along the riverbank, they stopped. "They're coming," said Lance, "but not too fast, must be confused. The water is a bit fast here but we'll make . . . "

That was as far as he got. A tomahawk swished through the air, bounced off of Turley's belt, taking along the rest of his raccoon cap. The impact spun him around and he fell to the ground. Lance whipped out his gun and fired at the charging brave, who toppled over Turley, falling over the bank and into the river.

"Turley, are you hit bad?"

"No, just stunned a little." He got to his feet with the other's aid. With his arm around the stunned man's shoulder, Lance half-dragged him as they started on the run again. The chase went on for about a half mile with the savages hot on their trail. Lance cut over to the water's edge.

"Quick, slide in." Up to their necks they went. They worked their way under a heavy thicket that grew out over the bank. One savage went by, then another. More coming up, looking here and there, searching. Minutes went by, and all commotion ceased.

Lance broke the silence with a whisper. "I'm getting careless of late, left the towels in my saddle bag." Before the other could make any reply, Lance hissed, "Hold it." Something was in the water up above. They could see the ripples, the moving braches.

"Could be an animal," whispered Turley. The other made no reply but kept staring toward the direction of the noise.

"Don't move--it's a curious Indian. When he parts the brush here and looks in, we'll give him a good drink of water," Lance whispered so softly that the other could barely make it out.

Cautiously, the intruder came nearer, slowly lifting the branches and looking under the heavy growth that hung out over the water. He kept an ugly looking knife above the water line as he half swam, half walked, toward sudden death. The ripples grew heavier. Slowly, two pairs of hands came to the surface of the water, ready to lunge out at the unwanted guest. The overhanging brush parted slightly. Lance struck out at the knife wielding hand, got a vice like grip around it and pulled the victim under the water with him. He felt the others' arm tighten around his neck, but only for a moment.

The brave's end came fast, as Turley's blade found its mark. Lance sucked in the air fast as he came to the surface but held on to the dead body. Approaching feet could be heard in the distance.

"The rest of them are on their way back," cautioned Lance. They waited silently, motionless. One by one they filed by, what was left of them. Finally they could hear them no more.

Lance let go of the dead man and made his way to the bank. Cautiously, he crawled to the top and extended his hand to Turley, who was now shivering a little.

"No towel, plus ice water for a bath. However, I will say this much for your hospitality, Winsor. You sure supply your guests with plenty of excitement."

"We'll not wait for any more," grinned Lance and added, "Good, let's get up to the cove for some rest and sleep."

"Lead the way, Captain," said Turley. "You've got company." A little over an hour elapsed before they neared their destination. The exact location of the cove was difficult to find, for the brilliance of the moon, which lit up the entire valley like day just a few hours before, was fast sinking over the horizon.

Lance stopped and threw himself on the ground where he stood, the other collapsed as if he was hit on the back of the head with the butt end of a gun. Panting hard, tired, they both laid there as if retiring from the night. The rest was brief, for not too far in the distance came the shuffling of horse hooves.

Lance slapped Turley on the shoulder and said, “Come on, we’re home.” A few moments later, they found their way over to the cove. The saddles and blankets were taken off the horses and placed in the shelter. Stripping to the waist, they spread out the wet shirts and coats and wrapped themselves in the blankets. Lance threw his off and started toward the animals.

“Where you going?” asked Turley.

“I’m going to take them back there a ways,” answered the other. “If anyone should run across them, we’ll have a chance to wake up before they come rapping on our door . . . with arrows.”

“Don’t you have anybody around here that’s neighborly?” asked Turley with a grin. Lance came back shortly, wrapped the blanket around him again and lay down, using the saddle for a pillow.

He started to say something about getting up early but stopped abruptly, for the other’s heavy breathing indicated the fact that he was well on his way to St. Louie, in his dreams. Moments later, nothing could be heard but the breathing of two tired men.

II

The early morning sun looked like a ball of fire, as it arose slowly over the mountaintops. The Big Horn country, in all of its glorious splendor, never looked more radiant than it did on this cool morning. Mother Nature's creatures of the wild went about their daily routine with the exception of at least one. A little chipmunk perched on a small pine tree gazed curiously down at the two sleeping figures that seemed at the moment to be completely without life.

A few hours later, a small herd of deer passed near the cove and suddenly put on a burst of speed, as one member of the sleeping two crawled out from underneath the harboring thicket. Lance snapped his head around in the direction of the noise but soon relaxed as he watched the deer disappear over a small ridge. He glanced back at his companion and noticed that the rumpus had no effect on arousing the latter. Reaching back to the saddlebag, Lance took out the small canteen, filled the cup of his hand with water and put it to his eyes. The next handful met Turley's face; he bolted up with the speed of a wild cat. Conscious of what was going on; he managed a grin and said, "Save the rest for coffee, I've got some beans in my saddle bag."

"This time, you be my guest." Lance laughed, as he proceeded to drag out his belongings.

The next hour found the men near ready to move out. Lance went for the horses and returned just as Turley finished shaving. Turley, stroking his chin and half muttering to himself, was noticed by the other who asked, "What's the matter? Forget how to shave?"

"No, just cursing the Indians and their tough hides. My blades are dull."

Once on their way, Lance waited for Turley to pull up along side and asked, "Should we be successful in this little venture, what are your plans?"

"Well," replied Turley, "I'll take the girl and head for Apache country, get my reward; need I mention where I'm going from there? Like I mentioned once before, wish you'd come along; there will be plenty of loot for the both of us.

"Won't be able to join you this trip," grinned Lance. "I've got plans for the future here in the Big Horn.

"You didn't tell me her name," put in Turley amusingly, as the other still wearing a smile, urged his horse on leading the way toward their destination.

About noon, they pulled to a halt near the banks of the river. Looking around in all directions, they observed nothing suspicious and then preceded down to water the horses.

"Good a time as any to fill the canteens," said Lance as he reached into the saddlebag. Upon turning, he laughed, as the other already had his out and was pouring the contents on his head. "You're quite a fellow for baths. Why don't you stop at Fort Laramie with me on the way back and we'll both have ourselves a good one."

"Not going to have much time, once I get the girl. But, I'll tell you what, in St. Louie we can both—"

"No can do," cut in Lance with a smile, and added, "You can't tempt me."

With that he turned, leading his horse up over the bank. The other followed suit.

Lance stopped and thought in silence for a moment, then asked Turley, "when you crossed over the mountains, you came into the valley by the way of Elk Pass, didn't you?"

"That's right," replied Turley, and he took out his map and showed it to Lance. "The trappers were going in that direction, so when I decided to go on ahead of them and wait for their arrival at the river, I headed straight for the pass."

"It would be wise to go down there and wait for them," suggested Lance. With a frown, he added, "don't think they are going to come up this far. That way we can tail them until they make camp. After the guide leaves to break the news of their arrival and the others settle down, we'll wait for the break, and then charge in.

"Sounds good to me," put in Turley. "Any time you're ready, Captain."

Lance smiled as he mounted his horse and asked amusingly, "When do I get promoted to general?"

"Just as soon as I go south with my prize," the other answered with a laugh.

Hours later, Lance pulled to a halt and pointed in an Easterly direction and said, "To the right of that ridge, is where the pass starts the down grade and comes out about a half mile from here. We'll go on a little closer and pick a spot, from where we can take in everything that goes on." The other nodded in agreement.

Mid-afternoon found the two scouts sitting with their backs against a tree and conversing about their adventures of the past. Every now and then they would steal glances in a backwardly direction.

"If I figured right," said Turley, changing the conversation, "they should be here any time now."

Lance got to his feet and looked out toward the pass, asking casually, "Wonder what the trappers were to get out of this deal?" Before the other could make any comment, Lance held his hand up and motioned for silence. He listened briefly, and then walked back to the tree.

"What'd you hear", asked Turley with a frown.

"Thought I heard a whippoorwill."

"Little early in the day for that bird to be chirping, isn't it?"

"We scouts, out of Fort Laramie, use that bird call for signaling," replied Lance. "Orders are relayed in that fashion at various times; I guess you used the same–" he didn't finish but half whispered instead, "listen."

This time the call was clear. The latter inhaled a lungful of air and returned the signal.

"A pretty good imitation if I must say so," put in Turley with a smile. The signaling went on at intervals.

A half hour later, both men were watching in the direction from which the last call came. They had not long to wait, for they spotted a solitary horseman slowly making his way through the dense forest.

Cautious, alert, ready for quick action, despite his years, and about fifty years old, one would judge. The heavy beard he wore blended in with the buckskin clothes. Knife and gun hung in his waist belt. The butt end of the rifle stuck out of its holster, the latter being attached to the forward end of the saddle. The weapons were nicked, worn, and long since lost the luster of the original color. A master and veteran Indian fighter, of the ole school. He pulled his horse to a halt, took out a piece of plug tobacco and bit into it, then hesitated, sitting there motionless, his piercing eyes never leaving the trail for a moment, and as another call from Lance, it drew the direct attention of the old veteran scout.

Satisfied completely that the call was indeed a familiar one, he finished biting off a piece of plug, put the remainder into one of the pickets and urged the horse forward. Over here, called out Lance, and stepped out from behind the tree. Turley walked over and stood beside his friend.

The oncoming scout flashed a big smile as he recognized Lance. "Wall, if it ain't the tender foot of the Big Horn. Knew it was you from the first time you answered ma call." Lance walked forward to greet his long time friend, and extending his hand in greeting, he said laughingly, "Is that why you came up like you were expecting to be ambushed by a band of Indians?" Then added, "I thought you were assigned to Cheyenne country permanently."

"Ain't got the hankerin' to stay put in one place too long, Winsor." Glancing at Turley, the newcomer added, "ain't seen him around afore."

"Oh, sorry," exclaimed Lance, as he laid his hand on the shoulder of the man in question. "This is Blade Turley. Blade, want you to meet an old friend and teacher of mine. Will Dawson."

Clasping hands, Turley said with a smile, "Right glad to meet up with a friend of Winsor's, Mr. Dawson."

"Wall now son," replied the other, "I'll recognize you as a friend just as soon as you forget about the Mr.," and laughed as he pulled a sack out of his saddle bag and threw it over to Lance saying, "Something to eat, fresh from the Fort, with the compliments of General Terry."

"Thanks," said Lance, and after a moments thought, asked seriously, "You didn't come by the way of the pass, did you?

"No, I didn't, followed the Oregon Trail for a spell, then headed north. Why did ya ask son?"

"We're expecting company," replied Lance. "Thought maybe you might have seen them on your way up."

"Nary a soul, who are—"

Lance cut him short and related the story from the beginning to end.

At the conclusion, the old scout ran his hand over the rough beard on his face and let out with a low whistle. "Wall now, I might join up with you two young'uns before going back to the Fort but for now, I have a bit of news for you Winsor."

"Was expecting something like that. Good or bad?" asked Lance.

"Could be both," replied Dawson. "I'm taking your place as head scout for General Custer." He paused briefly, waiting for a comment from Lance but got none, then continued. "You're going to be assigned to do the scouting also as an adviser to a newcomer to the Fort by the name of Captain Runter."

"What territory was assigned to the captain?" asked Lance, breaking his silence.

"Don't rightly know," replied the other, "kind of a secret I was told. How's it hit you son?"

"Don't mind at all," said Lance with a smile. "As long as it will be up in this territory; kind of like it around here."

"One more thing son, was told that if I found you, we whar to report back within a week if you found out what you came for or not."

"Well," said Lance, "we have a little time left and don't have to rush." He stopped talking and looked around for Turley who a short distance away was staring, more than anywhere else toward the pass. The latter turned, as the two men walked toward him and said, something's gone wrong, should have been here by now. "Only one thing to do," put in Lance. "Make ourselves home here and wait."

"Wall now, since we are about to wait around for a spell, how about digging in to that bag I brought along and see what we have for supper," suggested Dawson.

Once more the sun was on its way down. The late afternoon gave way to nightfall. Dawson lay on the soft moss fast asleep. Turley sat up against a tree with his legs crossed chewing on a piece birch twig, staring at nothing, lost in thought.

Lance stood a little distance away with his shoulder resting on one of the tall pines casually observing the foot of the pass. Turning, he walked toward Turley, saying "We'll have to stand watch tonight; I'll take the first when the time comes."

Turley nodded his head, then remarked, "Maybe they went up the river another way, sure should have seen some kind of sign by now."

The conversation awoke Dawson who sat up stretching and yawning like an old grizzly. "Nothing yet, I take it?"

"Not a sign," answered Lance. "We're going to change plans just in case we get a chance to attack after dark," he added. "Either way, we'll have to wait till they show up."

The evening shadows crept up slowly and disappeared with the passing of time. Once again, darkness covered the valley. Lance left his watch and walked over to the two sleeping men and aroused Turley.

"Want to take it over for a couple of hours?" he asked.

"Sure," replied the other. "And if anything breaks, I won't bother to knock. I'll arouse you fellows fast and furious like." With that he walked over to the lookout, at the same time taking out his tobacco sack and proceeded to roll himself a smoke. Several hours elapsed. Turley decided to continue the watch "can't sleep anyhow," he said to himself.

Suddenly he stiffened as the hoofs of a horse on solid rock attracted his attention. After reassuring himself that it wasn't his imagination, he quickly ran over and awakened the other two.

"There's a horse on the other side of the river making his way up stream, it may be the Indian." The three of them, crouching low, made their way to the riverbank. The moon wasn't up yet and it was difficult to see. Almost directly in front of them, the horse came out into a little clearing.

Lance whispered softly, "The horse has a rider." The horse and rider vanished into the dark forest again and the three scouts didn't utter a sound till the noise made by the animal died out completely.

Then Lance cut in sharply, "I'm pretty sure it was the Indian guide on his way to the camp. In that case the trappers and the girl should be somewhere between here and the pass. Now here's what we'll do; the animals we'll let stay right here, wade the river, once on the other side we'll spread out and work our way down. If and when they are spotted I'll give the signal to close in. Three calls of the whippoorwill will be it, any questions?"

"I'm ready," replied Turley, who was quite excited now.

"Suppose we don't surprise them and they give us a fight?" cut in Dawson.

"Well, whatever happens will have to be worked out from down there," answered Lance. "Let's go."

Lance led the way a short distance then cut sharply over to the water's edge. "Shouldn't be too deep here, let's give it a try." Lance slid in, the water reaching above his knees.

Turley made a comment as he went into the water. "I'm sure going to be plenty clean for my trip back to Texas, third bath in the past twenty-four hours."

"Wall now son, you're gonna have one more on me when we come back to get the horses," grinned Dawson as he spat a stream of tobacco into the water.

They reached the other side in short order and climbed out. The scouts were slow and cautious as they made their way toward the pass. Lance could see Turley's outline every now and then but failed to get a glimpse of Dawson who seemed to have vanished in the darkness of night. The men were about twenty-five yards apart.

Fifteen minutes later, Lance stopped short as he heard Turley call his name. It was more of a hiss than a whisper. Lance crept in toward the other and asked in a whisper, "What is it?"

Dawson just called, "Must be on to something, over this way." On nearing the old scout, the latter whispered, "Over there, a small fire, must be them."

"More than likely it is," said Lance and then gave fast instructions. "I'll go in from here. Turley, you circle around to the right, Dawson, you go to the left. Now remember, wait for my signal then close in fast. We've got to surprise them if we're going to take the girl without a fight. Let's go!"

Minutes later Lance crawled within a short distance of the camp and saw, for the first time, the trappers and the girl he heard so much about.

The trappers lay sprawled out near the fire discussing something but not clear enough for Lance to distinguish. Lance looked over toward the girl who sat with her back against a tree. She wasn't tied, a point in their favor he mused. She was pretty indeed, even from a distance. The shadows cast by the flickering flames played about her face. She looked tired as she gazed out into space. Still hoping for a chance to get away, thought Lance to himself. The lack of horses on the scene suddenly occurred to him. He wondered where they were but that thought was cut short as one of the trappers sprung up whipping out his gun and started to shoot wildly into the brush.

Turley was out in that direction somewhere, he unwillingly gave some sign of his presence, Lance figured. No time for planning now. He grabbed for his gun just as another exploded and the trapper who did the firing went down in a heap. The other two at the fire were up and dove in behind the trees. They were blasting away towards Turley. In the confusion the girl sprang up and was off like a deer running straight for Lance who waited for a moment then grabbed her by the feet. She went down with a thud, Lance charged out from behind a tree pinned her to the ground at the same time clasping his hand over her mouth.

The girl, startled by the turn of events, fought like a wild cat. They turned over and over in the brush but Lance held on. Guns were barking all over the place now, shattering the quiet of the night. To his left he could hear Dawson blazing away. Lance sensed the girl's body relax. He eased up on the tight grip he held on her. Suddenly she tore loose, twisted around and drove a knife toward Lance's chest. He lashed out with his hand deflecting the knife, which came down at an angle ripping through his clothes and cutting a long gash from the right of his chest to the upper part of his arm. Startled, Lance lost his senses for a moment. That was all the girl needed; she soon disappeared into the darkness.

Lance felt over the wound and noticed that it wasn't serious. Getting to his knees he whipped out his gun. The firing eased up quite a bit as the trappers were making their way deeper into the woods. Lance sized up the situation and decided to round up his two aids. He called out to Turley who responded quickly, "over here." Lance circled around and approached Turley who exclaimed, "Sure was worried about you fella, didn't get a glimpse of you since the shooting started.

Before Lance could make a reply, Dawson called out, "Where you at, Winsor?"

Lance answered back and Dawson came charging over. When he got to them Lance spoke swiftly; "They must be going for their horses, let's spread out once more and charge fast in the direction they went."

Lance got no farther with his plan as a muffled scream pierced the darkness, "it's the girl," half shouted Turley.

"Come on," cut in Lance and the three rushed toward the direction of the scream.

They didn't get far before the stomping of horse hoofs through the brush and trees reached their ears. They're circling around toward the river, let's cut through here and see if we can cut them off. They spread out a bit and rushed through the thicket. A moment later, Dawson blasted away at the horseman as they sped by directly in front of him. Shortly, Lance's gun barked as he got a glimpse of them. The trappers fired back madly at them but all was in vain for the trees and the heavy brush were the only ones to feel the impact of the straying bullets. Turley, who was at the extreme right, had the only chance to get in a clear shot but held his fire as the front horse had a double rider. Instead, he lunged at the rider's foot, held for a moment being dragged along for a few yards and then released his hold as the butt end of the gun crashed down upon his head. The riders vanished into the dead of the night.

Lance called out to Turley several times but got no answer. Going up the river a little ways, they found him stretched out along the bank. Lance quickly lit a match and noticed a trickle of blood on the side of Turley's head.

"It's not a bullet wound," he said to Dawson. Lance took off his coat, ripped a piece out of his shirt and wet the cloth in the water. He applied it to Turley's head, who, in turn, moaned softly. A short time later the trio sat on a fallen tree discussing the unsuccessful venture. "Well fellas," said Turley, as he put his hand to his bandaged head, "I sure messed it up bad. The shooting started when I tripped over a log."

"Wall now son," put in Dawson as he handed Turley his gun, which he found lying near by. "Sometimes things just don't work out and this was one of those times."

"It sure surprised me when the girl cut me up," cut in Lance. "Well any way it's something to remember her by."

"Since it was your knife Lance and she took it along, you can have one of mine," offered Turley.

"Thanks," said Lance.

"Well, if you fellows think that you can make it back to the horses, let's get started," suggested Lance, laughingly.

Dawson commented with a grin, "Afore we get there I think I'll be helping the both of you. But for now lead the way, Winsor."

Turley said as he slid off the log, "You've got company, Captain."

Lance turned to face the latter and said, "Sure thought I'd be general after this," and smiled as he laid his hand on the others shoulder. "However, there is still a chance for your gold and St. Louie,"

"Tell you about it tomorrow."

Dawson scratched his head as he followed the other two up the river. He muttered to himself saying, "Maybe I should put in for lieutenant," and spat out another stream of tobacco juice that hit a tree trunk with a splatter.

Lance slept little during the night. He was molding together a plan, a dangerous one, that fact he knew very well. In the morning they would pick up the trail of the trappers and the girl. If they came upon them, there would be another attempt to get the girl away from the trappers but Lance considered that possibility lightly. After last night's ambush, the trappers were sure to travel hard and fast until reaching their contact. That would mean a trip right into the heart of the Sioux Village. Once there, he would be the bearer of a message from the Fort. A friendly visit, most anything in the way of goodwill will do. Just in case the Sioux get any ideas about getting rough, he could tell them too that General Custer is not too far off on a routine patrol. At that point would be the only chance to try to locate the girl and plan a hasty exit. Then too, more information could be gathered as to their present attitude. Lance wondered why he was planning such a desperate attempt. Back to the Fort should be his next step. He answered that to himself. *Rescuing the girl was for Turley, of course.* Turley came a long ways and had little or no luck in achieving his purpose. Lance felt that he owed him another chance, but all his thoughts were merely being justified by using Turley as the reason. Something strange and mystifying came over Lance Winsor since he first laid eyes on the Indian girl. His mind wondered back to the trappers' camp where he first saw her sitting near the tree. She sat there like a sphinx staring out above the campfire. The beaded braid she wore around her head sparkled like diamonds in the sun. Her face was beautiful but with an expression of sadness. Far away from home, the long hard trip, Lance knew well the bitterness she felt. *No doubt about the girl hating the white man, especially now*, thought Lance as his mind wondered to the slash she made across his chest and arm. *After all, how was she to know that we meant her no harm,* he said to himself, justifying her actions. *Anyway, I'm doing what I can for Turley, why when I want to settle down out here there're girls back at the fort, now let me see just who would fit into the picture, Therese Della, and, ah yes, the sergeants daughter, right nice girl, who else now but that is as far as he got.*

"That's enough of this," he said half aloud, and turned over on his side pulling the blanket up over his shoulder. Discarding everything from his mind, Lance made an attempt to sleep but nevertheless, he allowed himself to visualize the face of the Indian girl. *Wonder what her name is,* he mused. And a little later he fell asleep with a smile on his face.

III

Early the next morning, Lance was relaying the plan while the three of them ate blueberries picked from the nearby bushes. After finishing he asked Turley, "What do you think, want to give it another try?"

"Well, I've got nothing to lose but my scalp and as close as I could figure you don't have much to gain by going up there, so I'll leave it entirely up to you. Say," exclaimed Turley before the other could make a reply, "you didn't change your mind about going to St. Louie did you?"

"No," answered Lance with a grin. "I'd like to help you get the girl; other than that, my business up there is but a social visit." The smile on Turley's face slowly disappeared as he put a handful of berries to his mouth and wondered just what the real reason was behind Lance's fantastic plan; but he pressed the issue no further.

"Always wanted to see this here Sitting Bull," spoke up Dawson. "Wonder if I should shave 'afore meetin' up with the chief."

"Now, wait a minute," cut in Lance with a grin. "Thought it would be better for you to come along a ways and then wait for us. Somebody should report the incident back at the fort, in case things don't turn out too well."

"Wall, maybe you're right son," replied Dawson. "But I ain't taking any orders from you till you become general, so like I heard Turley say last night, let's move along, you've got company, Capt'n."

Lance and Turley smiled broadly, the latter put his hand on the old scout's shoulder and said laughingly, "What is your real reason for coming along Dawson, got kin folk up in that territory?"

"Can't rightly say that I have a son," commented Dawson whose face saddened suddenly. "Married a Cheyenne and had a son, was quite sometime ago, both were kil't during a raid by a band of Shawnee."

"I'm sorry," apologized Turley. "Sometimes I say the wrong things."

Lance knew about Dawson's misfortune and felt sorry for the old scout, who, at the moment, saddled his horse in silence. *A wife and son is quite a loss to any man,* he mused. His thoughts went to Turley. *Suppose he doesn't get the girl. There would be no gold, no St. Louie. He, too, came a long ways and gone through a lot.* He wondered at the moment if complete failure would sadden his friend, and if so, to what extent.

Suddenly his mind wandered to the girl alone. Suppose everything failed again. He wanted to see her again, didn't he? Why was he planning this trip? *Don't try to cover the real reason, Winsor. Admit it, ever since that short meeting when you had your arm around her, felt her slim body, her hot breath on your face . . . something happened to you, Winsor, and now you want to tell her that you meant no harm, that you are just trying to help her get away so Turley can take her back home. Reasons, reasons, what is the real reason, Lance Winsor?* He answered that to himself: *just want to see her, that's all. Then I'll be satisfied. I'll rid myself of this feeling that's come over me.*

Turley and Dawson were both watching Winsor as he stood by his horse, motionless, staring out into space. Dawson cut the silence as he grinned at Turley and said, "That faraway look could mean but one thing: a woman. Is she pretty, Son?"

Lance snapped out of it as a slow smile crept over his face and answered. "She's pretty all right but I don't think she like me very well."

"Did the girl tell you that?" put in Turley amusingly.

"No, she didn't in so many words," answered Lance, and his thoughts flashed back to the long gash that was concealed by the heavy wool shirt he wore.

"Then you still have a chance," added Turley.

Lance mounted his horse and motioned to the others, "come on fellas, we're going visitin'."

They crossed the river and found the trail left by the trappers without any difficulty. Several hours later, Lance pulled to a halt, dismounted and proceeded to water his horse; the others followed suit. Lance frowned as he looked up stream and said, "It won't be long now before we reach the spot where the tribes were camped the other night. I would say that the trappers made their contact by now and made a hasty retreat to parts unknown."

"Wall," said Dawson as he slid out his rifle for inspection. "That means that we are going all the way up to Chief Sitting Bull's roost." Taking his eyes off the rifle momentarily he glanced at the younger scouts, asking, "How you young'uns fixed for ammo? I've got quite a bit here in my saddlebag. Just thought I'd mention it." He spat out some tobacco juice that hit the water with a splash, and added, in case we ain't welcome up there." He looked at Lance and commented with a grin: "Maybe the Sioux are more neighborly than the others."

"They sure are," answered Turley before Lance could make a reply. "Why, ever since I come up here they've been knocking on my back door with knives and arrows. All they wanted to borrow was my scalp."

Lance laughed as he mounted his horse and said, "let's go, fellows, before you change your mind." He advanced a few yards then jerked his mount to a halt as a knife sailed by him and sunk into a nearby tree. Before he could turn around, another sailed by and took its place near the first. As he turned around sharply, a slow smile appeared on his face. The other two sat on their horses and looked at him with an amusing grin. Turley then remarked, "Just to assure you that you've got a well trained rear guard, Captain." Lance turned and walked his horse to the tree, pulled out the knives, and handed them to their owners. Still smiling, he rubbed his horse and resumed the journey.

As time went by, they began to feel the heat of the sun. Every now and then one or the other would make a comment, sip some water from the canteen, mop the sweat off their brow, yet ever alert for signs that may give away the presence of the unknown. Finally they came upon the campsite that was used by the tribes a few days back. Looking around and finding no signs of life but the creatures of the wilds, Lance decided on the next move.

"We'll cross the river here and follow the trail left by the tribes." He snapped off a small limb from a birch tree, attached to the end of it a white piece of cloth he used for a handkerchief and tied the limb, in an upright position, to his saddle. This should help us from being attacked. Let's go. Lance's heart skipped a beat as he plunged his horse into the water, for his thoughts wandered back to the girl again. *Would she recognize me? Of course not*. But at least he hoped not. He didn't want her to betray them as the ones that broke in to the trappers camp the other night, for she was still unaware that they meant only to rescue her from what was to come. Lance tensed at the thought of the trappers being in the village. They could very well accuse them as the ambushers. Suddenly he pulled hard on the reigns and stopped the animal.

"What's the matter son," exclaimed Dawson as the other two pulled along side. Lance didn't have to answer for the sight directly in front of them cut short any comment. From the limbs of an oak tree hung two men. The feet were attached to the limbs with rope. Their hands were tied to stakes that were driven into the ground. Arrows protruded from their bodies and upon closer observation, they were dotted with knife-inflicted wounds. It was the trappers.

Lance broke the silence as he said, "Poor devils; little did they know that the reward was going to be . . . sudden death. Come on, let's cut them down." The blood soaked, scalpless victims were buried under rock piled graves.

After finishing the unpleasant task, Turley wiped the sweat off his face and said, "I've been wondering what the outcome of this deal was going to be! They should have known better than to come in here like this unless they didn't get a chance to carry out their plan, if they had one."

"The Apaches are just as bad," spoke up Lance. "If you take back the girl how do you expect to keep yourself from ending up like they did?"

"Well," answered Turley. "I planned on taking her to Fort Smith... they'll have to come up there to get her." Lance didn't answer but nodded in approval as he glanced over toward the old scout who sat on a boulder lost in deep thought.

Lance cut short the latter's thoughts by calling over to him and asked, "Tell us about it Dawson."

"Oh, ain't nothing. Just thinking that Injuns are Injuns. I seen this method of target practice used by the Shawnees." He motioned over to the stone graves of the unfortunate trappers.

Lance thought for a moment and then said, "From here on in, there is no turning back, if any of you fellows changed your mind."

"Are you going in?" cut in Turley.

"My flag of truce still ripples in the wind," said Lance in answer.

"The rear guard is ready," said Turley as he mounted his horse.

"They sure are," cut in Dawson as he bit off another hunk of tobacco. On his way to his horse he reached out with the plug and offered it to Turley. "This here stuff keeps your teeth clean," he said with a grin.

"No, thanks," said Turley with a smile. "I get my shirt front stained when I spit.

"Save some for Sitting Bull," said Lance amusingly. "We'll offer it as a peace token." The latter got up into the saddle and urged his horse forward.

Nothing disturbing occurred as time went by. They rode at a slow pace, watching, and waiting. They were expecting company as they drew closer to the not too far distant village, or at least Lance assumed that the tribes would settle down without penetrating too deep into the Big Horn. Late afternoon found the scouts entering a valley. Lance pulled to a halt and motioned his hand for silence. Except for the soft rustling of the leaves fluttering to and fro in the summer breeze, they heard nothing. "Awful quiet around here," said Lance. "No doubt we are getting close now; wouldn't surprise me that we've been spotted." He reached up and adjusted the truce flag. "Now remember, don't make any moves that may draw their fire. If they come in on us without using any of their weapons, we'll probably be relieved of ours and escorted on into the village. However, if they are going to be hostile, well, we'll have to make the best of it from there. Let's go."

Lance thought of the girl again. *If only I could make her understand that I want to help her, that is, if I get the chance to see her. Suppose she didn't want to leave!* Lance frowned at the thought, especially after her experience with the trappers. *They didn't dare treat her out of the way in fear that she would relate it to the chief,* he mused. Nevertheless, the girl was going to be hard to convince. *Time will tell,* he sighed, and he pictured her face in his mind. The girl vanished from his thoughts as he heard Dawson's voice from behind.

"Don't look around now, but we've got company. There are six braves on horseback following us." Lance didn't move his head but his eyes flashed as they moved from left to right. Deep among the trees he spotted more braves moving along with them.

"Lance," hissed Turley, "they're all over the place."

"I see them, just keep on riding and don't make any moves," replied Lance.

They rode on for several hundred yards and upon rounding a bend, Lance betrayed no emotion as he caught sight of about a dozen more waiting for their approach. "Keep riding," he ordered sharply.

As the trio neared the savage-looking band, one of them rode forward; apparently, he was a chief. He was young and strongly built and he wore a feather that protruded up over the top of his head. The war paint didn't help his savage-like appearance. Lance noticed the rifle the chief held in his hands with the barrel resting on the horse's shoulders. It was one of the best.

Lance put up his hand in greeting. The chief ignored the greeting and asked instead, "Where go white man?"

"I have message for Chief Sitting Bull," answered Lance, and wondered now if he would live long enough to deliver it to him. All the savages were bunched around the scouts now and looking them over with hatred in their eyes. One of them jerked the reigns roughly and rode over to the chief and half shouted something that mad Lance stiffen lightly, for he spoke and understood the Sioux dialect.

"They could only mean trouble and dead men don't make trouble," the brave told the chief.

"What's he saying?" asked Dawson under his breath.

"It's not in our favor," answered Lance as he kept a steady gaze on the chief and then left out a little sigh as the chief waved the brave aside.

"These men work for the great white father, it is not for us to decide." The chief raised his hand and pointed, saying gruffly, "go." The latter took the lead. The scouts and the rest of the band followed. Lance told the others what took place and now they were on their way to the village.

Dawson asked Lance as they rode along: "Is that Chief Crazy Horse?"

"No, it isn't," he replied. "Never saw this one before."

Several miles later, they came in sight of the village. The familiar sound of drumbeats could be heard in the distance. As the slow moving procession entered the outskirts of the camp, the scouts eyed each other but said nothing. They observed a huge fire. Savages danced around it yelling, working themselves into a maddening frenzy. Villagers stood by watching the intruders as they rode by. Some with hatred in their eyes, others just staring.

Dawson asked, from the corner of his mouth, "Wonder what the occasion is?"

"I don't know," answered Lance, whose lips hardly moved, "but I'm sure that it isn't a welcoming committee."

The chief put up his hand and motioned to stop, then said, "You come no more," and rode ahead.

"Keep your eyes open," Lance cautioned his friends. "We've got to find out where the girl is and make our move the very first chance we get."

"If she's here," added Turley.

Lance looked at Turley but hesitated to say anything as the chief came back and said gruffly, "come."

An uneasy feeling gripped the scouts as they rode by the fire and the screaming dancers. One of them broke away from the fire and came along side of the scouts, jumping like a mad man and shouting something that Lance couldn't understand. It was the weird looking medicine man of the tribe. He followed them a short ways then fell back as they approached a large tepee.

Once more the chief motioned for them to halt. He dismounted and went into the tepee.

"I think we are about to meet some of the big chiefs," said Lance. "Did you fellows comb your hair?"

"Wall' now, come to think about it I didn't even wash ma' face for the occasion," answered Dawson.

The conversation was cut short as five chiefs in full chief attire came out of the tepee and stood at the entrance with their arms folded.

Lance put up his hand in greeting and said, "I bring message to Chief Tatanka Yotanka, Sitting Bull, from General Custer."

Sitting Bull ignored Lance for a moment as he spoke to the young chief that brought them in. The latter came over and motioned the scouts off their horses and then led the animals away. Chief Crazy Horse's stare was anything but friendly and up to the moment he said nothing either. Turning his gaze back to Lance, Sitting Bull spoke, "General Custer...friend."

That was a lie indeed, Lance knew, as well as the one he was going to tell him now. "General say that his heart is light if Chief and his people are happy in new home. Custer say, great white nation wants peace with the Sioux nations."

The chief commented emphasizing his words, "White man - leave Sioux alone, no war."

Lance was about to ask if they could stay for the night but he had a feeling that the Indians would see that their visit was permanent. It was too obvious that the chief conversed coldly and without feeling. Crazy Horse whispered something to Sitting Bull and the latter faced the scouts and said, "wait" then reentered the tepee with the others following.

"Looks like they went in for a powwow," said Turley, who spoke for the first time since they entered the camp. "We're not going to finish what we came here for if they ask us to leave now."

"They're not going to ask us to leave," answered Lance. "More than likely they are deciding our fate. If it looks bad, I'm going to tell them that Custer is on patrol not too far from here. Hold it, here they come."

The chiefs filed out and faced the scouts once more. Lance wondered why the two chiefs showed no recognition although he had met them on several occasions before.

Speaking for the first time, Crazy Horse asked Lance "Where Custer now?"

"He and the regiment are waiting for our return," lied Lance, then added, "They are camped along the river." Crazy Horse looked over to Sitting Bull and the two of them exchanged glances. Lance knew what they would do now, send scouts out to the river and find whether or not he was telling the truth. That would involve a little time and that is exactly what he needed.

Sitting Bull spoke now as he pointed to the chief that met the scouts out in the valley, and said, "White Cloud, take wife, tomorrow."

Lance gave Turley a puzzling look as the chief ordered, rather than asked, "You. Stay."

The latter gave orders to White Cloud, who in turn motioned to the scouts and said, "Come." He led them to a large tepee, which was lofcated in the heart of the camp and motioned for them to go inside, then departed.

Lance spoke to Turley and asked, "Are you sure it was Crazy Horse who came down to the Apache Village? I believe it was White Cloud. He's the one that is to be married tomorrow."

"Can't say for sure," answered Turley, scratching his head. "But like I told you before, that's what we were told down there."

"Probably sent there by Crazy Horse, but it makes no difference who went down to the inviting," put in Lance, whose face now held a serious impression.

"Something is cooking besides deer meat for the wedding feast. What do you make of it all, Lance?" asked Dawson.

"They have no intention of letting us go," replied Lance, adding, "and I'm pretty sure that by tomorrow morning they'll know that Custer is nowhere near the river. If we're still here, more meat will be added to the pot, and that, gentlemen, will be us."

"We'll have to make a run for it tonight, with or without the girl," said Turley as he peered out through the opening of the tepee. Lance's pulse quickened at the thought of leaving the girl behind. It was because of her that he decided to come into this rattlesnake den. He's got to find out where she is somehow. A knife appeared in his hand as he walked over to the back of the tepee and began to cut small slits in the skin. "Whatcha doing?" asked Dawson curiously.

"We'll keep watching through these slits for any sign of the girl. If we can locate her, then our plans for an escape can be made." They observed the tribes' people milling about the camp. Lance spotted many horses at the far end of the village and fixed the location in his mind. An hour passed, yet no sign of the girl that they so anxiously awaited to appear.

Suddenly, Lance whispered quietly. "Someone is coming," and they waited for the intruder to appear. A brave pushed aside the flap and entered. He pointed to the side arms that the men wore and he went through the motions of disarming. Lance glanced at the other two and said, "Guess he wants us to take these off."

Reluctantly, they unbuckled their belts and laid them on the blanket that covered the floor of the tepee. The brave then motioned for them to follow.

"This boy ain't so smart," said Dawson, as he felt the handle of his knife that was covered by his coat.

"Maybe they want us to carve the meat," put in Lance.

"I would sure like to sink my teeth into some," commented Turley.

The fire burned brightly in the semi-darkness as they were being led toward it. The smell of roasted game reached their nostrils as it was being prepared. Seated around the burning embers were the chiefs, some women, and a handful of braves.

"Having quite a feast," said Dawson. "Right nice of them to invite us." And he spit out the mouthful of tobacco he was chewing.

As they neared the fire, Turley dug his fingers into Lance's arm. "Look over to the right; it's her." Lance's eyes flashed as he spotted her, and he let out a little sigh.

He quickly cautioned his friends. "Pay no attention to her whatsoever. We don't want to let them know that we've seen her before. They probably know about that ambush and suspect us."

He said no more as they made their approach and upon hearing them, Sitting Bull turned and motioned for them to be seated. Lance sat next to the chief, then Turley and Dawson next to the latter.

"Eat," spoke the chief. He reached over to a big wooded tray and picked out a well-roasted pheasant, which he handed to Lance. The latter tore off a leg and handed the rest to Turley and Dawson. Lance couldn't resist a glance at the girl. In order to avoid a direct look, he said to the chief, you have many things to eat, and swept his hand in a semi arc toward the food at the same time accomplishing his purpose. The other nodded with an affirmative grunt.

Indeed she was beautiful, Lance thought once again as his heart began to beat a little faster. For one that was to be married soon she certainly had a sad face. *Not her idea,* he mused. He wondered what she was thinking about.

Lance felt his pulse beat madly as he visualized an escape with her, safe and sound, away from the Sioux. *Then what Winsor*? Why did he keep thinking of that? Why? Why? *If they get out of here, Turley will take her home, and that's that. Is it Winsor?* His conscience kept taunting him with questions. *Is that why you took this desperate chance? To save her for Turley, so that he could get the gold, so that he could go to St. Louie. That's the way it was planned, there is nothing else!* he shouted over and over again deep within himself. *Or is it because you are in love for the first time in your life, Winsor, it's true, isn't it? Well, isn't it? No, No,* he argued, shouting within himself again. *Just can't be, I don't even know this girl. All Right Winsor, have it your way, perhaps you're right,* kept taunting the voice deep down inside of him. *But, I want to be on hand when you shake hands with Turley and say good-bye to the girl you risked everything for. Then you can settle down in the Big Horn like you always wanted to, all by your little self and eat your heart out, 'til you rot.* Lance was mad, the color drained from his face. He turned sharply and faced Turley.

The latter looked up at him as he sensed rather than saw the other's quick turn and asked questioningly, "Something the matter?"

Lance recomposed himself quickly and a slow smile appeared on his face as he remarked, "No, nothing's wrong, just wondering if you boys were enjoying your supper."

"Good food," answered Turley, without any mirth. He was still bewildered by the look on Lance's face. He discarded the issue from his mind as he listed to Sitting Bull conversing with Lance.

The chief asked questions concerning Custer's forces, the Fort, and looked directly at Lance when he asked if the latter saw anyone during his trip to the village. Lance betrayed no mention as he answered with a lie, "No." Crazy Horse said nothing, just stared into space. Lance's heart skipped a beat as he chanced another look toward the girl. She held a fixed gaze on him. His face reddened slightly as he reluctantly cast his eyes downward. He tensed slightly as the thought of recognition entered his mind again.

Was it possible that she knew that he was one of the ambushers? It was dark then. The shuffle was fast. Of course there was a fire but she hardly had a chance to get a look at him. Suddenly he froze. A cold sweat broke out on his forehead. For the first time he realized what she must have noticed. The knife slash that had cut open his coat that night was quite obvious. Would she betray them? He had no answer that would enlighten the dark moment. Lance informed Turley concerning the matter as he handed the latter some tobacco in pretense of offering him a smoke. They knew that at any moment the lid could blow off the pot and hasten their departure to the happy hunting grounds, if she chose to speak.

Any shabby excuse would be enough for these savages to do away with them. They were waiting for one anyway; such as the lie about Custer being camped along the river. Then they would know that their mission here was other than peaceful. Lance shuddered at the thought. If only she kept silent. His gaze fell upon the features of White Cloud who, at the moment, was engaged in conversation with Crazy Horse. They were both ruthless looking foes, he mused.

Suddenly, the two chiefs were on their feet. One of them motioned to where the women were seated and an elderly squaw who was seated next to the Apache girl arose and followed the chiefs to a spot far enough away to be out of hearing distance.

Turley stunned Lance as he whispered through the corner of his mouth, "I saw that squaw make some kind of sign a few minutes before when White Cloud glanced in her direction." The blood drained from their faces as they watched the squaw put her hand near the upper part of her shoulder. She was referring to the slash on Lance's coat, which indeed was obvious. Lance looked at the girl now with an expressionless face and she returned his gaze in defiance. Lance let his eyes fall downward again as he heard Turley swear under his breath, sure looks like our luck ran out.

Lance seemed to ignore that remark as he said, with a deep frown appearing on his forehead, "I don't think that she likes the Sioux very much, but she sure hates the white man. Fellows, I think she's given us away."

Dawson, who hadn't said much since he sat down to eat, remarked casually, "Ain't much we kin do right now; he stopped talking as he noticed the Indians coming back and then said in a quick low voice, "They're coming back."

The three scouts hastily relived their lives in the next few moments but were jarred out of their thoughts as the gruff voice of Crazy Horse split the dead silence. "You!" he half shouted.

Lance turned slowly around and looked up at him, then got to his feet, the other two following suit. Sitting Bull and the chiefs that were sitting with him were now up, and upon being told of the new developments, turned and faced the scouts. With his arms folded, he just stared at them apparently waiting for Crazy Horse to do the talking. The latter put his fingers through the knife slit of Lance's coat, took a firm grip on it and pulled with force downward ripping a large piece all the way to the bottom seam where it hung loosely, near touching the ground.

Lance's face reddened. He had the urge to drive his knife through the chief's heart, which was still concealed underneath the left side of the chief's coat; but Lance just stood there, eyeing the chief coldly.

"Knife put hole in coat. Where?" demanded Crazy Horse. Turley and Dawson looked at their friend and waited anxiously for him to say something that might ease the tension a bit.

Lance answered. "I had a fight with a soldier, back at the fort."

"White man lie," cut in White Cloud, as he pointed an accusing finger at Lance. He then turned slightly and pointed at the girl who still was at the other side of the fire standing near the old squaw. "Girl make hole with knife. You want girl. Why?"

Lance shifted his eyes in her direction and answered, "Never saw her before. I came here only to bring the message," lied Lance again. Whatever the latter said had no effect on the chiefs; they ignored him completely.

"You kill man braves, on river," cut in Crazy Horse angrily. "Now, you die." He issued swift orders. A dozen braves grabbed the scouts roughly and half dragged the reluctant men toward a group of trees. Their hands and feet were tied with rawhide and lashed around the trees. The medicine man began his wild dance around the fire again. Others were gathering dried limbs and leaves, placing them around the feet of the tied men. The camp was in a general uproar as some joined the dancers while others milled around to watch the beginning of the end of their white enemies.

Every now and then a dancing brave would break out of the circle and shoot an arrow at the helpless victims; another would throw a tomahawk. They came dangerously close. They were being tortured, before the final blow: they were to be burned at the stake.

IV

"Do you think that they will go through with it," asked Turley as he barely moved his lips.

"It certainly don't look good," answered Lance who had his eyes on Sitting Bull.

It seemed to Lance that the latter was arguing with Crazy Horse and White Cloud rather than just conversing.

"Looks like the meat I ate is going to be roasted twice," said Dawson, and swore under his breath. "Shore would like to see Custer marching in here this minute," he added, and frowned as a burning branch was thrown at them, which landed on the wood piled around them. It began to burn slowly.

They struggled with their bonds but to no avail.

A brave ran over and stomped out the fire. A few minutes later another burning limb was thrown onto the pile. This too was put out. This method of teasing went on for a while. Then the medicine man came dancing over and waved his stick of magic menacingly at them. Finally, everyone seemed to be milling around the chiefs.

"Wonder what they are up to now," spoke Dawson.

"It seems to me that they're not all in agreement about something," replied Lance. "We'll find out before long."

Turley cut in sharply, "Look over to your right; it's the girl and the old squaw."

Lance saw them just as they entered a small tepee and cautioned Turley, "Mark that tepee in your mind. If somehow there should be a chance in store for us, we're going to go by there and take one of them along."

"Winsor, if we ever get that chance, I say let's get the hell out of here and forget about everything else." Lance paid little attention if any to the latter's remark, for the position they were in now certainly seemed like there wasn't any time left for future plans, let alone contemplating carrying them out. Just how much time there was left to live depended on the outcome of the powwow that had been in session for the past few minutes.

"Gonna be over due at the fort, wither we get away or not," said Dawson, who with the others, was struggling desperately with the tightly tied bonds. "'Peers to me, that my first mission is gonna be the last for ma friend, Custer."

Lance looked over toward Dawson and cursed himself under his breath for allowing the older scout to make this trip with them. After all he had absolutely nothing to gain.

"I ain't complainin'," said Dawson, after noticing the other's glance. "Just want to work ma mouth a little since I can't get ma chew."

"Here they come again," said Turley as he tensed slightly with the others and waited for the oncoming savages. Coming within a few yards of the haggard looking scouts, they stopped.

It was Sitting Bull who spoke. "We wait one moon. Scouts come from river. White man tell no lie, you go." And he continued harshly, "White man lie, you die."

The color came back on to the faces of the scouts and they let out their breath ever so slowly. Their pulses pounded madly as the delay in carrying out the execution offered new hope. Sitting Bull motioned and the tribesmen left the scene, grumbling.

"Winsor," remarked Dawson, whose face had brightened considerably since the verdict, "shore got to hand it to you son. Once in a while a man has to lie and you sure lied about the right things.

"They are more scared of Custer then I thought," answered Lance. "The ole Sitting Bull is a foxy one," he added. "Wants to make sure that Custer won't find out that the Sioux was responsible for our disappearance. If it wasn't for him, the others would of hacked us apart by now and our remains would be just ashes in the dying embers."

Turley, whose mind was occupied until now with all kinds of fantastic escapes, said with a touch of excitement, "We have 'til dawn to break loose and I aim to get my hands free if I have to leave one wrist behind. Should we get that opportunity," he continued, "we'll head for the horses that are at the edge of camp and ride hard and fast."

"That plan is fine," remarked Lance as he cast his eyes to the ground. "You and Dawson do just that." He hesitated for a moment, then looked at Turley and said, I'll follow a few minutes later.

Turley looked at him questioningly. Lance offered no answer. "Look, Winsor," Turley tried to reason. "Believe me when I tell you that I've lost all interest in that gold. Just let's get out of here and leave the girl." He didn't finish as he continued to look at Lance curiously, and then asked, "Why do you insist on leaving with her?"

"Do you want to leave her with White Cloud and the rest of these savages? She came unwillingly, if you remember."

"It's because of her that we are in this tight spot," argued Turley. "She don't want our company, that's for sure. She gave us away, didn't she?"

He waited for an answer from Lance and he got it. The latter replied, "The plan still goes," and Lance winced as the rawhide dug into his wrists as he struggled to loosen them a little.

Turley pressed the issue no further, as the mystery concerning his friend's intentions grew.

"Wall," spoke Dawson, who just listened to the conversation 'til now. "Guess there will be three of us visitin' the tepee on our way out," as his eyes met Turley's. "You're right there Dawson," answered Turley in agreement and looked over to Lance and said, "Like it has been and hope to continue, Captain, you've got company."

Lance met Turley's yes and managed a faint grin but said nothing. That their friendship grew more with each passing day was obvious. Lance wondered how he would feel if he should he be on a mission sometime in the future and, upon glancing over his shoulder, see no

Turley, hear no comment such as, "Lead the way, Captain, you've got company."

He let the matter drop as a brave left the still burning fire and came within a few yards of them. He sat down facing the scouts.

"A guard," said Lance, through the corner of his mouth to the others. The sight of the prisoners was depressing. Their bewhiskered faces looked haggard. That the men were tired was obvious as their weight was held more by the bonds rather than their lashed feet. The clothing they wore was ripped here and there, especially Lance's, who was indeed in need of a new wardrobe. However, their feelings were contrary to their looks. New hope of escape had inspired them to an exciting pitch, although it certainly wasn't noticeable. Biding their time, they waited patiently for the villagers to quiet down for the night.

As time went by, the last of the stragglers slowly disappeared behind the flaps of wigwams and tepees. The once blazing fire was dying out as the darkness seemed to crush into oblivion the last of the burning embers.

The scouts worked feverishly in an attempt to free their hands. They tugged and strained and their slow moving action attracted little or no attention, as far as the half sleeping guard that sat before them was concerned. Within the hour, the guard arose, walked over and looked at the scouts in darkness. Satisfied that nothing was amiss, he turned and left them, disappearing into the dark of the night.

"No doubt that another will take his place," cautioned Lance.

"I may be able to work my hand free; it's only a matter of time," cut in Turley, excitedly.

"If we do," replied Lance, "we'll have to silence the guard first and then work fast." He said no more, nor did the others, as another brave appeared from out of the darkness and seated himself in front of them.

As time wore on, three pairs of hands twisted and strained in the darkness. The work was painful, physically as well as mentally. Slowly but surely, one man's hand began to ease out of the rawhide bond. Blood slowly trickled down the wrist, for the skin had been cut and bruised in the attempt to free the hand. One heart beat madly as the owner was aware of the fact that soon he would be free of the bonds. He stopped straining for a moment as he eased out a lungful of air and kept a vigil eye on the brave, who seemed to have sensed nothing suspicious. After a painful few minutes, the once tightly held hand finally slipped free. The end of the raw hide fell to the ground and hung loosely off the other wrist. His mind reeled for a moment as the thought of escape flashed all over him, but Lance soon checked himself. His hand was still semi-arced around the tree in back of him. He exercised his finders, wearing off the numbness that had set in. He inched it around in the darkness and finally let it drop to his side. Lance was aware of the guard's heavy breathing and assumed that he was dozing.

Lance let his other hand drop. A knife appeared in his right. Tense but cool, his eyes never left the brave as he cut the bonds off the other wrist. He didn't dare alert the others in fear of waking the guard. Taking a firm grip on the knife, Lance braced himself and made a wild cat like leap at the unsuspecting brave who hardly uttered a sound as the long blade sank into his heart. Before Turley and Dawson could collect their senses as to what took place so suddenly, Lance was slashing away their bonds.

"This is it fellows," he whispered swiftly. "Now listen carefully. Turley, you hang on to these bonds. Once we are in that tepee, you and Dawson tie up the squaw. Cut a piece off and anything you find in there and tie it around her mouth. I'll silence the girl somehow; we'll take it from there. Come on."

They made their way along the edge of camp to a spot where Lance had fixed in his mind as being directly in line with the sleeping quarters used by the squaw and the girl. He cautioned his friends once more: "I'll light a match just as soon as we get inside, pick out the squaw and work fast. Clasp your hand over her mouth the very first thing. One scream and we'll be facing the whole village."

Crouching low, Lance led the way. Everything was still and quiet with the exception of the crickets that seemed to pay no attention to the night invaders.

Past one wigwam, then another. The distance was short, but to the three men it seemed like the slow passing of years. Their thoughts were devoted to the present attempt. It had to be fast, sure, no slip-ups. They didn't dare think about what would happen if they were detected.

Suddenly, the three scouts dug their faces into the ground as a hoot owl cried out in the dark. They laid there motionless for a few moments, cursing the nocturnal prowler under their breaths. Observing nothing suspicious, they moved forward again. They began to breathe heavily as they pulled themselves in front of the flap of the small tepee. Lance reached into his pocket and withdrew a few matches. He took a final glance around in the darkness but saw nothing.

"Now," he whispered faintly. Cautiously he crawled in through the opening. Turley was along side and Dawson was halfway through when Lance lit the match briefly. The light startled the old squaw but before she realized that there were others present a strong hand was placed roughly over her mouth and muffled any scream that she might have attempted.

Once again, Lance had his hand over the girl's mouth. Again she fought like a wild cat. This time Lance was ready and he took no chances as his fist met her chin during the short struggle, she went limp in his arms. Lance felt that burning desire again. To hold her close and tell her that everything was being done for her. He felt a little ashamed as he realized that he hit her.

"Ready Lance," hissed Dawson.

"Yeah, let's make tracks. Turley," spoke Lance, "take a look around."

After peering out into the darkness for a few moments, Turley replied, "Can't see anything. Come on."

Lance half dragged the limp girl out of the tepee. Once outside, he laid her gently up over his shoulder and followed Turley toward the outskirts of the village where they first noticed the horses. Dawson kept them covered from the rear. His knuckles were white as he held the handle of the long knife with a vice-like grip. A sigh escaped his lips, for at the moment they had just passed the last wigwam and entered the tall pines.

Swiftly, he glanced over his shoulder for a last look. Everything seemed to be in order. He turned and followed the others. Their steps were light and fast, but a little shaky. Hearts pounded madly and the tempo of their steps increased, casting caution aside briefly as the foursome neared their destination. Finally, the outline of the animals appeared in the darkness. Lance was about to issue quick orders but stopped short as one of the animals whined, causing the rest of them to move about restlessly.

"Something disturbed them," whispered Lance, as a sickening feeling came over him.

Three desperate men stood still in a crouching position and waited in near panic. To add to their grief, a low moan escaped the lips of the girl.

Lance laid her down on the ground and Turley cut in with a hiss. "For God's sake Lance, clip her again." He was indeed desperate, as were the others, but Lance kept his head.

"I'll take care of her, now, don't worry," whispered Lance as he tore off the dangling piece that still hung off his coat. He swiftly tore it in half, tied one piece around the girl's mouth and tied her hands with the other.

Lance was about to lift the girl back to his shoulders as Turley's fingers dug into his arm. He whispered, "Listen. Horses."

Their ears picked up the thud of hoofs as they made their way toward the ones already tied to the trees just a short distance away. Cold sweat trickled down the faces of the men, who were so near yet so far away from their one chance of escape. Their eyes pierced the darkness in the direction of the on-coming horses. Suddenly, they appeared.

"Four of them," whispered Lance, faintly. The riders pulled alongside the other animals and dismounted. Tying their own horses to the trees, they lifted something off two of the horses.

It was Lance who whispered, "They are hunters, coming back late with a couple of deer." Their hopes grew as the four braves started toward the camp with the fresh meat.

The scouts' nerves were on edge and they knew that time was limited, for their escape would soon be detected. As the hunters disappeared into the darkness, Lance practically threw the girl over this shoulder and they half ran toward the horses and finally...escape.

Swiftly, he lifted her on a horse and hopped up on the horse's back behind her.

"Follow me," said Lance to the others. "And don't push the animals 'til we get out of here a little ways," he cautioned. At last, breathing the fresh air of freedom a hundred yards or so from camp, they were about to burst into speed when suddenly another horseman with a deer appeared directly in front of them after rounding a bend. They pulled to a halt cursing under their breath and Turley lost no time as he hissed, "Wait here." He crouched low as he made his way over to the unsuspecting hunter, who assumed at the moment that his friends came back to help him. The brave said something just as Turley sprang at him. They both fell off their horses, taking along the deer with them. "This one killed his last deer," remarked Turley as he jumped back on the pinto.

"You all right, Turley?" asked Lance.

"Yeah," was his quick answer and the scouts were fast on their way toward freedom and safety. Several miles out, Lance pulled to a halt.

"Watts' a matter?" asked Dawson excitedly.

Lance looked in the direction of the village and commented, "No doubt that they are on to us by now. We'll have to do our best to keep out of their way. If we can keep ahead of them for another five miles or so, we'll cut up north then push on toward the river and once we are across, head toward the Bad Lands on the other side of the mountains. That will be the safest way to Fort Laramie. We can't chance going back along the river, they'll search it from one end to the other and then there are the scouts who will be coming back this way, the ones sent out by Sitting Bull last night to spy on Custer." The others agreed without any comment and once again they were racing their horses madly.

Lance put his hand to the girls face and slid the gag off of her mouth. He didn't bother to untie her hands. His past performances cautioned him against it. Trouble enough riding double on a saddleless horse, he mused. That she was conscious now and aware of the fact as to what took place within the hour was obvious. She didn't slump against his arms, easing the burden. Lance wondered how her jaw felt. Up till now, his actions were that of an enemy. How could she think otherwise? *It must be quite a mystery to the girl as to the reason we took such a chance to get her,* he thought. Lance took the reins with his right hand and quickly encircled his free arm around the girl's waist as she slipped heavily to one side. He held her tightly, a little more than was needed. A faint grin appeared on his lips as her hair brushed his lips and at the same time wondered how large a force it would take to get her away from him now. His face became sober with the thought that perhaps it would take but one man: Turley. No doubt that the latter was making all kinds of plans by now. Lance released the girl and took hold of the reigns with both hands.

A short time later he pulled to a stop again.

"We'll cut up north from here," he said. "Got quite a ways to go before we can stop to rest up."

"How is your passenger doing," asked Turley? "Are you keeping her away from your knife?" And he laughed softly.

"Behaving like a kitten," answered Lance amusingly.

"But always ready to scratch," added Dawson. "Be careful son, I hardly think that she is on friendly terms with us."

The conversation ended there as a night owl, whose call was just a little too heavy, reached the ears of the scouts. They listened, as another one answered. "A couple of miles back, I calculate," said Dawson.

"Too close for comfort," said Lance in reply. "Come on, let's move on." Every now and then they could hear the calls but they grew fainter as the scouts rode on.

Hour after hour, mile after mile they pushed on relentlessly. Just before daybreak Lance pulled the horse to a stop. The moon was still in the sky and aided the men in locating a spot where they could bunk down 'til nightfall. Lance had no intention of traveling during the day in fear of being detected by the search parties that were out looking for them.

They'd come upon a cave and decided that it was an excellent place. At the entrance they dismounted. Lance put his hands around the girl's waist and lifted her off. She swayed against him as her legs buckled. He picked her up and seated her on a fallen tree.

"Turley," he called. "Stay with her 'til I get back. I'm going into the cave to see how far back it goes."

Once inside, he lit a match and advanced forward. Shortly he reappeared and said to the others, "There's enough room in there to harbor a regiment. Dawson, you come with me. We'll build a small fire in one of the crevices and move in, horses and all. It won't be noticed from out here," he reassured the others.

Finally, they came back out. Dawson led the horses in. Turley picked the girl up and started in with her, at the same time commenting, more to himself than to the others, "St. Louie, it won't be long now," and strolled in with a grin on his face.

A cold chill swept over Lance as he watched his friend carry the girl into the cave. He had a sudden impulse to rush in and tell Turley *. . . tell Turley what, Winsor? To tell him how this girl made you feel since you first met her? This girl that hates your guts along with the others. Once and for all Winsor, pull yourself together and forget about this nightmare. You've had a rough time in the past few days; you'll be all right once you get back to the fort.*

Dawson appeared at the entrance. "Come in and have a smoke, neighbor," he invited amusingly.

"I was thinking about just that," lied Lance, as he put his arm around Dawson's shoulder. "I accept the invitation."

Inside the fire burned brightly. Turley stretched himself out, as did Dawson. The girl sat leaning against a large rock with her eyes downcast.

"You fellows get some shut-eye," suggested Lance. "I'll take the first watch." He walked over to the girl and untied her hands. She didn't look up at him nor did she betray any emotion upon being untied. Lance sat down nearby and rested his back against the wall of the cave.

"Wake me up when you want to," said Turley, as he rolled over and rested his head on his arm. Lance nodded and then glanced at

Dawson who was stroking his chin. "I don't think I'd recognize you if you shaved off that beard," he said with a chuckle.

"Good way to keep hid when the wrong folks are looking for you," replied Dawson with a smile. "Wall," he said, yawning and scratching his grizzly looking head, "I'll get me a little shut-eye so as I can be fit for guard duty when called upon."

"Ever been to St. Louie?" Lance asked as the other slipped an arm under his head.

"No, I haven't," answered Dawson. "But accordin' to our friend Turley here, it's a right nice place. Why did ya ask? Don't tell me that you are hankering for the bright lights too?"

"No," laughed Lance. "Just asked out of curiosity."

"'Peers to me," said Dawson rather slowly with his eyes closed, "if Turley ever gets there with his pockets lined with gold, it won't be the gold he got for this here girl." Lance's face reddened as he flashed a quick look at Turley and sighed with relief, as he noticed the latter was sound asleep.

"Don't worry son, I knew he was asleep," and Dawson said no more. Neither did Lance as he wondered why the old scout made that remark.

Lance discarded whatever he had on his mind as he noticed the girl trying to make herself comfortable. Indeed he felt sorry for her. *Certainly went through a lot since she was first kidnapped by the trappers,* he mused. Lance found no answer as he wondered just how much more of this rough stuff she could stand. He wanted to comfort her, but how? *Come, come Winsor, you're quite the boy with the women make your move,* he urged himself. *The mere thought of her nearness sends you spinning doesn't it? Now is the time, Winsor. Go on over and try to explain that she won't be harmed and not to be afraid. If you could make her understand perhaps it would lighten her heart a bit. You sit there like a fool, Winsor. Yes, I know what you're thinking, that you would fight the whole frontier just to see her smile once. You're dreaming now boy, you're blood is on fire. Holding her close, are you not? Kissing her soft red lips. Whispering in her ear about your future plans here in the Big Horn aren't you? You like what you are thinking, you and I both know that continued his conscience. If only all this could become a reality hey Winsor? I dislike very much cutting in on your pleasant thought, my boy, but I must caution you once more, she's on her way home. Watcha going to do about it? You dreamer.*

Once again his conscience got the best of him as he snapped aloud, "Shut up." His voice startled the girl. She opened her eyes and looked at him. He felt the blood rush to his face and he cursed under his breath for answering out loud like he did.

Subconsciously, he got up and walked over to the girl who shrank back slightly as he came near.

Lance took his coat off, whatever there was left of it, and folded it several times. He placed it behind his head so that she would know that he wanted her to use it as a pillow.

Her face had an expression of fear; she was uncertain as to his intentions. She glanced toward the two sleeping men probably hoping that they would awaken. Lance sensed this as he managed a smile to reassure her that he meant no harm.

"Now don't be afraid," he said, and softly and slowly placed the folded coat behind her head. He placed his hand on her shoulder and forced the reluctant girl's resistance until her head rested on the pillow. Still smiling, he said, "Now you can go to sleep," and walked out to the entrance of the cave. The girl watched him as he walked out and a faint trace of a smile appeared on her lips. No doubt that she was bewildered by the friendly attitude of the man.

Slowly her eyes closed. Whatever wandered in her mind was still a secret, known only to her.

V

Lance inhaled a lungful of fresh morning air. It was daylight now and the busy creatures of the wilds were on their way. As tired and weary as he was, Lance felt good. He had a smile on his lips but was unaware of it. *Patience, Winsor, patience.* For a change, Lance agreed with his conscience. *Right you are, little fella, right you are,* he mused, and glanced back into the cave as he rolled himself a cigarette.

The sun was high in the sky and gazed lazily down at the solitary figure that was sprawled out daydreaming at the entrance of the cave. Blade Turley, Indian scout, at the moment unemployed, destination, Southeast of Big Horn. His face was expressionless as he looked out over the green valley and wondered if his dreams of St. Louie would ever become a reality. He admitted to himself that the country up here was the ideal spot to settle down in and the prospects for the future were bright. *Well, maybe I'll decide on what to do after the girl is back home and the gold is mine,* he mused. His thoughts were interrupted by Lance, who leaned casually against a ledge at the entrance of the cave.

"You're thinking of steak and apple pie," Lance remarked.

Turley looked at him with a grin and remarked, "You certainly can make an approach without making any noise." He added, "I could sure go for some steak; the apple pie is for dreamers only."

"Well, now, I don't know about that, fella. I know a girl back at the fort that can sure make the stuff. I'll give you an introduction when we get back."

"I'm going to hold you to that," said Turley, as he got to his feet. Looking at his bruised wrists, he nodded toward the interior of the cave and asked, "Are they still sleeping?"

"Just like kittens," answered Lance. "Didn't want to disturb Dawson, guess they're pretty well tuckered out." On glancing about, Lance commented, "Let's go down into the valley a little ways and see if we can locate some water and maybe if we're lucky, something to eat."

"I was about to suggest that myself," replied Turley, then added, "It would be a good idea to get Dawson to stand guard while we're gone." Lance nodded in agreement as he put a freshly rolled cigarette to his lips and beckoned Turley to arouse the old scout.

A moment later they returned and Dawson was grumbling like an old bear that was held fast by the jaws of a trap. He blinked his eyes as he came out into the sunlight, barking, "It's down right orn'y to let a man waste his time sleeping."

He looked at Lance, who was laughing at the sight of him, and said, "Why didn't you get me up when it was my turn, you young pole cat. If Custer should hear about this, he'd send me back to Cheyenne country."

Dawson became serious for a moment, saying, "As a matter of fact, he might do it anyway. We're going to be mighty late getting back," and he dug his hands into his pockets in search of his tobacco.

"I think that they will wait for our return, for a while anyway," said Lance, and went on to explain their intention for the time being. A short time later, Dawson leaned against a tree near the entrance of the cave and watched his two friends disappear into the dense forest. Time went on slowly as he waited with anticipation for their return. Dawson shifted his position where he was sitting leisurely and was startled momentarily as his eyes met those of the girl, who was standing within a few yards of the exit of the cave. He got slowly to his feet and managed a smile as he looked at the frightened girl. His eyes became a bit moist as he put up his hand slightly and said rather softly, "Now don't be afraid; we're not going to hurt you. You know, you remind me of my wife. Yes sir, young and pretty like yourself. She was an Indian girl too. Cheyenne as a matter of fact." He checked his emotions and felt a little embarrassed as he realized that this girl, perhaps, cared little for his conversation but much for a chance to escape.

He decided to coax her out and have her relax at the entrance, though he cautioned himself against staying too far away from her in case an attempt was made to make a run for it.

He advanced a step or two toward her pointing with his hand and said, "Come on outside and get a little sun." She hesitated a moment and slowly made her way to the outside and without further instructions, sat down. Dawson sat on a boulder directly in front of her and was now pondering on the idea of how to make her understand the whereabouts of Lance and Turley, among other things.

Suddenly, he sat up right and near fell off the boulder in amazement as he heard the girl's voice for the first time and in English.

"You marry Indian girl? Cheyenne?"

He looked at her wide eyed and exclaimed, "Wall' I'll be a grasshopper's twin," and scratched his grizzly head. "Wall' now, I can sure tell you a lot of things that you art'er know," he said excitedly. "Just let me check my shock first. Shore didn't expect to be talking to you in English." Dawson felt greatly relieved, now that the task of explaining was going to be easier.

Sill grinning, he asked, "What might yore' name be?"

The girl's fear and tension had seemed to vanish completely as she answered in a soft mellow voice: "Naomi." She gazed at Dawson with interest and smiled, as he started to relate the occurrences that took place from the very beginning, some of which he participated in, others told to him by Lance and Turley.

By late afternoon, the two men were slowly making their way back to the cave. Lance was dragging along a small deer that he had knifed and Turley had his coat sleeves filled with water. Coming within seeing distance of the cave, Lance stopped and said to Turley curiously, "I don't see Dawson."

"Must be in the cave checking on the girl," said Turley. Edging their way up to the mouth of the cave, they stopped and looked at each other in silence.

Lance peered into the darkened cave and called out, "Dawson."

"Hold it," snapped a gruff voice. "Don't move and stand where you are."

They looked up toward the direction from which the voice came but could see nothing. Obviously, whoever it was must be hidden behind the ledges up above the cave entrance Lance thought, as he cursed the string of bad luck they were forever encountering. Their tension relaxed a bit as a roughly clad figure stood up behind one of the ledges pointing the business end of a new rifle at them. He was a white man.

Lance managed a mirthless smile and said, "Howdy, thought you were Indians at first."

"Just as well be," answered the gruff voice. "You scouts don't fit into our business."

His eyes never left the scouts as he snapped an order, "Hardy, you go on down and search them." "Wade," he shouted. "Come on out and help Hardy."

Another figure arose from behind a ledge and made his way down, following out his orders. The eyes of the scouts fell upon another henchman as he swiftly came out of the cave.

"They're gun runners," said Lance under his breath. In another few moments they were relieved of their knives. Lance's expression was stone like as he demanded more than asked. "What did you do with our friends?"

The one that did the talking and who was obviously was the leader answered, "Don't worry about them for now, you're going to join them in a minute," Then he snapped, "Tie their hands, get them inside, then tie their feet."

As they were led in, their grief grew as they saw the girl and Dawson bound and gagged. A tough spot to be in again, a pitiful sight.

That the girl was being abused again enraged Lance to a feverish pitch. If ever again they were on the loose, Lance shouted deep within himself, he would never leave her out of sight. He cursed himself over and over again for taking Turley along, but then again, these men had rifles, probably would have turned out the same way. One of the outlaws walked over to Dawson and the girl and took the gags out of their mouths.

"Wall, son," blurted out Dawson, who was indeed madder than a hornet. "I let these orne'y critters get the best of me. Why, if I had my shootin' iron, they would have been blasted right out of the valley."

"Simmer down pop," said the outlaw leader. "Or you won't be fit to cook our supper."

"Untie him, Wade, and have him unhide that deer. Stay with him, en' if he makes a wrong move, shoot off his beard."

The more Lance looked at the girl, the worse he felt. His emotions got the best of him and he said to the leader, who reentered the cave, "This girl don't have to be tied; she's harmless."

"I'm giving the orders here mister," and added with a sickening grin, "I'll untie her when I'm ready."

Lance mashed his teeth together as the blood drained slowly from his face, but he said no more. He glanced at the girl who was looking at him and for the very first time had more than a faint smile on her lips. His pulse quickened as he smiled back at her and she let her gaze fall downward. Her smile amazed him. He noticed too that the frightened look on her face had vanished. The hate in her eyes that was so noticeable was gone. Wonder what made her change, he mused. Lance pondered over the change but was unable to come up with a logical answer. He glanced toward Turley, whose facial expression was anything but bright. The latter was eyeing the new rifle that lay across the lap of one of the renegades. The other two outlaws went out of the cave again and aided Dawson in the preparing of deer for a roast.

Lance gazed at the one guarding them. *Rather young to be mixed up with these gun runners. Can't be more than nineteen or twenty,* he mused. Lance waited until the guard met his gaze then asked, "Where did you fellows get the new rifles?"

"Don't answer that," came a sharp command from the mouth of the cave. It was the leader's voice and he now came in toward them as he fingered the point of the knife he held in his hand.

"Look mister," he said to Lance rather sarcastically, "I'll do the answering around here. If you want to know anything, you just ask me."

"I'm asking," replied Lance smoothly.

"Ain't none of your business," he replied.

Lance ignored that and continued the conversation. "Hog tying us like this seems to be senseless. Why don't you let us go on our way and you fellows go about your business?"

If Lance had anything else on his mind he didn't say it as he watched the outlaw stare at the girl with a beastly grin. His gaze left the girl and as he turned he said to Lance, "You scouts are going to do a little visitin'. You're going to meet up with Crazy Horse." He waited for that to sink in then continued, "No doubt that you boys did away with a few of his braves in your time and maybe he wants to settle a little score. Anyway, the less there are of you fellows around, the better it will be for his operations and better for our business too."

He took a few steps toward the exit and stopped. Turning, he looked at Lance again and added, "We'll let the chief decide on yore' fate." And with that he walked out of the cave.

"By the looks of things, his intentions don't favor us in the least bit," spoke Turley.

"Up till now," replied Lance. "I sure thought that things would work out a little better than this. That fellow is sure bent on getting us out of the way."

Silence fell upon the interior of the cave as the men thought in sheer desperation on a way to escape. Rifles, six shooters, and knives against their bare hands. *Sure looks bad,* mused Lance to himself. As he gazed at the young guard an idea suddenly struck him.

It's worth a chance Winsor, after all you have no choice under the circumstances. Go ahead man, give it a try, he urged himself. He glanced toward the outside and noticed the outlaws and Dawson were busy preparing the fallen deer.

Lance broke the silence as he spoke casually. He turned toward Turley but whatever he had to say was indeed meant for the ears of the guard, who would be the easiest to deal with in any respect.

"Being a scout for the military and working under General Custer has sure been a great adventure. Plenty of excitement when out on a mission. Good place to sleep, excellent food when we're back at the fort."

Turley, unaware of Lance's intentions, looked at him curiously, and thought that his friend sure picked a poor time to be reminiscing. Lance continued without letting Turley make any reply.

"I always looked forward to the dances and all those pretty girls. They can sure bake apple pies...and the sergeant's daughter, she's got her eye on you."

Turley managed a grin as it occurred to him now that Lance was up to something other than reminiscing. He decided to play along, but kept silent.

Lance nodded toward the guard and said, "Now if I were as young as this fellow here, I think that I would join the military and have plenty of fun and excitement. That's the place for a good young healthy fellow, like this boy here. Not gun running."

The guard kept silent and Lance knew that what he said had some effect on him.

"If the military ever catches up with these fellows they'll stretch them to the highest pine tree in the valley."

The boy became a little nervous as he swallowed hard. He dug his hand into his coat pocket and brought out a sack of tobacco.

Lance continued, "It sure would be a poor way to die young, and all for nothing. This boy would be a good one for Custer's regiment, and who knows, maybe work himself up to be sergeant or lieutenant in time." He looked at the guard and said as an afterthought, "Any of these men your kinfolk?"

The boy shook his head in answer. It was in the negative.

Turley cut in as he eyed the guard, and said, "Better listen carefully, boy. I don't think that you will get another chance like this to clear yourself with the law and head for better days."

The guard said nothing as he lit the cigarette he made and shifted his eyes toward the outlaw leader as he entered the cave.

"Everything all right, Wade?" he asked gruffly.

"Yeah, nothing's amiss." he answered.

Satisfied, the leader glanced briefly at the girl and walked back out. Lance and Turley eyed each other in relief, for they certainly didn't know what to expect. At least for the moment, the boy kept silent regarding their intentions. Taking advantage of the situation, Lance continued to push the issue.

"Look, Wade," Lance paused, "cut us loose and give me your rifle. We'll make a stand, and if we get away, I promise you that you'll get back home or come down to the fort with us and join the military like we said and you'll be cleared once and for all of any wrong doing. How does it sound?"

Lance and Turley were a bit excited and waited anxiously for a reply. The boy cast his eyes to the ground and swallowed hard again, but said nothing. Disappointed, Lance wet his lips and asked, "Would you stand by and watch those men harm this girl?"

The guard glanced at the girl in embarrassment and let his eyes fall to the ground slowly, still making no reply.

"Are you going to let them take us in and stand by while Crazy Horse and his savages burn us at the stake? You'll be a murderer as well."

The guard shifted his position and paled slightly.

"Think hard fellow," urged Lance. "We don't have too much time left." He said no more as the others entered the cave.

"All Right you," said the leader to Dawson. "Untie your friends' hands and give them some of this meat." He handed him a canteen of water. "Hardy, cut up that meat," the leader ordered and the latter went about slicing up the freshly roasted deer.

They ate in silence. The outlaws glanced casually at their captives every now and then but said nothing as they went about eating their meal. The girl ate very little and the scouts less, for the farthest thing away from their mind at the moment was hunger.

Lance looked at the young guard and wondered what was going on in his mind, for he too ate little and chewed on the venison rather reluctantly. If only the boy would come over to their side, pondered Lance, they would have a chance to get out of this mess.

He shuddered at the thought of being taken back to the Indian camp. He glanced over to the girl, as he did so often and a sudden urge came over him at the moment to make an all out deal with the outlaw leader but he relaxed slowly, for he realized that bargaining with the gun runner under the circumstances was useless. That the leader had personal plans for the girl was quite evident. Lance cast the unpleasant thought from his mind; he knew that if he didn't, he'd lose control of his inner self.

The long silence was broken by the leader as he spoke. "What's the matter? Don't you like Pop's cooking?" With that he got up from where he was sitting and said, "All Right Hardy, tie 'em up, the party's over."

With their hands and feet tied again, the trip back to the village seemed to be inevitable.

"Wade," said the leader. "Keep a sharp eye on them, we'll be back shortly," and motioned to Hardy. The two of them left the cave.

Lance lost no time as the two outlaws disappeared and said rather mildly to the guard, "If you're going to do anything to help us and rid yourself of this mess, now is the time. They're going to come back soon for this girl. Are you going to just sit there and let them harm her?"

The guard sat there as if paralyzed with his eyes to the ground but made no answer.

Turley took over as he sternly said, "If this girl were your sister, would you still do nothing?"

Dawson, who caught on quickly and added, "She's just a girl son, can't defend herself with men like that out there."

The attempt to win the young guard over came to a climax as the outlaws re-entered the cave. A fiendish grin appeared on the leader's lips as he looked at the girl and then made a sweeping glance towards the now heavily breathing scouts. They knew more than sensed just what was going to take place. The leader spoke to the one called Hardy. "Take her outside."

"Now wait a minute," half shouted Lance. "Let the girl be. I'll make a deal with you."

"Shut up," snapped the leader sarcastically, "I'm not interested in making deals with scouts."

As the outlaw lifted the struggling girl, in desperation Lance attempted another try to reason with the leader. "Hold on you," he shouted to Wade, but got no farther as the outlaw leader kicked viciously with his knee that caught Lance on the side of the head and he fell backward semi-consciously.

"I don't want anything out of you fellows," roared the leader as he pointed a finger at Turley and Dawson, "Or you'll be getting' the same thing."

With that warning, he left the cave. Lance braced himself on his elbow and shook his head.

"You all right Lance?" asked Turley anxiously.

"Yeah, I'm all right," was the reply, and he glanced around the cave. Slowly, he turned and gazed at the guard, whose forehead was now breaking out in sweat. The latter breathed fast and heavily as he stared out toward the entrance of the cave. If any of the scouts had anything on their mind to say, they didn't. For at the moment, the young outlaw slid his hand slowly underneath his coat and came out with a knife.

With their hearts pounding madly, waiting with anxiety for some kind of answer for the sudden appearance of the knife in the guard's hand, they hoped against hope and prayed, that whatever he was about to do would be in their favor.

The boy took one last look toward the outside and slowly slid off the small boulder on which he sat. Suddenly, he charged over to Lance and feverishly began to cut the bonds. The sudden turn of events spirited the scouts to a high pitch.

"I knew you had it in you," spoke Lance quickly. "Here, let me have the rifle," and put his eager finger around the trigger. "Cut them loose," he ordered softly, and cautiously crept toward the entrance of the cave.

Like a big cat ready to pounce upon an unsuspecting victim, Lance crouched near the entrance, straining his ears for some disturbance that would betray the location of the outlaws and the girl. He heard nothing. Growing impatient, he edged his way out of the cave cautiously and hit upon an idea how to attract the attention of the outlaws but it never materialized.

A rifle shot split the silence. The screaming slug sailed past Lance's head and sprayed him with particles of dirt and stone as it tore into the wall of the cave. Lance dove behind a boulder and heard the riflemen shout at the tope of his voice, "Darton, high tail it up here pronto! They're loose."

Peering out toward the direction of the surprised outlaw, Lance saw him briefly as he hugged a big pine tree and chanced a quick shot at the renegade. The latter concealed himself completely behind the giant tree and didn't return the fire. *Waiting for the other to come*, mused Lance.

The others were loose and at the moment crouching low near the entrance. Lance looked over his shoulder and managed a slight grin as he noticed the ever-ready Turley held a knife in his hand. Dawson had his hand on the boy's arm as they crouched there and was saying something to him. No doubt the latter was frightened and was quite concerned as to the outcome of the present situation. He would be dealt with harshly if his newly found friends failed in their attempt to make an escape.

"Lance," Turley called over to his friend. "Keep them busy, and I'll try to get out of here and work my way in behind them. If nothing else, I'll have them worried a bit."

Lance nodded in agreement, and as an afterthought asked Wade if he had any more bullets.

"Not on me," replied the boy half-heartedly. "They're in my saddle bag."

Another rifle barked and the slug screamed madly as it ricocheted off the wall and buried itself deep within the interior of the cave.

The shot came from his right. Lance knew that Barton, the leader, was up here now and he felt a bit relieved at the thought of the girl being safe, at least for the time being. Lance decided to work his way in the general direction of Barton if he got the chance, for the girl was obviously behind the leader somewhere.

"Hardy" shouted Barton. "Start closing in and fill 'em full of lead."

Lance took advantage of the moment and advanced from boulder to boulder, then threw himself on the ground as a slug whizzed by above him. Lance was well aware of the predicament he was in. There were only four shells left in the rifle and he didn't dare waste any. The outlaws opened up in earnest as a hail of bullets blasted the mouth of the cave. Concerned about his friends, Lance looked toward the cave and noticed that they were gone. They must have moved back in, thought Lance. He was about to move to a higher position so that he could get a clearer view, when suddenly, the bulky form of the outlaw Hardy came into view as he dashed wildly across a small clearing in an attempt to reach a concealment a few yards away from the mouth of the cave. Lance brought the rifle to his shoulder like a flash and fired. The outlaw stopped dead in his tracks and collapsed like an empty sack. Bullets screamed madly around Lance as he huddled close to the ground.

The leader, Barton, was no doubt frantic, thought Lance. Now that his comrade was gone, the outlaw would surely change his plans, and Lance wondered at the moment what the renegade would do next.

The firing stopped abruptly.

Lance got to his knees and peered about through the openings of the rock formations. Suddenly a shot rang out and the bullet shattered the bark on a large tree about fifty yards below him. It occurred to him now that either Turley or Dawson was in possession of the fallen outlaw's rifle and upon spotting Barton, took a shot at him.

Like lightning, Lance sprang to his feet at the same time whipping his rifle to his shoulder and fired at the remaining outlaw, who left his hiding place and was dodging from tree to tree like a half crazed fugitive being closed in on by a posse. The shot made the outlaw dive in behind a fallen tree, but only for a moment. Lance got another glimpse of Barton as he dove over a small embankment and disappeared. Lance cautiously circled around the spot where he last saw the renegade but saw no signs of him. He looked back in the direction of the cave and wondered where the others were. He decided against calling out to them in fear of betraying his position.

Suddenly, he tensed, as the thought occurred to him that Barton may be heading toward the girl and was going to use her as a shield in an attempt to get away.

He moved fast, crouching low as he made his way over to the embankment and was about to go over, when suddenly a loud gruff voice split the silence as it urged a horse forward with the aid of a slap on the animal's flank.

Lance froze, as the wild scamper of horse hooves crashed through the dense forest. It relieved him slightly that the sound was only of one horse on the move, but just as fast paralyzed him at the thought that the rider could be riding double. He lost no time as he scampered swiftly in the direction of the get-away horse. A few moments later, Lance spied the remaining horses tied to the trees. Dashing over to where they were, he stopped abruptly and let out a sigh of relief and at the same time managed a little smile as he looked at the girl who was still tied and again had a gag in her mouth.

Lance laid the rifle down and pounced to her side and a frown appeared on his forehead as he noticed the wild look in her eyes. He got no farther as a voice snapped, "That's all, Mister. Sit down and don't move, or I'll blow your head off."

"Barton," Lance hissed to himself. He sat down limply like a man that just awoke out of a bad dream only to find it all a reality.

"I sorta thought that you would fall for that gag," said the outlaw with a smirking grin.

Lance was well aware of the fact that he had thrown caution to the wind by allowing himself to walk into this predicament, but he was at a loss as to the reason Barton chose to stay on rather than make an escape, which was certainly wide open.

"Now fella," snapped the outlaw. "You do just as I say or I'll finish you and this here girl off pronto, savvy? Holler to your friends and tell them to come down here. Tell them that everything is all right. Go on."

Lance shouted to Turley and Dawson, calling them by their names and following through with the rest of the instructions.

A hundred yards away, a voice answered in return; it was Dawson.

Barton slid behind a tree directly behind Lance and cautioned once more, “The end of the barrel is pointing at your head fella, no mistakes,” and added, “just in case you are wondering what I’m going to do, I’ll tell you. Gonna take you all in like I planned,” and he let out a low sickening laugh.

After he caught his breath, he added, “I’ve been wondering how you fellows got loose, but that don’t matter now does it?”

It seemed to Lance that the outlaw was enjoying the fact that at the moment, he was master of the situation. Lance felt the business end of the gun being pressed against the back of his head as the oncoming Dawson neared the trap. The pressure of the barrel ceased as the renegade concealed himself entirely behind the tree.

Dawson lit up with a smile as he noticed Lance sitting there and said as he advanced nearer, “Wassa matter, you tired? Seems as though I miss out on all the fun, you young hellion.” Dawson stopped short and his smile vanished from his lips as the outlaw leader stepped out from behind the tree slightly with the rifle pointed at the old scout.

“All Right, Pop. Join your friends and sit down. You look tired too.”

“Well I’ll be . . . ”

“Shut up and sit down,” snapped Barton. Then he added, “Where are the others?”

“Why, I don’t know where Turley is,” answered Dawson as he looked at Lance. “But you and your partner shot up your young friend. He was kil’t on the spot.”

Dawson said no more, as the outlaw snapped, “Shut up, Pop.”

“You,” ordered Barton, jabbing Lance in the back. “Holler up to your friend and tell him that I got the three of you covered, and if he don’t show up here with his hands high in the air in one minute flat, I’m going to blast all three of you right here and now. Start talking mister and talk convincingly.”

Lance and Dawson eyed each other and were breathing rather heavily. Lance called to Turley and followed orders once again. Everything became silent as the echo of his voice died out in the valley. There came no reply from Turley. The tension grew with each passing moment. Lance made another attempt but his voice seemed to fall on deaf ears. Although Lance didn't betray his emotions, he was slowly becoming desperate and turned his head slightly toward the outlaw in an attempt to visualize the latter's position and perhaps as a last resort make a lunge at the leader's rifle.

"Go ahead mister," hissed Barton. "Give it one more try. This is his last chance and yours."

"Look feller," spoke Dawson as he turned and faced the outlaw. "Our friend may be dead up there, ain't seen him since the shooting started. 'En if that's so, then he ain't going to come no matter how much you call him."

"That's your tough luck," snapped the leader. "I don't aim to take any more chances. He either comes down here pronto or you'll all stay here permanent like. Call him," he snapped at Lance as he pointed the rifle at him nervously.

Lance prayed to himself as he mustered a lungful of air and hoped against hope that his friend would answer and ease the terrific tension that had once again come over them in the past few minutes. Once again, Lance called out to Turley. Deadly silence was the only answer. Their hearts pounded madly and the grief on their faces showed up plainly. There was nothing else to do but to make a wild lunge at the renegade when he stepped out from behind the tree; Lance knew that he had to chance that as a last resort.

Dawson and Lance eyed each other and the blood in their veins seemed to freeze, as the click of the hammer as it was being drawn back into firing position, indicated that the outlaw was indeed going to carry out his threat. He appeared from behind his concealment and retreated a few steps then snapped harshly, "You can thank you friend for this," he said, as he slowly raised his rifle.

He was too far back for Lance to make any kind of attempt that would be anywhere near successful. The scouts' minds were blank as they braced themselves helplessly and awaited the roar of the rifle that would forever hasten their departure from the green valleys of the Big Horn.

It took but a split second for Lance to decide to make the move that he surely thought would be fatal. He spun around with lightning speed and was on his hands and knees, ready to spring, expecting to meet head on with the blast from the rifle, but it never came. Lance froze in that position in amazement as he looked at the outlaw Barton.

The renegade stood limply against a tree. The barrel of the rifle he clutched in his hands, pointed downward. The expression on his face was blank and his beady eyes stared out into space. Dawson, who made a move a moment later after Lance, stared at the sight wide-eyed and moistened his lips. Slowly, the body of the renegade sagged forward. He buckled at the knees and fell forward on his face at the same instant; Lance snatched the cocked rifle before it hit the ground. Just what took place within the past minute was now a clear picture in the minds of the two scouts as they saw the big knife sticking out of the outlaw's back.

In their bewilderment, they managed faint smiles as they hastily scanned the area behind the fallen gunrunner and their smiles widened as they spotted Turley leaning against a tree, nonchalantly. Before they could say anything, Turley remarked, "Rear guard Turley coming on in," and he advanced toward them.

Lance recomposed himself and rushed over to the girl, took the gag out of her mouth and untied her bonds.

Turley, on the scene now, remarked, "I don't know fellows, you get yourselves in the most awful predicaments when I'm not around," and laughed softly as he threw an arm around the still bewildered Dawson.

Dawson wet his lips and grinned as he said to Turley, "Why, you young coot, wassa big idea waitin' so long to get here? We near got our heads blown off by this here son of a –" he stopped when he glanced at the girl, and then said "—rattler."

Turley laughed as they walked over to Lance who was trying to desperately say something to the girl.

Dawson went over to the girl's side and put his arm around her shoulder. Lance looked at Turley with a grin and remarked, "Looks like he knows more about getting along with the women than we do."

"Fellers," said Dawson, "I have a bit of a surprise for you. I want you all to meet up with the prettiest little girl that ever walked on the green moss of the Big Horn. Her name is Naomi." He pointed at the two scouts and said to the girl, "This here is Lance Winsor, and this one is Blade Turley."

The girl smiled shyly as she looked at the two young scouts who were a bit taken by the pleasant turn of events.

"That's not all," spoke Dawson with pride. Looking at the girl, he urged, "Say something to these fellers."

"Now look Dawson, don't embarrass—"

"Quiet boy," cut in Dawson, "Where's your manners? Can't you see that the lady wants to say something?"

"Sorry," said Lance, and eyed Turley.

"Go ahead, little one." Dawson urged the girl again.

The expression of surprise on their faces was indeed obvious as they heard her soft, mellow voice for the first time. She smiled at the old scout as she said, "Dawson . . . tell me . . . everything. My heart . . . is . . . light."

"There, how do you like that?" Exclaimed Dawson with a big grin.

"From here on the going will be much easier," said Lance. As he smiled at Naomi, that mystifying feeling seemed to grip him all over as she smiled back at him. Lance's smile slowly faded as Turley remarked, "Our trip back to Texas is sure going to be a pleasant one, now that we know our little friend speaks English."

Dawson, who suspected Lance of having more than a friendly attitude for this girl, watched him from the corner of his eye. He wondered at the moment what the outcome would be should his suspicions concerning Lance be confirmed. Suddenly, the men tensed, as a faint call of a crow reached their ears.

"It could be that they heard the rifle shots," said Lance soberly.

"Injuns, all right," cut in Dawson.

"We can't chance staying here until dark," remarked Lance. "We'll have to push on now."

Turley walked over to the dead outlaw and yanked the knife out of his back.

"Turley, untie the horses with the saddles and one of ours, I'll ride that one. Inspect the bags and see how much ammo they have."

"When we ride out, let's go by the cave and pick up that other rifle," suggested Dawson.

"It only had one shot left in it and I fired that one."

"I was tending to the lad up there and plum forgot it when you called for me to come down here," said Turley.

"What happened to the boy?" asked Lance as he jammed his newly possessed rifle into the sheath that was strapped tightly to one of the saddles.

"Well," replied Dawson. "The boy got hit in the head when they opened up on us, never uttered a sound."

"Too bad," said Lance as he stared out over the trees. "Sure wanted to repay him for helping us out."

"Ready, Captain?" asked Turley, who was already up on his horse.

"Yeah, let's get going," replied Lance.

Lance walked over to the girl and smiled down at her. "Don't get out of my sight anymore; it's not nice for a lady to be tied up all the time." There was something else in her eyes besides spark as he gently lifted her into his arms and held her there momentarily before setting her up into the saddle. Dawson eyed Turley, as the latter stared at Lance soberly with a frown appearing on his forehead.

Friend Turley is beginning to catch on, said Dawson to himself as he scratched his grizzled head.

He distorted Turley's thoughts intentionally as he spoke to Lance. "Your guards are ready, Captain," he said, and noticed that Turley's facial expression remained the same.

Lance mounted his horse and urged it forward. They rode up to the cave and halted. The old scout dismounted and disappeared into the cave. Lance and Turley followed suit. Once inside, Lance examined the wound that had caused the death of the young boy. "Let's build a stone grave around him," he suggested, and then added soberly, "it's the least we can do for him." During the course of the task, the call of the crow reached their ears at intervals.

"Getting closer, those redskin devils," remarked Dawson.

Lance glanced toward the outside of the cave and got a full view of the girl sitting on the horse. *Winsor, you fool,* he shouted to himself.

Keep that girl close to your side. Do you want her to be abused and tied up again? Or something worse? Especially now. I think she likes you Winsor. Remember how you felt when you lifted her in your arms and she smiled at you? You do. Then stay with her do you hear? Stay with her.

Dawson watched Lance for a moment as the latter stared in the direction of the girl. The old scout tensed slightly at the crow call that echoed through the valley, not too far distant. It disrupted Lance's thoughts too, for the latter issued hasty orders.

"Let's move out before we get trapped in here again." He took a step or two, then stopped, for he noticed the frowning expression on Turley's face a moment before. He turned toward his friend and asked, "Something wrong?"

"No, not a thing," replied Turley, as he brushed off the dust that covered the front of his coat. "Just been wondering about those red-skins out there," he lied.

Lance turned and the others followed him out. They mounted their horses and were off again heading now in an easterly direction. They rode hard for about an hour, and Lance, who was in the lead, pulled to a stop. "Been trying to spot the gun-runners' trail," he said. "Can't pick up a sign anywhere."

"Do you figure there were more of them?" asked Dawson.

"I think so," answered Lance. "They must have a wagonload of guns out here somewhere and probably another man or two watching it. No time to look for them now, he added. We'll get caught up with for sure."

"Haven't heard the call for some time now," spoke Turley, as he wiped the sweat off his forehead.

"I noticed that," said Lance. "No doubt by now they found a few things that took place back at the cave. From here on, they'll follow us in silence." Lance frowned as he looked in a backwardly direction and added, "We'll hear them again if they spot us. It'll be the signals for an attack."

"Let's not give them that chance, Winsor," said Dawson, as he loosened the rifle a bit in its sheath.

"Don't aim to," said Lance, as he managed a slight grin. "If we don't soon get back, you and I will be looking for a new job."

"In that case, I'll go along to St. Louie with my friend Turley here," replied Dawson, as he spat another stream of tobacco juice that changed the course of a beetle that was headed toward an ant hill.

Lance smiled at Turley, then looked at the girl and asked, "Are you all right?"

She smiled lightly and nodded her head in the affirmative.

Lance urged his horse ahead and the four of them pushed on through the timber. As time went by, the sun disappeared behind the mountains and darkness set in. Although progress was slowed up a bit, the foursome rode on relentlessly. Lance wanted to get away as far as possible from Sioux country before settling down for a well-earned rest. His thoughts were of the girl most of the time. He was amazed at her endurance, which seemed to be endless. Nevertheless, she certainly must be tired, he mused. He finally pulled to a stop upon reaching the top of a mountain they had just climbed.

"There it is," exclaimed Turley, as he got a glimpse of the moonlit waters of the Big Horn River. He put his hand on Lance's shoulder and pointed between two giant trees.

"It's the river all right," agreed Lance.

"Let's go on down and cross it. We'll make camp on the other side."

VI

A half hour later, they pulled up in between some large boulders and dismounted.

"We'll have to chance a small fire for a while," said Lance.

"I'll make it," volunteered Dawson, and went about gathering dried limbs. He had the fire going in short order.

Lance and Turley unsaddled the horses and threw them down near the small blaze.

"How long do you expect to stay here Lance?" asked Turley.

"Four or fire hours at the most," answered Lance.

"I'm sure anxious to get going," said Turley. "Things are starting to take shape."

Lance felt an empty feeling in the pit of his stomach but managed to say without betraying his emotions, "I'm going to have the sergeant's daughter hog tie you when we get back to the fort and see if we can't get you to stay around here for a spell."

Turley hesitated for a moment, then looked Lance squarely in the eye and asked, "Why?"

Lance's face grew red. He wasn't quite sure why Turley asked that question. "Oh," replied Lance. "Just don't want you to leave the country. Anyway, I need a good partner. I intend to start a little ranch somewhere along the river."

Whatever was on Turley's mind, he didn't say. Instead he commented, "Sounds good, maybe I'll join you when I leave St. Louie."

Lance looked at the girl as she rested against a boulder. Her face was expressionless, and he wondered what occupied her thoughts.

"Why don't you two pole cats get some rest and quit gabbing," cut in Dawson, who was now preparing a place for the girl to sleep. "It's high time that I stand guard anyway."

"I'll stand the first one," said Lance. "Want to do some thinking. You can take the second."

Dawson grumbled but didn't argue the point.

"One more thing," said Lance as he ran the palm of his hand over his face. "We'll stand our watch down by the river. Our chances will be a lot better should anyone try to cross."

Lance picked up one of the rifles and inspected it briefly. His mind was more on the girl than the inspection for he had intentions of saying something to her before leaving. He had nothing special to talk about at the moment. Just wanted her to say something or perhaps see her smile again. It would give him a thing or two to dream about while he guarded the camp out there in the moonlight. He turned, took a step and stopped abruptly as Turley sat down beside the girl.

"Well, Naomi, how does it feel to be on your way home?" he heard Turley ask.

As if he forgot something, Lance walked back to one of the saddles and fumbled around in one of the bags waiting for the conversation to continue.

He was well aware of the fact that the nearer they got to the fort, the more uneasy he felt. Lance felt a sense of relief when Naomi asked a question instead of answering Turley's.

"We . . . go home . . . soon?"

Lance noticed that the girl didn't smile, nor did she seem enthused.

"Yep," replied Turley. "We'll be going back right soon."

"Expecting a war?" asked Dawson, as he eyed Lance slipping a handful of cartridges into his pocket.

"Never can tell," replied Lance with a smile slapping the old scout on the back. "Get some sleep; I'll be waking you up right quick." Lance hesitated a moment and smiled at the girl.

"You look sleepy," he said. She smiled back at him shyly but didn't say anything.

"Don't wander too far," said Turley as he looked up at Lance. And added musingly, "Wouldn't want to find us all tied up again."

Lance said nothing as he smiled at his friend, and walked out toward the river. Dawson watched Lance disappear into the darkness and then glanced briefly at Turley and the girl. The young scout seemed to be quite eager to talk to the girl about the trip back to Texas. With a frown, Dawson laid his head on one of the saddles and pulled the blanket up over his shoulders. He didn't fall asleep quickly, for a lingering thought kept prying on his mind. *Winsor wants the girl for one reason, Turley wants her for another. The question is,* he mused, *does she want Winsor or is she looking forward to home.* Dawson discarded the matter from his mind as Turley came over and laid down a short distance from him. With the exception of a few nocturnal creatures, the great forest slept in silence.

Another guard, high up in the skies, kept the valley well lit with its bright rays that cast flickering shadows along the rippling stream of the Big Horn. A solitary figure sat facing the stream, lost completely in his thoughts. They were disturbed and he tensed slightly as three deer suddenly appeared out of the forest and trotted into the water. He watched them as they drank the cool water. Every once in a while the creatures would look up, perk their ears and listen. A short time later, the deer made a hasty retreat and disappeared into the darkened forest. Wonder what scared them, mused Lance. He scanned the area but saw nothing suspicious. About to settle back against the tree, Lance glanced back over his shoulder toward the camp and suddenly sprang up with the swiftness of a cat. He noticed the outline of someone coming toward him from the camp. His heart skipped a beat and his heart raced madly as he recognized the intruder. It was Naomi. Upon seeing Lance, she walked over to him slowly. He put his hand tenderly on her shoulder and asked, "What is the matter? Something wrong?"

Looking up at him, she said, "I could . . . not sleep." If ever there came in a man's life the very depth of love, the urge to want someone, to protect someone, one to call his very own, this certainly was the time for Lance Winsor.

Snap out of it Winsor, say something, don't just stand there.

He recomposed himself and said, "Come over here and sit down." Lance sat down beside her and wondered momentarily why other girls never excited him like this girl did.

You were never in love before Winsor, but you are now, aren't you boy?

She had her head against the tree and slowly turned it toward him. The shadows flickered across her face and the sparkles in her eyes danced about like the shining stars high up in the skies. The soothing south wind caressed her lovely face as it flowed gently by. The faraway cry of the night bird seemed to blend in with the loveliness of the moment.

Lance got the sudden urge to kiss those lips, to hold her close, tell her that nothing else in the world mattered but the two of them. He wanted to tell her that he loved her, that he wanted to marry her. Everything that he has done was because of her.

Go ahead Winsor, this is the time, he urged himself. His head was spinning and he knew it. Slowly he bent his head towards hers. They were only inches apart. Naomi didn't move. She just looked at him. Lance advanced no farther as the thought occurred to him, that perhaps this girl wasn't in love with him. The spell broken, Lance drew back slightly and placed his shoulders against the tree.

You fool Winsor, you fool. When do you expect to find out if she likes you or not? When she's gone?

Lance was jarred momentarily, as Naomi broke the silence. "I . . . don't want . . . to go home. My . . . heart . . . is heavy." She looked at Lance pleadingly for an encouraging answer. Lance was bewildered and sighed unnoticeably. The burden that he carried on his mind was suddenly relieved. Now that he knew she didn't want to go back was certainly in his favor.

Winsor was inspired beyond imagination and betrayed his emotions very little if any, as he asked, "Why don't you want to go home?" He breathed a little heavily as he waited anxiously for her to answer.

"I know . . . my father . . . was hurt in ambush. Dawson . . . tell me . . . my father . . . died."

Lance noticed that the expression on her face had turned to sadness. He put a hand on her shoulder and said, "I'm sorry about that."

"I have . . . no body there . . . now." She continued, "I should like . . . to stay . . ." She hesitated momentarily and Lance's heart skipped a beat, then she added, "Here."

Winsor, did you hear that boy? Press the issue, go on, don't stall, he shouted to himself. You're going to find out just how she feels about you if you ask her why she wants to stay up here. Lance hesitated for a moment, for he wasn't sure that her answer would be in his favor and that thought chilled him. Lance sighed a little as he bent slightly toward her and tensed. He could feel the blood rush up to his face, and finally asked, "Why do you want to stay up here, Naomi?"

With her head still resting on the tree, she turned slightly and faced Lance squarely. His pulse pounded madly as he waited with anticipation for the answer that would heighten him to the top of the world or crumble his dreams to the very depth of despair.

She didn't answer verbally, and Lance was about to ask her again, when all of a sudden his very being was filled with the sweetness of life itself as he felt her hand slowly circling his. Lance could feel his heart crying out for her as he placed his hand on her face and slowly bent toward her. Lance never met her lips for he suddenly sprang up and half dragged the girl behind the tree with him, as a screaming arrow sunk deep into the tree upon which they leaned.

The turn of events angered Lance as he fired shot after shot across the river. The crack of the rifle shattered the stillness of the night and the echo carried far and wide dying out as it sailed over the darkened horizon. The commotion brought Dawson and Turley out in a hurry.

Rushing toward Lance, Turley was about to ask Lance what the trouble was. The answer came to him through another source, as an arrow sailed by him tearing into the outstretched limbs of the trees.

"Darn their ornery hides," grumbled Dawson. "I was just beginning to sleep peaceful-like."

"Back in behind the boulders," ordered Lance swiftly as he circled his arm around the girl's waist and dodgingly retreated.

"You stay right here and don't move," Lance cautioned Naomi as he led her behind a large boulder.

"Turley," he ordered. "Guard this end. I'll take the other. Dawson, saddle the horses fast!"

"How many do you think there are?" asked Turley.

"I don't know," answered Lance, as he strained his eyes watching for some sign of the intruders.

Dawson was grumbling for all he was worth as he went about swiftly preparing the animals for travel. The men tensed with alertness, as the low sound of a hoot owl came to them from the direction of the river.

"Blasted injun trouble makers," mumbled Dawson.

Another owl call was heard in answer, not too far distant to the right of Turley.

"Lance," hissed Turley in excitement. "Some of them are on this side of the river."

Lance was well aware of the fact as he glanced over to Turley's position and called out softly to Dawson, "Are the horses ready? We've got to get out of here fast."

"Just about," answered the old scout, and then added, "you better come on down and fill your pockets with these here bullets. Looks like we'll be need'n 'em plenty."

"They don't often attack at night," remarked Lance, as he took a few boxes of cartridges that Dawson shoved at him. "Bet my next month's pay," he continued, "that the leader of that band out there is White Cloud."

"Must be mad as a hornet after stealing his bride to be," said Turley hastily as he fingered the trigger of his rifle.

"Naomi," Lance half whispered.

The girl got up swiftly and came over to his side. Lance lost no time as he swept her off her feet and placed her onto the saddle. He hopped up on his saddleless horse and the other two mounted theirs.

"Now look," cautioned Lance. "Keep down low and follow me close. We'll try to head down the river a ways and then head up over the mountain. At this point it's much too steep for the horses to climb."

Suddenly, they tensed to a feverish pitch as a savage let out a blood curdling scream and jumped on Dawson, who at the moment was the nearest to him. The old scout ducked and the savage bounced off the horse's rump and fell against one of the boulders. The attacker, who was fast getting back up on his feet, spun around crazily as the impact of the bullet tore into his side and he fell to the ground without uttering a sound.

"Come on, let's go," said Lance quickly, and headed his horse away from the stony area toward the haven of the deep forest. He advanced but twenty yards, when all of a sudden a hale of arrows tore at them from the direction of the river and two of the horses screamed wildly as their feet buckled under their riders, sending them sprawling headlong into the brush.

"Quick, back behind the boulders," Lance shouted.

Lance and Turley, the fallen riders, sent a barrage of bullets towards the river as they dodged brokenly making their way back to the rock concealment. Dawson snatched the reins of the girl's horse and rode swiftly behind the boulders. He jumped off the animal rather than dismounted, and at the same time fired point blank at an oncoming savage whose life suddenly came to a violent end as the shot sheared off the top of his head.

"Any of you hurt?" asked Lance with anxiety as he and Turley came charging in.

"Little short of air, that's all," replied Dawson, who was breathing fast and hard.

"You all right Naomi?" asked Lance softly, as he placed his hand on her shoulder.

"All Right," she answered looking up at him.

"What's the next move, Captain?" asked Turley, as he sucked in a lungful of air.

"I'm afraid that we'll have to leave the horses here and try to escape on foot." Lance walked over to a boulder and peered out toward the river. Turley scanned the other end of the stone concealment.

After a few minutes, Lance walked back to where Dawson and the girl were standing and said, "Got awful quiet, sudden like." He jammed a few cartridges into the magazine of the rifle.

"Do you think they will attack in force?" asked Turley.

"I don't think that they have much of a force out there or else they would have before this," replied Lance. "Another point in our favor," he continued, "is that they are without rifles. Now let's take whatever we can and make an attempt to get up over this mountain. We'll have to keep low and do some crawling and if we're lucky, we may get away without being detected."

In a minute they were ready and Lance clasped Naomi's hand in his and led the way up toward the steep grade. They stopped suddenly as a sharp voice startled them. It came from the direction of the river, and in broken English.

"White Cloud . . . want girl . . . you give girl . . . you go." Lance pressed his lips together which went white as they formed a thin line. He clasped the girl's hand tighter and drew her to him slightly. Her forehead touched his shoulder and he thrilled to her nearness.

His lips formed into a smile as he said to himself, "The whole Sioux nation couldn't get her now, fella."

"What you going to answer," asked Dawson in anticipation.

Lance sucked in a lungful of air and shouted, "You wait, I ask girl if she will go."

He turned to his friends. "Come on, let's go," he whispered quickly and advanced forward. They made their way up the rugged slope in silence. A full five minutes elapsed before the voice down by the river finally blurted out again.

"Girl come now, we wait no more."

The climbers stopped and looked down at the river through the trees. The stream looked beautiful in the moonlight from up at that height. The night seemed quiet and peaceful at the moment but they knew better as they observed nothing. A deadly menace was lurking along the banks of the Big Horn and at any moment their absence would be detected.

"They are going to get mighty curious shortly as to why we didn't answer," whispered Lance. "Let's keep moving."

Lance helped the struggling girl along. They pushed on relentlessly. About halfway up the mountain, Lance stopped and looked up at the almost vertical slope that be-fronted him. "Impossible to climb any farther," he said to the others. "Much too steep. We'll have to continue to along the side here until we come to a spot where it's passable."

"Look," exclaimed Turley. "In the river."

"They're coming across, blast their ornery hides," blurted Dawson, who was indeed panting hard.

The moon was high in the sky and the Indians were easy to detect in the bright waters as they cautiously made their way across.

"Must be seven or eight of them that I can see," said Lance. "All Right fellas, let's move, and keep a tight grip on your rifles."

Continuing along side of the mountain, the going was much easier. About a half hour later, Lance halted for a brief rest. They near collapsed to the ground, however, welcoming the cool soft moss as they stretched their tired bodies out on. Lance looked over the terrain in back of him and noticed that the steep grade continued. He wondered how much farther they would have to go before they could cross over the top of the mountain. Certainly don't want to mix with those renegades down there again if I can help it, he mused. All was silent.

No one spoke, nor did they care to at the moment as they laid there like babies in the woods retiring for a good night's rest. Suddenly, their bodies became tense as the old familiar owl call reached the reluctant listeners.

"Down by the river and a little to the right of us, I would say," whispered Lance.

The men bolted to their feet as another call came from a distance in back of them, but at the same level.

"Don't these Sioux ever sleep?" snapped Turley sarcastically. He was indeed annoyed at being on his feet again so soon, as were the others.

"Let's wait for them here," said Dawson gruffly, as he gripped the rifle tightly. "We'll put them to sleep permanent like."

Lance paid little attention if any to the raving scouts, as he planned the next move.

"Now listen," said Lance to the others. "We can't go up yet. So we'll have to continue in the direction we were headed. Got to go fast or they'll catch up with us. That we want to avoid if possible."

Lance took the girl by the hand, and once more led the way along the mountainside. The owl call signals began to get a little closer as they advanced. The ones heard down by the river seemed to be much closer to them as time went on. A short time later, Lance stopped briefly and said," There is no doubt about it now, they're sure of our position. We've got to head down toward the river and throw them off our trail for a while. Our chances are a lot better down there anyway."

Dawson grumbled something under his breath that was meant for Indian savages only.

"We're still alive, following you, Captain. Lead the way," commented Turley anxiously.

Lance did, and as he cut down the mountainside at an angle, he thought warmly of Turley, for not once did his friend question his decision during the entire venture thus far. Never the leader, this Turley, always the guard, and a mighty good one at that. A considerable amount of time elapsed during the retreat toward the river and the calls signaling came from high up in the back of them. Once again Lance stopped and remarked, as he gripped the rifle with his left hand and his right slipped around the girl's shoulder as she fell against him in sheer exhaustion, "I think that they are confused, we left them back there a ways."

"They'll be on to us 'afore long," remarked Dawson.

"You are right there, Old Timer," agreed Lance. "We'll go down to the river, make our way along the bank and get far enough away so that we can rest up. We're not going to be able to take too much of this any more." Lance was thinking about Naomi, as he drew her tightly to him.

Once along the water's edge, the going was much easier for the already over-burdened hearts of the hard going foursome. Within the past hour, the signaling stopped completely and finally Lance made his way into a heavy thicket and halted. Once again four tired bodies laid down to rest. Lance took a deep breath and said wearily to the others, "Try to get some sleep. I'll stay awake as long as I can, then wake one of you."

Several minutes later, everything was quiet and still. Lance rubbed his eyes and blinked them several times, letting them rest on the girl's face. That the moon was still in the sky was evident as the rays peeped through the heavy brush. Tired and weary as he was, Lance got the urge to kiss the girl's cheek. He glanced casually at the two scouts and eased slowly over to the girl. He bent down and kissed the corner of her mouth. Lance seemed to become alive again as he felt the soft warm face of the girl. Suddenly, he realized that she wasn't asleep as her hand reached his face and held it tightly to hers.

"Naomi," whispered Lance softly, and then eased away from the girl as Turley rolled over on his side. Lance took another look at the girl as he picked up his rifle and smiled with satisfaction, then strode on out toward the river.

VII

Nearing the river's edge, Lance stopped and looked cautiously about. Observing nothing suspicious, he lay down upon the soft moss and sighed heavily. Fingering the rifle momentarily, he let it lay at his side satisfied that it was in readiness, if needed. He clasped his hand together and placed them under his head. The moon was bright and high in the sky. Lance gazed at the stars as they seemed to dance about in the blue and his thoughts went back to the Indian girl whose sudden appearance in the Big Horn had changed his plans and course entirely. The soft ripple of the stream and the chirp of the crickets seemed to blend in with his thoughts. Slow but sure, the magic powers of the sandman will overcome the strongest of men, the wildest of beasts, and Lance Winsor was no exception, for his eyes closed slowly as his weary body gave way to the ever-welcoming slumber.

An hour went by, and then another. Nothing seemed to disturb the silence of the night. Not even the soft cry of a nocturnal bird whose forlorn calls went unanswered as it called out repeatedly somewhere up in the tall pines not too far distant. Should any of the scouts have been up and about at the moment, they would have aroused the others and quickly be on their way of escape. Any one of them would have distinguished those calls as signals made by the red man. Indeed, White Cloud must certainly be furious, for he led his braves on relentlessly in search for the girl who was to become his wife and the hated scouts who stole her out of the village the eve before his wedding.

It could have been the dead still of the night that caused Lance Winsor to stir slightly, and upon doing so, he slowly opened his eyes. His mind wasn't clear as he lay there semi-conscious and wondered momentarily where he was. Suddenly he tensed; he reached for his rifle and sprung up on his feet as another call, high up to his right, reached his ears and penetrated them for the first time. He lost no time in arousing the others and swiftly explained the situation.

Dawson was his usual self as he grumbled, "Let's make a stand and blast those ornery injuns once and for all. I'd like to sleep one night through for a change."

"We'll talk about that one some other time," said Lance. "Right now let's get out of here fast or that bushy hair of yours will get a good combing in the morning and it won't be you running a comb through it as it hangs as a trophy in some Brave's tepee."

Turley laughed as he grabbed Dawson by the hair and said, "This would be quite a trophy at that. I'd get quite a price for it in St. Louie."

"This boy has injun blood in 'em," grumbled Dawson, "or else he's gone plumb loco."

He faced Turley and said, "You all right son?"

Turley laughed as he slapped the old scout on the shoulder and at the same time Lance cautioned for silence, as the call that came from the right of them seemed much closer.

"They don't know our exact location," said Lance to the others as he stopped short of the riverbank. "However, I do believe that they are aware of the fact that we are no longer up at their level." They listened in silence to the signaling and huddled momentarily, ever so cautious before continuing along the route of escape.

"They are working their way down the side of the mountain," said Lance.

A frown appeared on his forehead as he continued. "If we follow the river, they are bound to run into us and if we go back up, we stand the same chance."

"Well Dawson," cut in Turley. "We're in for another bath, you need it anyway." Turley grinned as he waited for the old scout to make a reply but Lance cut the matter short.

"Let's cross here; we don't have too much more time."

Dawson grumbled something under his breath and made his way to the edge of the water. He was first to step in.

"Hold it," said Lance quickly as he held Naomi and Turley back and waited for the old scout to appear on the surface of the water.

Suddenly, there was a break in the water, and Dawson, gasping for air, exclaimed, "Damn blast this river. Can't never tell where it's deep."

Lance and Turley grinned as they pulled him out of the water. The smile on their lips died swiftly and the expression on their faces became serious as the signaling began again and at the moment much too close for comfort. Lance swiftly issued orders.

"Quick, over here, let's get this into the water." The three put their shoulders against a fallen tree that had lain dried and withered in the sun and inched in toward the water. The task of getting it into the river left them breathless but finally the soft edges of the bank gave way and slowly the heavy tree slid into the water.

"All Right," said Lance between breaths. "Let's get in and hang on to the tree.

Keep swimming with one hand, and we'll try to get it out to the middle."

The already wet Dawson slid into the cool water again, this time hanging on to the tree. Turley got in and then Naomi. Lance swiftly looked about in the semi-darkness and found a large limb. He lost no time placing one end against the trunk of the tree and pushed it out into the current. Discarding the limb, he slid into the water and swam over to the floating tree. Inch by inch they struggled with it, trying to propel it out toward the middle. Suddenly, a savage let out a yell as he came out to the edge of the river.

"They're on to us," whispered Lance quickly. "There are heavy rapids not too far from here, if I remember correctly. If we can make it, they'll have to give up the chase for the mountain is steep along the rapids and I don't think that they will make an attempt to climb it."

If Lance was going to say more, he sure decided to let it go for the time being as he ducked under the water along with the others, safeguarding themselves as the screaming arrows splintered the floating tree.

The savages kept yelling and shooting their murderous arrows as they kept pace with the floating foursome. The scouts and the girl kept coming up for air at intervals. On one of the occasions, Turley said between breaths, "Looks like this is an all out affair this time. The way they are shooting they don't care whether they hit the girl or not." Turley winced and snapped his head to one side as an arrow sailed past him near taking along his natural hearing aid.

A short time later, the four of them peered out over the trunk of the tree wondering just what was in store for them next. The shooting ceased and the wild chatter along the riverbank indicated a change in tactics or probably a new plan of attack. Lance paid little attention to the latter as the noise of the rapids became more distinct. His anxiety grew to an explosive pitch at the thought of reaching the rapids, for there was the gateway to the final escape.

Lance was jarred from his thoughts as Dawson exclaimed, "Look, some of those savages are getting into the river."

Lance took a fast look for himself. Satisfied that the old scout wasn't seeing things in the dark, he asked Naomi, who clinged to the float next to him, "Are you all right?"

"Yes," she answered, and her face held an expression of anxiety.

"Now listen," he cautioned. "You hang on to this tree as long as you can. I'll try to get back here before we reach the rapids." She nodded her head in answer.

He managed a smile and said, "Now don't you worry," as he swam around her and made his way to the rear of the tree trunk.

"There are about four or five of them swimming out toward us," said Turley as he snapped his head to one side shaking some of the water loose. Lance turned and glanced in the direction of the rapids whose ever-increasing noise was more than welcome even though certain dangers still lurked in the fast, rock-infested waters. Devoting his attention now to the oncoming savages, Lance submerged himself and came up on the other side of the trunk. He lifted his water-soaked rifle out of the water and laid the stock end of the weapon across his shoulder.

Turley followed suit as Dawson muttered in disgust, "I lost my rifle when I first got into the river back there."

"Don't worry 'bout that now, Old Timer. You stay close to the girl and use that big knife of yours should any of them slip by us."

"Lance," cut in Turley. "Over to the right."

Lance turned in time to see the leading savage disappear underneath the surface, then bob up again, much nearer a few moments later. "Let them come all the way in," cautioned Lance in low tones. "Don't let go here unless you really have to." He worked his hand downward until it reached the end of the barrel. In the semi-darkness Lance could see the pursuer quite clearly. The roar of the rapids increased his already racing pulse. He had the urge to steal a quick glance toward Naomi before going over the rough waters but the nearness of the savage erased all thoughts.

Turley felt quite warm in the cool water as he watched the second savage swimming cautiously toward them. He, too, held fast to the barrel end of his rifle and was ready for action. Right now, he would have traded his trip to St. Louis for some dry powder.

Lance stared at the attacker nearest to him as the latter stopped swimming momentarily and floated with the current. Confused as to a way of attack, thought Lance.

Suddenly, the Indian disappeared and Lance knew what to expect. The red skin was going to come up under him. To battle the enemies now, Lance braced himself, leaning heavily on the trunk of the tree, and lashed viciously with his feet. The moments seemed like hours as he tried desperately to come in contact with the Indian's body.

Suddenly, there came an outcry from Dawson. "Lance!"

Lance let go of his rifle and reached for his knife as he made a desperate scramble toward the struggling Dawson and the girl. Whether the savage passed him up on purpose or became confused underneath the water was a matter quickly discarded by Lance at the moment, for the thought of harm befalling the girl and the old scout drove him into a feverish pitch.

"Naomi," he called in desperation, as he half climbed upon the tree trunk.

"Over here," she answered gasping for air, as her head bobbed up in behind a stubby limb of the floating tree.

"You all right?" he asked quickly.

"Yes," was the answer.

"Make your way back to the rear of the tree, fast." At the same time he searched in vain for some sign of Dawson who seemed to vanish with his attacker, a secret held by the raging rapids just a short distance ahead. Slipping an arm around Naomi's waist as she struggled toward the rear of the trunk, Lance felt a sickening feeling in the pit of his stomach.

"Turley," called Lance to his friend.

There was no answer.

"Turley," he shouted. The anguish in his voice was obvious. He looked out over the rough waters but saw no one. Grief stricken, Lance held on tightly to Naomi and braced himself, wrapping his free arm around the trunk of the now fast-moving tree. The mad moving rapids rolled the large float back and forth as if it were a twig. The two clinging figures bobbed in and out of the water hanging on desperately, for now it was a matter of endurance.

Lance wondered just how much of a pounding they could take. They had a long weary struggle behind them, with very little rest and just as much food. Suddenly, the tree rammed a large rock. The impact caused Lance to lose his grip on both the tree and Naomi. He lost his senses momentarily but soon regained them as he reappeared on the surface splashing madly about like a drowning cat looking for some sign of the girl.

"Naomi!" He shouted in desperation and at the same time got a glimpse of her in the still moonlit waters, as she held on frantically to a limb of the tree. Lance reached out and held fast to a limb of the tree float as it spun around. New life seemed to engulf him as he made his way along the trunk toward the half-drowned girl. Finally, getting within reach of her, he slipped his arm around her waist again and half-lifted the girl out of the water. Her head rested on his shoulder and she panted hard and fast, for within the past few minutes she was subject to a lot more water than air. Her heavy breathing reassured Lance that she was all right, with the exception of drinking more water than necessary. He held her tightly and put his lips to her wet head. His arm was near numb as he kept it circled around the trunk. The other around the girl, floating down the river in the dead of night.

Tired, hungry, sleepless. Not very romantic, thought Lance, but if things turn out like I want them to, it certainly will be worth it.

He felt a sudden pang within himself as his thoughts flashed back to his missing friends. Lance was indeed sad and tried to keep the thought from his mind. He pressed the girl closer to him and her arm tightened about his head slightly. He discarded the idea of breaking loose and swimming to shore. Better wait until they got nearer to shore, Lance thought to himself, for he was well aware of the girl's physical exhaustion and didn't want to over tax the little strength that he still possessed unless he really had to.

About another mile down the river the tree suddenly spun around and zigzagged momentarily as it scraped the bottom of the now slow moving waters. Lance, conscious of the fact, slowly eased himself downward until his feet touched the bottom. He stood there for a minute trying to keep his balance, for his arms and legs were nearly numb. Finally, he gathered all of his strength and made the attempt to wade to shore.

The struggle seemed like hours before he was able to set Naomi down on the soft grassy bank and Lance fell down beside her. The two weary figures lost consciousness in less than a minute and the river seemed to look upon them in triumph as it went down through the canyon, for she was rough and vicious indeed; in her attempt to snuff out the life within the two resting bodies, to keep her company as she made her way toward the great waters that lie far beyond the horizon.

Dawn approached the Big Horn country a few hours later. The moon had gone on its way to another part of the world, hiding within it the secrets of the night.

Lance Winsor awoke, rubbing his eyes as he sat up. Chill had over taken him otherwise he would have continued the much needed rest. He looked sadly at the motionless girl who was indeed a pitiful sight. Reluctantly, he went about the task of waking her for it was imperative that they seek a place of hiding to elude the pursuers should they wander down this far, by choice or otherwise, and too, the hot sun that would cast its heat throughout the valley.

Lance Winsor had plans for a lot more rest before another nightfall. A few minutes later, the pair headed up toward the mountain. The struggle was slow, for Lance half-carried the weary girl. They stopped at intervals for a short rest. The climb to the top seemed endless but they pressed forward painfully. Finally, they reached the top. Once again, out of breath, and out of strength. Lance led the girl to a thicket of pines, slowly eased her down and dropped down beside her. Not a word was said as they lost consciousness again. They laid there motionless, undetected by the busy creatures as they scampered about their daily tasks. As the hours went by, the day became hot but the two slumbering figures were aware of nothing as they continued their sleep underneath the tall pines.

The day wore on to late afternoon. The once brilliant sun was slowly edging its way toward the horizon. A deer, nibbling on some laurel, suddenly perked up its ears, as the faraway cry of a whippoorwill faintly echoed out in the valley. The animal was motionless for a full minute, then resumed the meal, satisfied that nothing was amiss.

Minutes later, the animal's head bobbed up again as the cry echoed through the valley. The deer let out a snort and started to walk away from the laurel bush confused, but stopped suddenly and looked back as the cry was repeated. The animal waited for another echo, which seemed to have alarmed him but it did not come. A moment later, he scampered away, disappearing among the tall timber. Lance Winsor opened his eyes and stared up at the tall trees. The events that had taken place slowly re-entered his mind.

Getting up on his elbow, he turned slightly and gazed at Naomi. The color in her face was back and the tired haggard expression was completely gone. He placed his hand on her shoulder lightly and had the urge to hold her closely to him, tell her that this was the end. He wasn't going back to the fort. Together they would seek the presence of the on coming settlers, get some equipment and go down the river a ways, starting the future he had planned.

There must be someone who can marry us among the settlers, he mused. Lance's dream carried him away as he thought of a best man and at this moment the smile vanished from his lips for he had hoped that Turley would do the honor. Saddened by the thought of his missing friends, he got to his feet and looked around the area. He wondered just what took place back there in the rapids. His friends disappeared so suddenly. *Of course the river became quite fast at that point,* he mused. *Maybe they . . .?* The thought that Turley and the old scout may have reached the shore suddenly shot through his veins.

He realized that the scouts had their hands full with the swimming savages and if they eluded them, maybe they couldn't get back to the fast-moving tree as it sped down the treacherous rapids. New life engulfed Lance as he made his way over to a small stream that trickled in and out among the rocks. He washed his face after drinking some of the cool water and went about looking for some berry bushes.

A lot of time had gone by since the last meal and at the moment, anything edible would do, he mused. Lance spied a patch of berries, then went back and aroused the sleeping girl. She was bewildered for a moment but smiled presently, as the events of their harrowing experience re-entered her mind. Lance smiled down at her as he helped the dazed girl to her feet.

"Well, how do you feel now?" he asked.

"Very much better," she answered.

"How much we sleep. . ." asked Naomi. ". . . many days?"

"No," laughed Lance. "I would say about twelve hours. I know where there is some nice cool water and something to eat. Today you are my guest, come on."

Lance put his arm around her shoulder and they walked over to the mountain stream. Quenching her thirst, she got to her feet and slowly looked about the present area. The expression on Lance's face became sober as he noticed Naomi staring about, for he knew, more than guessed, why the puzzled look appeared on her face.

"They're not here," said Lance, before she could ask the question. Naomi looked at Lance questioningly as she walked slowly toward him.

He explained the turn of events that took place at the rapids. She stood before him with her head bowed. Her face was sad, as Lance put his hand under her chin and tilted her head.

"Our hearts are heavy now," said Lance. "But there's still hope. Perhaps they were lucky as we were, and made their way out of the water."

"I did not know," she said softly. "My head was not too clear."

Lance managed a faint smile and said in agreement, "I think that you were out completely but I am still amazed at your endurance."

Lance turned slightly and pointed toward the berries. "That is the best the mountains have to offer. Shall we eat?"

He watched the girl as she picked and ate the berries. There was no doubt in his mind that this was indeed the girl for him. He had admitted that to himself many times before. From the very first time that he had set eyes on her, back at the trapper's camp, she had fascinated him. Lance felt a bit uneasy, not knowing just how much she cared about him, if at all. She must care a little, he said to himself. After all, hasn't she stuck near him ever since they got away from the gunrunners up at the cave? And the way she looked at times, especially when he near kissed her back at the river just before the Indians attacked the first time.

Once and for all Winsor, he said to himself, there will never come a better time than now to find out how you really stand.

"What are you thinking?" asked Naomi, as she looked at Lance with a smile. Her sudden question caught him off guard but he managed a smile and decided to go about the matter in another way.

"I was wondering what you were going to do up here in the Big Horn country," answered Lance.

He watched her face, trying to detect the hidden answers that could ease the approach as to what he had on his mind, or else force him to discard it. A faint trace of a smile still lingered on her lips as she cast her eyes to the ground.

"My heart would be sad if I go back now," she said.

There was a reason why she wanted to stay, Lance pondered to himself, that's for sure, but he certainly made no headway in clearing up that reason. Lance felt a sudden pang in the pit of his stomach but only for a moment as it suddenly occurred to him, that she didn't leave the Sioux village willingly. But her actions since then caused him little concern as far as the next question was concerned; nevertheless, he held his breath slightly as he asked, "Did you want to stay at the Sioux village?"

"No," she answered softly. "I did not want to stay."

Lance let out a soft sigh and his hopes grew intensely.

"I was afraid," she continued. "The night you came in the tepee and took me away. I did not know why until . . . " she hesitated for a moment, then added ". . . your friend Dawson told me. Now, only here, my heart will be happy."

Naomi got to her feet and her dark eyes flashed as they met Lance's. She let her eyes drop and walked a dozen yards in the direction of the river far below, then stopped, gazing out over the valley.

Fool, fool, shouted Lance to himself, as he got to his feet. You must be the reason why she wants to stay. You saw how she looked at you a moment ago. Go ahead boy; lay your heart out in the open. You must be sure this time, there is nobody else.

Something seemed to chill his insides as he slowly turned and gazed at Naomi. He stood there a full minute. The thought that suddenly tore him apart, was indeed a possibility, and his lips moved but uttered no sound, as they formed the name Turley. Face it Winsor, you've got to find out now. You couldn't feel any worse than if she told you that it was Turley. Brace up man, you could be dead wrong. Must I remind you that it was you she almost kissed? Then why, said Lance to himself slowly, is she staring out there as if the one she loves may still be alive down in the valley? Then again Winsor, wasn't she waiting for an answer just before walking away, and you sat there like a fool?

I know it's the ever cautious Winsor, want to be sure that you don't make a fool out of yourself. Lance walked slowly toward the girl. Once his hopes were high; then just moments later, the world is collapsing at his feet.

During his short walk, Lance thought of the battles he had participated in; there was always a chance to win, but he could never battle for a girl who was in love with someone else. Once again, he held his breath as he walked up behind the girl and softly laid his hands on her shoulders. His head tilted slightly forward and his lips brushed the back of her head unnoticeably.

"Naomi," spoke Lance evenly. "You have given your heart to someone, right now you seem to be sad. Is it because of . . ." Lance Winsor never finished as his hands grasped the girl's shoulders firmly. His body became tense as he stared out over the valley and hoped against hope, that his ears were not deceiving him. What he thought he had heard before was now indeed a reality as the call of the whippoorwill echoed up over the mountain.

"Did you hear that," said Lance, as he focused his eyes in the direction of the call.

Naomi turned and faced Lance questioningly. Lance looked at her, smiling slightly. The question he was about to ask her a few moments ago would have to wait a while. Perhaps not too long; Turley may be with Dawson. It would hurt Lance to see Turley take Naomi if that's the way it had to be, but Lance would endure it all, just to see his friend safe and sound.

"There is only one man that can make that call so perfectly," said Lance with a brace of anxiety in his voice. "Dawson."

Naomi's face brightened up at the thought that the scouts may be alive and followed Lance over to the edge of the downgrade. Lance cupped his hands over his mouth and duplicated the call of the whippoorwill. The echo carried far and wide as it made its way to the rugged corners of the valley. Before it died out completely, a call in answer came ringing up over the mountaintop.

"My heart is happy for you," said Naomi, as she stepped to Lance's side placing her hand on his arm. Lance placed his hand over hers and smiled but his eyes were sad.

"I am to," he said.

Lance, eager to get a glimpse of Dawson, turned away from Naomi and scanned the area below him. His pulse quickened as the calls came nearer. Small beads of perspiration formed on his forehead as he waited with anxiety, for there was no way to determine whether or not Dawson had company.

Lance returned the calls at intervals.

Time seemed to drag on ever so slowly. Patience is a virtue, and Lance certainly abided by the old prophecy, for at the moment his eyes flashed as he caught glimpse of a climbing figure.

"There," said Lance to Naomi, with a bit of excitement in his voice, as he pointed at the on coming figure. "It's Dawson all right."

Naomi's face brightened as she caught a glimpse of the old scout. Lance refrained from calling out to Dawson just then for he waited with anticipation for another form to appear into view. A minute or two later, Lance called out to Dawson, "Over here," for he was convinced that the old scout was alone.

Lance turned toward Naomi and said soberly, "There is only one of them."

He noticed the sorrow in her eyes as she looked at him but the girl made no remark. He took hold of her hand and said, "Let's go down there and help him up."

Dawson's face brightened as he noticed the two of them making their way toward him. He threw himself down on a dried leaf bed and between breaths he managed to exclaim, "Well I'll be darned, I was . . . pretty sure . . . that I'd see you again . . . but I kinda . . . lost hopes . . . for the little one."

"I think that you can outdo any one of the elements," laughed Lance as he made his way over to Dawson and wrapped an arm around his shoulder. You sure look like the 'ole river rat himself. Been swimming of late, Ole Timer?"

Lance continued his laughter, for Dawson looked a sight.

"Why you young coot," blurted out Dawson. "Have you taken a look at yourself? You crawled out of the same river not too long ago."

Dawson looked up a Naomi who stood a short distance away smiling at him and said, "Sure pleased seeing you again little one. Come over here and sit down by me."

She walked over and sat down along side the old scout shyly.

"My heart is happy . . . to see . . .you are well," she said softly.

Dawson put his arm around her shoulder and exclaimed, "You sure get prettier by the day. Never did spec't that you and me would finish the talk we had back there at the cave when we run into those gunrunners."

Lance's thoughts flashed back to the cave. He was well aware of the fact, that it was Dawson who eased the girl's mind as to the reason she was taken out of the Indian village. Ever since then she was easy to get along with and stayed near him through out the rugged trip.

Lance gazed up toward the top of the mountain, paying no attention to the conversation between Dawson and Naomi. He was bitterly accusing himself for being an idiot. You had your chance up there and failed. By now you would have known whether she loved you or not. How much longer are you going to go on burning your insides apart before the answer comes to light? Why prolong the issue, it must be you that she loves. It was you who created that dream about her being in love with Turley.

Turley, the thought of him erased everything else momentarily. It occurred to him now that Dawson never so much as mentioned the welfare of his friend.

He himself didn't mention Turley in hope that the old scout would bear some glad tidings as to the young scouts' whereabouts. Looking at Dawson now, he waited for the latter to finish answering a question that Naomi had asked, and then cut in before their conversation continued.

"Dawson," spoke Lance soberly. "Have you seen anything of Turley?"

The old scout gazed at Lance for a moment, then said, "Why, that young-un can whip a pack of wolves and walk away. I could near bet my next month's pay that he'll be chargin' in on us one of these times. Right now I could eat some laurel and not fret about it."

"Let's go on up over the top and have a look around." He helped the girl to her feet and then asked Lance, "When did you two eat last?"

"We'll join you now," said Lance. "There's a lot of berries up there." Dawson took the girl by the hand and started toward the top. Naomi glanced at Lance over her shoulder and smiled slightly. He winked at her and returned the smile as he followed close behind. Lance pondered over the fact that Dawson seemed unconcerned when asked about the missing Turley. He was still weighing the matter as they reached the top and headed toward the berry patch. Dawson still held the girl's attention, talking faster than a medicine man who was trying to get rid of snake oil. He was retelling his story of his narrow escape from the rapids after getting rid of his Indian attacker.

"Yes sir, by George, I drank me enough water down there to keep a herd of cattle going for a week. After draggin' myself out of that dast blan river, I collapsed like a sack of wheat and the sun was up pretty high when I come to. Well sir, I looked around and saw nar'y a sign of any one, so I headed down stream trying to locate the tree trunk."

He hesitated for a moment and scratched his mud-caked beard. It seemed to Lance that the old scout related his venture somewhat amusingly.

"Go on," urged Lance, as he reached over from a sitting position and pulled off a hand full of berries from one of he bushes. Lance put the berries to his mouth, but got no farther, nor did Dawson with his story, for suddenly a soft drawl broke in on them from a short distance away.

"Wonder if you folks can scrape up a meal for an old weary traveler?"

Quickly, they turned with smiling faces toward the direction from which the voice came; to them it was indeed a familiar one. Leaning against a tree, with his thumbs hooked in his belt stood Turley, grinning like a six year old at his birthday party.

Just as Lance sprang to his feet, Dawson blurted out, "Damn blast you, you impatient pup, I ain't finished my story yet. Now you went and spoilt everything," and he shook his fist in the direction of Turley.

Lance walked swiftly toward the on coming Turley and the two young friends threw their arms around each other's shoulders. They conversed briefly and walked back toward the other two.

Turley broke away from Lance and made his way over to where Naomi was now standing. Upon reaching the girl, he flung his arms around her and placed his cheek against hers, giving her a terrific hug. Releasing the girl, he looked down at her and said, "It takes a mighty good girl to save a man like Winsor from drowning," and he winked at Lance, who regarded them with a smile. Lance felt a little better as far as Naomi and Turley were concerned, for the reunion certainly didn't seem much more than a friendly one. However, uncertainty still existed within him as he let out a sigh and said to himself, time will tell Winsor, time will tell.

Discarding the matter completely, Lance addressed Dawson amusingly. "You ole Cheyenne ambusher. Why didn't you tell me that Turley was near by? Why I ought to . . . "

"Now hold on, you young wild cat," cut in Dawson with a grin and twinkle in his eye. "We wouldn't come up here side by side, not known for sure who was up here, so we decided to spread out a little."

The old scout glanced at Turley amusingly and continued.

"So I told the young one here to hold back a little after I met up with you, sorta wanted to surprise you. But the blan fool spoil't it all."

He shook a finger at Turley and the dust flew out of his mud caked chin as his head bobbed back and forth, "I was only in the middle of my story . . . "

He said no more as the two young scouts laughed at the sight of him. Naomi sat down beside Dawson and said with a faint smile, "Do not be angry, their hearts are happy, like yours."

"I know, I'm not angry," said Dawson as he put his arm around her shoulder. "Especially since I rounded us all together again."

Lance winked at Turley after that statement, and then asked, "What happened after you left the float?" Not waiting for an answer, he added, "I called out to you several times but you seemed to have vanished in to the night."

"I didn't hear you at all," replied Turley. "For one, the rapids were quite noisy and at the same time one of the Indians had a vise like grip on me and was sure dead set on dragging me under with him. Anyway, I managed to break loose and floated down quite a ways before I managed to get to shore. Like the rest of you, I was in no shape for further travel. After sun up, I located the float snagged in the shallow waters.

While wading across, Dawson spotted me and he made his way down toward the float. We located a fresh trail and figured that it was you and Naomi."

"Well," cut in Dawson. "Seein' that you young'ens arn't going to shave or tidy up, we'd better get movin while there is still some daylight left. What's yore plans, Winsor?"

Lance wrinkled his brow and looked out over the terrain in front of him. After a few moments of silence, he answered. "I think that it would be wise to cross over the mountains and head down into the flat country. There are settlers moving in on the ranges and our chances of getting food and possibly horses should be good. It's still a long ways to the fort and we'll need both."

"We're going to need something under our belts long before that," cut in Dawson. "I ain't had a waist line so thin since I was twenty one."

VIII

The young scouts chuckled amusingly as they helped Dawson and Naomi to their feet and once more began their journey on foot. After covering several miles, Lance, who was in the lead, stopped suddenly and held up his hand, motioning silence.

They listened anxiously, trying to determine the noise that came from the other side of a laurel patch a short distance away. Lance took out his knife and cautiously made his way to the edge of the laurel. He advanced along the heavy thicket at the same time motioned for the others to follow. Going but a short distance, he stopped again as the cause of the disturbance was observed. The others crept up to him and followed the direction of his out stretched arm.

Two bucks were engaged in a terrific battle for life. Dawson grinned and smacked his lips as he watched Lance creep up on the unsuspecting animals. The latter palmed his knife as he got within throwing distance but waited momentarily for the deer to interlock antlers. At that precise instant, Lance threw the knife with speed and accuracy and the deer collapsed as the keen edge of the blade entered the neck of the animal. The other scampered off wildly as the ambushers came into view.

"That's what I like about Winsor," beamed Dawson. "Always manages to find food just about the time a mans ready to keel over, and might I add, keeps ya well bathed on these here trips."

"By the looks of you," said Lance, "I'm going to have to find another river and let you soak for a couple of hours."

Lance and Turley grinned as the old scout remarked, "I'm in favor of that, but make sure that it is nice and shallow. I'm not hankerin' to be no pirate. Near got my fool self drowned in the last one."

They went about the task of cutting portions of the deer away. "Seems to me that we have enough," said Lance as he looked over the pieces. "It won't be long before night sets in and we may as well cover a little more ground before we settle down and get this meat over the fire."

Turley remarked to Dawson, "Now don't you go eating this meat raw as we go along, you may go vicious."

Turley laughed as Dawson blurted out, "Why you young coot, in my time I've eaten more raw meat than you have eaten fried and I ain't gone loco yet."

Lance picked up one of the pieces of meat and said to Naomi, "We haven't eaten formal since we dined with Sitting Bull." Glancing at the old scout with a grin, he added, "Dawson will do the cooking."

"No I ain't," half shouted Dawson. "I did my chef's work back at the cave when those outlaws forced me into it and now I aim to be strictly a guest, by dern."

"I'm glad you feel that way," cut in Turley, laughing. "I haven't felt the same since."

Dawson had an answer for that but Turley cut him short as he called over to Lance. "We're ready, Captain," and slapped the old scout on the shoulder, who in turn muttered something under his breath which Turley chose not to question in fear of thinning out Dawson's sense of humor.

As nightfall began to close in, the going got rough. Upon entering a likely area, Lance halted the others near a small spring and decided that the night would be spent there. They lost no time in preparing the set up for the roast. Lance took a small metal box from out of his pocket as a frown appeared on his forehead but it soon vanished when he removed the lid and found the matches to be in useable condition.

A short time later, a night bird perched high up in one of the trees and stared down at the foursome sitting around the campfire as they filled their empty stomachs with venison.

Lance watched Dawson as the latter looked over his shoulder every once in a while. "I hardly think that we are going to have company tonight," said Lance after one of Dawson's backward glances. "Whatever was left of that band of braves back there are probably on their way back to the village to reorganize, I would say."

"Reorganize," exclaimed Dawson. "What for?"

Lance hesitated for a moment then answered. "As long as White Cloud knows that Naomi is alive, he'll be on the prowl looking for her. His personal feelings and the fact that he would be a disgrace to the villagers if he gave up, will keep him coming."

Lance and Turley both watched Naomi and her eyes fell on the embers of the dying fire.

Dawson wrinkled his brow as he stared out into the dark night and broke the silence that had befallen them. He spoke slowly of an event that took place far back in the past. "I had to fight a young Cheyenne chief once. Got cut up bad before I finally kil't em. Later I married the girl we fought over. Right pretty girl too, just like the little one here. 'Peers to me that some day one of you will have to tangle with White Cloud and settle the matter once and for all. He'll find out where the girl is and make the challenge at the right time."

Dawson scratched his beard as he looked at the two young scouts and added, "When it's all over, the victor walks away with the prize, the other will be dead."

Lance looked over to ward Naomi and said soberly, "Should that time come and Naomi still wants to stay with us, I'll be ready for White Cloud."

Naomi lifted her eyes and looked at Lance managing a faint smile, then glanced at Turley as disagreed with Lance. "Seems to me that Lance done more than his share in helping me and Naomi to get going on our way back to her home. Should the chief one day cross our trail, it will be me that the chief will have to contend with."

Lance turned and faced Turley with a grin and said, "You made me captain. At that time, I'll give the orders. Then again, my knife is sharper than yours."

Turley laughed as he remarked, "In that case, I'll quit your command a day ahead of time."

Dawson stroked his bushy chin as he eyed the two young scouts and wondered how much longer it would be before Turley found out that Lance was in love with Naomi. It suddenly occurred to him that perhaps he was aware of the fact. The old scout eased out of a slow sigh as he again glanced toward Turley with a look of doubt.

Breaking the silence once more, Dawson remarked as he got to his feet and stretched out his arms, "You young-ens get some sleep so as we can get an early start in the morning. Ma' food digests real slow like, so I am to take the first watch this time."

Turley cut in with a grin, "When I come over to relieve you, I'll wake you up."

"I ain't fell asleep on a watch yet, you young coot. As a matter of fact, when you do come my way, be sure to pronounce my name right and wear a big smile or else the others here will think that you were mauled by a grizzly come mornin'."

Lance and Turley laughed lightly at the old scout's remark as they went about preparing their beds. Shortly, Lance took off his coat, whatever was left of it, and placed it around Naomi's shoulders. As she laid down upon the soft leaves, Turley removed his coat and placed it about her feet. She smiled up at the scouts as they both gave her a wave of the hand and made their way towards their own beds. A few minutes later, silence fell about the camp as they settled down for the night with the exception of one of them, whose sharp eyes and alertness has helped keep him alive throughout the many dangers encountered as an Indian scout.

Dawson glanced at the sleepers for a moment then seated himself against a large oak in readiness, come what may.

IX

About noon the next day, four pairs of eyes scanned the flatlands eagerly as they halted atop the last of the mountain chain. Lance's sharp eyes fell upon a small dust cloud far out in the flats and he pointed his finger in the direction saying, "That cloud of dust can be made by a wagon train."

"I hope it is, by darn," cut in Dawson. "I'm shore hankerin' to get some horse flesh under me. I've had me plenty of exercise of late."

"What are the chances in getting some horses?" asked Turley, directing the question at Lance.

The latter frowned as he kept a steady gaze on the dust cloud and answered, "Depends on who they are and what they are willing to part with. However, we're sure going to give it a try. Come on, let's get down there."

An hour or so later, the foursome walked leisurely toward the on coming wagon train, which was confirmed now, as a fact by Lance for he could see the lead wagon slowly take shape as it stirred up the dust behind it.

Once again time seemed to drag slowly along, as they waited with anticipation to come in contact with the newcomers. The full length of the wagon train finally came into view.

Dawson whistled in bewilderment and then exclaimed, "By the looks of that train out there, everybody has left the east." He glanced at Turley and added with a grin, "You're going to be mighty lonesome in St. Louie, boy. There ain't no body left back there."

Turley smiled slightly but made no comment, nor did his expression betray his thoughts concerning the city mentioned.

"They've spotted us," spoke Lance quickly as he noticed three horsemen break away from the wagon train and ride toward them. "We'll wait for them here."

Riding within fifty yards of the scouts, they slowed their horses to a walk and then advanced slowly with their rifles out and ready for action.

"Howdy," greeted one of the horsemen as they pulled to a stop a short distance away.

"Hi," said Lance, returning the greeting.

The three roughly clad figures looked over the scouts questioningly then stole a quick glance at the girl. Lance guessed that the one who greeted them was the train boss and spoke to him, saying, "We've been out on a mission up in the Big Horn. Had quite a tumble with the Sioux. Lost our horses and had to make our escape on foot. We're on our way back to Fort Laramie." He paused. "My name's Winsor," and he extended his hand, which the leader grasped firmly.

"Mine is Bacon, I bossed this here outfit up from Kansas."

"These are my friends," said Lance, continuing the introductions and explained briefly the presence of Naomi. Addressing the leader Bacon, Lance asked, "Where do you expect to stake out?"

"This is just about as far as we are going to go," replied Bacon. "We've been told that the area on this side of the mountains will be patrolled by the army and that interference by the Sioux will be limited."

The leader glanced over his shoulder and then addressed one of the horsemen, Jim. "Ride back and halt the train." He smiled broadly as he added, "Tell them all, this is it."

The rider took off his hat and yelled gleefully. Spurring his horse, he rode wildly toward the caravan with the good news. Bacon watched the rider gallop away, then turned toward Lance and said, "From what you told me, I 'spect you folks are mighty anxious to get back to the Fort, but I sure would be obliged if you would stay 'til morning. We need to know a lot about this here area and I figure that you boys can help us out on the right foot. Anyway, you can use a good rest and a couple of good hot meals in your stomachs will get you off to a good start."

Dawson's eyebrows lifted upon hearing the suggestion and grinned as he exclaimed, "Wall now, we've been lookin for your kind of a neighbor for quite a spell." Glancing at Lance he asked, "What do ya say, Captain?"

"With Mr. Turley's approval, we'll accept the invitation," answered Lance as he smiled at Turley.

"Under one condition," smiled the latter as he glanced up at Bacon. "Do you have a barber in this outfit?"

"We've got most everything," chuckled Bacon as he dismounted. Addressing Lance, he said, "Help the little lady on the horse and we'll get her down to the outfit."

Shouting and laughter greeted them as they neared the wagon train. Men and women surrounded Bacon, slapping him on his back and shaking his hand, congratulating him on his leadership during the long and rugged campaign.

Bacon smiled broadly as he put up his hand and shouted, "Folks, it's going to take a little time to stake out claims, start building our homes and whatnot. We're going to talk it over and decide things in a mannerly way, but for right now we'll make camp right here where water is a plenty and get that long needed rest we've been looking forward to."

A roar of approval cut Bacon short and he put his hand up again motioning silence. As it quieted down again, the leader continued, "As you have noticed by now, we have company. They are scouts from Fort Laramie and know the situation out here quite well. They're going to stay with us 'til morning, so let's show them some of that eastern hospitality." The men milled around the scouts eagerly and fired question after question at them. The camp was filled with excitement as preparations were made to celebrate their safe arrival to the side of their newly found home.

Bacon shouted to Lance and motioned him over to one of the wagons. Beside the leader stood two women. The leader smiled as

Lance walked up to them and said, "I'd like you to meet my wife, and daughter Mary Lou." He gestured toward the women. "This is Mr. Winsor."

"It is indeed a pleasure . . . " said Lance smiling, " . . . to meet two lovely ladies out here in the wilderness. Welcome to the Big Horn."

The women nodded in greeting, smiling shyly.

Bacon's hand was in the air again as he motioned for the other scouts to come over. Lance watched Turley as he was being introduced to Mrs. Bacon and her good-looking daughter. Her honey colored hair and brown eyes blended neatly with the tan colored dress she wore. Turley's expression was that of surprise and approval. Lance hastily excused himself as Dawson answered one of Bacon's questions and went over to Naomi who had dismounted and was walking slowly toward him.

Smiling down at her, he said, "Don't look so scared, these people are our friends. Come with me, we'll see if we can get you something else to wear. We're invited to a party tonight."

Lance related Naomi's presence to Mrs. Bacon and her daughter, and the women accepted her warmly.

"You fellows come with me," said Bacon. "We'll find something for the three of you to change into over at the store wagon." The scouts spent their time getting themselves cleaned up and conversed continuously with Bacon, who was bent on gathering as much information as possible concerning the Big Horn country.

Late afternoon, the scouts, Bacon and three members of the outfit rode away from camp for a look around the area. Darkness was beginning to set in as they re-entered the camp. Dawson's eyes lit up as the scent of roasted beef and fowl reached his nostrils. He looked around in delight, as he watched the busy settlers getting ready for the occasion.

"Ain't seen anything like this since my Aunt Nell married up with Buck Tooth Jim, back in Missouri."

The others laughed and dismounted. Lance patted the horse's mane as he gazed up toward the darkened mountains. Bacon was about to make a remark but hesitated as he noticed the sober expression on Lance's face. Walking over to Lance, he asked "Something wrong?"

"No," answered the scout, who turned and faced Bacon. "But I think that it would be a good idea to have the camp guarded just in case the smell of roast beef attracts the attention of prowlers." The scout reached inside his saddle and pulled out a canteen to give his horse a drink of river nectar.

"Winsor, that's been taken care of. Been cautious all along the way and I aim to be that way for quite a spell."

"Just checking," remarked Lance, smiling.

'Well," said Bacon as he glanced toward his wagon. "Let's go on up and see if the women folk are ready for supper."

Upon rounding one of the wagons, Lance's heart skipped a beat. He slowed almost to a stop before resuming his pace, and his eyes lit up at the sight of Naomi. She was wearing one of Mary Lou's dresses. Her hair was combed straight back and tied with a ribbon that hung neatly at the back of her neck. Her black eyes flashed and she smiled slightly as she caught sight of Lance. His new shirt and trousers, in addition to a barber's haircut and shave, was quite a novelty to him, and more so to Naomi, whose expression of approval was indeed obvious.

Bacon put his hands to his hips and looked at the three women in admiration, and exclaimed, "There never were three prettier women in any wagon camp. You girls are sure ready for the party."

"I've covered a lot of territory in my time," cut in Dawson with a grin. "And I must say that I agree with Bacon to the hilt."

After a few more comments, they headed toward one of the fire pits. During the course of the meal, Lance watched Turley amusingly as the latter stole more than his share of glances at Mary Lou. He felt a bit foolish, for his thoughts wandered back to the lack of aggressiveness that he had displayed within the past few days concerning Naomi.

Lance was convinced now that Turley's affection toward the girl was but a friendly one as he watched the latter progressing with conversation toward winning over the friendship of Bacon's daughter. His thoughts left him suddenly and a smile brushed his lips as a four-piece string band went into action.

Laughter and merriment filled the air. Couples walked and ran up to the spot where the dance was to begin. The caller for the band placed the dancers into position and then shouted, "We need another couple. Come on you Missouri ridge-runners, one more couple."

Lance noticed Turley saying something to Bacon and assumed that his friend asked permission to dance with Mary Lou. He was right, for Bacon answered with a smile and Turley lost no time getting up and helped the girl to her feet. Lance looked at Naomi, who sat next to him and noticed her slight smile but her eyes hinted a bit of sadness. He knew what she was thinking at the moment. The white man and the Indian were fighting bloody battles. Here she was, an Indian girl in white man's camp. Lance knew just how she must feel even though the Bacons had treated her warmly.

He sensed her uneasiness, although she betrayed that fact little, if any. Noticing Lance's gaze she looked at him and smiled. Lance refrained from continuing his thoughts by the way of conversations and asked instead, "Do you know how to do that dance?"

"No," she answered softly.

"I thought that perhaps you did since you lived near Fort Worth. Would you like to try it now?"

Her answer was negative as she shook her head slightly.

"All Right," said Lance. "We'll make it some other time. I'm a good teacher."

She looked up at Lance and held his gaze for a few moments, then turned slightly and stared out into space. The smile on Lance Winsor's face faded as he still kept his eyes on the lovely Indian girl, whose questionable look but a moment before added to his confusion concerning the true feelings the girl had toward him. He brushed his brow with his hand and let out a sigh that was well-marked with anxiety.

Lance glanced up as Dawson addressed him gleefully, "Winsor, it's about time you got up and gave the ladies a turn."

Lance was certainly in no mood to dance but he knew that there was no way out, for he had to show his respects to the female part of the Bacon family.

"Choose your partner, Mr. Dawson," said Lance with a grin. "And if Mrs. Bacon is willing, with Mr. Bacon's approval, I'll join you in the next round."

A short time later, Lance went into the two-step with Mrs. Bacon, as did Dawson with Mary Lou. Every once in a while he would glance at Naomi. He noticed that her expression was a sober one as she conversed with Turley, whose ever present smile was at the moment replaced by a serious expression as he stared out into space. Lance felt uneasy as he tried to detect the topic of conversation, which was obviously far from amusing. After the dance, he reseated himself next to Naomi but chose not to ask anything concerning the troubled looks that they wore on their faces a few minutes before.

A short time later as Lance danced with Mary Lou, he noticed that on one occasion Naomi was gone from the spot that she held during the course of the evening. The lovely girl he was dancing with would have been a treat under other circumstances but at the moment he was waiting patiently for the music to end. As the band went into another chorus, Lance checked his emotions and smiled down at his partner but he had the urge to grab one of the fiddles and smash it over the caller's head.

Finally, the music stopped. He walked the girl back and thanked her for the dance.

"You dance well for a mountain climber," remarked Turley smiling at Lance.

"I had a good partner," said Lance with a grin and then walked over to where Dawson was sitting after excusing himself.

"Where did Naomi go?" he asked the old scout curiously.

"Said she was going for a little walk," answered Dawson, and pointed in the direction of a large oak tree.

Once more Lance excused himself and disappeared into the darkness. A few yards from the edge of camp, he spotted her resting with her back against a tree looking up toward the darkened mountains. She tensed and turned her head quickly in the direction of his approach but relaxed as she recognized Lance whose features were made quite obvious by the brightly burning campfires. A faint smile formed on her lips as Lance walked up to her. He looked at her and smiled. Indeed, she was the queen of the party; as a matter of fact the queen of the Big Horn as far as Lance Winsor was concerned.

Once again he had the opportunity to tell Naomi just how he felt about her and find out once and for all the unanswered questions that burdened his troubled mind. He was aware of the fact that she too had something on her mind, for the grave look on her face while conversing with Turley was quite obvious.

Evading a direct question concerning her feelings toward him, he said instead, "You're not having too much fun for a celebration such as this, perhaps you feel like I do, don't care too much for parties."

She turned her head slightly away from him and once again looked out over the darkened area as she said softly, "You, Dawson, Turley, have been nice to me. Your friends here have been nice too. But I have seen others stare at me, some with hate in their eyes. I know what they are thinking. I am Indian. Even now, they are not at peace with my kind of people." She turned and faced Lance, adding, "You are wise in the ways of the Indian, you are wise in the ways of the white man. You know that of which I speak is true."

Lance felt a bit uneasy, for the topic of conversation at the moment was far from the one he expected to major in. Trying to ease the girl's mind concerning the matter, he checked his emotions and spoke softly, as if the matter was incidental.

"It isn't that bad. After all, these people just came from the east and they don't know too much about us out here. I would say that their reactions are based on the many stories that they have heard. You just wait 'til we get back to Fort Laramie. The people will be different down there."

Lance looked down at Naomi and smiled, wondering if he had eased the girl's mind concerning the matter with his last remark which, he well knew, held little truth, if any.

"I have been to Fort Worth with my father many times," said Naomi. "We were not welcomed. As I am not welcomed here, it will be the same at Fort Laramie."

Lance let out a little sigh as he was aware of the fact that it would be useless to continue pursuing this lost cause. The subject he wanted to discuss above all seemed to be drifting farther and farther away.

This was it. He was going to wait no longer. He'd pour out his feelings and tell her of his plans. She would either return his love or reject it. His heart beat madly as he placed his hands on her shoulders. She lifted her face to his and Lance had the urge to kiss her before saying another word, but instead tensed and his head reeled momentarily as Naomi finished saying, "It would be best, that I go home to my people."

Lance drew back slightly and his hands dropped to his side. Well Winsor, said Lance to himself, this could be an indirect answer to you question. But you're still not sure, are you? Flickering shadows played across their faces as Lance looked at the girl questioningly but she offered no explanation concerning her sudden change in plans other than the attitude taken by the white man toward the Indian, friendly or otherwise. Lance hid his disappointment well and pressed the issue in hope that there still remained something that he could say or do that would keep the girl from making the trip back to Texas, especially after telling him that her heart was set on staying up here in the Big Horn.

Lance spoke softly as he said, "You told me the other day that remaining up here was your wish. Remember, you don't have to stay or live where there are a lot of people. The country is big. There is plenty of room for everyone."

"What you say is true," said Naomi, cutting in on Lance. "But soon, you will be gone, then I shall be alone. My heart is heavy, now that I speak of going back, but it will always remain here." She hesitated momentarily and dropped her gaze toward the ground, then continued slowly. "For I have given it to someone, but he does not know."

Lance waited a long time for the answer he was soon to learn. He failed several times in his attempts to uncover the girl's feelings in the past. Was it because of his slow approach? Or was it because of the way he felt then, as he felt at the moment?

Hesitating, for fear that the answer wouldn't be in his favor, Lance tensed slightly and readied himself for the answer that would start his plans concerning the Big Horn country into becoming a reality or continuing his present job, as Indian scout, out of Fort Laramie.

"Who have you given your heart to Naomi?"

Lance breathed very slowly as the girl brought her head up and faced him squarely. Her dark eyes sparkled and a faint smile brushed her lips as she answered softly, "You."

Lance Winsor accepted that as if it was the answer he expected. The pensiveness, anxiety, and above all the burden he had carried within himself up to now vanished completely. He smiled down at her and placed his hands on her shoulders, which didn't stop there but went on to encircle the girl, drawing her ever so close to him. He put his cheek against hers and then kissed it slowly making his way toward her lips. Lance was aware of the fact that this method of affection was not the way of the Indian, but he said out loud, you're going to learn little one, you're going to learn and he seemed to lose all his senses as his lips met hers.

He drew away slightly, then kissed the corner of her mouth. He began to talk softly as he once again held her face close to his. "Ever since the first time I saw you at the trapper's camp, something came over me. Now I never want to get over it. I've wandered far beyond the horizons, always reaching out for something, but it was never there."

Naomi's eyes were closed as she nestled close to Lance. Her facial expression was tinted with happiness, for she too was relieved of a burden that saddened her heart to the depths of despair. She had fallen in love with a white man. An Indian fighter at that. Naomi was well aware of the fact that the chances for this man's love were mighty slim, especially with her being of Indian origin. The sudden turn of events had shaken her pleasantly, as it did Lance Winsor.

Lance put his lips to the side of her head as he continued. "I've gone over a lot of trails, climbed the highest of mountains, but not until I met you did I know exactly what I was really looking for. It was because of you that I went into the Sioux village. Because of you that I have lived in anxiety since." He drew back slightly and smiled as he added softly, "I've pictured this often, and hoped that it would become a reality. When we get back to the fort, we'll get married. I'll quit my job and you and I will go down to a spot I have picked along the Big Horn River and start that ranch I've been thinking about. Now tell me, how does that sound to you?"

She smiled slightly as she looked up at Lance and said in answer, "I do not know many words, like you, but you will understand, when I say my heart will be with yours, until the moon will come no more, over the mountain, for us."

If ever Lance Winsor wanted a girl to be his alone, body and soul, it was at this moment, Apache Indian girl, Naomi. He drew her to him once more and kissed the parted and willing lips tenderly. The rest of the world was lost to them momentarily as they clung to each other.

"Winsor, Winsor," called a voice coming from the direction of camp.

Lance reluctantly stepped back a ways from Naomi and said to her with a grin, "I don't think that I will ever dislike Dawson as much as I do right now. Feel like tying that beard of his into a pinto's tail and drag him around camp."

"Over here Dawson," answered Lance, as he made out the form of the old scout coming towards them.

"Party's about over back there," said Dawson as he walked up to the couple. Bacon wants to have a talk with you. I told him that we wanted to borrow some horses and..."

He stopped short as he eyed Lance and Naomi, for the smiles on their faces and the glint in their eyes was obvious that the conversation between the two was other than what they would eat for tomorrow morning's breakfast. He knew that Lance was in love with the girl and would be ready to bet his next month's pay that the girl loved Lance. Scratching his grizzly head he said, "'Peers to me that I've barged in on some personal business."

"Yes you have," replied Lance as he placed his arm around Naomi's shoulder, "and I'm glad you did now. Dawson, I'm going to leave all the scouting to you, unless you want to come along with us and be my foreman. Naomi and I are going to be married."

The old scout smiled but showed no surprise as he placed one hand on Naomi's arm and the other on Lance's, saying, "I'm mighty glad that it turned out like this. Been watching you two for a quite a spell now; that's why it comes as no surprise. As you know I married a Cheyenne girl once." Dawson's eyes watered a little as he added, "The little one here always reminds me of her."

Dawson changed the subject. "Might take that foreman's job at that.Might get lonesome after the four of us being together and gone through what we did."

The last remark reminded Lance of Turley.

"Dawson," said Lance. "I think that it would be best to keep this quiet for a while. This will certainly hinder his plans as far as his trip to St. Louie is concerned."

"Wall now, he wouldn't take it too hard a the moment," remarked Dawson, as he tugged at his whiskers. "Been keeping steady company with Bacon's daughter all night." The old scout grinned broadly as he finished, "Might not go back to the Fort with us, that young-un. Anyway, son, don't you fret none. I'll feel him out a little at a time on our way down to the Fort."

Lance let out a little sigh at the thought of the outcome, then let the matter slip from his mind as he remarked, "Let's get back to camp and see if we can get the horse deal settled."

The celebration was about over. The settlers began to thin out as they headed toward their wagons to retire for the night. A few remained, standing around the dying embers of the once brightly burning fires, chatting amongst themselves. Turley and Mary Lou sat at one of the fire pits, conversing. Upon hearing the Bacons, who were waiting for them, Dawson remarked, "The party's never over for the young-uns, 'peers to me, always have to round them up like stray cattle."

"Didn't you ever wander off at a party, Mr. Dawson?" asked Mrs. Bacon amusingly.

"Wall now, I can' t right say that I did," answered the old scout. "Her Pa always made me the chief cook at these here parties."

Dawson seemed to enjoy the laughter that followed his last remark and was about to continue with another, but it died on his lips, as a howl of a lobo wolf echoed throughout the valley. From high up in the mountains came another, then another. The men eyed each other knowingly.

Lance turned toward Naomi and smiled down at her assuringly as she returned his glace with an expressionless face, for she alone of the women knew what that was and what it meant. Turley was up and now eyed Lance as he neared them with the girl.

"Well, I guess the women folk are ready to retire," said Bacon. "I'd like you fellows to ride around camp with me, if you will. Want to check and see that everything is in order."

"Certainly," answered Lance, as Dawson and Turley nodded in agreement. Mrs. Bacon put her arm through Naomi's and with her daughter soon disappeared into one of the wagons after bidding everyone goodnight. Bacon, satisfied that the women were out of hearing distance, faced the scouts and asked in low tones, "How big a force do you think they have up there?"

"Well," said Lance. "I hardly think that there are many of them. As a matter of fact, I'm surprised that there are some around here so soon. The main tribes are beyond the Big Horn River. I would say that White Cloud left a few of his braves behind to do a bit of scouting."

"For one thing," cut in Dawson. "They will be back in force now that they know that you people are here. They'll try to get a lot of things you have here in this outfit."

"The area will be patrolled by the military," assured Lance. "Under the circumstances I don't think that you will have too much trouble in getting started out here."

"Hope not," said Bacon as he motioned the others toward the horses. "Although we can sure give them a hot welcome. Got plenty of rifles and ammunition."

"I'd like to borrow some rifles and horses for our trip back to the Fort," said Lance. "I guess Dawson mentioned it to you before."

"Yes, he did," said Bacon with some concern.

"We'll need them as we go along up here and I'll see that they are returned to you by one of the patrols that come up this way," cut in Lance.

"You may be scouting for that patrol," remarked Dawson as he eyed Lance.

"Fine, then that matter is settled," said Bacon as he urged his horse forward.

Lance wondered if the old scout took him lightly when he told him that he was quitting the military after getting married. His thoughts left him as Bacon pulled to a halt near one of the men on guard and issued further orders.

Out of curiosity, Lance asked Bacon, "That wagon out there broke down?"

"No," said Bacon slowly as he ran a rough hand over his chin. "It's owned by two fellows that joined up with us right after we started out. Kept pretty much to themselves during the whole trip. As a matter of fact I didn't notice either one of them at the celebration tonight."

"What kind of equipment are they hauling," asked Lance.

"The usual things a fellow would need on starting a ranch," replied Bacon.

"The reason I asked," said Lance, "is because a couple of days ago we ran into some gunrunners who were on their way to make contact with the Indians. At the time I thought that they had a wagon load around in the area somewhere but we failed to find it. Guns could be brought up by the way of a wagon train without being detected and smuggled over to the Sioux."

"Come morning, we'll have a look around if you wish," remarked Bacon. "Wouldn't want any rifles reaching the Indians through my help, even if it was indirect."

Once more the horses were urged forward and headed back towards Bacon's wagon.

Two pairs of eyes kept a steady watch on the disappearing horsemen as their hands eased up on the tightly gripped rifles they held in readiness. The occupants of the forlorn looking wagon breathed a little easier, for the disaster that had passed them by, at least for the time being. "Let's get the hell out of here while we still have a chance," hissed the shorter of the two.

“Shut up, you fool,” snapped the other. “Do you think that I came all the way up here with this stuff just to leave it here and run?”

“But they’re coming back in the morning for . . . ”

“Let them come,” cut in the other. “The rifles are well hid and I hardly think that they will tear the wagon apart after seeing all the equipment on top. You keep your mouth shut; I’ll do all the talking when they get back up here in the morning. After that we’ll just play around with the rest of the settlers and wait till Barton gets here as we planned.”

X

The early morning hours found the camp alive as the settlers busied themselves with the many chores that awaited them. A short distance from the edge of camp, a girl walked toward one of the numerous springs that trickled down off the mountain. A smile appeared on her face as she began to fill the pail that she carried, for her thoughts wandered back to the night before. After filling the pail, she sat down on a large rock and began to hum a tune softly as she stared out into space. Indeed her thoughts were about someone that pleased her fancy, for the look in her eyes indicated that fact. Finally, she let out a little sigh as she got to her feed and reached down for the pail. Mary Lou was startled momentarily as a strong hand slid down over hers and a voice asked softly, "May I?"

The girl relaxed as she recognized the voice but her face held a light shade of crimson upon facing the man who held her thoughts but a few moments before: Turley.

"You have learned the ways of an Indian scout well," she remarked shyly. "I didn't hear you come up at all."

"I wasn't too quiet," said Turley smiling. "You were deep in thought. If I asked what you were thinking about, would you tell me?"

She tried to hide her embarrassment and hoped that he wouldn't press the issue as she answered, "Perhaps at another time."

"Do you think that there will be another time?" he asked rather softly. Her smile faded slightly as she met his gaze.

"If you're interested enough to know, then there will be another time, Blade Turley."

Turley's pulse beat rapidly as he looked down at the lovely girl and wondered why he was filled with excitement. After all, he had known the girl for only a day. Before Turley could continue with the conversation, a call came for Mary Lou from camp.

"We'd better go," she said. "Some of this water is for coffee and they are waiting for it. You're going to have breakfast with us this morning, aren't you?"

"Only if I can sit next to you," said Turley with a grin.

"You can," she said softly.

Dawson, who was saddling a horse near Bacon's wagon, hesitated momentarily upon noticing the young couple entering the camp together. He squinted his eyes and stroked his beard, muttering to himself as he gazed at the couple. "If we stay up in these parts much longer, I'll be headin' back to the fort all by myself. Pretty little gal though, might pretty little gal."

Shortly after breakfast, Dawson led the four horses, which he had saddled, up to where the others were waiting. Rifles, ammunition, and food were placed in their proper places. Dawson bit off a piece of his newly obtained plug tobacco. Lance noticed him and remarked with a grin, "I think that you like that stuff better than roast beef."

"Wall now, I would say that the beef keeps me alive," said the old scout with a twinkle in his eye. "But this tobacco keeps me going strong and furious like. Wanna try some?"

"No," said Lance, laughing. "I'd need a beard like yours to keep from getting my shirt front stained."

"Now don't you bother growing one, son; I'll do the chewing. And once more, in a situation like this all you have to do is follow this beard of mine and you'll get where you're going, en if you're ready capt'n, I'm ready to lead the way."

They thanked the Bacons for their hospitality and assured Bacon himself that everything would be returned as promised. Bacon mounted his horse, as did the others, and all of them held a smile as their eyes rested on Turley and Mary Lou who were lost in conversation a short distance away.

Turley, suddenly conscious of the fact that silence had befallen the once talkative group, turned slightly and his face betrayed his embarrassment as he noticed the smiling faces. “Didn’t know we had company,” said Turley with a smile. He turned to Mary Lou and whispered, once again, “Like they say back in the east, we have a date. Don’t know when, but I’ll be back.” The girl gave him a reassuring smile that she would be waiting. It was obviously clear, for her big brown eyes failed to conceal the fact.

As they waved goodbye and headed toward the other end of the camp, Turley looked over his shoulder for one last look at the girl who left little room in his mind for such thoughts as bright lights along the dusty streets of St. Louis. “We’ll mosey over to that wagon casual-like and have a look around,” said Bacon. Glancing at Lance, he added, “I think you will find everything in order.”

The latter nodded in approval but said nothing as he kept his gaze on the two occupants of the wagon. They were engaged at the moment, unloading some of their equipment. As they neared the two roughly-clad figures, Bacon called out in greeting, “Mornin.’”

“Mornin, and a pretty one at that,” said the taller of the two as he walked toward the horsemen.

“Friends of mine, stopped in yesterday on their way back to Fort Laramie,” said Bacon nodding towards the scouts. They nodded slightly, and the other put up his hand in greeting.

“Sure nice to know that you gents get around up here once in a while. Mighty rough country I understand,” said the newcomer as he eyed Lance.

“Shouldn’t be too bad on this side of the mountain chain,” replied Lance. “However, one can never tell.”

It appeared to Lance that the tall stranger was far from being a gunrunner, that he was more so a rancher. His manner and speech was that of a well-polished gambler. Lance stole a glance at the back of the wagon every now and then and noticed that it was jammed with implements needed for farming and ranching. Little did he realize, that if the tall man was a gambler, he was making use of his profession at the moment with a bluff as he conversed nonchalantly, for the hidden rifles that were worth a fortune in gold, and his life were at stake.

"Didn't see you gents at the party last night," remarked Bacon.

"We're not too good at dancing," replied the other as he nodded in the direction of his partner, who was near a small fire preparing something for breakfast. "But should another occasion arise sometime in the future I hope that we get an invitation, especially if these gents are back up this way. Might get into some might interesting conversation."

We're going to have coffee; won't you fellows join us?" he added quickly, changing the subject.

The gunrunner at the fire swayed slightly and the blood drained from his face as he cursed his tall partner for pressing his luck, but relaxed shortly and eased out a sigh as Lance remarked, "Thanks, I'm afraid that we can't make it this trip. We're way overdue at the Fort. Perhaps some other time."

"You gents have a standing invitation," said the stranger. "We ought to be settled by the time you get back this way and when you do, look us up."

"We will," said Lance, as he motioned farewell with a wave of the hand and urged his horse forward.

As they got out of hearing distance, the short member of the gunrunning duo got up and walked over to where the other was standing with a wide smile on his face, exclaiming, "Have you gone mad sticking your neck out like you did? Near died a couple of times."

The tall one turned and faced the other with a cunning smile on his lips and said, "When you play with a stacked deck, you know just how far you can push your luck. We won, didn't we?"

After bidding Bacon adieu, the scouts and the girl started their last but long trail to Fort Laramie. The going was much easier now: horses, plenty of food, and with each passing mile, farther from Indian country. At the close of the first day's travel, the foursome relaxed as they camped near the edge of a small stream. That Turley was in deep thought since leaving the settlers camp was quite obvious, for at the moment, Dawson winked at Lance with a grin as he nodded his head slightly toward the silent Turley who sat motionless with a faraway look in his eyes.

"I think that Turley here would look right nice behind one of those plows that I saw in one of Bacon's wagons," chuckled Dawson. "As a matter of fact, Bacon will be needin' a top hand afore long."

Turley discarded his thoughts and glanced at Dawson, then Lance as a slow smile appeared on his lips. The old scout pointed a finger at Turley and said, "Take a good look at that boy, he has the marks of a sod buster. Tell me son," continued Dawson with a sly look in his eyes as he addressed Turley. "Ever think of doing some farming? 'Afore yesterday, that is?"

Lance grinned as he noticed Turley's face become red, and he wondered momentarily just what effect Bacon's daughter really had on his young friend.

"I'm a rancher at heart," answered Turley with a smile. "Yesterday hasn't changed anything."

He kept his eyes on the amusing Dawson as the latter remarked, "Don't rightly know about that. Couldn't get a conversation started with you all day. Maybe your mind wasn't on Bacon's plow but it sure was on something else that belonged to him. Yes sir," continued Dawson as he stroked his beard. "I could see the bright lights of St. Louie slowing fading away. How soon you coming back this way son?"

Lance and Naomi smiled at each other as they listened to the ribbing in silence. "Well," answered Turley. "That depends on a lot of things." Motioning toward Lance, he added, "Winsor here plans on starting a ranch down along the river someday. Might be tempted to drive a herd of cattle up from Texas and give him a good start."

"Mighty good excuse to get back up in this country again," cut in Dawson. "But it seems to me that it would be much easier to get to the Fort and in a day or two start back to Bacon's camp with these horses."

"Now that's a better excuse than yours . . . " He hesitated for a moment then said in conclusion, " . . .to get back into the dance."

Turley eyed the old scout with a smile and asked, "What do you want me to admit, that Bacon's daughter put her brand on me?"

"You don't have to admit that son," answered Dawson with a big grin. "The mark shows plainly."

"This could go on all night," said Lance laughingly as he got to his feet. "You two can debate the subject tomorrow; there'll be plenty of time."

"It will be the same tomorrow," remarked Dawson as he spat a stream of tobacco juice into the brush causing a red squirrel that lurked underneath to blink it's eyes madly as it scampered swiftly away. "Won't be able to wrench a word out of him."

The small camp settled down to rest once more. They all laid there in silence staring up at the stars in the heavens. Whatever their thoughts, a secret to them alone. Pleasant ones though, for the sand man could see faint traces of a smile on their lips as he labored to clear their minds of their thoughts and make way for slumber.

XI

Fort Laramie, frontier arsenal, was a busy place this hot spring afternoon. Newly arrived rifles, ammunition, and other supplies were being opened and stacked high in the powerhouse. The blacksmiths were noisily pounding on their anvils. The many horses were being equipped with new shoes for the coming trip in which the animals played a major part of transportation, which would be long, hard, and rugged. The entire scene within the walls of the fort was obvious: preparing for battle. That something was brewing, other than an ordinary routine patrol or hit and run attack, justified that fact by the sudden appearance of Major Reno's and General Custer's forces, the latter ordered up from the Cheyenne frontier.

A session was being held in quarters that belonged to General Terry: the supreme commander of Fort Laramie. Seated around the table, other than the general, was his staff, General Custer, and Major Reno. General Terry addressed the others solemnly. "Gentlemen, I prolonged this session on Captain's Benteen's behalf. He arrived at the fort about an hour ago. I judge that he has rid himself of dust and beard by now. He has been informed of the session and should be here at any moment. Incidentally, Captain Benteen is a replacement for the late Captain Brown, who died in action up at the Dakota Wyoming border several weeks ago. He will head part of my forces in the coming campaign."

A knock on the door interrupted the general who, in turn, urged the intruder to enter. As Captain Benteen entered, Terry made the necessary introductions and the new arrival took his place at the table. Terry started anew as he let out a sigh, which had a faint touch of disappointment, for the subject first to be discussed was a major factor in his plans: intelligence.

"A short time ago, I sent one of my best scouts up to the Big Horn country to gather information as to the exact location of the Sioux. A little later, I sent another up there to try and locate the first to relate a message." Terry hesitated a moment and glanced toward Custer, then said, "I believe you know Winsor, General."

Custer nodded in the affirmative.

"The other was your old scout Dawson. Unfortunately, neither one has been seen or heard of since. However, we'll give them another day or two and in the event they fail to show up, it will be necessary to send out scouts again, for the information concerning the exact position of the Sioux is vital, as all of you gentlemen know."

Custer's eyes were downcast at the moment for the news was disheartening. Not only was Dawson an old scout with whom he had fought side by side in many a battle, but as well and more, an old friend. Custer went on. "Under the new treaty, the Sioux were to move well into the Big Horn country; however, they failed to abide by some of the rules. During their push westward, they plundered and killed, hitting our patrols on sneak attacks and as you know on one of these occasions was fatal to Captain Brown."

Terry picked up a glass of water and drank from it, then continued. "It is a known fact to us now that the tribes are being agitated and primed into a warlike behavior by two of the leading chiefs, Sitting Bull and Crazy Horse. I have been ordered to wipe out the Sioux resistance once and for all. That is why you gentlemen are here under orders with your forces. Have you any idea how large a force the Sioux can muster?" he asked the question to the table.

"With the information I have at hand," replied Terry, "I would say that they will outnumber our forces three to one: however, that point being near incidental since we are better equipped." Terry paused momentarily and his face became serious. He turned slightly and stared out through the opened window. "There is the possibility," he said, "that the Sioux will try to get some outside help."

Facing the men at the table again, he added, "That information was given to me by one of the Sioux outcasts we have here at the fort. In any event, we'll have to move and plan cautiously." Getting up from his chair, Terry walked toward a large map that was draped over the rear wall of the room and beckoned the others to join him.

"At present, I'll outline the plan briefly and discuss the territory into which we will venture. To most of you, the country up there will be new, but an old story as far as the reason for going there is concerned." Pointing to a spot northwest of the Big Horn River, Terry began to explain the situation. "This is the country where the main tribes of the Sioux should be congregating. When we are ready to move out, General Custer and his forces will proceed to the Big Horn River, cross it, and then move northward until making contact with the enemy. I will be about half a day behind you with part of my forces. The reason for the lag is to offset the Sioux as far as our strength is concerned. Major Reno will lead his men north on the east side of the river an hour or so behind my forces. Captain Benteen will proceed north along the east side of the mountain chain, which will take him and his men a considerable distance from our place of attack; however his mission is to combat any resistance that may confront him in that particular area. Recently, a large wagon train went up into that territory and they are sure to get repeated visits from the Indians. From there the captain will advance westward over the mountain chain and drive whatever Sioux there are in that territory into the oncoming forces of Major Reno. Eventually, we'll all meet somewhere west of the river for our final attack. There will be daily meetings to discuss our plans thoroughly, any questions for now gentlemen?"

A loud knock on the door silenced the group momentarily. "Come in," urged Terry as he looked in the direction of the door.

An orderly came into the room, saluted, and said hastily, "One of our scouts just came back with some news of the missing scouts and . . . "

"Send him in," the General cut in quickly.

The men eyed each other in anticipation. They stood there tensely as they waited for the scout to appear. A moment later, a dust-covered scout entered the room and after a hasty greeting related the news, "On my way back to the Fort, I ran into Winsor and Dawson. They should be here within the hour."

Eyes brightened and slow smiles appeared on the faces of the men. "They have with them," continued the news bearer, "another scout, never saw him before, and an Apache Indian girl." Terry looked at Custer questioningly.

"I don't know the answer to that one myself," said Custer. "But if she is Apache, I must say she certainly wandered far from home. Are you sure that they went up to Sioux territory?" asked Custer amusingly.

Terry smiled as he stroked his chin and replied, "I'm beginning to wonder about that myself."

Several miles north of the fort, four riders wiped the sweat and dust from their eyes as they dismounted near a small stream. "Wonder what kind of reception we'll get," remarked Dawson, as he dunked his head into the cool water.

"You'll probably be demoted to a stable boy," replied Lance, laughing.

"Maybe so," said Dawson. "But in that case there will be two of us, like I told you 'afore."

Turley stepped up to the two men and placed his hands across their shoulders and said smiling, "It grieves me to see you boys worrying about your jobs. Should anything go wrong, you can depend on me to see you through."

Lance laughed as the old scout squinted at Turley, saying, "What are you going to do, hire us out to Bacon?"

"Nope, I'll take you two along to St. Louie and . . . "

Turley stopped short, saying no more as his smile diminished to a slight grin, for he was looking at Naomi who gazed at them with uncertainty.

Lance eyed Dawson momentarily then glanced at Turley. He was on the verge of telling the young man about his plans concerning Naomi but decided that this wasn't the place or the time. Walking over to where the girl stood, Lance smiled down at her and said, "A few more miles and there will be new subjects to discuss and new faces to look at. As a matter of fact, I'm going to insist that Dawson here shaves his beard so that we can all see what he really looks like."

"Ain't a main in the territory that can shave this beard off and live to see what lies beneath it," remarked Dawson as he mounted his horse.

"I think that it would be wise to let it stay on," cut in Turley. "What lies under that briar patch you call a beard may scare the women folk to death."

Dawson ignored the last remark. A slow grin appeared on his lips as he watched the others mount, then he said, more to himself that to the others as he fingered his beard, "Come to think of it now, I may get it trimmed a mite. There's some mighty pretty women folk down there at the fort."

The others smiled broadly as they urged their mounts forward. Lance noticed the old scout was still motionless, lost in pleasant thought. "Hey Romeo, coming with us?" Dawson looked and Lance with a twinkle in his eye, turned his head and spat out a stream of tobacco juice.

"Darn fool boy, askin' me silly questions."

Upon nearing the fort, the inhabitants milled about the gates waiting for the once missing scouts to enter. Naomi reached over and placed her hand on Lance's arm. He looked at her and wasn't surprised to see her face tinted slightly with fear. Lance knew just how she felt, for most of the people within the walls of the fort hated her kind of people.

He squeezed her hand tightly and said reassuringly, "Now don't you worry, everything will be all right." She smiled slightly and her eyes brightened as Lance winked at her like he so often did. She held her head high as they went through the gates, for not every day did the inhabitants of Fort Laramie gaze upon an Indian princess who could pass without question as the queen of Indian country. The scouts were greeted warmly by friends as they dismounted. Questions were many but answered scantly for higher authority awaited their presence.

An orderly rushed up to the scouts and addressed Lance and Dawson, "General Terry requests your presence immediately."

"We'll be there in a moment," replied Lance and he looked toward the dwellings that were located at the far end of the fort. He turned addressing the two scouts. "You fellows wait for me here; I'll be back in a minute."

Lance put his hand to Naomi's arm and said, "Come along with me. I'll take you over to some friends. Now don't worry about anything; they'll treat you fine." He reassured her again as they neared one of the cabins.

The door flew open and an elderly woman rushed out exclaiming, "Lance Winsor, my gosh, how you do worry us sometimes. Sure takes more than Indians . . ." She stopped short as her eyes fell on Naomi's features momentarily but held her smile as she continued, "You're safe anyway. Certainly good to see you again."

"Nice seeing you again, Mrs. Tuffs. I'm due at the General's quarters, and in a hurry. I wonder if you would do me favor?"

She sensed what he was about to ask and smiled at Naomi. "Anything for an old friend of the family. What would you like?"

"First of all," replied Lance. "I'd like you to meet Naomi. Naomi, this is Mrs. Tuffs, the best apple pie baker in the territory."

"You needn't mention anymore about it, Lance Winsor, I took the hint," laughed Mrs. Tuffs.

"I wonder if you would mind taking care of Naomi and let her stay with you during her short stay here at the fort?"

"I certainly will, and she is welcome, you know that."

"Thanks," said Lance. "Her trip was long and rugged, she needs some clothes and . . . "

"Never mind saying anymore, you just leave her to me," cut in the kindly old woman as she put her arm around Naomi's shoulder. "Come dear, let's get you inside and . . ."

"By the way Mrs. Tuffs, Naomi speaks very good English."

"My, what a pleasant surprise," exclaimed the delighted woman. "Now I'm going to find out what you've been up to all this time."

Lance smiled but said nothing as he watched them go through the open doorway. Naomi looked back over her shoulder and smiled at Lance and then hesitated a moment longer as her eyes seemed to be focused on something beyond him. As the door closed, Lance was about to turn around when suddenly a feminine voice halted his movement.

"Hello Lance, it's nice to see you again, especially after the rumors I've heard around the fort."

Lance turned slowly and faced the girl, smiling slightly.

"Hello, Helene, this ought to teach you a lesson about rumors, often they are contrary to the truth."

Her blue eyes flashed in the sunlight and Lance noticed a trace of a frown appear on her forehead as she remarked, "You brought company with you this time; she's very pretty."

The girl still held her smile and looked at Lance questioningly. Although there had been nothing serious between them in the past, he felt a sense of uneasiness, for in the past few weeks he'd changed his future plans considerably.

"I'll tell you about her sometime," said Lance as he noticed Dawson waving to him. "I've got to leave now, they are waiting for me at the General's quarters. Say hello to your mother and dad for me."

"I will not, Lance Winsor," she said teasingly. "But I will tell them that you are coming over later on."

"You caught me off guard," laughed Lance. "I'll be over later."

With a wave of his hand, he hastily made his way toward the scouts who were in waiting.

"Darn fool boy," grumbled Dawson as Lance approached them. "Messin' around with woman folk while the general is waitin'. What do you want us to do, get hung up before we can fill up our bellies?"

Lance grinned as he said, "Let's go," and followed the orderly. The occupants within General Terry's quarters had the looks of surprise, bewilderment, and admiration as Lance finished the story concerning his last mission.

"That was quite an ordeal, yes, quite an ordeal," remarked Terry glancing at the scouts. "But going into the Sioux village like you fellows did and live to tell about it, especially under the circumstances, is indeed nothing short of a miracle."

"Tell me Winsor, just what prompted you to go all the way into the village when you already had the necessary information?"

Lance felt the blood drain from his face as he glanced at Dawson then Turley. He had no intention of misleading the general and answered, "Other than added information, the venture into the village was a personal one."

"If I may add," cut in Dawson. "Mr. Turley and myself volunteered to go along. We were curious to see what Sitting Bull and Crazy Horse looked like."

"Excellent," remarked Custer. "Now you can introduce the chiefs to me when we run across them." The others around the table laughed as Dawson squinted at Custer with a grin.

Once again, Terry went over the plans briefly for the benefit of the scouts. Questions were asked, comments were made by most everyone but Lance Winsor, who sat there listening half-heartedly, for within his mind he was going over his personal plans that were contrary to the plans being discussed by Terry. Lance was finished scouting. He had to tell Terry today. Now. He wondered how the General would take it, especially at a time like this when every man will be needed for the oncoming battle against the Sioux. His thoughts were disrupted as Terry asked, "Any questions for now, Winsor?"

"No, not at the moment," replied Lance and held Dawson's gaze as the latter stared at him. There was a question in the old scout's eyes and Lance knew what it was. *When are you going to tell him that you are going to get married and that you are quitting as a scout?*

Lance Winsor's emotions were disturbed greatly as Terry said in conclusion, "I need not stress farther that every man, every available scout, has their work cut out for them. The possibilities of outside help for the Sioux are now a reality. That source of information from the Sioux outcasts has been confirmed since the return of Winsor and Dawson. All of you here will be entrusted in leadership, a vital role in the oncoming campaign. Until tomorrow then, when we shall continue familiarizing ourselves with the plan and iron out the rough spots. I call the session to a close."

Custer put his hand on Dawson's shoulder and remarked, "I think that you and I have a lot of reminiscing to do. Why don't we go over to my quarters."

Before Dawson could answer, Custer leaned toward the old scout and added in low tones, "I've got some aged bourbon to go with it."

Dawson's eyes glinted as he remarked with a smile, "General, I accept the invitation whole-heartedly; there is something about your hospitality that just sets me afire."

Custer laughed amusingly as he got up from the table. He said a few words to Terry, who was engaged in conversation with Lance and Turley and then left the quarters with Dawson.

Terry faced the two young scouts again and remarked, "Mr. Turley, I assume you are freelancing at present. I wonder if you would be interested in a job scouting for one of our forces."

Turley eyed Lance for a moment, but other than a smile, the latter offered no indication of approval or otherwise.

"Well," replied Turley tugging away at his chin. "I hardly know how to answer that at the moment. You see general, I came up from Fort Worth on a personal mission and had plans of my own, but since then, certain events have occurred that near obliterated my original plans completely."

Lance flushed as he stared at his friend and for the first time sensed that Turley knew a little about his intentions concerning Naomi. He also wondered if Turley make that statement because of his interest in Bacon's daughter.

"However, I appreciate the offer and if I could have until tomorrow to make my decision I'll . . . "

"Certainly, my boy," cut in Terry. "Just take your time, there is plenty of it left and if I may add, in addition in connection with the offer, you'll scout along with Winsor for Captain Benteen."

The scouts glanced at each other smiling.

"Should Turley accept, General," Lance remarked, "half of your troubles will be over; they don't come any better."

"Alight then gentlemen, until tomorrow," said Terry, his voice tinted with approval.

Once on the outside, the scouts refrained from discussing anything that went on within the General's quarters as they made their way over to the cabin issued to Lance and Dawson in the past.

"Not bad, not bad at all," remarked Turley as he looked over the interior of the large cabin and proceeded to roll himself a cigarette.

"You bunk here with us," said Lance. ""As you see, we've got most everything here." Lance opened a large drawer and took out a new buckskin outfit. Handing it to Turley, he remarked, "You'll need these, whether you go south from here, or north." The scouts held each others' gaze, for the last remark was an indirect question. Lance took advantage of the present privacy with his friend to press the issue that burdened his mind, revealing to Turley his intentions concerning Naomi. Before either one of them could make any comment, a knock on the door diverted their attention. Lance frowned slightly, for the untimely interruption only prolonged the touchy matter that had to be faced sooner or later.

Walking over to the door, he opened it.

It was Helene holding on to an oversized coffee pot.

"Hello again."

"Come on in," said Lance, managing a smile.

"Mother insisted that I bring this coffee over. I don't know why she did, but I didn't protest the idea," she remarked, laughing.

Lance flushed slightly as he stole a glance at Turley and noticed the latter grinning with an amusing glint in his eye.

"Helene, I'd like you to meet Mr. Turley. Turley, this is Miss Baker."

Lance took the pot of coffee from Helene as she exchanged greetings with Turley and placed it on the stove.

"Haven't seen you around before," remarked Helene as she smiled at Turley. "Came up from Texas a short time ago," said Turley.

"Where did you fellows find that pretty Indian girl?"

"You certainly make good coffee," cut in Lance as he sipped on some of the brew. "Won't you two join me?"

That her question went unanswered was quite obvious to the girl, that the scouts evaded the subject intentionally.

"No, thanks, none for me now," replied Helene as she went toward the door.

"Thanks a lot for the coffee," said Lance as he walked over to the door and placed his hand on the latch.

"Compliments of the Bakers," replied Helene with a smile and added, "See you all later."

As Lance opened the door, Dawson, who was reaching for the outside latch, missed it and stumbled through the doorway, falling flat on his face.

"Darn fool boy," grumbled the old scout as he raised himself on his elbow and scowled up at the two laughing scouts. He pointed a finger at them but checked himself as he noticed Helene for the first time and said instead, "Howdy Miss Baker. You shore are a welcome sight."

Lance and Turley helped the old scout to his feet.

"Thank you Mr. Dawson, did you hurt yourself?" she asked.

"Shucks no," replied Dawson. "I do things like this to keep me in shape.

"Been to a party, Old Timer?" grinned Lance.

"Wall now, if you must know, I did have a few with Custer while we talked over old times but it wasn't very much. It ain't even reached my stomach yet."

"I believe that," said Turley laughing. "Most of it is still in your head."

"Some day, I'm going to put that young coot over my knee and give him a sound thrashing," said Dawson more to himself than to the others as he caught sight of the coffee pot.

Facing the girl, he remarked, "That coffee is going to taste mighty fine. I see you haven't forgotten us."

"No, I haven't," she replied smiling and she glanced at Lance whose face took on a shade of crimson, for he sensed that Turley's eyes were on him after that remark.

"Well, I must be running along," said Helene. "See you all later."

Once more her remark was directed at Lance as she looked at him for a moment, then with a wave of her hand, departed through the open doorway.

"Nice gal, that Helene," said Dawson as he took a cup off the shelf. "If I were a mite younger, you coots wouldn't have a chance with any of them."

"I don't know about that," said Turley looking at Lance. "Her eyes sparkled every time she looked at Winsor here."

Lance returned Turley's gaze with a sly grin and once again wondered just how much his friend knew. He sensed that the latter was quite amused for some reason. Perhaps Turley knew that he was in love with Naomi and now that Helene appeared on the scene realized the embarrassing situation.

"Maybe so," said Dawson as he sipped on his coffee and looked at the scouts over the brim of the cup, "but she ain't his type."

"I've been around Winsor of late," said Turley, "and we've talked about girls but I'm still at loss as to the kind of gal he would go for."

"Just what is your type, Lance?" asked Turley as he kept his eyes on the cigarette he was rolling.

"I like the camp fire type myself," replied Lance as he poured himself another cup of coffee.

"Well, we found out one thing," said Turley.

The latter struck a match and looked at Dawson as he lit the cigarette, saying, "He goes for the dark headed ones."

Lance felt the blood rush to his face for Turley's last remark convinced him that the latter was pressing the issue for something more than just plain conversation. Dawson was aware of the fact, for quite a while, that the two scouts would have to face each other concerning Naomi and wondered at the moment if the time had finally come. He bit into a fresh piece of tobacco as Lance sat down at the table and remarked, "You may be right there, but I've known some light haired girls that could be placed in that category."

"I was only referring to the campfires we sat around at and ones that we've seen since you and I first met."

Lance finished drinking his coffee, crossed his legs and leaned back in the chair. He had evaded this moment for quite a while for reasons he thought logical at the time but was now ready to fight Turley verbally to the bitter end and hoping at the same time that the outcome would not be a bitter one, for he liked the young scout who shared the many dangers with him in the short time they had known each other.

"Turley," said Lance with a slight trace of a grin forming on his lips. "You have narrowed it down to a point where it could involve but one person, Naomi."

Dawson squirmed in his chair uneasily as he watched the two scouts eyeing each other, for the both of them took desperate chances to free the girl, first from the trappers, then finally from the Sioux. Both of their futures involved the beautiful Indian girl. For Turley she represented a fortune in gold. For Lance she was the girl that he loved and wanted for a wife. In the beginning the situation was entirely different but since then, fate had stepped in and changed the course, which led to the matter now being discussed in an air of tension.

Dawson chewed his tobacco slowly as his eyes shifted from one scout to the other and waited impatiently for Turley to answer. The old scout's jaw stopped moving as Turley replied. "You're right Winsor, I'm referring to Naomi. Certain things within the short past led me to believe that the two of you are more than just interested in each other; however, I brought up the subject out of curiosity, not knowing for sure." Turley kept his gaze on Lance as he puffed on the cigarette then added, "You are aware of the fact that Naomi is the reason for my being here, and I still have plans."

"Turley," said Lance as he crushed out the cigarette he was smoking in a wooden ashtray shoved across the table to him by Dawson, "You've come a long way and succeeded in your venture, up 'til now.

I refrain from the thought of discontinuing our friendship or meddling in your affairs directly; however, whatever happened since you and I crossed trails concerning Naomi and myself is something that couldn't be helped."

"You talk as though you're quite serious about the girl," said Turley as he got up from the chair and stood before Lance.

The latter hesitated for a moment then answerer, "I am."

"How serious?" asked Turley.

"We're going to get married," replied Lance as he got up from his sitting position and faced Turley, not knowing exactly what to expect, for the scout from Texas not so much as batted an eyelash upon hearing his friend's last remark.

Dawson expected something to explode as he sat there motionless, but he was ready to intervene should the two young scouts differ bitterly over the matter being discussed.

The old scout relaxed slightly as he noticed Turley's gaze drop downward and he waited for him to say something that would betray his feelings one way or another.

Suddenly, Turley walked slowly toward the door. He opened it, then turned and faced the scouts who were watching him with a puzzled look. Turley's grin widened a trifle but he said nothing as he stepped out and closed the door.

Dawson sighed in relief as he kept his gaze on the closed door along with Lance, but he too was a bit confused by Turley's silent attitude concerning the event that took place but a moment ago.

"Darn if I can figure the boy out," said Dawson breaking the silence. "I expected him to go into a rage but all he did was grin. Might be burning inside though, reminds me of you a lot."

Lance glanced at the old scout then walked over to the stove and brought the coffee pot back to the table.

Dawson pointed a finger at him and remarked, "No matter what is going on, you and Turley always wear a grin."

"I know you young coots pretty well, but most people would find it hard to figure out how you fellows feel or what you are thinking about at times."

"Right now I'd like to know what Turley had on his mind just before he walked out."

Dawson dragged the pot across the table and began to fill his cup.

"Where do you suppose he went," he asked Lance.

"I don't know," answered the latter with a frown.

Lance rolled a fresh cigarette, lit it, the proceeded to take off his shirt. "I think we ought to get cleaned up, he said casually. "Going visiting tonight. Want to come along? That apple pie ought to taste awful good."

"Don't have to ask me twice, you young coot," remarked Dawson as he filled a large basin with water and placed it on top of the stove. Walking over to his bunk, the old scout sat down and began to take off his boots.

A frown appeared on his forehead as he looked up at Lance saying, "Son, I don't want to nosy into your business but I think that you ought to see the General tonight and tell him of your plans that include quitting the military. Ain't no use dragging it along."

Lance's face became serious as he said rather softly, "I'll go see Terry tonight."

Dawson scratched his bushy chin and squinted at Lance remarking, "The General is shore going to hit the ceiling when that bit of news soaks in, especially at a time like this."

Lance faced the old scout and said, "I'll admit that it is a poor time to be backing out, but there is no other way."

"I think that you ought to make another way, Son."

Lance's face was expressionless as he faced the old scout and asked slowly, "Why?"

Dawson grabbed a towel and flung it over his shoulder, saying, "Son, I know what you have already thrashed out in your mind and the answers that have met your approval. You don't care what anyone thinks about your quitting now and too that you can get along without their help. You can leave all that behind you, I agree, but can you live with yourself from here on in knowing that you have quit the military when you were needed most of all? Can you move into the Big Horn country with your intended wife and live in peace and contentment with the thought that others have fought and died for the land that you are going to stake out while you stepped aside and waited for the all clear signal?"

Silence befell the two scouts for a full minute. It was Lance who broke the stillness.

"Anything else, Deacon?"

"Just wanted to point out a thing or two," replied Dawson."Didn't mean on doin' any preachin."

Lance put his foot upon a chair and continued wiping his face and neck at the same time remarking, "Just where would you suggest that Naomi stay while I'm gone, here at the fort?" You know as well as I that the cool treatment she would get here from most of them would cause her a great deal of grief and sorrow, need I mention the possibilities of other undesirable occurrences she may have to put up with?"

Dawson rubbed his chin and remarked "The Bacons would take care of her for you, of that I'm sure."

Lance hesitated for a moment then said, "I believe that you resent my quitting the military, Will."

"No, I don't," said the latter slowly. "You'd be moving into a hornets' nest if you went up the river now. Them redskins would burn you to the ground before you got the front wall of the cabin up, amongst other things, like getting yourself and the Mrs. kilt, being up there all alone."

Dawson got o his feet and walked toward the wash basin. As he poured some of the water into a pan he glanced at Lance who seemed to be lost in thought. He added, "Another thing that stands in your way and always will until one of you are dead is White Cloud. Have you forgotten him?"

Lance took his foot off the chair and walked over to a dresser taking out some fresh clothes. He let out a sigh remarking, "Will, you should have been an artist, you certainly paint a sad picture."

"It's not a new one," said the old scout. "I believe that you have been looking at it quite often during the past week."

The latch turned in the door; the sound drew their attention and they gazed at the intruder as he came in to the room. It was Turley.

He walked slowly over to the table, poured himself some coffee and sat down.

Lance and Dawson looked at each other momentarily then continued changing their clothes. They waited for Turley to break the odd silence but he said nothing as he glanced at one, then the other with a grin, and casually rolled himself a cigarette.

Whatever was on Turley's mind, Dawson decided to drag it out as he started the conversation by asking, "When you going to get cleaned up, Son? There's some apple pie in the fort that is awaiting our attention."

Turley hesitated momentarily before answering. He put the cigarette to his lips, lit it and inhaled deeply.

Lance watched him curiously and was at a loss as far as a logical answer concerning his friend's attitude was concerned. Up to the moment he gave no indication of approval or otherwise and Lance was more than eager to settle the matter once and for all. He decided to press the issue along with Dawson but differed with the old scout's method by coming to the point.

"Turley," said Lance as he took a step toward the latter who now turned and looked at Lance with an amusing grin.

Before Lance could continue, Turley raised his hand and cut him short, quickly saying, "Hold it, Captain. I have yet to answer the bearded gentlemen who just cast a tempting invitation my way."

"Wall now," cut in Dawson with a big grin. "I haven't been called a gentleman since I slipped in the mud back in Missouri and Mrs. Perkens, the mayor's wife, stepped on me to get over the puddle."

Lance let out a sigh and walked over to the table to sit down. He decided now to let the others talk, for the situation sure took an abrupt turn from the tension that filled the room about a half hour ago. Now it was a humorous conversation that seemed to be drifting away from the subject he wanted to discuss.

Turley laughed as he got up from the chair and walked over to where Dawson was standing and put an arm around his shoulder saying, "Will, I'll accept that invitation since I've decided to stay around here for a while."

Lance frowned slightly as he leaned back in the chair and waited anxiously for Turley to continue, for he wondered at the moment just what his friend was up to other than going out for some air about a half hour ago.

"Wall now," remarked Dawson, "I was sort of hoping you would, for more reasons than one."

"Yes, I know," said Turley slowly as he turned and faced Lance. "I'm now a member of General Terry's forces and will do my scouting with the captain here. And another thing I'd like to say at this moment, I guess it's the proper time, congratulations, Captain. I'm not the type to get sentimental, but I will say sincerely that I have no regrets and offer the best in wishes for you and Naomi."

"Thanks," said Lance as he got up from the table and walked around toward the others. "You've certainly taken me by surprise and, if I may add, made things a lot easier fella. There were times when I thought of this moment and wondered what kind of weapons you would suggest for the duel."

Turley remarked, laughing, "Sorta glad it turned out this way. Don't have to go south anymore."

"Or east," cut in Dawson as he gazed into the mirror inspecting his freshly cut beard.

"For the lights of St. Louie have gone dim and gave way to the bright fire that burns brilliantly up at Bacon's camp."

Dawson seemed amused as he watched the scouts through the mirror, for he too was more than happy by the pleasing turn of events.

"Looks like our friend has everything mapped out," said Turley with a smile. "Can't do a thing without him knowing how it's going to turn out."

"Plain as day," chuckled Dawson. "Like the handwriting on the wall."

"Watch this man," remarked Lance to Turley amusingly. "He is a troublemaker."

"Which reminds me," said the old scout as he turned around facing the other two, "I'm going to get into trouble with my stomach if I don't start filling it up soon. I met up with Mr. Baker just 'afore I came back from visitin' with Custer and he told me that we are all invited to come over tonight." Dawson stroked his beard and said as an afterthought, "Come to think about it, he didn't mention supper."

He looked at Turley with a scoff and remarked, "Don't just stand there grinning like a coot. Get yourself cleaned up and let's get on over there; maybe we can barge in afore they put the supper dishes away."

Lance walked over to the window and looked out. The activity within the walls of the fort failed to disrupt his thoughts of the man who occupied his mind at the moment, Turley. Not once did his friend argue a point, or differ in opinion. He followed his leadership ever since they met. More than once Turley turned the tide when everything else seemed hopeless. With each passing day their friendship became warmer. Lance wondered many long it would continue after he was told about the plans that would forever rob him of the reward in gold. He kept the secret from Turley until the bitter end and tonight it was made known to him. *Perhaps it wasn't much of a secret at that,* mused Lance as he sighed easily. *For it was Turley himself who started the issue.* Once again the easy going, ever ready Turley simplified the matter that could have ended their friendship and perhaps ended in bitter resentment. Instead, he bowed out nonchalantly as if the sudden end to his plans were incidental.

Lance was indeed happy about the outcome. A trace of a smile appeared on his lips as he turned and glanced at his friends.

"Making plans, Captain?" remarked Dawson as he put on a clean buckskin coat. "You stand there like you were deciding the next move against the Sioux."

"He certainly don't look like the head scout for Benteen in that attire," cut in Turley. "Flannel shirt, blue trousers, looks more like a farmer or a rancher, doesn't he," laughed Turley as he looked at Dawson.

Lance's face became crimson for only Dawson and Naomi knew of his plans of quitting the military. Before he could make any comment, the old scout said rather casually, "He ain't going to be with us anymore."

Turley's smile faded slowly as he looked at Dawson questioningly.

"That's right son," said the old scout as he put his hand on Turley's shoulder. "Looks like it's just you and I from here on in. Winsor here is quitting the military."

"Is he serious?" asked Turley now looking at Lance with disbelief.

"Yes, I told him that I was quitting," answered Lance with a touch of embarrassment.

Turley's disappointment was obvious but he offered no comment. Lance knew that it was useless to try saying something in regard to justifying his actions, for the two men that looked at him without betraying their emotions would accept nothing in the way of an excuse for quitting the military in time of need. He broke the awkward silence by changing the subject completely. "If you gentlemen are ready, we'll go pay our respects."

Opening the door, Lance waited for the others. Dawson hesitated before stepping out, tugged at his coat collar and asked, "How do I look for the occasion?"

Lance managed a grin and said, "If it wasn't for your voice, I wouldn't recognize you, must be someone around you've got your eye on."

"Wouldn't tell you if I did," said the old scout with a twinkle in his eye, and went out. Turley stopped near the door and the two friends faced each other. Lance expected a cool remark of some sort now that the other was aware of his quitting the military, among other things that he did that didn't flatter his friends' plans. But once again he was wrong concerning Turley's attitude toward his decisions as the latter spoke rather softly.

"Winsor, I have never questioned your decisions or asked for reasons in the short time we've known each other and I'd like you to know that the ones made known tonight are no exceptions. However, my future missions up in the Big Horn won't be the same without the captain."

A bit of mist covered Lance's eyes as he smiled slightly and said, "Thanks."

Lance followed Turley out with a saddened heart, for the predicament that had befallen him certainly left his mind in a state of confusion. Although he had already related his plans, Lance tried to convince himself over and over again that his decisions were just, but deep down within the depths of his soul the aggressor of meek justification was slowly shattering his present stand. His thought faded away as Dawson grumbled, “A man could starve waiting for you two . . . can’t see for the life of me how you coots are going to get along without each other.”

Nothing more was said as they made their way over to Mrs. Tuffs’ cabin. Late evening found the Bakers, the scouts, Mrs. Tuffs, and Naomi seated in the large living room. Excitement filled the air as Dawson related one of his hair-raising adventures that took place back in Missouri.

“There I was, at the edge of the cliff, the giant grizzly comin’ at me full speed . . . ”

Dawson took another mouthful of apple pie as Mrs. Tuffs exclaimed in anxiety, “For gosh sakes Mr. Dawson, what on earth happened?”

“The bear died of fright,” cut in Lance with a laugh.

“Pay no attention to these young coots,” remarked the old scout. “Neither one of them is worth a sack of wheat without me being along side of ‘em.”

Everyone enjoyed the humor as they focused their eyes on Dawson, again waiting for him to continue.

“Well sir, I had but one choice, and that was to jump off the cliff into the river below which I judged at the time to be about three to four hundred feet.”

Lance and Turley grinned as they eyed each other.

“Those big hungry jaws near got me as I leaped off the cliff but I made it and swam to shore.”

“I kept you from drowning several times back at the Big Horn,” cut in Turley. “That river you jumped into must have been about two feet deep and you walked out.”

Laughter filled the room as Dawson scowled at Turley. Though gaiety flooded the interior of the dwelling and everyone seemed to be enjoying themselves, there was one whose heart failed to ring with laughter. Her many glances at the Indian girl, whose eyes sparkled brightly when looking or talking to Lance on occasions, confirmed her suspicions: that there was more between the girl and the man that she secretly admired, she was more than a friend who was rescued on her way back home.

Helene's thoughts wandered back into the past and a slight smile touched her lips as she thought of the first time she met Lance. They danced together on occasions, went for short rides outside the fort; the many pleasant hours they spent together chatting about the craziest things. *After a while you fell in love with him, didn't you Helene,* she said to herself. *You changed from admiration to love, but he didn't, did he? You've given him all the chances in the world and at times your love was quite obvious but he always failed to take advantage of the situation. Yes, always the same Lance the gentleman. I know, you hate to admit it,* she said to herself. *He just didn't care for you that much but you weren't going to give up, were you? Of course not. Again you waited for his return. This time you were really going to pour on the charm.*

Helene sighed slightly as she thought of the best of her charms that she already put to use, but to no avail. *Helene,* she continued conversing with her inner self, *now don't you fret about that. You're a woman, surely you'll find a way out.* Again a slight smile brushed her lips as she exclaimed to herself, *you've got it, I knew you would, just dress up the old charm a bit and present it differently this time.* Her moment of glory in coming up with a warmly approved solution was short lived as her inner voice called out rather cautiously, *Helene, you are letting your dreams carry you off. Haven't you forgotten something?* Her face became sober and her brow wrinkled slightly. *Yes Helene, you are right. The Indian girl isn't going to help you in your cause, is she? Let's be frank now. Two people don't look at each other like you've seen them do if they were only just friends.*

Helene's face grew white as she pressed her lips together and shouted within herself: *but she is Indian! Lance wouldn't marry an*

Indian girl. Wouldn't he, Helene? Especially a beautiful Indian girl like her. Need I mention Dawson? He married a Cheyenne. Remember handsome Sergeant Grim? He brought back a Pawnee and married her right here at the fort. It's an old story Helene. Suddenly her inner emotions burst and she screamed deep down within herself. *I won't let her have him, do you hear? I won't let her have him.* Without thinking, she snapped her head slightly and faced Naomi squarely, the latter was staring back at her rather curiously. Helene felt the blood rush to her face as it occurred to her that the other must have been watching her facial expressions. She quickly recomposed herself and managed a smile wondering at the same time if the Indian girl had read her thoughts aided so plainly by her facial expressions but a moment before.

Naomi returned the smile the turned quickly and accepted a cup of coffee that Mrs. Baker offered her. This was indeed a gala night for Dawson as he delighted in telling tall tales that drew hearty laughs and chuckles. Lance and Turley cut him short with a bit of ribbing at times like they did so often.

"Tell me Dawson," remarked Baker. "What story lies behind that beard that you don't seem to want to get rid of?"

"Well, now Baker, there is quite a story attached to it, and besides, tobacco juice, insects, and the usual dirt," cut in Lance laughing.

The old scout grinned that comment off as he remarked, "There's one nice thing in having these two youngins along as sidekicks. They never let you think seriously, as a matter of fact, they never let you think."

Dawson got up from the chair, more to stretch his legs than anything else, pointed a finger at Lance and Turley and said, "Let me tell you what these coots did on our last trip up to . . . "

The old scout stopped abruptly as a loud knock sounded on the door. Baker got up and opened it. Upon recognizing the intruder, Baker bade him in.

It was Terry's orderly, who upon entering said apologetically, "Sorry to bother you at this time of the night."

"That's quite all right," replied Baker.Then he asked, "Something wrong?"

"Not that I know of," answered the orderly. "However, I was sent out by General Terry to inform Mr. Winsor, that the General has received a message from one of the guards out at the gate given to him by one of the members of a small Indian party."

The scouts looked at each other as the orderly continued. "They wish to speak to the three scouts that have visited the Sioux camp about a week ago."

"What about?" asked Dawson.

"They wouldn't say," replied the message bearer.

Lance had an idea and he was aware that Naomi knew too as she looked at him understandingly. "Now don't you worry," he said to her softly. "I'll be right back."

The scouts excused themselves and left the dwelling. As they made their way to the gate, Dawson remarked, "White Cloud sure didn't waste any time, the red skin buzzard. Wasn't too far behind us I would judge. Had I known that he was so close I sure would have suggested to ride on through instead of camping last night."

"You wouldn't have gotten an argument," replied Lance. "This sure is a surprise to me."

Turley said nothing as a cold chill crept up his spine at the thought of what could have happened if the Indians had caught up with them unsuspected.

XII

As they walked out through the gate they stopped abruptly. They scanned the faces of the four braves on horseback whose features showed plainly in the light cast by the fire at the roast pit, but the chief was not among them. One of the braves holding on to a lance, which had a white piece of cloth attached to the top end and rode forward a short distance and halted his horse.

"White Cloud say . . . in three moons . . . he will send here." The brave pointed to the spot where Lance stood, then continued. "Much gold . . . " He hesitated for a moment, then said quickly in a gruff voice, "We take girl."

Dawson and Turley eyed Lance as they waited for him to answer. An expression of defiance appeared on Lance's face along with a cool grin as he stared up at the brave and shook his head in the negative. The moment was tense and the scouts were ready for any violence that may be attempted, however, they hardly expected anything to occur under the circumstances.

"You no give girl?" asked the brave, scowling down at them.

"No," replied Lance sternly, his lips hardly moving.

The brave quickly removed the peace flag from the lance and then threw the sharpened spear into the ground inches away from Lance's feet.

Lance never moved a muscle as he held his ground. The brave urged his mount around, and with the others, rode off into the darkness.

Dawson snatched the spear and pulled it out of the ground. Fumbling with it momentarily, he gazed out into the darkness in the direction of the disappearing braves and said slowly, "There will be no escape, or peace for you son, as long as that savage breathes. There never will be room enough for the both of you along the waters of the Big Horn."

Lance made no reply as he stood there with his thoughts, nor did Turley, who watched his friend closely, trying to detect the effect, if any, the incident had on Lance.

"Excuse me gentlemen," said a voice near the gate. "General Terry requests your presence at the conclusion of your business at hand."

"One of us will be there in a moment," replied Lance, whereupon the orderly made a hasty retreat.

"If you fellows don't mind," said Lance, his face becoming quite sober. "I'd like to explain the incident, among other things, to the General. Alone."

"Go right ahead," said Dawson as he put an arm around Turley's shoulder. "We'll mosey back to the Bakers' for another piece of that pie."

As Lance turned to go, Dawson called out to him whereupon the other stopped and looked back at the old scout questioningly.

"That new buckskin outfit that you got a short time ago will look awful good on you, especially if you're Head Scout for Captain Benteen."

Lance smiled but said nothing as his eyes lingered on his two friends momentarily; he turned and walked up toward headquarters.

"Fool boy," remarked Dawson with a big grin. "What made him think that he could stand by and watch his sidekicks march off without him."

"You mean," said Turley, whose face was all smiles, "... that ... "

"Exactly," cut in the old scout. "When we go, the captain will be in the lead."

Arms over each others' shoulders, they walked off in the direction of the Bakers'. A short time later, Lance reentered the Baker dwelling upon finishing his business with General Terry. They all looked at him questioningly, and it appeared to Lance that neither of the scouts related the exact reason for the appearance of the Indian party. He managed a smile and said, "No cause for alarm. The matter is incidental. I wish to apologize to the Bakers for imposing on their hospitality this far into the night."

"Nonsense," remarked Mrs. Baker. "It was indeed nice to have all of you back here again."

As they bade each other goodnight and started through the open doorway, Helene quickly walked over to Lance and remarked, "Since you've been away I haven't had much practice riding horses. Are you going to have time to give me a few more lessons before you leave again?"

"I hardly think that you need practice," said Lance, smiling down at her. "As a matter of fact I've always considered you one of the best."

She looked up at him with a glint in her eye, and asked, "Does that mean no?"

Lance knew that this girl cared for him more than he wanted her to and that she would have to be told about Naomi. He didn't want to hurt her feelings anymore than he had to and it certainly wasn't the time or place to relate the secret.

"All Right," he said. "You pick your horse, and in a day or so I'll race you out to the wall."

"I'll be looking forward to it," she said with a smile of satisfaction. The light in her eyes as she spoke to Lance didn't go unnoticed, for another pair of eyes, dark and expressionless at the moment, watched the incident through the open doorway.

Minutes later, Lance said to Mrs. Tuffs as they neared her cabin, "I'd like to speak to Naomi a few minutes. She'll be right in."

"On one condition," remarked Mrs. Tuffs. "You must come over for one good dinner with Mr. Dawson and Mr. Turley before you all leave here again."

"We wouldn't miss it for the world," replied Lance, smiling.

"Fine then, that is settled. I'll be waiting for you dear," she said to Naomi, then she left the young couple and entered the cabin.

Lance put his hand on Naomi's shoulder. The other hand he placed gently on her face then let it slide smoothly back across her temple. He controlled his emotions as he looked down at her adoringly. His whole world, his future was wrapped up with the girl that stood before him. She was his. He had claimed her and she had accepted his love in the not too far distant past. He wondered now what effect the change in plans would have upon her. If she loved him, she would understand. She would wait until he had cleared all the barriers.

"We don't get too much of a chance to be alone," he said to her softly.

"Soon, it will be different," she said as her dark eyes flashed in the semi darkness.

The smile on his face slowly faded away. He placed his arms around her and drew her tightly to him saying, "Little one, there is something that has to be done before we can go up the river like I told you that we would back at Bacon's camp. You will have to try to understand. If we go now, there will never be peace and happiness for you and me." Lance paused momentarily, perhaps waiting for a comment, but none came from the girl who snuggled against him without betraying any emotion.

"I will have to go with the military once more in this campaign against the Sioux. Then there is White Cloud, and you know as well as I do, until he is dealt with, we will have to keep looking back over our shoulders." Lance pushed her back slightly until she met his gaze, then continued, asking, "Would you want to see Dawson and Turley march away to battle while I ran the other way?"

He looked at her questioningly, waiting for her to say something that would bring light her silent thoughts. An empty feeling engulfed the pit of his stomach as it did several times during the discussion, for the thought of her being contrary concerning the turning of events lingered in his mind. Lance held his breath as she finally broke her silence, saying, in a soft warm voice, "I have given my heart to you. It will be happy when you are near. It will be sad when you are gone. Naomi will always be waiting for your return."

Lance's facial expression changed from anxiety to a deeply emotional one as his arms enfolded her, drawing her close to him as if his very being depended upon her nearness. His lips yearned for the ones so very close to his but he stayed away momentarily, filling himself with every desire before giving away to the thrill of the kiss, which up to a short time ago he thought could only exist in imagination aided by creations that mythically exist within the walls of deepest fantasy.

"Now ain't that touching." The voice came from one of the nearby buildings. Lance drew back quickly upon hearing the sarcastic remark and said to Naomi, "Go in; I'll see you tomorrow." He kept his eyes on the girl until she disappeared behind the door, then turned slowly around and scanned the area for the intruder.

His eyes fell upon two guards leaning against one of the cabins; they were obviously making their rounds when he and Naomi were interrupted. Lance was furious as he walked slowly toward the guards. The one that made the remark nudged the other with his elbow and said, "What do you know Bill? We have a Squaw man in our midst."

Lance kept his head as he neared them and eyed them coolly. A cold grin that was anything but amused appeared on his lips.

"Haven't seen you fellows before. New around here, are you not?" asked Lance without any mirth.

"Yes we're new around here," answered the talkative one sporting a sarcastic smile. "But we've been around plenty elsewhere."

"You haven't learned much, I notice," remarked Lance coolly. "Out here you mind your business and keep out of other people's way. You've made a bad start as far as I'm concerned, but I'm willing to forget the incident."

"Well now," cut in the other. "That's right nice of you, ain't it Bill?" he asked the other laughingly.

Lance was raging within himself but managed to control himself. "Listen, fella," said Lance slowly. His voice was even, but colder than the icicles that hung off the cabin roofs in mid-winter. "If this occurs again, I'll be ready to teach you the hard way."

After a moment of silence, the guard, who was sliding a small twig from one corner of his mouth to the other, replied with a little less sarcasm and without mirth. "I'll be looking forward to join one of your classes, Teacher."

Lance widened his grin a bit, saying, "One class is all you're going to be able to attend." With that he left the guards who stared after him until he disappeared in the darkness.

The days that followed were busy ones for the scouts and most everyone else at the fort. Patrols were constantly moving in and out, other scouts going and coming off their missions. Outside the fort, drills and maneuvers were an ever present sight. A few more days and the long march north to seek out the ravaging, plundering Sioux, led by the relentless savage of them all, Sitting Bull, would begin. Within the walls of Lance's cabin, a dozen scouts sat around facing a large map that was hung up on the side of the wall. They listened eagerly as Lance pointed out strategic areas up in the northwest wilderness.

Once again the busy orderly appeared and informed Lance that his presence, along with Dawson's and Turley's, was requested by General Terry immediately.

"That will be all for today gentlemen," said Lance. "We'll continue tomorrow and iron out some of the rough spots."

A few minutes later, the scouts entered Terry's quarters.

"Gentlemen, I had you come over at this time to advise you of a change in command. Captain Benteen is attached to my forces as of now and his replacement has been assigned to Captain Drume who was sent here at my request." After the necessary introductions, Terry addressed Lance. "The captain will need all the added information you can give him, in addition to familiarizing himself with the territory up north. The country will be new to him. I'd appreciate the extra effort."

"I'll do my best, general," replied Lance assuringly.

"Dawson," said Terry addressing the old scout. "I had you called over especially to meet the captain. He is the son of Major Drum. "An old friend of yours," he said smiling.

"Well, now," remarked Dawson. "I was sorta anxious to ask the captain if he might be a kin to the Major. The Major and I got more Cheyenne then there are buffalo out on the range."

"He told me quite a bit about you," said the captain with a smile, "during some of his short visits back east."

"The General might have more important business at the moment. With his permission, I suggest we all go over to the cabin for a little more discussion on the subject," remarked the old scout enthusiastically. Terry chuckled as he walked to the door and then stared after them in silent approval.

The morning was cool and bright. Activities at the fort had long since been in progress. Two riders rode out through the gates and then urged their mounts to a gallop, racing on toward a well situated about a mile from the fort. Minutes later, Lance held back his mount, allowing Helene to reach her destination first.

"There you are, Lance Winsor," she exclaimed laughingly. "That's the third time I've beaten you out here."

"No two ways about it," said Lance smiling as he helped her dismount. "You are without question the better rider."

They sat down on one of the large stones that encircled the well and gazed down ino the water below.

"Do you believe in wishing wells?' she asked.

"I've never given it a try," said Lance, amusingly. "So I don't believe or disbelieve the stories of the existing magic powers that is said to be within the depths of a well."

"Now is your chance. Want to try?" she asked, facing Lance with a glint in her eye.

He chuckled softly as he gazed at her momentarily, then said, "It's funny how women believe in hidden powers. Tell me," he asked, "how much time would you give this well to fulfill your wish?"

"That depends on a lot of things," she replied with a grin, and eyed Lance who seemed to be quite amused.

"What happens if it should fail completely? Would you forget about the wish?" asked Lance as he added a few inches of distance between them.

"That would depend on what it was," she said gazing into the well. "If it failed here, then I would have to resort to other means, that is if I find it worth my while."

"Well," said Lance chuckling. "You go ahead and make a wish and let me know sometime how you made out. I'm curious to know if anything besides stone and sand lie beneath the water."

A faint trace of a smile appeared on Helene's lips and her eyes sparkled madly in the sunlight as she leaned toward Lance remarking, "You are in a much better position than all the wishing wells in the world to help me with my wish."

She was much closer to him than Lance desired and he was angry with himself for allowing the matter to go this far instead of getting to the point at the beginning. He didn't want to hurt her anymore than he had to, and at the moment his mind was racing to put together the words that would sound logical in bringing this one-sided romance to an understanding. Helene kept swaying toward him and her lips were but inches away. He knew what she was attempting to do but his mind seemed to function improperly. Lance felt the blood rush to his face and knew that he had but a moment to say something that would end the uneasiness he felt if not the embarrassing situation. "Helene..."

That is as far as Lance got, for the girl, who sat so near him stopped further conversation as her lips met his. Lance's face became sober as he slowly drew backward and kept his gaze on the beautiful blue-eyed girl before him. He thought of others that would go to extremes for a chance like this with Helene. But to him, it was time wasted.

His heart belonged to another and at that moment he thought of Naomi. He felt a sense of shame for allowing it to happen, although he didn't encourage the incident at all.

She smiled at him but with a look of dismay for his reaction was contrary to her expectations. Her facial expression didn't change as the thought of Naomi entered her mind. The thought of Lance favoring the Indian girl to her angered Helene to a feverish pitch but she failed to betray her emotions as she kept her smile. *We'll see about that*, she said to herself. She broke the moment of silence by remarking, "It certainly took a long time for that to happen. You amaze me with you shyness."

"Helene, it's not a question of shyness," said Lance trying to shake off the uneasiness he felt. "Something happened a short while back that has changed the future considerably."

"Would it be Naomi?" she asked with a faint trace of a smile still lingering on her lips.

Lance looked at her squarely and answered. "Yes, it's Naomi."

Her wide smile at the moment puzzled Lance. "I'll admit that she is beautiful. But I think that your adventures of late in which she was involved have you weaving a fictitious story. Lance Winsor," she said slowly. "I do believe that you are infatuated."

"Helene, if I told you that I was in love with her, would you believe that?"

She got up and walked a short distance then stopped, turning to face Lance.

"No I wouldn't," she answered with a look of defiance.

"All Right," sighed Lance. "We'll let time answer that one."

He was about to get up and considered the issue closed but changed his mind momentarily as Helene walked slowly toward him wearing a smile that could be credited to a cunning schemer.

Curiosity, more than anything else, kept him in waiting.

She walked up to where he was seated and placed her hands up to his neck and fumbled with his coat collar.

"All Right, Lance. If that's the way it is and if it's going to remain that way, then I wish the both of you all the luck in the world and your share of happiness."

Lance eased out a sigh and was relieved at the thought that the matter was going to end a friendly one, but his relief was short lived as Helene continued.

"However, since you've always been the gentleman, I know that you will listen to my bid, which I know at the moment you consider a lost cause."

Contrary to the past, her aggressiveness surprised Lance immensely and at the moment he wondered if he knew this girl as much as he thought he did.

"I've been in love with you since the first time we met. I've been too ladylike in the past, to a fault, and perhaps now to my regret. Just in case you find one day that you don't really love the other girl, I want you to know I'll be waiting."

"Helene."

Lance said no more as she put her finger to his lips. "Every man needs a girl," she said after hesitating briefly. "Someone to come back to, especially off those wild and lonely ventures." Her fingers caressed the back of his neck, then his ears the latter becoming crimson, not from the caressing, but from her next remark.

"Sometimes a lot of time is involved before two people find that they are really in love and then decide upon marriage. If such is the case now, then I m willing to do anything, anytime you wish, starting right now."

He took her hands away from the back of his neck and stood up, saying, "I'm sorry, Helene. Don't waste your time on me." He felt sorry for this girl and much sorrier that he had come out here to the well. "There are others that would move mountains just to engage you in a minute's conversation."

"I don't want others," she said slowly. "I want you."

Suddenly, Lance caught sight of a moving object a short distance up the side of the mountain.

"Helene, mount your horse fast," he snapped. "We've got visitors."

An arrow swished through the air and buried itself in the trunk of a tree, causing the horses to shift about uneasily. He got hold of the excited girl and placed her up into the saddle. Slapping the horse on the flank, he half-shouted to Helene, "Ride back to the fort, fast."

Lance yanked his rifle out of its holster and ducked in behind the tree. He fired several rounds in the direction of the moving object which he first saw but at present saw nothing, nor were there any arrows coming this way. *White Cloud's scouts still hanging around*, he mused. He knew, too, that they would keep the chief well informed of Naomi's whereabouts. He wondered now if it would be wise to take Naomi up north to the Bacons'. It would be another hard trip for her, in addition to being much closer to the revenge-seeking Indian chief.

Lance discarded the thought for the time being as he backed cautiously toward his horse. Keeping his eyes on the heavily brushed area at the foot of the mountain, he mounted his horse and urged it into a gallop in the direction of the fort. A few hundred yards from the fort, a girl on horseback sat still and gazed back toward the spot that she left hastily but a few minutes before.

Indians back there, she mused. *Must be the same ones that Dawson mentioned the other night. Said something about chief White Cloud wanting Naomi for gold.* Her blood rushed through her veins in a radiant heat as a thought suddenly occurred to her. A grin, matching her cunning mind, appeared on her lips and new hope surged through her body like a bolt of lightning through space. She urged her mount forward and headed for the destination intended as she noticed Lance racing toward her at full speed. She waited for him at the gate where Dawson, Turley, and others from the fort questioned her concerning the shooting that had taken place shortly before she rode up to them.

"What happened out there?" asked Dawson.

"Ran into a few Indians that are scouting around," replied Lance.

"Still hanging around," remarked Dawson as he gazed out toward the mountains.

"Turley, will you walk Miss Baker up to the house?" asked Lance. "I'm going to report the incident to the General."

Lance managed a smile as he glanced at Helene and said more to his two friends than the girl, "I'll see you all later." He turned to go but stopped short and faced the girl again saying, "Seems like I could never beat you in a horse race. I guess you're just a born winner."

"I intend to stay that way," she replied with a smile that only Lance knew the meaning of. Lance disregarded the remark as he waved his hand slightly and started his walk towards headquarters. Halfway to his destination, a familiar voice caused Lance to come to an abrupt halt.

"I noticed that you had a new pupil in class today, Teacher. Quite a class you are putting together, all girls, no boys."

Lance knew that the voice belonged to the soldier that was on guard duty the night he had walked Naomi and Mrs. Tuffs home from the Bakers. Once again he walked up to the soldier who seemed to amuse himself with remarks that were quite touchy as far as Lance was concerned. He stopped within a foot of the other and eyed him coolly. The soldier stared back at him nonchalantly. A slight grin brushed Lance's lips as he said, "Perhaps you misunderstood me the other night, fella. I told you that classes would be open for your convenience at any time and I take it that you insist on learning the hard way."

"I hardly think that you could teach me anything," said the soldier as he hooked his thumbs in his belt and looked at Lance in defiance. "But I'm willing to learn, Squaw man."

The last remark angered Lance beyond control. This time he failed to control his emotions, nor did he try very hard. Suddenly, he lashed out with his left arm, the blow striking the other in the pit of the stomach at the same time bringing his fist upward connecting with the jaw. His right arm was already on its way and landed solidly on the soldier's jaw. The impact sent the latter backward, tumbling over bales of canvas, finally ending up between a couple of them. Lance rushed over to continue the fight but was convinced that the fallen man had no desire to go on, as he laid there motionless like a fisherman taking a nap on a hot summer day. Soldiers that were present during the incident looked at Lance casually but said nothing. Two of them went to the aid of their fallen comrade in an attempt to revive him.

"When he wakes up," said Lance as he adjusted his belt, "tell him that classes are still open if he cares to continue his education." He turned to go then stopped short momentarily as he noticed Turley and Dawson standing a few feet away from him, like a couple of cougars ready for action.

"Still guarding the rear, just in case, Captain," said Turley slowly.

Lance smiled at them understandingly and, like many times before, felt that he had achieved a few valuable things in life that he had valued highly, two of them being the friendship of Dawson and Turley.

"If you gentlemen are serving coffee, I'll join you shortly," he remarked and continued on towards Terry's quarters.

XIII

Once again the sun sank slowly beyond the horizon. The shadows of the night crept in and around the fort, indicating the fact that another day had gone by, another day closer to the battle when the blood of warriors would run freely among the clear waters of the Big Horn.

A guard stationed up in the tower shouted in a loud voice that drew a lot of attention and excited most of them. "Two riders approaching." Minutes later, two dust-riddled scouts rode in through the gates and lost no time getting to Terry's quarters.

"Looks like they spotted trouble somewhere along the trail," remarked Dawson as he and the younger scouts watched the newcomers disappear behind closed doors.

"If that is the case," said Lance with a frown, "we'll know about it before long."

"What are the chances that Sitting Bull would come down here with his forces and strike first?" asked Turley.

"I've got my doubts there," answered Lance. "He is aware of the strength down here and I'm sure that he would much rather have it out in his own back yard."

A knock on the door interrupted the conversation. The scouts glanced at each other for a moment, then Lance said, "Come in," as he sprang from the chair and walked toward the door. Their glances at each other but a moment before justified their thoughts, for the man appearing through the doorway was Terry's orderly.

"The General requests your presence gentlemen at eight o'clock sharp," said the newcomer.

"Bad news?" asked Lance with anxiety.

"Indian trouble up north, I believe it's around the new settlers camp that went up."

"We know where that is," cut in Lance.

"We'll be there at eight, son," said Dawson to the orderly as he kept is eyes on Turley.

The latter stared down at the floor as he methodically rolled a cigarette. Lance closed the door after the orderly departed and walked back toward Turley who slowly placed the cigarette to his lips. Upon striking a match which he held for his friend, Lance remarked, "I think that the settlers can take care of themselves until we get up there; they have plenty of rifles and ammunition."

Turley smiled at Lance understandingly but made no comment. He was aware of the fact that his friends knew of his concern regarding Bacon's daughter and was at the moment reassuring him that things would turn out all right.

"As a matter of fact, we'll know just what is taking place up there once we see the General."

Within the hour, those that were requested to appear at headquarters were present and awaiting Terry. Moments later he appeared and greeted the men whose chatter quieted down to complete silence as they waited in anxiety for him to disclose the news that was brought in by the scouts. The seriousness of the matter showed plainly on Terry's face as he began speaking in an even tone.

"Gentlemen, I have a bit of bad news that will unfortunately hasten your departure up north. The Sioux are harassing the settlers constantly and the alarming addition to the situation is that they have plenty of rifles. They need help right away, plus the fact that the source through which the Indians are obtaining the rifles has not been identified. Captain Drum, you will have your regiment fully equipped and ready to move out in the morning after tomorrow. You will be ahead of schedule as far as our previous plans are concerned but will continue to follow them out on the date already set. However, in the mean time, you will aid the settlers in their strife. I shall brief you on personal instructions tomorrow, Captain. Gentlemen, you all have a lot to do, personal and otherwise, and only a short time to do it in. I'll not keep you any longer; however, if any of you have any questions, I'll be glad to answer them if I can."

There were more questions than the General anticipated, for no one made an attempt to leave.

The next day was indeed a busy one at the fort. Captain Drum lost no time in getting his regiment and equipment into shape. Near the end of the day, all was in readiness and the excitement grew with the passing of each hour. No one seemed to notice the dark haired girl as she stood leaning against a porch post, gazing far out over the fort, lost in thought. No one but the soldier who received a sound thrashing a day or so ago by Lance. He placed a box of ammunition he was carrying into one of the wagons, looked around casually and proceeded to walk toward Naomi. His presence startled the girl as he remarked, "Not bad for an Indian girl. What is your name?"

She stared at the man before her in annoyance but said nothing.

"I just stopped by," he continued, "to find out if you wanted a message delivered to some of your kin up north, before they are wiped out that is."

The soldier disregarded her silence saying, "I don't care too much for Indians but I could change my mind about some of the women folk." He took a step forward then stopped as Naomi backed up toward the door. His smile was wide as he shrugged his shoulders and remarked, "No sense in running away from a little conversation."

"That's right fella," said a voice in back of him. "You can have that with me, and more if you wish."

The soldier turned and faced Lance squarely, then exclaimed, "Well, well, if it ain't the teacher. Something tells me that it's time again for classes."

"That's right. It will be held outside the gate, now," said Lance in even tones.

“Glad to oblige,” said the other. “However, it’s only right that the teacher should know his pupil by name. Yours is Winsor, I know. Mine is Stenton,” said the other amusingly.

Lance eyed the soldier and was taken by the humor which seemed out of place in the matter. He admitted to himself that he didn’t exactly dislike the man but he certainly needed adjustment.

Stenton bent slightly forward and with a wave of the hand said, smiling, “After you, Mr. Winsor.”

“I rather you go first,” said Lance. “You may not follow.”

“Don’t you worry about that,” said the other still holding his smile. “I’m going to keep you company, and I’m ready this time. But I’ll give you a chance to back down.”

Lance managed a slight grin, saying, “To the gate, Mr. Stenton.”

The soldier smiled at him for a moment then turned and walked toward the gate.

Lance gave Naomi a wink and said, “I’ll see you in a little while,” and proceeded to follow the soldier. Once on the outside, Lance was about to reason with the man verbally, but the other soon put an end to any verbal reasoning as he lashed out with his fist that glanced off Lance’s jaw. Lefts and rights were exchanged as they lashed at each other viciously. A right hook caught Lance on the side of the head and he went down.

The other pounced up on him and they rolled around in the dust, striking madly at each other. Five minutes later there was quite an audience witnessing the battle, including Dawson and Turley. The fighters were up on their feet now, circling each other. Lance knew that his opponent was weakening and concentrated on the other’s weakness, which he found to be the stomach. He let the soldier come at him swinging, each time averting the blows by side-stepping or ducking, waiting for that opening to come. And on one occasion it did.

Lance stepped in and landed a hard right to the stomach, then a left to the same place. He brought his right back then forward with lightning speed that landed squarely on Stenton’s jaw. The latter collapsed like a bushel of wheat and once more several of his aids ran over to revive their fallen friend. One of them came over to Lance, who was breathing heavily, and said, "Since we're all riding north together, I would like to put in a word in behalf of my friend there," and he motioned toward the fallen man. "He isn't half as bad as he puts on to be; I can't figure what's got into him of late."

"Well," said Lance between breaths. "If he behaves himself, I'll see that he gets his diploma." Then he added, "He is a much better fighter than he is a bad man."

"I hope that this ends the classes for you two," smiled the soldier.

Lance managed a grin as he nodded in agreement then left the scene with Dawson and Turley.

"Well," remarked Dawson. "Not much time left before you coots start headin' for Sioux country. Better not stick your necks out too far once you get up there. I won't be around for a spell to guide you two hellcats like I did on our last trip."

Lance looked at the old scout before lathering his face for a needed shave. He smiled but made no reply, for he sensed that Dawson's voice lacked the usual humor because of the same thought that he and Turley also had on their minds.

The parting of ways was near at hand. Perhaps not for long but nevertheless, quite effective for the three men that were so attached.

"Don't you worry, Will," said Turley as he slapped the latter on the back. "We'll be waiting for you up along the river before we wade across. Got to have somebody to show us just how deep the waters are."

"If you're referring to the night that I accidentally slipped in and lost ma' rifle," replied Dawson with a glint in his eye, "Why . . . "

"Accidentally slipped?" exclaimed Turley, grinning.

"Either that, or else you pushed me in," remarked Dawson.

"Who are you two going to rib tomorrow?" said Lance chuckling as he walked over to his bunk.

Silence befell them momentarily as they drifted away with their thoughts. As Lance finished dressing, he remarked, "Let's not keep Mrs. Tuffs waiting with supper. Should be ready by now. I'm going to stop over at the Bakers' for a minute to bid them farewell before going over to Mrs. Tuffs'."

"I owe them that myself," said Turley. "I'll go along."

"Just to keep you two from letting the supper go cold, I'll tag along," remarked Dawson yanking his coat off the back of a chair.

Late evening found Dawson and Turley bidding Mrs. Tuffs and Naomi goodnight.

"I'll be along shortly," said Lance as he walked his friends to the door. Mrs. Tuffs left the room and went into the kitchen understandingly.

Naomi looked up at Lance with eyes of sadness. He smiled slightly as his gaze wandered about her beautiful face, photographing every detail in his mind. At least he would have that much with him until his return. Finally he placed his arms around her and drew her to him. His kiss was soft and tender and the way she responded made Lance feel that his dreams of finding a good woman and settling down throughout the years were not just idle thoughts, for they were beginning to become a reality. He drew back slightly and said softly with a hint of satisfaction in his voice, "You sure are learning fast."

"The soldier is wise, when he called you the teacher," she said with a trace of a smile appearing on her lips.

"His lessons were kind of rough and I hope that classes with him are over." He drew her close again and his lips brushed her hair as he remarked, "But classes with you will go on and on, that is, if you want to attend."

She backed away slightly and looked at Lance, smiling and nodding her head in the affirmative.

"When I get back, we're not going to waste much time here. We'll get married, pack up and leave for the river."

Her eyes dropped downward as she asked slowly, "Does the light-haired one know? She too seems to have Lance in her heart."

"She knows. I told her," said Lance reassuringly. "Now don't you worry about anyone or anything."

Lance frowned as he gazed across the room. His lips were pressed against her head and his arm tightened about her.

"This sudden move up north has cut everything short. I wanted to outline everything to you in detail before leaving, but it will have to wait. Now little one, I want you to stick to the fort and close to Mrs. Tuffs. She will take good care of you until I get back. I've got to go now but I'll see you in the morning before we leave."

Their feelings were mutual: sad, but understanding.

Naomi looked into Lance's eyes momentarily then her hands brushed across his face. Her face neared his and her lips touched his face, then the corner of his mouth. From there Lance took over as he held her tightly and showered her with kisses that rated highly with Naomi who approved of the method of affection practiced by the white man. He drew back slightly and looked down at her admiringly.

"One day soon, little one, our hearts will be light, there will be no more parting. Whatever trails there will be to ride, we'll be riding them together. You just stay the way you are, all right?"

She smiled up at him and nodded her head in the affirmative. Lance bade Mrs. Tuffs goodnight and accepted her invitation for breakfast.

"Oh, I near forgot Dawson and Turley," she remarked. "They are invited too."

"I'll tell them," said Lance as he opened the door. He gave Naomi a reassuring smile.

Her eyes were shining brightly as she smiled back at him but faded away as the door closed behind him.

Mrs. Tuffs realized the girl's sorrow. She put an arm around her waist and said reassuringly, "Now, don't you fret none, Naomi. Everything will turn out fine, just you wait and see. I've got some hot tea made. Let's go into the kitchen and have some. You can tell me the rest of that story you started the other day."

Early morning found the northbound patrol in readiness. Captain Drum was given last minute instructions by Terry, who was flanked by Custer and other military personnel. A large part of the inhabitants milled around the outside of the gate, waiting to bid farewell to loved ones and friends. Lance and Turley inspected their new rifles once more then shoved them into their sheaths. Dawson, who was talking to several scouts, called over to Turley and motioned for the latter to come over. Several minutes later, Captain Drum mounted his horse and issued a command.

Lance was about to get on his horse but stopped momentarily as a soft feminine voice said, "Don't forget what I've told you, Lance. Everything sill goes. I'll be waiting, just in case you change your mind."

Lance looked at Helene for a long moment then said with a grin, "You don't discourage easily."

She shook her head slightly to the negative but said nothing as she smiled at him. He mounted his horse and looked at her, saying, "Goodbye, Helene." She bit the inner part of her lip and her eyes seemed to be dancing in amusement as she stood there, silently watching Lance ride toward the conversing scouts.

Another sharp command by the captain caused a shuffling of feet and the metallic clanging of sabers as the horses were being mounted.

"Well," remarked Dawson as he extended his hand to Lance, "don't seem right to be left behind, but I'll be joining you before long and once more. Don't you two coots go moseying around 'til you see the tail of my buckskin cap fluttering in the wind."

"If by chance you hear a shot and that tail goes flying away with the bullet you'll know that I's around," cut in Turley laughing.

"You ain't going to rest after that until you replace it," warned Dawson amusingly.

A final command by Captain Drum set the outgoing patrol into motion. The scouts waved to old Dawson as they urged their animals forward. Lance turned in his saddle and looked toward Mrs. Tuffs' cabin. He singled out Naomi, who looked at him from across the way. Lance gazed back long and hard at the girl that he had allowed to dwell alone in his heart. His eyes were a bit misty as he rode out through the gate and wondered if that would be the last look at the girl he loved so well, for the oncoming campaign offered little in the way of an assurance of a safe return. His moments of despair were relieved a little as Turley rode alongside and remarked, "This is my final bid to be best man, Captain."

"Should that day come," said Lance as a smile brushed his lips, "then you've talked yourself into wearing a new tie."

They eyed each other understandingly and then rode to the front of the patrol.

Two days later, Helene knocked on the door of Mrs. Tuffs' home. "Why, come in Helene," said the elderly woman. "Naomi and I are having cake and coffee, won't you join us?"

"Thank you," she said as she walked into the room. Upon seeing Naomi seated at the table, Helene greeted her smiling. "Hello, Naomi."

Naomi returned the greeting with a smile. The women chatted about the outgoing patrol and Helene was quick to acknowledge Naomi's sadness and sided with her concern.

"Well, I don't think that he will be gone too long," remarked Helene casually. "But in the meantime you should keep yourself occupied." Her eyes lit up as she continued. "I have a suggestion that will do the both of us a lot of good. We'll do a lot more horseback riding and today is good a time as any to start."

"Oh, no," exclaimed Mrs. Tuffs. "It isn't safe to go riding about and I don't think that Lance would like that at all."

Naomi looked at Helene and was rather puzzled concerning the latter's friendliness towards her, for she was aware of the fact that Helene cared for Lance too.

"Well, I thought I'd ask since I so like to go riding and thought perhaps the idea would be appealing to Naomi," remarked Helene casually. "We wouldn't wander off too far from the fort," she added with a hint of anxiety.

Mrs. Tuffs looked at Naomi and asked, "Would you like to go dear?"

Among other things, curiosity played the major role concerning Naomi's answer as she replied, "I would like to go, but only if you say yes."

Helene sighed slightly as she lifted the cup to her lips and waited for Mrs. Tuffs to answer. The elderly woman answered rather reluctantly, "Well I guess a bit of fresh air would be good. You can't stay cooped in here all the time, but don't you girls ride too far off."

"I'm glad," said Helene with delight. "I don't like to ride around alone and talk to myself. I'll have the horses saddled and we'll go right after lunch. Will you be ready then?" She asked Naomi with a smile that seemed more like a smile after victory rather than a friendly one.

"Yes," she answered, "I will be ready."

The afternoon sun bore down in and around the fort as the two riders rode out through the gate. They proceeded northward for about a half mile then circled the fort in a wide arc. A half hour later, Helene pulled the mount to a halt saying, "There is water a short distance from here. We'll go over and water the horses then I'll race you back." Naomi nodded in the affirmative and the girls urged their mounts forward. Naomi learned nothing personal from Helene, for the latter's subject of conversation was strictly of a feminine nature. Helene wasn't concerned with Naomi's feelings one way or the other. Her idle conversation was merely a way to kill time without causing suspicion as to her real intent. Helene's brow was wet with perspiration as they rode slowly forward, for her plan had worked perfectly up to the moment. It was time to go into her next act, for she spotted the well where Lance fought off the Indians just a few days ago. She pulled her mount to a stop again and put her hand to her head in an act of faint.

Naomi glanced at the girl as she swayed slightly in the saddle.

"You don't feel well, Helene?" she asked with anxiety.

"Seems like I have a dizzy spell of some kind," she answered rather brokenly. "I just can't ride any farther."

She slid off the horse feebly and sat down on a rock.

Naomi came to her side and started to wipe the perspiration from Helene's brow.

"I'll be all right," she said, managing a slight smile. "But a little water would help. Would you get me some?"

"I shall get you some," replied the unsuspecting girl. "Where is the well? I do not see it from here."

Helene got up slowly as she brushed her hair back with the sweep of her hand and pointed toward a spot at the foot of the mountain, saying, "It's over there, near the trees. You will find a pail hanging on one of them."

Naomi glanced about the saddles momentarily and then mounted her horse. Looking back down at the other, she said with a smile, "I will be right back.

Helene was aware of the fact that Naomi was looking for the canteens that usually hung somewhere around the saddle, but their absence wasn't questioned by the Indian girl. She had taken them off back at the fort, according to plan. Her smile was without mirth as she watched the Indian girl ride away. Her heart raced madly and her eyes kept a steady watch now for a moving figure that must be somewhere nearby in order for her plan to become a complete success.

Ever since they left the fort, they were the focus of several pairs of eyes that scanned the area from atop of the mountain. Helene's body became more tense with each passing moment. Her lips quivered and she bit into them as she saw Naomi dismount. She held her breath, waiting for something to happen; for if her plan were to succeed, it had to happen now. "Now," she said out loud in a fit of anxiety.

Suddenly her body became relaxed, the blood left her face and she paled. The knuckles of her hand became white as she clinched a tight fist around the reigns. Her moment of potential glory shattered to a million pieces as she caught sight of Naomi carrying the pail toward the horse. With failure in sight, Helene sat down on the rock again and buried her face in her hands and uttered brokenly, "They're gone."

Helene's disappointment was short, however. A new plan along the same lines was already forming in her mind to be carried out sometime in the near future. She knew very well that as long as Naomi was around, her chances with Lance Winsor were very slim, if that; for the desperate attempt to eliminate the girl as a competitor was certainly a priority.

The approach of the horse from the direction of the well distracted her attention. She waited until the animal stopped and slowly took her hands from her face. Helene was about to make a remark as she looked up, but the words never came. Instead her mouth fell open and her face was covered with bewilderment as she stared at the riderless horse. A sudden pang of hope surged through her. She snapped around and looked in the direction of the well. Nothing stirred, nothing moved as she kept her gaze on the spot where she had last seen the girl. A smile appeared on her lips as the thought of the sudden turn of events, in her favor, finally penetrated her mind. Her smile widened as she moved quickly and got up into the saddle. She rode over to the other animal and grasped the reigns, then faced the mountain again. The rider sat in the saddle like a sphinx and after several minutes decided that her mission this afternoon had come to a successful climax. She urged her mount forward, in the direction of the fort. Every once in a while, Helene would glance back over her shoulder, and then smile with satisfaction.

Halfway to the fort, she rode in behind some boulders and decided on her next move. *Better wait about an hour*, she mused, *before reporting the incident. By that time, the Indians will have a head start.* She was sure that a posse would be formed but more than sure that the search would be brief. Helene spent the hour thinking about Lance. *Surely by then his wounds would be healed concerning the loss of Naomi*, she mused. Then she could continue without interference toward achieving her goal, with our without the aid of the wishing well.

Finally she mounted her horse and stared back toward the mountain once more. She felt a sense of shame as she realized for the first time that her deed of the afternoon had been a ruthless one, selfish in nature, blind concerning the consequences that the others involved would have to endure. Helene relied on the old proverb as a means of justification as she said to herself, *All is fair in love or war.*

Moments later she was racing toward the fort. Upon reaching the gates several soldiers rushed toward her as they noticed the riderless horse and one of them asked, "Something wrong?"

"Yes," said Helene excitedly. "Indians, they got my girlfriend," and pointed in a backwardly direction. Dawson, who was discussing the long absence of the girls with Mrs. Tuffs, noticed the commotion at the far end of the fort. Mrs. Tuffs drew in her breath quickly and put her hand to her mouth, for she, too, noticed the riderless horse.

"Something is wrong," exclaimed Dawson and rushed off toward the gate. Upon seeing the old scout, Helene dismounted and said with tears in her eyes, "Indians grabbed Naomi and took her away."

"Where did it happen," asked Dawson rather sternly.

"Near the well," answered the girl brokenly.

"They didn't bother you?" questioned the old scout.

"No," she said as she applied a handkerchief to her eyes. "They left me alone."

Dawson looked long and hard at the crying girl in front of him, then went quickly toward Terry's quarters. With Terry's consent, the scout had a posse formed in quick order and headed with them toward the spot of the ambush. Hours after darkness fell, the posse returned to the fort, their search for the Indian girl unsuccessful.

Once more Dawson knocked on the door at headquarters. Terry motioned him to a chair and the scout related the unsuccessful attempt to contact the ambushers.

"We've picked up their trail, but as darkness closed in, we were forced to give up."

Terry tapped his fingers on the table as he gazed at Dawson and remarked slowly, "I understand that Winsor had intentions of marrying this girl on his return to the fort."

"That's right general, he had."

"And," continued Terry, "I know that you and Winsor are the best of friends and the expression you have on your face at the moment leads me to believe that you also have something on your mind that you want to relate to me on behalf of your friend."

"Among other things," said Dawson with a slight grin, "you're a mind reader, General. I sure would appreciate your approval."

"That depends on the nature of the request," remarked Terry. "Go on."

"I would like to leave right away to report this incident to Winsor. Might be able to catch up with the patrol before they reach the settlers' camp."

"Do you realize what a hardship that would be to you to go way up there then ride all the way back here again? By that time we'll be about ready to move out of here as planned."

"I ain't figuring on riding back," remarked Dawson as he lit a match and put it to the end of a cigar that Terry placed between his teeth. Terry glanced at the old scout for a moment then drew on the cigar. He blew out a mouthful of smoke then said, "I believe that I'm a little ahead of you Dawson. You are suggesting that I approve your stay up in that territory and that you will meet our forces along the river during their march northward."

"General, you have my word that I'll be on hand in plenty of time and I'll be at the foot of the pass, which will be plenty far from Sioux territory."

Dawson looked anxiously at Terry and waited with anxiety for the latter to answer.

Terry thought in silence for a full minute and then called for his orderly who appeared in short order.

"I want you to tell Custer that I request his presence immediately." Facing the old scout, he said, "Dawson, you are the lead man for Custer. You can go, with his approval of course. Mine is obvious." Dawson's eyes lit up upon hearing Terry's answer, for he had no fear of his plan being disapproved by Custer.

XIV

At the end of the fourth day of travel, the patrol bedded down for the night. Flickering shadows danced about the camp as the glow from the dying embers penetrated the darkness of the night. Some of the soldiers were preparing their beds, others sat around the remaining fires. At one of them sat Lance, Turley, and Captain Drum. They were discussing the possible tactics used by gunrunners in smuggling arms to the Indians.

Lance stared out over the camp and remarked, "We'll check on those fellows just as soon as we get up there."

"Do you think that they were working alone?" asked Drum.

"I've been giving that a lot of thought," replied Lance. "And the more I think about it, the more I am convinced that they were tied up with those fellows we ran across while making our escape from the Sioux."

"I agree with you on that count," cut in Turley. "They were paving the way for the load that was coming up, but I must confess that when we looked over that wagon, it certainly looked like anything but a carrier of weapons."

"Nevertheless," said Lance, "there could have been plenty of rifles under that farm equipment that was on top."

Suddenly Drum put up his hand indicating silence.

They looked at him questioningly and after a few moments he remarked, "Little late for the whippoorwill. Way past his bed time, I would say. Maybe I'm hearing things, especially, after all the stories you two have been telling me and the signaling you use . . ." said Drum as he got to his feet, "I think I'll turn in for the night, but not before I have another cup of coffee. Want to join me?"

"Sure will," answered Turley, and then asked Lance, "how about you?"

"My weakness," he replied and got to his feet.

They stopped short and stood motionless, for the cry of the whippoorwill echoed faintly through the valley. The scouts eyed each other then glanced at the captain, who asked, "You two know more about this sort of thing than I do. Have any idea who it could be?"

Before any of them could answer, the call came again and it was more distinctive. "It's coming from the direction of the fort," said Lance finally.

A troubled look appeared on his face as he added, "I'm pretty sure it's Dawson."

"Dawson," exclaimed Turley. "If it is, he's certainly ahead of schedule and on the wrong side of the river."

They stood in silence staring in the direction from which the calls came, each unable to suggest a logical answer concerning the incident that now confronted them.

"Let's go over to the edge of camp," said Lance. "I want to answer those calls."

The signaling went back and forth for the next half hour and finally the outline of the horseman appeared in the darkness as he raced toward them. The rider slowed up as he noticed the three figures walking toward him, then walked his mount up to them.

"Just in time for coffee, Dawson," remarked Drum upon recognizing the old scout.

"He'll only get some if the news is good," cut in Turley laughingly.

"Looks like we can't get rid of you for long," said Lance as he slapped Dawson on the shoulder then added, "But you didn't come up for the ride, Will."

"You have a message from the fort?" asked Drum.

"It's not a message," said Dawson reluctantly. "It's news and all bad . . . for Winsor here."

Lance tensed and the blood drained from his face for he had hoped against hope since he recognized Dawson's call, that whatever his mission up here wouldn't concern Naomi; now he was sure that the news was of her.

"Naomi?" asked Lance slowly.

"Some of White Cloud's braves got her," answered the old scout as he mopped his sweating brow.

Lance felt a pang as it darted about his heart but his face betrayed no emotion. He cast aside the bitterness he felt a moment before, for he wasn't the type to grieve over the past, instead he had quickly come to a decision concerning his next move to remedy the situation if possible.

"Captain," said Lance soberly, "I'm ready for that coffee. I'd like to talk to you."

"Certainly," said Drum. "I'd like to say now that I understand your predicament and am sorry about the news."

"Thanks," said Lance.

Turley put his hand to Lance's shoulder and said, "nothing I could say that would help, but there is a lot I could do. When you head for the river, I'll be right behind you."

Lance faced Turley and smiled warmly at his ever faithful friend, then at Dawson who rated just as highly, as the latter remarked, "I already have plans as to just how we're going to intercept those buzzards, sort of planned it out on my way up here."

"You've got to go back to the fort, Will," said Lance. "There won't be . . ."

"I had that all arranged with Terry and Custer. I'll join you fellows and the captain here and have that coffee. I know that you're anxious to hear the whole story."

The muscles in Lance's face tightened as he listened to the incident that had his heart crying far out into the night, for the one whose very heart at the moment is crying silently in hopeless despair. Lance gazed into the embers as Dawson finished and asked, "They didn't bother Helene at all?"

"No, they didn't," replied Dawson. "Like I said, she was quite a distance away." Lance smiled coldly as he kept his eyes on the fire but refrained from mentioning his theory of what actually could have taken place. For he suspected Helene had deliberately led Naomi into the trap.

Lance discarded the matter from his mind and glanced at Captain Drum, saying, "Captain, I would like to have a leave of absence for a few days, starting right now."

Drum filled his tin cup with hot coffee in silence. He seemed lost in thought. Lance wondered if he would have to leave on his next venture against the wishes of Captain Drum as he waited patiently for his answer. Finally Drum faced Lance saying, "Winsor, I understand the predicament that you are in. The nature of your business being a personal one, I find it just to make an exception in your case. I'll allow you three days. At the end of the third, I'll expect you to report back to me at the settler's camp. Mr. Turley knows enough about the territory to see us through until you get back. I wish you a lot of luck and hope sincerely that the climax of the mission will glow with success."

"Many thanks, Captain," said Lance. "I certainly do appreciate it."

Turley looked at Lance with a frown then glanced at Drum saying, "They're going to need a little help down there, Captain. I was sort of hoping that I could go along."

"I'm sorry, Turley. I've got to have someone with me that's been up here before. I believe that Winsor and Dawson can manage, as I was led to believe there are only three or four Indians in that band."

"You've seen the smoke signals along the mountains as we came up here," argued Turley. "There'll be others along that river to contend with besides the ones that have Naomi."

"Mr. Turley," said Drum in even tones as he set his cup down on a log. "We happen to be on a very important military mission which we must accomplish and at the moment we haven't yet reached our destination. I have already made one exception; I cannot make another."

Lance placed his hand on Turley's shoulder and said, "I'd like to have you along with me on this trip, but we're in with the military now and I wouldn't want you to quit or get fired before aiding in the first task." He shook Turley's shoulder slightly and added, "You just help the captain stir things up when you get to the camp. I'll be back to help out."

A grin appeared on Turley's face, for the thoughts that entered his mind were far from being in favor of the Captain. Turley nodded his head slightly in the affirmative and said, "Perhaps you're right, but I'll be seeing you shortly."

Lance realized the significance of the last remark but made no comment as he turned and walked toward the horses.

A short time later, Lance and Dawson were up in their saddles and fully equipped. Bidding farewell to Turley and Drum, they urged their horses forward and headed toward the mountains.

Several hours elapsed since the departure of the scouts. A solitary figure arose from his sleeping position and stole softly toward the horses. He looked cautiously about, observing nothing suspicious, and began to saddle his mount. His hand slid over to the sheath and rested momentarily on the butt end of the rifle. Satisfied that all was in readiness, he slipped one foot into the stirrup and was about to mount the animal when suddenly a voice cut short his actions, saying rather softly, "Going for a little ride, Mr. Turley?"

Turley swore under his breath as he recognized Captain Drum's voice, but checked his emotions as he stepped down off the stirrup and faced Drum, who stood but a short distance away.

"Captain," said Turley. "You sure are learning fast; didn't hear you come up at all."

"I suspected that you would be pulling out tonight," remarked Drum. "And if I may add, against orders. I understand the strong friendship that exists between you and Lance and the predicament that he is in, but you came up here to perform a duty for the military, under oath, I needn't remind you, for you are well aware of the fact that your duty under the circumstances comes first above all."

"I know that, Captain," said Turley, as he walked toward his superior. "And I'm not running away from it. Whatever has to be done at the settlers' camp can be done without a few of us for a couple days. You know that as well as I do."

"That's beside the point," remarked Drum rather sternly.

"One moment, Captain," said Turley sharply. "There is no use in dragging this thing on. I know that if I leave here without your consent I'll never get another job with the military and you can go ahead and do whatever you please concerning myself, but I want to ask one more time to let me have a few days to help Lance out in his cause. And I want to make this promise: when I return, there won't be another man in this outfit that will stick more closely to you and help you out in the coming campaign to the bitter end. You won't regret it, Captain; you've got my word."

Drum stood there motionless and silent as he faced Turley in the darkness. A slight grin brushed his lips as he remarked finally, "I'd like you to come with me for a minute."

Suspicion engulfed Turley as to the captain's intent. He hesitated briefly, then decided to follow Drum out of curiosity. There was no conversation between the two as they disappeared into the darkness, but Turley was on guard and ready to resist any attempt that might detain him from making the trip to the river.

The next day was hot and clear. The blue waters of the Big Horn sparkled in the sunlight as it rippled slowly along its way. Once again two figures scanned the silent valley below in anticipation. After minutes of observation that failed to detect any form of human life, one of them spoke rather casually. It was Lance. "Do you think we've missed them?"

"Hardly," replied Dawson as he bit into a piece of plug tobacco. "I rode hard and fast coming up here with little sleep. If my calculations are near correct, I judge that they'll be coming along here sometime after daylight."

"They may be riding the back trails on the other side of the river range," said Lance frowning. "In that case, we'll miss them."

"Maybe," said Dawson as he peered through squinted eyes, "but I don't think that they will. They know that the patrol is headed North toward the settlers' camp, otherwise they would have taken the Oregon Trail part ways in order to get to the river here. Since those Indians know that, they'll take the easiest way up here and that's along the waters. Anyway, we're going to have to chance that."

Lance's face was expressionless as he stared down into the valley, but his body was tense and would spring into action like a wild cat at the first sight of a red man. Within himself, he was torn apart and would not heal until Naomi was safe by his side. He vowed to himself, as he stood there motionless, that if anything happened to Naomi because of the red man, he would wage a one man war against the Indians as long as life existed in his being.

The bitterness that he felt at the moment was plainly inscribed on his face. Dawson sensed the feeling that his friend possessed at the moment and decided to ease the matter a bit, if possible, by suggesting, "Better we go down to the river now and get ready for those buzzards. Can't tell, might be showing up earlier that I expect."

Lance made no reply as he looked at Dawson, but shook his head in the affirmative.

A short time later, they rode on to the river's edge and dismounted. Observing nothing suspicious, Lance began to roll a cigarette. Glancing at Dawson, he remarked, "I'll go to the other side, directly across. You conceal yourself here and get a little sleep.

Should anything occur, I'll awaken you fast."

"I'm wide awake, Son," said the old scout as he slid his rifle out of the sheath and added as he inspected his weapon. "And I don't aim to sleep til I see that girl again."

Lance managed a smile and looked warmly at his friend, then rode across the shallow water to the other side. Lance sat with his back against a tree for about an hour, growing impatient with the passing of time. Suddenly his body tensed and all thoughts left him as the racing of hoof beats pounded madly as they ran swiftly over the rocky banks of the river. His pulse beat rapidly as he sprang up and peered cautiously in the direction of the noise.

A frown appeared on his forehead for the oncoming rider was alone. Quickly he raised one finger for Dawson to see, indicating the fact that the rider was alone. Lance ran into the thicket and laid his rifle down. With the swiftness of a cat, he was back and started to climb a heavily branched pine tree whose limbs stretched out over the riverbank. He yanked his knife out in readiness and in a crouching position, waited for the unsuspecting brave to ride by. Dawson had his rifle trained on the red skin just in case something went amiss. Moments later, Lance set himself as the brave drew near and jumped down on him just as the rider passed underneath. The impact of Lance's weight caught him squarely and the victim with his attacker hit the ground solidly. They grappled with each other, rolling over and over, finally ending up in the river. Lance intended to relieve the savage of his knife, thus avoiding killing him so that he could question the brave concerning the other members of the band. But the brave had no intention of favoring Lance's idea, for he fought like the savage that he was. To avoid taking any more chances, Lance took advantage of the opportunity offered at the moment and thrust his knife into the brave's midsection. The latter relaxed his death grip that left Lance gasping for air.

Dawson, who rushed across the river the moment Lance made his leap remarked, "'Pears to me that you wanted this one alive, else you could have got him when you jumped."

"Yes I did," admitted Lance as he breathed heavily, then looked at the Brave floating in the water. "I wanted to question him but I hardly think that he is in the mood right now."

Dawson frowned as he glanced down at the brave, then went over and dragged the body close to the bank. Lifting the head out of the water he exclaimed, "I thought I saw this face before, why, he's one of the four that came to the fort that night. Do you recognize him?"

Lance paid little attention to the dead man's face until now and his eyes lit up with new hope upon recognition.

"Must be one of the ambushers," he said glancing at Dawson.

"That's right, Son. Looks like we're in luck."

The old scout pushed the corpse under a clump of bushes and said, "I'll go back across; They can't be too far behind."

Lance walked back to the tree where he was seated previously and was about to lay down when suddenly the mad splashing of water caught his attention. He snapped around quickly but made no attempt to move forward as Dawson, who was rushing toward him motioned with his hand and said excitedly as he came up over the bank of the river, "They're comin', but we're going to have a rough time! There's a whole bunch of 'em."

"We'll have to worry about that later," said Lance. "Right now let's get set and take them on. Is Naomi with them?"

"Didn't get a chance to look 'em over out there," said Dawson hastily.

"Come on," said Lance, edging his way toward the river. "Let's see what we have to contend with."

As they laid there peering out over the bushes, Lance whispered without betraying his emotions. "Naomi is with them."

"Yeah, I see the little one," said the old scout, acknowledging the fact. "But look at the size of that band. Must be a dozen at least."

"Must have picked them up along the way," remarked Lance. "They certainly have scouts all over the territory."

"Sitting Bull ain't going to get caught nappin', that's for shore," remarked Dawson.

"Will," said Lance as he took one more look at the oncoming band. "We'll have to shoot fast and straight. A lot will depend on how many of them we can knock off before they can organize. It wouldn't be so bad if Naomi wasn't here but . . . "

"Don't worry, Son," assured Dawson. "If she gets an opening she'll take care of herself."

Lance perked up his head as the sound of the approaching horses cautioned him against any more conversation.

"Let's get back in there; but don't open up until I do," said Lance. "Then let them have it. I want to make sure that they retreat back down the river. Ready?"

"Ready," said Dawson and he spat a long stream of tobacco juice in the direction of the riding savages.

Hidden behind the tress but not too far from the river, the two scouts waited, their bodies tense and ready for action.

Lance thought of Turley. What he wouldn't give to have him here at the moment. He cursed himself for not making an attempt to convince Drum that he would need him badly for this occasion, but justified that thought by not knowing at the time that he would have to contend with a band of savages rather than three or four that was assumed to be with Naomi.

He stiffened and discarded any more thought as he caught sight of the rather slow riding band. Lance brought the rifle to his shoulder and waited for them to come into full view. Slowly the procession moved closer, unaware of sudden death that soon was to reach out with its ugly fangs. Lance could hear his heart pounding faster as one brave appeared, then another. He waited until most of them were in clear view, and then he fired.

The shot split the silence of the valley like the crack of thunder just before the streak of lightning bolts through space. Dawson's rifle barked a split second later. The blazing weapons took their toll as four of the braves became potential travelers, their destination: the happy hunting grounds.

The horses reared up on their hind legs and squealed in fright as excited hands pulled savagely on the reigns. The savages were in a state of confusion, trying to get out of the line of fire as they desperately retreated to the rear. The scouts ran down toward the river and watched the retreating red men as they rode madly in the direction from which they came. Lance's knuckles became white as they tightened around the rifle and his face held a mixture of anger and hate, for he spotted Naomi among the hard-riding Indians. He knew well the abuse that she had taken of late and more of it at the moment. The thought tore his insides apart but he couldn't do anything about easing her grief at the very moment. The one thing that helped ease his tortured heart was that Naomi must be aware of the fact that there are others around who may be trying to help her. That would ease her grief a little, said Lance to himself.

"They stopped, the ornery buzzards," said Dawson, breaking the silence. Then he asked, "What do you think they will do now?"

"I believe they will come sneaking through the woods on foot," replied Lance. He frowned slightly, adding, "I noticed several of them with rifles. I certainly didn't count on that."

"Maybe they're out of ammo since they did no shootin'," remarked Dawson.

"Maybe, maybe not," said Lance. "We caught them by surprise; they didn't have much of a chance to do anything."

"They're dismounting," exclaimed Dawson as he chewed feverishly on his wad of tobacco.

"They've decided on their next move no doubt," said Lance. "We'll see shortly."

Several minutes later, the band disappeared into the forest. Lance looked at the old scout and remarked, "We're going to have company soon."

"Just rarin' to show my hospitality," said Dawson as he spat against the side of a tree, tobacco juice splattering in all directions.

"Will, get my horse," suggested Lance. "And go up ahead a little ways. Now, if things get out of control forcing us into a hasty exit, we'll ride to the other side of the river and make tracks before deciding our next move."

The old scout nodded his head understandingly.

As the minutes wore on, the scouts lay hidden in the thicket several dozen yards apart, awaiting the foe whose savage attack at any moment was inevitable. Lance was weighing their chances in the event of a retreat, but the thought left his mind suddenly as he caught the motion of a red skin darting from one tree to another. Dawson's gun barked once, then twice.

Lance cut loose as more forms began to appear. Finally a roar of a rifle from up above.

Lance swore under his breath for he had hoped that the old scout was right about the ammo. Arrows began to sail by, screaming the message of death. The firing became furious as the darting figures moved closer. One of the savages screamed wildly as he ran down the side of the mountain toward the still concealed scouts.

Lance waited until the savage was but a few yards away before pulling the trigger. The attacker spun around wildly, crashing into a tree, bouncing off like a rubber ball and ending up in a heap near the river bank. As the Indians began closing in, bullets and arrows began to take effect for suddenly Lance shouted, "Dawson, work your way into the river. We've got to get to your horse. Can't make it to mine anymore."

Lance crawled toward the river hastily and slid in upon reaching the water. Dawson was already in and scrambled toward Lance, at the same time blasting away at the too-near red man. They continued the firing as they crawled backward in the shallow waters, trying desperately to reach the other side before their lives were snuffed out by the savage foe.

The Indians took advantage of the scouts' retreat and began to close in more rapidly. Dawson was in a sitting position in the middle of the stream, loading and firing his weapon as fast as he could. Lance was near him, on his knees and crouching low, blasting away like he never had before.

The situation was desperate. The move backward was ever so slow. Lance gave a quick thought to making a run for it but realized that turning their backs now would mean almost certain death.

Dawson's yell added to his already grieving mind as the old scout pointed in a backwardly direction. Lance took a quick glance over his shoulder and a million knife wounds couldn't have more effect on him as he saw a horse racing madly up the river carrying on its back two riders, and one of them was Naomi. Lance spun around in the water and fell flat on his stomach. Whipping the rifle up into shooting position he aimed at the savage and realized this was probably the last shot that he would ever make again for time was running out. The thought that the savage would get away with Naomi if he missed near paralyzed him and it didn't console him any knowing that he wouldn't be around any more to continue the search for her. He squeezed the trigger slowly and kept a deadly aim on the target. A rifle barked, another, then another, a split second later a body crashed from its hiding place and dove at the savages leg, pulling him off the horse that he was seated upon with Naomi a moment before. Lance's eyes widened as he noticed that the ambusher was wearing a military uniform. Suddenly he realized that the firing was coming from his side of the river. A voice shouted to him from up the river; it set Lance afire. Lance snapped his head in the direction from which it came and saw a figure crashing through the water, his rifle barking furiously.

"Turley," whispered Lance as a grin brushed his lips. Lance got to his knees quickly and looked over to where he last saw Naomi. A great burden that weighed him down within the past few days left him suddenly as he noticed the soldier hurrying the girl toward a large tree to safety. Sparked to life again, Lance spun around and trained his rifle toward the other side but slowly brought it down again as he noticed Dawson still sitting in the water grinning like a kid wearing his first Sunday suit.

"Never did think those Indians would get us," he remarked.

Lance grinned back saying, "Liar." And then he emptied his rifle in the direction of the fleeing braves, or what was left of them.

Lance got to his feet and started eagerly toward Naomi's place of concealment. The happiness that he felt, after nearly being one of the victims who was within the grasp of the black fangs of death, helped clear his dazed mind and body. He finally became conscious of the intense firing that continued and realized that there were others besides Turley and the soldier in the rescue party. Lance glanced back at Dawson, who started to walk toward him at the same time biting into his water soaked plug, and remarked, "Wonder who else is here with Turley and the soldier."

"Wouldn't surprise me none if it was the captain," answered the old scout as he slipped the tobacco back into his pocket.

Lance made no reply as he gazed toward the mountain trying to spot the riflemen. He caught sight of Naomi as she stepped from behind the tree and everything else vanished from his mind as he subconsciously started to wade the remaining part of the river. She walked slowly toward him. There was no smile on her lips but her face held the expression of bewilderment and sheer surprise, for the girl was still dazed by the sudden turn of events that she no doubt had given up as a possibility during her recent encounter with the Indians.

The love that Lance had for this girl was plainly written on his face. He said nothing as he neared her. There was no need for words for their eyes related all that there was to tell. Naomi lifted her hands slowly toward him, whispering softly, "Lance," as if she was still uncertain of reality.

He took them in his and drew her slowly to him saying, "Everything is going to be all right, little one, don't you worry none. From now on when I can't be around, I'll have you guarded if I have to hire part of the military." He was aware of the fact that she was still shaken badly by the ordeal she had to endure.

Suddenly she let out a little cry and encircled her arms around his neck holding on to him tightly. Lance held her as if he'd never again release her from his embrace. His lips brushed the top of her head, then her temple. He let his mouth linger on her cheek at the same time whispering her name softly, "Naomi."

They clung together as if this was the last time that they would ever see each other again. Finally, he kissed her mouth and let his lips linger there momentarily. Lance became aware of the fact that the side of his face was wet. A frown appeared on his forehead as he looked at her closed eyes. Suddenly a strange but desirable feeling swept over him and it affected him emotionally. His heart cried out to her, *Naomi, Naomi*. What he had just seen was a rarity among Indian women; Naomi was crying. Moments later Lance was aware of someone standing but a short distance away.

He glanced at the intruder who smiled slightly with a look of admiration on his face.

"Didn't mean to intrude Winsor," said Captain Drum, apologetically. He walked toward them, "but before anything else is said, I'd like to say this much. As long as I live I will never regret coming down here to the river, especially under the circumstances. Should I wander to the far corners of the earth, I shall carry with me the outcome of the incident that occurred down here. I have learned wisely, from the both of you, and Dawson out there. Where there is life, there is hope. I am indeed happy for both of you."

Lance was deeply impressed by the captain, whose appearance on the scene added to his surprises, and especially the warm attitude displayed by the military man at the moment.

"Thanks" said Lance, as he looked at Drum questioningly, for he was still at a loss as to the captain's presence after the stand the latter took concerning the matter the night before.

"Captain," said Lance "I don't know why you decided to make the trip, but I'm certainly glad that you showed up when you did with the others."

"Well," remarked Drum running a hand over his chin. "I'll cut the story short and just say that your friend Turley would have made a good lawyer."

His face took on a serious expression as he added, "At the time I underestimated the odds that you and Dawson may have to contend with down here." A smile brushed his lips as he hesitated momentarily then continued, "Several hours after you left, I walked upon Turley saddling his horse. We had quite a discussion. I gave instructions to my sergeant and asked for two volunteers, and here we are."

Concerned about Turley's actions of the night before, Lance remarked, "I hope that your confidence in Turley hasn't dropped off too far, Captain."

"Certainly not," cut in Drum. "As a matter of fact it increased."

The already amazed scout smiled with satisfaction upon hearing the captain's remark, then said, "Naomi, this is Captain Drum."

She managed a smile and bowed her head slightly.

"Indeed a pleasure ma'am," said Drum who already had his hat in his hand. "And I'd like to say that if ever again I can help in rescuing a lady, I'm sure she won't be prettier than you are."

Naomi just smiled shyly.

"Hey, up there," shouted a voice. It was Dawson's. "It's safe to come down," he heckled. "We chased those buzzards away."

"In that case we'll come down," chuckled Drum.

Upon nearing the river, Dawson greeted Drum, saying, "Welcome to the Big Horn, Captain. You shore are getting around fast-like."

"Exciting place," said Drum, smiling.

"Shore is," agreed the old scout as he rushed toward Naomi and greeted her with a bear-like hug.

Lance and Turley smiled at each other understandingly, for their thoughts at the moment would take hours to express verbally. He put his hand on Turley's shoulder saying, "One of these days we are going to swim this river without being forced into it."

"I'm looking forward to it," remarked Turley chuckling. "Should be a novelty."

Lance turned his gaze upon the soldier who put an end to the savage that rode behind Naomi during the seemingly hopeless situation. Lance was much too busy at the time to show surprise upon recognizing the man as the one he fought with back at the fort. Now he wondered just what prompted the soldier to volunteer in this particular case.

Lance walked over to the soldier, who grinned at him with a look of satisfaction that indicated that his deed for the day was well done.

"Stenton," said Lance. "Your presence down here comes as a surprise to me. However it's beside the point at the moment. I was certainly glad when I saw you appear out of nowhere and yank that Sioux off the horse. This is rather a mild way to express gratitude to you and the others, but I'd like to say many thanks."

"Looks like everything turned out for the best," replied Stenton. "And it's good to know I was of some help. Anyway," continued the latter as a broad smile replaced the grin. "I wanted to see what it would be like to fight with you rather than against you for a change." He extended a hand to Lance, then added, "I'd rather it be like this permanent-like."

"So would I," replied Lance as he gripped the outstretched hand.

The second volunteer was introduced to Lance and the conversation flowed freely for a few minutes.

Drum, who was conversing with Dawson, Turley, and Naomi, called over to the others saying, "Getting late, gentlemen. We can still cover a few miles before sundown."

"I still have a few days left before joining up with Custer down here, Captain. I'll ride back with you fellows and get my fill of beef," remarked Dawson.

"Glad to have you along," said Drum as he placed his hand on the scout's shoulder. "I can always boast of being a personal friend to the master of the frontier."

"Thems' mighty nice words, Captain," said Dawson, "but you might get an argument from these two coots on that score."

"I've got to agree with the captain there," remarked Turley, smiling.

Lance walked toward them saying, "No use going over to the other side for the horse. They probably took the horse with them."

"You and Naomi take mine," offered Dawson. "I'll ride the one without the saddle."

"You'll only hold us up," cut in Turley chuckling. "I can see you sliding off as we go along."

"That little pinto couldn't shake the water off his back, let alone Dawson, the man that tamed the devil's horse, the wildest bronc that ever roamed the Cheyenne territory," said the old scout, boastfully.

"I recall that horse," remarked Turley thoughtfully. Then he squinted at Dawson saying, "The animal had three legs, I believe."

The group laughed heartily and turned their attention toward the scowling Dawson who ended the subject by saying, "'Peers to me that you're going to end up plumb loco, Son, plumb loco." And he shook his head as he started toward his mount.

Although Dawson took a lot of ribbing from the younger scout, he nevertheless had a soft spot reserved especially for him.

As Turley walked by, he slapped Dawson on the shoulder and asked, "Still buddies?"

"May as well be," he replied. "Someone has to keep you from going astray." He spat out a stream of tobacco juice that caught a fly squarely that was perched on the tip of the horse's ear.

Turley laughed heartily at the incident and looked up at the old scout who sat on the bare back of the animal rather amused saying, "Will, you amaze me with your accuracy."

"I spat in an Injun's eye one time and it saved my life. Just you go on and get on your horse, young feller, and I'll tell you more about that one."

"I'll be right with you," chuckled Turley, and he disappeared into the thicket.

XV

Late in the afternoon on the following day, the weary group neared the edge of the settlers' camp, which was still intact due to the consistent attacks by the Sioux. The sergeant, who was in charge of the patrol during Drum's absence, rode up in a cloud of dust and saluted his superior, who in turn returned the motion.

"Any trouble?" asked Drum, expecting the worse.

"No trouble, sir," he replied. "Everything is under control. We had but one raid since our arrival. The Sioux seemed to have vanished."

Drums eyes brightened and the frown that he had been sporting during the day disappeared upon hearing the good news. He glanced at Lance and smiled, the latter returned the smile understandingly, for he was quite concerned about the captain's predicament should anything of major importance have occurred during his absence. The trip to the river, for whatever the purpose, would have been inexcusable under the circumstances.

"Your quarters, sir, are at the far end of the camp."

"I'll be right with you, Sergeant," said Drum, then addressed the others. "Gentlemen, I know that you have friends up here and are anxious to go about your personal business. However, I'll await your presence at my quarters, say about nine o'clock?"

"Pardon my interruption, sir," apologized the sergeant, "but whenever they are ready, I'll show them to their tents; they are all set up."

"Well then," said Drum, "until nine o'clock," and gave a short wave with his hand. He halted his horse abruptly and turned in his saddle and smiled at Naomi, saying, "should Miss Naomi get the urge to go riding again, I would advise her to consult Lance first. He in turn will advise me where upon I'll round up the patrol, including our scouts, and we'll all go out together. We'll take no more chances."

She smiled at Drum and then dropped her gaze shyly upon noticing that she held everyone's attention, some with a grin, others just smiling.

"See you later," said the captain again and rode off with his men.

Several riders approached just as the scouts started toward the wagon masters' quarters. One of them shouted happily as he neared them. It was Bacon.

"Sure am glad to see all of you again," he beamed as he rode up. "The stories we heard sure had the womenfolk all riled up." He looked at the girl, remarking, "They sure can't change the looks of you Naomi. You're one tough little gal, yes sir. The womenfolk are sure going to be mighty glad to see all of you. Let's mosey on up to the wagon. The beef is still warm."

"Bacon," cut in Dawson. "All the way up here I had but one thing on my mind. . . "

"Roast beef," said Turley.

Dawson opened his mouth but got no farther as Lance cut him short, "And plenty of it."

"Darn fool boys," said the old scout scowling. "Never will let me finish my speech."

As they approached Bacon's wagon, which had a few tents added to the crude homestead since their last visit, Turley's eyes roamed about anxiously for Mary Lou. Mrs. Bacon appeared at the doorway of one of the tents and her outburst was one of joy as she tearfully greeted the scouts and hugged Naomi in a motherly fashion.

"Land sakes child," she exclaimed. "Your endurance must be endless, but I must say, you look fine even though you went through all that hardship."

"Mrs. Bacon," said Lance. "I must impose on you again. Naomi's clothes are rather worn from her travel and . . . "

She cut Lance short as she looked at Naomi, exclaiming, "Just you wait and see the pretty buckskin skirt and jacket I made especially for you. Sort of a wedding present.

Did it take place yet?" She asked rather slowly, for she was uncertain of the truth.

"Not yet," answered Lance. "But it will take place before very long."

"Here in camp?" Asked Mrs. Bacon anxiously.

"Right here in camp," replied Lance as he held Naomi's gaze.

Turley waited patiently for the conversation to end. The anxiety on his face was obvious concerning the question he was about to ask Mrs. Bacon but she turned quickly facing him and spoke first, "Mr. Turley, if you should walk in that direction," she pointed over his shoulder, "the third wagon from the end, and run into Mary Lou coincidental-like, would you . . . "

"Mrs. Bacon," cut in Turley. "You read my mind. Thanks, see you all later."

With a wave of his hand, he was off wearing his best smile.

"Now there's a bright young fellow who joined up with the military to fight the Indians, so he said," remarked the old scout with a grin. "But he ain't foolin' ole Dawson."

Turley was about halfway to his destination when he saw Mary Lou round one of the wagons and walk hastily in his direction. Her eyes flashed upon noticing the young scout who in turn stopped in his tracks and waited for her approach. They were more than happy to see each other again and it was written plainly on their faces. For a few moments they stood there looking at each other then Turley broke the brief silence saying, "The last time I felt like this is when I saw you last."

"Then I'm happy," she said softly, "because I'm more than glad to see you." Her face was that of concern as she continued. "When I heard what happened, I guess that I was still in a daze 'til just a few minutes ago when one of the men came to us with the news back there that everyone that went to the river just came into camp safely, including Naomi. Oh, I'm so glad," she said rather brokenly. "Poor Naomi, the things she's gone through."

"I could tell you all about this and what happened since I left here if we were to go for a walk later on," suggested Turley smiling.

"That sounds a little like a hint, Mr. Turley," she said with an amused glint in her eye.

"I was under the impression that we had a date the very first time you came back.

Just making sure that you didn't get yourself attached while I was gone," he said and took her hand in his as they started toward the Bacons' wagon.

The scouts and the military personnel met at the appointed hour. Drum spread out a map on the table at the same time remarking, "I'll relate the instructions given to me concerning orders which we'll carry out during our short stay here at the camp. One of the orders in particular is to send out an advanced scouting party over the mountains to the river, first to get a direct route so that the patrol won't be held up because of unforeseen barriers. And secondly, to find out the strength of the Sioux that maybe lurking somewhere in the mountains on this side of the river. That is the reason why we were sent up here in this campaign against the Sioux. Of course, another factor, which is of importance, is the patrolling of this area in aid of the settlers. A small detachment will remain behind to guard the camp here on the day we push across the mountains in force to meet the ones that will be on their way north. Now then, any comments gentlemen?"

"Yes," replied Lance reaching into his pocket for his tobacco pouch. "Suppose we run into unexpected strength in the mountains, and because of that are unable to keep the appointment at the river on time?"

"Should that occur," replied Drum, "our failure to appear at the river will be of little concern because our patrol is not included in the direct attack on the main forces of the Sioux. Our job is to engage the enemy, if any, that may be waiting in ambush. Terry wants no force of any size attacking his forces from the rear when they clash head on with the Sioux. However, if we make the river on time then our duty falls in the category of rear guard. Whichever way you look at it gentlemen, our task is a rugged one."

Dawson chuckled softly and the glint in his eyes indicated the fact that something amused him. He looked and Lance and Turley who were already eyeing the old scout curiously, and remarked, "I've led many a campaign in my time as head scout and never 'afore have I a bunch of wildcats for a rear guard, including the captain here and some of his boys. The Sioux won't know what hit 'em, them ornery buzzards, got a taste of it the other day. Now don't let what I said go to you're heads, you might get careless and slow down a bit." He put his fingers up to his beard and stroked it lightly then added, "I ain't hankering on parting with this just yet."

"Don't you worry about that," said Drum, chuckling. "We'll see to it that it doesn't leave your chin."

"Just can't see why he is so proud of that tobacco stained brush," said Turley amused as he addressed Lance.

"This beard was sought after by many of Cheyenne," said Dawson. "As a matter of fact, one of the braves wanted to marry a chief's daughter and the only way that he would get his consent was by hanging my beard up in the chief's teepee."

"Poor girl," continued the old scout who was still fumbling with his chin. "Must have died of a broken heart by now. I've got another story that I'd like to tell you but we'll make it another time. The captain here still has unfinished business to attend to. Didn't mean to cut in on you like I did 'afore, Captain," said Dawson apologetically.

"It didn't hinder a thing," assured Drum. "As a matter of fact I'd like to hear some more of your adventures and I'll make it a point to remind you when we get a little time again. Well," said Drum, addressing the group, "I think that we have everything straightened out. Tomorrow morning we'll start our way across the mountains and plan a route for the near future. Those of us here, including a few more men, will undertake the mission. Dawson, of course, is unattached at present and his stay in camp should be a restful one."

The old scout looked at the smiling Drum and remarked, "Captain . . ."

Turley cut him short, saying quickly, "I'll bet my next month's pay that he wants to come along."

Dawson dug into his pocket and came up with his plug tobacco and offered it to Turley saying, "Here, fill you mouth with some of this. It'll keep you quiet for a while. Maybe I can do my own talking for a change."

The old scout's mouth parted slightly in amazement as Turley took the tobacco from the outstretched hand and bit a portion of it off. He started to chew on it slowly, handing the rest back to the still bewildered scout whose lips took on a wide grin, exclaiming, "Well, if that don't beat a polecat all to pieces. Knew all the time that there was something that you and I agree on, Son," said Dawson. In delight he slapped Turley on the back, the latter coughing viciously after near swallowing the distasteful wad of tobacco. "Go right ahead and finish what I've started to ask the captain, for me."

Turley shook his head in the negative pointing at the same time to his mouth, indicating the fact that his jaws were quite occupied at the moment.

"Excellent," remarked Dawson as he winked at Lance. "For a minute there, I thought it wouldn't work."

Turning toward the captain who attempted to hide his amusement by brushing his lips with the palm of his hand, he said, "Now then, Captain, we can finish our discussion without any more interference."

Chuckling filled the air as Turley dashed through the open flap of the tent with his hand clasped over his mouth.

The early morning sun began to edge its way up over the horizon. Those that were up this time of the day went about their chores, but every now and then they would glance with a frown in a westerly direction. Some would mutter to themselves, others making comment, for the smoke signals that arose high above the mountains were the object of attention.

Near the far end of camp, the captain and some of his men, including the scouts, looked soberly at the smoke that reached far up toward the blue of the sky.

Drum broke the silence, addressing Lance he asked, "What do you make of it?"

"Could be one of many things," he answered. "It would be rather difficult to pin it down to one particular thing. That we'll find out when we get into the mountains."

Lance faced Drum, remarking, "Captain, your responsibilities in the campaign are heavy, which you in turn are well aware of. I think that it would be wise for you to remain behind instead of chancing the trip."

"Winsor," replied Drum, as he kept his gaze on the mountains. "I appreciate your concern, and I must admit that you are quite right in a sense, however my lack of experience in Indian warfare and my uncanny desire for adventure aids me in making decisions which I feel are just. I have men in my command that depend upon my ability to make decisions that will help pull them through when the going gets rough. The more I can learn, the better their chances are in staying alive."

Drum faced Lance with a smile and added, "Perhaps I should have been an Indian scout, like yourself."

The captain placed a previously rolled cigarette to his lips, and then continued. "Lieutenant Briggs is quite familiar with the plans and will precede accordingly, should something go amiss. Now then gentlemen, finish your last minute business and we'll move out within the next half hour. By the way Winsor," remarked Drum as an afterthought. "Those fellows that you talked to me about a few days ago, I'd like to look them over before we leave."

"They're gone," said Lance.

"Gone, away from camp? Where to?"

"Bacon told me last night that they left here the same day we did. Said that they wanted to do a little scouting around back toward Powder River way."

"Has Bacon seen them since?" asked Drum.

"Yes, once," replied the scout. "They asked him if there had been any newcomers in camp and seemed disappointed when Bacon told them that there had been none. They hung around for a few hours and then disappeared. Haven't been around since."

"Seems to me," said Drum, as he gazed out toward the horizon, "that they are associates of the ones that you fellows had trouble with up at the river. You told me at the time that you suspected them and now that we've found out more about them, I'm inclined to agree with you."

"I hope we're wrong," said Lance soberly. "The Sioux already have rifles. Another wagon load could make things that much worse."

"Nothing we can do about that at the moment," said Drum as he let out a sigh. "Well, I'm rather anxious to get started; see you gentlemen shortly."

Bidding farewell to those that were to stay behind seemed to be a daily occurrence in this era of friction. Turley and Mary Lou stood behind one of the larger tents, lost in conversation.

"Well," said Turley, "I guess that they are waiting for me. One of these days we'll be together long enough to say everything that we have to say to each other. Up to now, time certainly has been limited."

"One of these days," said Mary Lou softly and with deep concern, "You may not return from one of the missions."

"In that case," remarked Turley as he drew her to him. "You and I will have this much of an understanding." Holding her tightly, he kissed her long and hard, releasing her only at the mention of his name that drifted by from the other side of the tent. He tore himself away from the girl, took a few steps, then turned and faced her again saying as an afterthought, "And should the occasion arise, just tell the boys that you are now attached to Blade Turley, permanently."

He untied the reigns of the already saddled horse, and with Mary Lou walked to the front of the tent. Mrs. Bacon handed Dawson a large piece of beef wrapped in cloth, which he took and slid into the saddle bag.

"Something to soften the Sioux with?" asked Turley as he grinned down at him from atop of his mount.

"No Sioux is going to fill his belly with this while I'm still alive," remarked the old scout as he mounted his horse. "As a matter of fact, you ain't either if you misbehave on this here trip."

Dawson bit a piece of tobacco from his freshly opened plug then offered it to Turley, saying, "Have some of this boy. It'll help you keep in line."

"No, thanks," grinned Turley. "Not my brand."

"Ready, Son?" asked Dawson addressing Lance who was talking to Naomi. "I believe the captain is about due to send for us."

"He's riding over this way now," remarked Turley as he noticed Drum circling a string of wagons.

Lance put his hand on Naomi's shoulder and said, "One more thing: don't leave camp under any circumstances. If you fall into the hands of the Sioux again, we may not be lucky the next time."

"I will not go," she said softly, the look in her eyes reassuring the fact.

He looked at Naomi for a long moment, and then winked at her. Stepping into the stirrup, Lance mounted his horse just as Bacon rode up.

"Good morning," he greeted, tipping his hat.

"Many thanks for the side of beef that you sent over last night."

"Don't mention it," replied Bacon. "Too bad that you have to leave so soon or else we would really put on a roast."

"Perhaps some other time," said Drum. "As a matter of fact, I'll take that as an invitation so that I can have something to look forward to."

"Roast it is then," said the wagon master, "when you fellows return."

"You just bear that one in mind," remarked Dawson to Bacon. "We'll be back."

"Mention food, and he'll come back from anywhere," cut in Turley.

After bidding farewell, the captain urged his mount forward, and Dawson followed suit. Lance said a few words to the Bacons, and then smiled at Naomi once more, saying, "I'll be back little one."

He started off with Turley but the latter turned his mount abruptly and stopped at the mention of his name by the girl he just said goodbye to. She ran over to him and held out her hand in which she had a small handkerchief with a rose attached to it, saying "I'd like you to take this with you just in case you run across some of the female members of the Sioux tribes. I want them to know that you are taken."

Turley smiled down at her admiringly as she slowly slid the token into his side pocket. A moment later he urged his horse forward and galloped toward the others. After issuing last minute instructions to his lieutenant, Drum motioned the small detachment forward.

Several hours later, they pulled to a halt atop one of the mountains. Drum unfolded a small map and asked Lance, "Do you think we are up far enough to avoid coming out at the canyon part of the mountains?"

Lance looked over the map, then remarked, "I would say that we are about here," he pointed to the area on the map with his gloved finger. "Almost in line with the upper end of the canyon, however, it would be wise to proceed in a northwesterly direction. The meeting point is quite a ways from there."

"All Right," said Drum as he pocketed the map, "we'll carry on." He noticed Dawson spit out a stream of tobacco juice as the latter kept a careful eye on the surrounding area.

The old scout was motionless and seemed to be summing up the situation. "Something on your mind besides Indians?" asked Drum out of curiosity.

"Just Indians, Captain," replied Dawson, whose face remained expressionless. "Might be running into some soon. Fresh signs all over the place."

"It would be best to stick to the clearings as much as possible," remarked Lance. "And avoid running headlong into an ambush."

Drum nodded in agreement, and motioned the detachment forward with the wave of his hand.

On one occasion, Lance pulled his mount to a halt for a conference. He glanced about the area up ahead, and then remarked, "The ravine up there would be the easiest way to the other side of this mountain. Would save a lot of time and trouble. Keep a sharp look around you and be on the alert. Might save some of your hats from becoming full of holes."

He looked at Dawson with a grin and added, "Or maybe a chin."

They all managed a smile as they looked at the old scout, but too all realizing the seriousness of the situation.

"If you are ready, Captain," said Lance, "we'll push on through."

"Ready," replied Drum, more to himself than the one asking the question. He sat motionless in the saddle, gazing up toward the mountain with a frown appearing under the brim of his hat.

Dawson chewed steadily on his wad of tobacco as he watched Drum, for he sensed the nature of the captain's thoughts.

"They're around, Captain," remarked the old scout slowly. "You can feel their presence after a while without seein 'em."

"I know exactly what you mean," said Drum, and urged his horse forward.

Upon reaching the ravine, Lance suddenly threw up his hand, halting the others as a bird call from atop of the mountain echoed softly throughout the area. They sat there in silence, listening to the calls that seemed to go unanswered. The signaling stopped abruptly and the men eyed each other momentarily.

"What do you make of it, Lance?" asked Dawson as he spat out some of the tobacco juice.

"Whoever that signal was meant for apparently did not answer in fear of revealing their position," answered Lance thoughtfully.

"Might run into a force of 'em on the other side," remarked Dawson as he peered at Drum watching for his reaction.

"Maybe, maybe not," said Lance, as he too, waited for the captain's decision.

Drum listened to the discussion in silence and pondered over the matter thoughtfully. Finally, he took his hat from his head and wiped the sweat from his brow with the back of his hand. "We're not too far from the river now. The route we followed this far is a good one up to this point. If we turned back now, I would feel confident that the remainder of the trip to the waters could be made without too much difficulty on our return trip; however, one factor remains, and that is the strength of the Sioux in the area. Gentlemen, we'll go on as planned."

As Drum motioned the detachment forward, Lance faced the old scout, remarking, "Will, you have a hard trip to make after this one, I think."

"The captain already did the thinking," cut in Dawson as he spat to the ground again. "Just you follow me, Son, and we'll see what lurks on the other side of this here ravine."

"Dawson," remarked Turley as he rode along with the old scout. "Whenever you are around we can always expect Indians. You must have something they want."

"Maybe so," said Dawson as he ran his hand over his chin. "But they ain't gonna get it."

The detachment rode cautiously along, ever alert, for the deadly hiss of an arrow or a wild scream of a bullet was expected at any moment as they pressed forward. Their eyes scanned the area for some visible sign of the enemy, but the red man seemed to stay clear of their sight. Near the end of the ravine, the men tensed as a call echoed over the top of the mountains.

"Keep riding and sound off if any of you get a glimpse of any of them," said Lance sternly.

The bodies of the men were tense and their faces held the expressions like those of the hunted as they neared the other end. Deadly silence befell the area as slow moving horsemen rounded the sloping mountain and moved out into the open valley ahead. They began to breathe a little easier, for the open valley offered an advantage in case of an attack: it obliterated the chances of an ambush.

Suddenly the silence was broken by Lance as he snapped, "Keep on riding and don't make any moves; don't do any firing until given an order to. Up ahead, behind the boulders, a little to the left of the patch of small pines."

All eyes focused in the direction given by Lance and none failed to see the band of Indians that sat on horseback behind the rock barriers. Although only parts of the band were exposed, it was nevertheless obvious that the red man made their presence clear to detection.

"Now what are those sneakin' coyotes up to," muttered Dawson. "Seems to me that if they were going to attack they would have done it before we got into the open like this."

"What do you suggest, Winsor?" asked Drum, who kept a steady gaze on the Indians ahead of him, for he was suspicious of a hostile movement on the part of the savages at any moment.

Before Lance could answer, Stenton hissed from the rear, "Captain, Indians in the back of us."

The scouts, along with Drum glanced, backward and noticed about a half a dozen braves following them at a slow pace.

They all faced forward again with the exception of Lance who frowned deeply as he stared at the pursuers. As Lance turned around, Turley remarked, "Maybe they ran out of arrows, a fist fight with them would be quite a novelty."

"We may not even get that," said Lance thoughtfully.

"Quite a change in tactics, should your statement prove to be true," said Drum as he looked at Lance questioningly.

"These Indians belong to Chief Big Bear's tribe," said Lance.

"If I remember correctly," cut in Dawson, "they are part of the Sioux clan."

"That's right," said Lance, "but Big Bear has always been less aggressive than the others. I've known him a long time and been at his camp on a dozen occasions."

"An Injun is an Injun, Son," remarked Dawson. "Wouldn't trust 'em too far."

"Just keep riding and don't make any moves," ordered Lance loud enough for everyone to hear.

They were almost abreast with the band that still sat motionless in back of the boulders but to the right of them about a hundred yards.

"They ain't made a move yet," said Dawson as he glanced at them through the corner of his eye. "Seems like we're riding right into a trap, must be something on ahead or else they wouldn't let us ride on through like this without a shuffle of some sort."

"We'll find out before long just what smells in the wind," said Lance. "However, at the moment we have but one choice, and that is to keep moving."

"Winsor," remarked Drum. "There is something about the braves back there that had a distinguishable feature which enabled you to pin them down to one particular tribe."

"There are many ways to tell one tribe from another," said Lance without waiting for the direct question. "In this case it happens to be the color of the lance they are carrying. Bright yellow. Big Bear's trademark."

Turley, who kept a sharp eye in a backwardly direction, cut in on the conversation saying quickly, "The braves that were behind those boulders are joining the others. Looks like they are all coming along for the ride."

Suddenly the sound of beating drums from somewhere up ahead quickened their already racing pulses.

Dawson eyed Lance and remarked, "The last time we were in the same predicament, it was Sitting Bull we rode in on. Sure hope you are right about Big Bear. Stand a better chance, I'd say."

Lance made no reply as he eyed Turley, who returned the gaze understandingly, for they knew well what lay in store for them should any of the other Sioux chiefs be in the vicinity.

The detachment rode atop a small hill and suddenly the shuffling of the horses as they were jerked to a sudden stop caused the dust to fly in all directions.

"Keep riding," half shouted Lance, "or we may get a hot reception."

Their reaction was caused by the sight that met their eyes as they reached the top of the hill. A large Indian camp lay directly in front of them. The detachment moved on reluctantly. Their hearts pounded madly and seemed to keep in time with the beat of the drums as they neared the village. Lance sighed slightly as he looked out over the camp, noticing the women and children, but was still confused as to an answer to the tribe's presence on this side of the river.

"One thing in our favor," he remarked, breaking the tentative silence, "is that we're not riding in on a war party."

"Sure can't figure this one out," said Dawson. "This here tribe is moving east instead of west."

"We'll have the answer shortly," assured Lance. Then he added, addressing Drum with a slight grin, "Your first visit to an Indian camp. Do you feel neighborly, Captain?"

After looking over the odds, Drum replied, "I rather feel that there is no other choice."

The inhabitants, who had long known of the presence of the detachment in the vicinity, stood about watching the intruders as they rode toward the center of their camp. Lance strained his eyes, trying to get a glimpse of the chief whose absence at the moment added to the curiosity. He felt a sense of relief upon failing to recognize anyone in the camp thus far and anxiously hoped for continued failure concerning the matter.

Near the center of camp Lance pulled his mount to a halt and the rest of the detachment followed suit.

"'Peers to me that the welcoming committee is in no hurry," remarked Dawson, as he watched Lance gaze around the camp with a frown.

"Maybe they're deciding on what approach to use," said Turley with a grin. "They don't get such distinguished guests every day."

"Neither does Sitting Bull, yet he almost kept us there permanent-like," replied Dawson, whose stream of tobacco juice caused a small cloud of dust to shoot upward as it hit the ground.

"Perhaps this is the committee coming in now," cut in Drum as he motioned toward the oncoming horsemen that entered the camp.

"They are the ones we saw back in the hills," remarked Lance as he eyed them curiously.

A few moments later, the leader of the band pulled to a halt a short distance away. He said something to the others, and then rode slowly forward, raising his hand in greeting.

Lance put his hand up saying, "We come as friends. We want to speak with your chief, Big Bear."

The brave answered in the Sioux dialect. Lance understood enough of it to carry on a conversation. After a full minute he turned to the others and said, "The chief and some of his braves are out on a hunt. He's expected back at any time."

"Ask him what the chief and his tribe are doing back on this side of the river," said Drum rather anxiously.

The conversation with the brave was very short.

"Won't give any information," said Lance. "He said that whatever we wanted to know would have to be answered by the chief. I don't think that we have too long to wait; it'll be dark before long. Let's dig into our saddlebags and have something to eat."

"Good idea," said Drum. "And if they don't give us any trouble, we'll pull out of here right after we've talked with the chief and head back."

"Providing the chief is willing to part with the information that we want," added Lance.

"I guess that I'm being a bit optimistic," replied Drum. "Perhaps your friendship with the chief in the past was the reason for my hasty statements."

Lance understood how Drum felt, especially being in an Indian camp for the first time, whether it was friendly or otherwise.

"Captain," said Lance as he dug into his saddlebag. "I'm as anxious as you are to get out of here. There is something about an Indian camp that I could never get used to and I never tried to find out what it was. Because of that I'm always on guard, always cautious. You stay alive longer."

Drum looked at Lance and smiled, saying "That one goes to the top of the list, Winsor, I'll not forget it."

The men stood near their horses, eating in silence. Every now and then they would glance toward the outskirts of camp, eagerly looking for some sign that would reveal the near appearance of the expected chief.

Impatience among the men was obvious as they scuffled about restlessly, passing along a few words now and then. Dawson, who peered out over the top of his saddle watching the actions of the inhabitants, remarked, "I've been in many a Injun camp 'afore, and noticed many a savage eye looking over ma' scalp, but in this here camp we are being plumb ignored."

"Make one wrong move and we'd find out how conscious they are of our presence," said Lance causally.

"Just don't make that move," grinned Turley as he laid his hand on Dawson's shoulder. "The barbers are pretty rough here."

"I think the chief is coming now," exclaimed Drum as he pointed to the outer part of camp where a group of horsemen rode toward the village at a fast pace.

"Quite a hunting party," remarked Lance as he made his way to the front of the detachment. "Must be about twenty of them."

"Looks like the chief had a bad day," said Dawson. "Can't see any game strung along the saddles."

As the horsemen neared the edge of camp, Lance tensed and all hope of leaving the camp peacefully vanished as he recognized the leader of the band. He felt a tight grip on his arm and turned facing Turley, saying, "I know, it's White Cloud."

Suddenly the chief threw up his hand wildly, and his horse reared high on its hind legs as he tugged madly on the reigns. The entire band came to an abrupt standstill. Hatred flashed in his eyes, and the war paint that streaked his face added to the sinister sneer that appeared on his lips upon recognizing the scouts.

"He looks plumb loco," said Dawson, as he watched the chief closely. "Might bust things wide open around here any minute."

"Should be mad enough to," said Lance. "We've certainly given him a lot of trouble since taking Naomi from the village."

"Any suggestions?" asked Drum. "They'll be coming up here at any moment, I would say."

"Keep the men away from their arms," cautioned Lance in answer. "But get into action quickly should they choose to start something."

"They're coming all right," said Turley.

The remark caused all eyes to rest on the oncoming procession. The men were tense and alert, ready to go into action in a split second, for they all understood the circumstances, and too, that the savages who confronted them were painted for reasons contrary to a peace parlay.

They stopped about a dozen yards away. White Cloud's sneer was obvious as he glanced at the scouts. He let his eyes rest on each one of them for a moment or two, then shouted gruffly to one of his braves, who rode to his side, coming up from the rear. He asked the brave a question in Sioux dialect. The brave pointed to Lance.

"What did he ask?" whispered Drum to Lance without moving his lips.

"He wanted to know which one of us refused to give up the girl back at the fort. The brave that pointed at me was the speaker at the time," replied Lance in undertones as he kept his eyes glued to the chief.

Lance wondered if the time had finally come for the show down with the wild looking White Cloud, who suddenly jarred him out of his thoughts as the chief pointed at him and shouted gruffly, "You have girl. Where?"

Lance found it necessary to lie at the moment, for if White Cloud made an attempt to get Naomi, he certainly was in no position to help her.

"Girl is at the fort," replied Lance, hoping that the chief was ignorant of the fact, but that was short lived as the raging chief shouted back.

"White man lie!" He urged his horse forward slightly. The animal danced about wildly underneath the half-crazed savage.

The tension mounted to a feverish pitch. The scouts were well aware of the chief's anger, for they had repeatedly added to his grief on occasions within the short past. At any moment, they expected the Sioux leader to charge at them with his horse, but the scouts held their ground. They did, however, flinch at times as the animals fore legs came within inches of them as it pranced around.

Once more the raging chief yelled, "Girl not in soldier camp. Girl in white man camp, here," and he pointed in the general direction of the settler's camp. He spun his horse around in crazy fashion and once more faced Lance, shouting, "You come with White Cloud. We go to white man's camp." He hesitated for a moment, then continued.

"No get girl, you die." He swept his hand swiftly in a motion that covered the entire detachment.

"Take him up on that," said Drum quickly between clenched teeth, "We'll follow close behind and wipe out this renegade once and for all."

"It wouldn't be that easy, Captain," replied Lance, without taking his eyes off the chief. "He would leave the greater part of the band to guard the detachment."

Before any more was said, White Cloud urged his mount forward, reached over toward Lance's horse and took hold of the reigns. A cloud of dust arose as the horses scampered about wildly due to the rough guidance of the impatient savage. He issued swift orders; four of his men broke away from the bank and rode to his side.

Lance turned slightly and eyed Drum saying, "The rest of them stay here."

"Bad habit of mine, being optimistic," remarked Drum slowly.

White Cloud cut the conversation short as he said to Lance gruffly, "You come. We go now."

He threw the reigns that he held in his hand toward Lance and they dropped, dangling loosely underneath the horse's neck, for Lance make no attempt to catch them. The tension mounted as the detachment eyed Lance waiting anxiously for his next move.

The chief acted quickly, which left little time if any to concentrate on a plan concerning the untimely event. Lance had no intention of going, for he knew that if he left the detachment behind, they probably would never ride again over the green mountains of the Big Horn.

To stay may mean the same fate, but that remained to be seen. Lance eyed the chief coldly, remarking, "Girl no go with White Cloud back to village."

The muscles in the chief's face tightened as he stared at Lance. His eyes flashed hatred and his lips formed into a sneer as he shouted savagely once more, "She go."

Lance stood there in defiance and shook his head slightly, replying, "No go."

From the corner of their eyes, the men glanced at their rifles that had remained in their sheaths and were ready to get them into action at the first command.

White Cloud spun his horse around wildly and rode to the nearest brave that was in the possession of a lance. He grabbed the weapon out of his hand, rode back a short ways and like a raging maniac, and threw it toward Lance, the blade entering the soft ground inches away from Lance's feet.

The scout grasped the spear and pulled it out of the ground slowly. His face was expressionless as he raised the weapon with both hands and brought it down across his knee, snapping it in half. Throwing the lance into the dirt, directly in front of the chief, he took off his coat.

Drum looked at Dawson and Turley questioningly.

It was Turley who spoke, "He's going to fight with the chief."

As Lance unbuckled his gun belt, he spoke to Drum through the side of his mouth. "Keep the men alert, this may be the start of a small war."

White Cloud was already off his horse. He shouted an order to one of the braves, who quickly threw a tomahawk over to the chief.

He pulled his own out of his belt and walked out into the open. Lance felt the handle of his knife. Satisfied that it was secured in its sheath, he walked away from the detachment and faced the waiting savage who threw one of the tomahawks to the scout. He caught the weapon in mid-air and gripped the handle tightly. For a moment, his thoughts flashed back to Naomi. This was his chance to eliminate the savage who had caused her a lot of sadness ever since his visit to the Apache village. He knew, too, that this moment would have to be faced, and that he would have to be the victor in order to live his life with Naomi without being constantly pursued by the relentless renegade that confronted him at the moment. His thoughts left him suddenly, for the snarling savage began to move toward him.

Lance went into a crouch, tense, waiting, watching the Sioux leader's every move. Like a flash, White Cloud spun around, making a complete revolution and when he faced Lance again, the tomahawk was already on its way. The chief's crazy tactics nearly proved disastrous to Lance, for he barely got out of the way of the weapon as it hissed wildly past his head and ricocheted off the trunk of a tree a short distance away.

Lance recomposed himself quickly, but was unable to throw the tomahawk that he still held firmly in his hand, for the savage had charged in on him at the same time that he heaved the weapon.

White Cloud had already pulled his ugly looking knife from the sheath that hung loosely at his side and slashed wildly at Lance's head. Lance dropped the tomahawk as the blade of the chief's knife penetrated the skin on his hand. With the speed of lightning, his own blade appeared into view. Weaving and dodging, the scout managed to side step the charging Sioux who came at him relentlessly again and again, trying for the right moment to put a quick end to the scout who had caused him more grief than he cared to endure. The savage grabbed at Lance's knife hand and held on at the same time slashed wildly with his own.

Lance grasped the chief's wrist, but not before the blade skimmed across his face. He winced slightly as he felt the hot blood trickle down to his neck. Stumbling about in their struggle to stay alive, the fighters went down, hitting the ground with an impact that scattered the dust in all directions. Lance was aware of the fact that one slip would mean the end of his career as a scout and otherwise, for never in his life had he had to fight a man so savagely.

His opponent fought with all the hate, strength, and cunning that can be stored within a human body at one time.

Lance felt the blood trickle down over his mouth. His wrist was sticky and hot. At one moment he thought he saw a glint of satisfaction in the chief's eyes as his face neared his. Lance was conscious of the fact that his opponent found it more difficult with each passing moment to keep the hold on his blood smeared wrist. Taking advantage of the situation, he mustered all his strength and wrenched the hand free and in the same motion brought the blade streaking across the chief's chest. The latter screamed like a wild beast as he fought desperately to regain his hold on the scout's knife hand.

Lance slashed at the savage's hand and the blade found its mark. The startled Sioux let out another cry as his weapon fell into the dust. Once more Lance gathered all his strength and turned the frenzied Indian upon his back. He grasped the near-crazed chief by the neck and braced him on his knees. New strength surged through the scout's body, for the moment of the final victory was his. As he raised his knife for the blow that would forever cut short the ruthless activities of the renegade, he froze instead, his knife hovering in the air, for suddenly a sharp command reached his ears coming from a short distance away.

His hand descended slowly as he turned around in the direction from which the voice came. Lance's face held the expression of one who fought desperately for a lost cause as he noticed the one who had given the command that had saved the life of his opponent. It was Big Bear.

Very few noticed the chief ride into camp, for most of them kept their eyes on the battle. Lance felt himself being lifted off the bleeding White Cloud, whose wounds seemed to be of little effect as he scampered to his feet and rushed over toward Big Bear who was still seated on his horse looking rather disturbed concerning the incident.

White Cloud, panting hard, spoke to the old chief gruffly. Their conversation grew into an argument.

Drum and the scouts were discussing the incident.

Turley poured some water on a piece of cloth and started to wipe the blood off Lance's face.

Dawson, looking in the direction of the arguing chiefs, remarked, "Big Bear didn't do you any favors by showing up when he did. You had that Injun where you wanted to get him for quite a spell. What are they arguing about, Son?"

"As much as I can gather," replied Lance, whose breathing was still a bit faster than normal, "White Cloud insists that we are his prisoners. He wants to take us back to the Sioux village across the river. We have to answer for taking Naomi away, among other things."

"Big Bear don't seem to favor him," said Drum, glancing toward the chiefs. "I hope that I'm not wrong in my calculations again."

Lance gazed at the Indian leaders blankly, for his interest was in their conversation, which seemed to grow louder with each passing moment.

The men of the detachment looked at Lance with faces of anxiety, for his interpretation of the conversation thus far seemed favorable. Lance's face brightened slightly as he saw Big Bear point in an outwardly direction, his voice becoming loud and demanding.

"Is it as good as it looks," asked Turley, whose question was directed at Lance.

"Luck is with us, for the time being anyway," replied Lance. "He's ordering White Cloud and his braves out of camp. Said that he wanted no trouble with his race or the whites."

White Cloud lost none of his rage as he walked swiftly to his horse and leaped up on the animal's back. He raced his mount within yards of the detachment and shouted wildly, "Before many moons, white man's blood run like river." The maddened chief urged the animal around roughly and with the wave of his hand, ordered his band to move out. With White Cloud in the lead, they raced out of camp in a cloud of dust.

"To me, that remark signifies but one thing," said Drum, as his gaze followed the riders. "The Sioux are ready for Terry."

"You're right, Captain," said Lance slowly as his thoughts still lingered on the parting chief's last words. "And I hope that White Cloud is wrong."

Big Bear dismounted, and with some of his men, walked toward the detachment. He put his hand up in greeting. Lance returned it, managing a slight smile. The chief's facial expression was that of deep sadness, rather than the usual hardened features that signified hatred toward the white man whenever engaged in conversation, although, Big Bear and Lance had always been on friendly terms in the past. The chief spoke slowly and in low tones: "Sun go behind mountain many times since I have talk with my young friend."

"It is good to talk to Big Bear again," said Lance rather warmly. "The chief is wise in many ways. I did not know that the chief and his people were on this side of the river."

The chief turned and faced in a westerly direction and pointed toward the now setting sun and said, "Many smoke clouds past river. There are many tribes. Sitting Bull and Crazy Horse fill my people's ears with war."

The chief stood erect, folding his arms to let them rest on his chest. He looked every bit of the great chief that he was. His next remark could have been a boastful one, but it wasn't meant to be, for his eyes failed to sparkle with glory and the expression of sadness remained as he continued. "I have led my people in many wars, some time win, some time lose. Big Bear have seen his people die. Always, after war, Big Bear and his people follow sun. Indian win nothing. I come back here when war over. We go back across river." He swung his arm in an arc and continued. "My people, stay in peace."

An expression of sadness engulfed the detachment at the moment, for the old chief's words were spoken without bitterness or resentment as he related in short a story filled with grief but a moment before. Lance spoke softly with an expression of understanding. "The chief has spoken wisely. The people of the great Sioux nation would have saved themselves a lot of grief if they had listened to the words of wisdom spoken by Big Bear a long time ago."

"Words, my son," said the old chief, "will not stop chief like Sitting Bull and Crazy Horse. When all chief like them go, then peace will come."

Lance decided on a question or two and wondered at the moment if Big Bear would help him with some information.

"Does the chief know if other Indian nations have come up to help the Sioux?" asked Lance.

Big Bear turned slightly and gazed out over the camp as if pondering over the question, but answered readily. "Sitting Bull send message to other tribes to join war council. Cheyenne, Pawnee, Apache, no come."

Lance glanced at Turley who already had his eyes on him, for the chief's statement verified Turley's story that he had related to him when they first met concerning the Sioux's invitation to the Apache chief.

"Then there is only Sioux," remarked Lance more with satisfaction than surprise.

"But there are many," replied the chief.

"Are there more Sioux on this side of the river beside your people?" asked Lance.

"No," answered the chief. "Sioux tribes far from river."

Lance turned and faced Drum saying, "That about winds it up, Captain."

"How about White Cloud? He may have a force hiding out here somewhere," remarked Drum.

"White Cloud have twenty braves, no more," said Big Bear before Lance could ask the question.

"What is he doing here?" asked Lance as if waiting to hear another answer than the one reason that he knew for certain.

"Want girl," replied the chief. Then he added, "White Cloud much trouble; better you leave camp in dark." Lance nodded in agreement.

"Soon we eat, have much meat," said the chief, motioning toward the fire pits. He turned and walked away issuing orders to some of the braves.

"For some strange reason I've lost my appetite," remarked Dawson, eyeing the braves that were cutting the venison.

"You didn't lose it," said Turley. "That pot of yours is filled to the hilt. You've been digging into the saddle bag ever since we started this trip."

"I was checking my ammo," said Dawson biting into a hunk of tobacco. There was a twinkle in the old scout's eye as he offered the plug to Turley, saying, "Here, have some of this."

Turley shook his head in the negative, and with a grin, said, "Still trying to poison me."

The others watched the two amusingly but lost none of their anxiety to leave the camp as they waited patiently for darkness to close in. The cry of the whippoorwill echoed throughout the valley. A slight trace of a smile appeared on Lance's lips as he gazed around the area that was slowly being blanketed by the twilight of the night.

Dawson, who was lying around with the others, got to his feet upon reading Lance's thoughts and walked toward the young scout who stood near the horses. He was still staring out into space.

"It always seems peaceful when you hear that little feller calling out there," remarked Dawson.

Lance shook his head in the affirmative as he glanced at the old scout, smiling, but made no comment.

"Sometimes I wish this was all over," continued Dawson. "Been thinking about going along with you and Naomi, that is, when you two go down the river permanently."

"Will, I certainly wish that you would, and I say that on behalf of Naomi too. She has a soft spot in her heart for you. You were the first to ease her troubled mind after getting her away from White Cloud."

The old scout's eyes became misty and a smile creased his bearded lips. He spoke softly, saying, "I'll never forget the first time she smiled back there just 'afore Barton and his gang jumped us. I told her not to be afraid, that we were only trying to help her. We took to each other like water and thirst."

Dawson rubbed his chin with the back of his hand at the same time remarking, "Don't want to meddle in your affairs, Son, but I shore would like to see you two young ones get hitched up."

Lance cut him short, remarking, "I was going to wait until after the campaign." Putting an arm around the old scout's shoulder, Lance continued. "Will, be prepared to attend a wedding, tomorrow."

"Tomorrow," exclaimed Dawson in surprise. "Why boy, you won't be fit for anything but sleep. We won't get back 'til morning sometime."

"Are you trying to put this wedding off and spoil everything for me?" cut in Turley as he and Drum walked up to them extending their hands to Lance in congratulations.

"Not trying to spoil a thing, you eavesdroppers. Winsor caught me by surprise," remarked Dawson with a twinkle in his eye.

Drum took off his hat and scratched his head, saying, "Never thought that I'd be congratulating you in an Indian camp, and especially under the circumstances."

"Captain," remarked Dawson as he nodded toward Turley, "when this one gets married, don't be surprised if it takes place in Sitting Bull's camp. Never know what's going to happen out here."

The conversation ended abruptly upon noticing Big Bear approaching them. He stopped a few feet in front of them and pointed in the direction in which the raging White Cloud and his braves headed when they left the camp. He said,"White Cloud camp not far. My brave see. You go Black Mountain." The chief then pointed in an opposite direction.

Drum turned to Lance asking, "How much time would be lost by going the way the chief suggests?"

"Not too much," replied Lance. "Once we get over the mountain range we could cut across the others and head toward our destination. Under the circumstances any time lost would be work avoiding a battle with those renegades out there since we still have a lot to accomplish within the next few days."

"That's settled then," said Drum. "Any time you're ready, Winsor."

After bidding the old chief farewell, the detachment moved out under the cover of darkness. Hours went by as the sleepless men rode on through the night relentlessly. On one occasion, Lance pulled to a halt near a small stream. The water sparkled brightly in the moonlight as they led their mounts to the small stream. The cool water was refreshing as they drank and dunked their heads. Perspiration was unavoidable, for the pace was fast and rugged. Drum spoke to Lance, asking, "When do you expect to divert from the present course?"

"When we get to the valley below," replied Lance. "We've done pretty well thus far. How are the men?" he asked.

Before Drum could make a verbal check, Turley cut in quickly saying, "Everyone seems to be in good shape with the exception of this fellow here," he slapped Dawson on the shoulder and chuckled slightly as he continued. "With the captain's permission, I'd like to tie this man to his saddle; he's been weaving badly in the last hour or so."

"Pay no heed to the fool boy," remarked Dawson. "Starting to talk like a loco Injun. I guess the trip is too much for him."

"Will," cut in Lance, smiling. "How much will you offer to have this fellow lashed to a tree so that you can get at him with a mule whip?"

The light of the moon aided in detecting the grin that appeared on the old scout's lips as he remarked, "When I can't handle this loco weed by myself, I'll lay aside my knives and guns and admit that my time has come. You ride in front of me," he motioned to the grinning Turley. "Ain't going to give you the chance to yank me off my horse and then tell everyone that I fell."

"All Right," replied Turley as the others chuckled. "If you get any fainting spells, just you call me and I'll come tearing back to give you a hand."

Suddenly the conversation ended abruptly as a rifle barked somewhere down in the valley. The echo roared through the wooded area like angry thunder on a stormy night. The men held on to their reins, tugging sternly in an effort to check the frightened animals as they reared about uneasily. The detachment waited in silence, expecting to hear more of the shooting, but it failed to continue. The lone shot added to the mystery of the source or why it was fired. Curiosity engulfed the faces of the men as they waited in anxiety for one of the scouts to come up with an answer that would throw some light on the matter.

It was Drum who broke the silence. "What do you make of it, Winsor?"

"Rather hard to determine that at the moment," replied Lance.

"What would you suggest under the circumstances?" asked Drum. "Go down into the valley as planned?"

"No," replied Lance. "It would be wise to cut south right here on top of the mountain. The shot came from the right of us, down in the valley. By staying up here, we could avoid any unnecessary conflict that may confront us down there; also, we could easily spot a campfire should there be one."

"White Cloud," uttered Drum, as the possibility of his presence suddenly entered his mind.

"I don't think so," said Lance slowly. "First of all, I doubt that he knows that we left Big Bear's camp. And if he were after us, I hardly think that he would betray his presence, especially with a rifle shot."

"The shot could have been an accident," said Drum as he took his hat off and ran a hand through his hair.

"Could have been, Captain," said Lance sighing slightly. "But I'm rather doubtful about that. I suggest we move out in single file and ride cautiously for a while. Should we fail to detect anything within the next three or four miles we'll cut down to the valley and continue as planned."

The detachment moved along at a slow pace. The bright rays of the moon found their way through the wide spreading branches of the big pines and cast flickering shadows about the features of the riders in the night. The air about them was filled with suspense but none of them betrayed the fact as they rode along in silence. Everyone strained their eyes for some sign of life that surely existed somewhere below them; however, with the exception of a few night birds, the trip across the mountain was uneventful.

Lance finally halted his mount and scanned the moonlit valley. Dawson pulled up along side of him and remarked, in low tones, "Could have been like the captain said, an accidental shot. Not a sign of any kind down there."

"Nevertheless," said Lance frowning. "That shot was fired in this vicinity somewhere."

"Going to cut down here?" asked Drum in tones that were just above a whisper.

"This spot is as good as any to start down the grade. However, Dawson, Turley, and myself will go down on foot and have a look around. If we fail to run into anything, I'll give three short owl calls for the all clear signal. We'll wait for you and the men down there. On the other hand, should a sudden burst of rifle fire jar you out of your thoughts, come down fast and join the party."

"We'll be ready in any event," replied Drum dismounting.

The scouts took their rifles out of their sheaths and with a motion from Lance, proceeded down the mountainside. They had leaned well from the many experiences as Indian scouts, for they were almost noiseless in their attempt to reach the valley below. About halfway down, the scouts stopped and looked cautiously about.

Turley leaned close to Dawson and whispered, "If this keeps up, you're going to get very little sleep if any before you start the trip to the river to meet Custer."

Dawson tapped the young scout on the arm, saying, "Son, when this is all over, I'm going to go along with Lance and Naomi and spend the rest of my days just resting lazy-like along that Big Horn river."

Dawson stopped short the conversation as Lance motioned for them to follow, and silence befell them again as they renewed at a slow pace the trip to the bottom of the grade. In a semi crouch, they followed each other cautiously and made their way forward in single file like the roving deer looking for water and food in the dead of night. Near the bottom, Lance suddenly veered off his course and stepped in behind a large pine tree. The other two drew in close beside him for his act was met with curiosity as Turley asked in a whisper, "Latch onto something out there?"

"I don't know," whispered Lance with uncertainty as he peered from behind the tree. He raised his hand and pointed in a direction slightly to his right, saying, "I thought perhaps that flickering out there was caused by the moon, but it seems to be playing around in that one particular spot."

"Campfire," exclaimed Dawson, just above a whisper. "Bet Turley's next pay on that."

"Then you're not sure," said Turley. "Otherwise you would bet your own."

"Just want to help you get ahead, Son," remarked the old scout as he spat on the ground.

"Let's go a little further and find out," said Lance as he started away from the concealment. Less than fifty yards was covered when suddenly the scouts threw themselves to the ground, for a short distance away flames of a small campfire came into view as they rounded a thicket of laurel.

"Whoever is out there ain't expecting company with that fire a goin'," remarked Dawson.

"I agree with you there," said Lance as he strained his eyes trying to detect some sign of life.

"Can't make out anyone from here, said Turley, pushing himself up with his hands.

"We'll crawl in a little closer," said Lance. "We'll find out whose camp that is soon enough. Let's go."

"The crawling vanguard is right behind you, Captain," said Turley, slapping Dawson on the shoulder slightly.

The old scout glanced at the smiling Turley for a moment, then started to move along after Lance. As they neared the outer edge of the wooded section, Lance stopped and laid still, for the sound of muffled voices came to them faintly. Not being able to detect the voices clearly, he glanced around for a place of concealment that would enable them to stay out of view and at least get a look at the campers.

Upon noticing a large rock up ahead, he decided to chance going that close to camp and motioned for the others to follow. Once behind the rock, they eagerly peered out from the side of it and as they did, the answer to the mysterious shot that was fired during the night became obvious, for a deer was hung up to one of the limbs of a tree.

A portion of the animal was cut out and at the moment being prepared by those huddling around the fire. Their already beating pulses quickened as they watched the unsuspecting campers, of which, four of them were Indian and the other two were whites.

"Know what I'm thinking," whispered Dawson.

"I've got the same thought," replied Lance.

Turley's suspicions were at the same level, for he suddenly dug his fingers into Lance's shoulder and pointed in a direction beyond the fire, exclaiming softly, "That could be the wagon."

Lance strained his eyes and after a moment replied, "It could be."

"That's it all right," said Dawson after a close observation. "They've got that wagon pretty well concealed."

"As much as I can see of those two, they could pass as the fellows we looked over back at Bacon's camp some time ago," remarked Lance.

"If that is a wagonload of guns," said Turley, "they're not going to give it up without a fight. What kind of an approach do you have in mind?"

Let's go back a ways before discussing the issue," said Lance thoughtfully. "We'll need the other men."

Slowly, they edged their way back out of sight of the glows of the campfire.

"Turley," said Lance as he took hold of the latter's rifle. "Go back up and explain the situation to the captain. Tell him to leave one man with the horses and come down here with the others. We're going to bust that camp wide open if we have to."

"Don't start tearing the place apart until I get back," grinned Turley as he got to his feet. "Wouldn't want to miss anything."

"Do you have enough left in you, Son, to make it back up there? If not I'll go," said Dawson with a smile that was concealed by the darkness.

"Better that I go," replied Turley, whose humorous voice was just above a whisper. "It would take you till daybreak to reach the top of this mountain. By that time those fellows would be gone." Turley chuckled softly as he turned and disappeared into the darkness. Complete silence blanketed the mountainous area as the two scouts peered about cautiously from their laying position.

Flickering shadows played to and fro across the branches of the trees, for the brightness of the moon was at its height in glorious splendor. The soothing south wind flowed gently by, seeking new horizons, for tonight it was indeed king among the various winds that roamed the greens of the Big Horn. Even the night birds were silent at the moment, perhaps taking a little time to marvel at the magic of the night, or another reason that is known only to them, like intuition of the coming violence.

Not all was in harmony, for underneath a large tree stood a sinister figure whose dark eyes glanced slowly about in search for something that had aroused his suspicions. He was naked with the exception of a piece of buckskin that hung loosely from his waist halfway down to the knees and a pair of moccasins. A large feather protruded skyward from the back of his head and in his hands he held on to the deadly weapon of the white man: a rifle. The brave walked slowly forward a few yards, then stopped, glancing about in every direction. As time went by, he moved about less, for his suspicions were being hampered by confusion as he failed to detect any sign of the intruders. On one occasion, the Sioux stopped abruptly. Something had attracted his attention, or at least he thought so, for he stood there like a sphinx, listening in uncertainty. Minutes passed before he finally made another attempt to go forward. He took one step, then suddenly sank slowly down to one knee. The brave exercised caution rather than haste as he brought the rifle butt to his shoulder and aimed at the figure that was clearly outlined in the semi-darkness.

The target was Dawson.

XVI

It was their whispering voices that had attracted the brave while prowling around guarding the camp. The brave's suspicions were confirmed when he spotted Dawson's form as the latter got to his feet in an attempt to shake the drowsiness that had overtaken him while he rested on the inviting bed of soft moss. Little did the old scout know, as he stretched and yawned, that in a moment or two, he could be laid to rest in peace forever more under the protecting shade of the tall pines. A steady finger encircled the trigger of the weapon and pressure was applied by the gunman. It eased slightly as the old scout bent down momentarily, then straightened up again this time facing in the direction of the concealed ambusher.

The veteran scout shuddered slightly as a strange feeling came over him, for it occurred to him, that at the moment everything seemed to be deathly still. He was about to remark something to Lance, who was still sprawled out on the ground, when suddenly he spun around facing the mountain upon hearing soft footsteps approaching.

The rifle was still aimed at him, but the eyes of the one who held it were focused to the right of him, for he too heard the tread of footsteps.

As the outline of Turley and the others came into view, the barrel of the gun descended slowly, and the Indian moved backward slowly. Finally he got up into a crouch and hastily scampered in the direction of the camp.

Once again Dawson shuddered, and he wondered at the moment just what had caused the uneasy feeling that he sensed. *Shucks,* he said to himself. *Had this feeling afore,* and he cast the matter from his mind as the others neared him.

"Just about ready to go after you fellows," remarked Dawson. "Didn't think Turley could find his way back here. Mighty good thing you didn't have to come back alone, or you'd have never made it."

Turley smiled slightly as he breathed heavily, but made no reply.

"Looks like we'll be held up for a while," said Drum to Lance as the latter gave Turley back his rifle.

"How far is that camp from here?" he asked.

"About a hundred yards or so," replied Lance.

"I've been thinking about the type of approach you were going to use," said Drum. "Those fellows out there with the Indians may not be the gunrunners you suspect."

"We'll give them an opportunity to identify themselves," said Lance. "However, we're not going to take any chances . . . that is, any more than we have to. Now here is what we're going to do," said Lance, addressing everyone. "We'll go up ahead to a spot where we can see the flames of the fire. At that point, you men will spread out. Pace yourselves at about twenty five yards or less if you have to in order to at least see the outline of the fellow next to you. From there on we will crawl to the edge of the woods after I give the signal. I'll motion to the one next to me and he in turn will pass it down the line. Once we reach our destination, I'll call out to the campers. Whatever happens from there on remains to be seen. Any questions?"

There were none, and after a moment of silence, Drum said, "We're ready, Winsor."

Once again the detachment moved out on one of their many missions, this time on foot in the dead of the night. Tired, sleepless, forever treading toward the unknown, their endurance seemed unlimited. After long minutes of cautious maneuvering, they reached the spot from where the scouts first noticed the campfire.

After lying there motionless for a few minutes and not detecting anything suspicious, Lance got up on his knees and peered out from behind a laurel bush.

The two other scouts, along with Drum, followed suit and glanced out over his shoulder. Their piercing eyes failed to find any sign of the once brightly burning campfire.

The moon above seemed to smile in amusement as it gazed down upon the bewildered faces of the men who huddled closely in silence.

"Finally," Lance whispered softly without turning his head, "something is in the wind; I could smell it. The fire has been put out."

"Perhaps we're not in close enough," said Drum, trying to ease the already mounting tension that he himself more than felt.

"We saw it clearly from this spot before," remarked Turley, whose voice was scarcely above a whisper.

Dawson's jaws moved slowly as he chewed on his tobacco. Through squinted eyes he took in the area in silent thought. Finally he voiced his opinion concerning the matter as he remarked in low tones, "Don't know just how they got on to us, Lance, but I'm pretty sure that they know that someone else is around beside them."

"I agree with you, Will," replied Lance. "I have a feeling that they're in waiting, and just as soon as we're spotted, all hell is going to break loose."

Suddenly, Lance snapped his head around and hissed, "Hold it." He listened for the sound that had attracted his attention to repeat again. The shuffling of horse hoofs, as they dug into the dry leaf beds could be heard faintly.

Lance came to a conclusion quickly and lost no time expressing his thoughts verbally. "They're hitching a team to that wagon, and at the moment it looks like we're right about its contents. We've got to move in. Take your positions as planned and remember, if they are on to us, there may be some of them close by. Be alert and keep looking around. If anything so much as smells like an Indian, fire, and don't bother asking questions. With your approval, Captain, we'll move in."

"Take your positions, men," ordered Drum, in whispering tones.

They lost no time in placing themselves as planned and at the precise moment, Lance gave the signal that started the night raiders toward the silent camp of the assumed gunrunners. They progressed to the edge of the wooded area whereupon Lance stopped his progress forward and glanced around for some sign of the enemy.

He saw none, nor did he hear any movement on the part of the animals that was heard but a short time before. His gaze was trained in the direction of the wagon that was observed previously, but his eyes failed to pick up the bulky outline. *Either the fire helped before, or they covered it heavily with branches,* mused Lance.

Deciding to work his way toward the spot where he first saw it, Lance motioned to Turley, who was the nearest to him, to follow. He progressed slowly as he circled around the center of the camp. His breath came a little heavier, for his anxiety to contact the hidden enemy grew with each passing moment. He was aware of the fact that sudden violence would shatter the silent valley with a thunderous effect just as soon as one side or the other is noticed, and the echo would scream far out over the peaks of the Big Horn.

Cautiously he inched his way toward a heavily bowed pine tree whose shelter at the moment concealed a grim reaper of death: the enemy, one of the hunted. He stood on one of the limbs, crouching, waiting. An ugly knife was grasped in one of his hands. His silence and stillness were stonelike as he waited patiently for the unsuspecting scout who had been under the Sioux observation for the past few minutes.

Just as Lance pulled himself up the trunk of the tree, the savage leaped off the limb and let out a scream that would chill the spine of a Kodiak bear.

Like a flash of lightning, Lance threw himself to one side, ending up in a sitting position. His finger found the trigger and the rifle barked just as the attacker sprang up from his fall. The impact of the bullet spun the savage around and he crumpled in a heap at the scout's feet.

A volley of shots from the other side of camp tore in around Lance as he threw himself in behind the trunk of the tree. The calm night had suddenly turned into a thunderous roar as flaming guns marked the positions of the hunters and the hunted. A fire arrow sailed into the brush, igniting the dried twigs and leaves. Several more reached their destination and the bright fires lit up the camp area like the noonday sun.

"Pull back in," shouted Lance at the top of his voice as he saw Turley dodge in behind a tree after emptying his rifle.

"Captain!" shouted Lance again. "Get your men back into the woods."

Drum's voice came loud and sharp above the crackling of the wild-burning fire. The light exposed the men of the detachment clearly as they scrambled in a disorderly fashion toward safety. Lance and Turley moved back in slowly, blasting away furiously.

Drum was hatless as he and Dawson fired across the camp relentlessly.

"Back here," shouted Lance as he edged his way to the rear reluctantly.

The firing stopped as they got out of range and Lance lost no time in reorganizing the group. Their faces were covered with sweat and smeared with soot as they dropped to the ground near Lance.

Rifles were being reloaded without hesitation, for each one of them knew that the fight had just begun: in addition to their injured pride, the soldiers had had to retreat.

Lance spoke quickly and was brief in detail. "We'll circle around toward the wagon which will take us away from the fire. Stay closer together this time and keep following me. We'll get to the other side and blast them out of there. Was anybody hit?" asked Lance as he glanced at the heavily breathing men.

"No," answered Drum as he ran a hand through his hair. "Luck was with us this time."

"I hope it stays around a while," said Lance. "Let's go," he said, springing to his feet and starting the second attempt to put a finish to the untimely venture of the night.

Once again the valley became quiet, but the crackling of the fire that seemed to be simmering down was the only evidence at the moment that violence had been a visitor.

As the detachment neared the edge of the wooded section, Lance motioned them to the ground, then motioned for them to follow as he started to crawl forward on his stomach. Suddenly, the wild pounding of hoofs and the creaking of wagon wheels as they came in contact with stone broke the stillness of the moment.

Everyone halted automatically as Lance pushed himself quickly to his knees and peered out over the tops of the bushes. He sprang to his feet and at the same time shouted to the others, "Quick, over to the edge, we've got to stop that wagon."

The horses raced madly toward the open part of the once quiet camp, pulling the wagon that bounced into the air on occasions as the wheels came in contact with rocks protruding through the surface of the ground.

A volley of shots from the men of the detachment smashed into the crazily careening vehicle. The driver, who held on to the reins from in back of the seat, jumped up over it and lashed out at the frenzied animals with a whip. Lance already had his sights on the assumed gunrunner and pulled the trigger.

The impact of the bullet, as it found the target, knocked him out of the seat and he disappeared as he fell out of the fast moving wagon. Suddenly, one of the front wheels came off and as the spoke dug into the earth, the back end of the wagon flipped up into the air, turning completely around and smashing to the ground, settling on its roof. The team of horses continued on after breaking away from the dismantled wagon and increased their speed as the remaining outlaw band opened fire from the upper end of camp.

"They moved up to the other end for some reason," remarked Drum, as he lost no momentum in reloading his rifle.

Lance, who lay next to the captain, replied as he kept blasting away, "I believe that they were waiting for the wagon to come by, and were going to pull out of here in it."

"They're coming back this way, the fools," remarked Dawson.

"Those crates you see out there are worth a lot of gold," said Lance as his mind was already considering the next move, for he realized that the enemy intended to fight to the finish. He winced and buried his face into the soft leaves as a bullet smashed the outer edge of a tree nearby spraying his face with flying bark.

"Captain," said Lance as he wiped the debris off his face with the sleeve of the coat, "send a man back and have the horses brought down. We're going to have to blow up the rifles and ammunition. Can't leave them here, nor can we take them with us."

Drum called to one of his men, who upon receiving the instructions, quickly disappeared into the darkness. The tempo of the firing increased with the advance of the enemy. That there were only four of them bucking the odds aroused their curiosity.

"Kind of brave out there, aren't they, coming in on us like they are," remarked Drum.

"They could be expecting company," cut in Turley as he reloaded his rifle.

"I've already given that possibility some thought," said Lance, quickly getting up on his knees facing Drum. "Captain, take your men and circle around toward them and keep them plenty busy. Turley, you go along with the captain and his men. Stenton, you and Dawson stay here and keep me covered. I'm going to try and get those crates out there."

"Kind of dangerous, Son," remarked the old scout quickly. "They might put a bullet into one of those powder kegs with you out there and blow it sky high."

"I hardly think that they will do it on purpose," said Lance peering out across the way. "They want those crates intact."

As Drum and his men moved away, Dawson asked, "What could White Cloud have wanted at Big Bear's camp?"

"Just routine, I would say," said Lance thoughtfully.

"I have a hunch that he was on his way out to this camp to pick up the rifles. If I recollect, he told Big Bear that you had the girl and he wanted to get her back, with your help, that is," said Dawson.

"Naomi was not the object of his mission when he rode into camp last night," said Lance as it suddenly occurred to him that the firing had ceased. He peered across the terrain, which was still lit up by the slowly diminishing fires, then continued. "He saw an opportunity to kill two birds with one stone after he rode in on us. Force me to go with him to get Naomi, while the detachment stayed behind at the mercy of his renegades, and which I believe now, part of which would have been sent to this camp to pick up this load."

"In that case, since Big Bear cut short one of his plans, he'll be riding out here with full force, probably not 'afore morning though. White Cloud made camp before we left."

"He could have found out that we left and by which route," cut in Lance.

"The way you have things figured out," said the old scout, "makes me believe that we're going to have to move mighty fast."

"Too bad Big Bear stopped that fight last night," said Stenton looking toward Lance, "we wouldn't have to worry about him bustin' in here now. That Injun is sure crazy."

"Sure is," sighed Lance, "Big Bear prolonged that issue."

Suddenly, rifle shots split the air as they barked madly across the way. Stenton sprang to his knees, but Lance motioned him back down saying, "We'll keep down and out of sight; the chances of getting out there will be better if they don't know that some of us are back here, at least part of the way, before they spot me. Don't open up until they've spotted me."

Lance started to move out, crawling slowly. Working his way toward the overturned wagon, he crawled along steadily. Lance knew that it was just a matter of time before being detected, but if he could make it to the boxes safely, it would only take a minute to set the charge.

Drum and his men are sure making it hot for them, he mused, as he neared the halfway mark. He considered himself lucky thus far, for there hadn't been a shot fired at him.

Lance had been detected but the strategy at the moment by the enemy was to eliminate the scout by means other than chancing a fatal hit with direct firing. The gunrunner ordered one of the braves out of the wagon to wait for the unsuspecting scout. The Sioux faded back into the brush and came up in a direct line with the wagon in between himself and Lance and made his way out to the overturned vehicle.

As Lance neared his destination, he got to his feet, and in a crouching position rushed the remaining distance in short order and threw himself behind the boxes. Quickly, he broke open a small keg of powder and began to prepare for the blast.

From the back of the canvas that was once the roof that sheltered the now scattered ammunition, a long feather came into view, and then the head it was attached to. As the dark eyes came into view, they flashed momentarily upon observing the enemy, then quickly disappeared behind the outstretched portion of the canvas.

Stenton got a flashing glimpse of the brave, and said quickly to Dawson, "There's an Injun behind that wagon. I'm going out there." He was on his way before Dawson could get in a word.

He hit the ground as a volley of shots tore into the ground around him. Dawson opened up and zig zagged brokenly, following Stenton who was up again making his way toward Lance. The latter was out of sight as he buried himself between the boxes.

The Sioux observed Lance's position and crept toward the scout with a knife gripped tightly in his hand. Coming up behind Lance who was but a short distance away, the Sioux exposed himself as he made a wild lunge with his menacing weapon. At the same time Stenton, who was waiting for just such a move, shouted, "Look out Lance."

Stenton fired without aim, and the bullet caught the brave in the chest and he collapsed in a heap near the spot where Lance was before throwing himself to one side the instant Stenton gave the warning.

Suddenly the burst of rifle fire from the upper end of the valley captured the attention of the scattered detachment for a moment. It came as no surprise for the possibility that had been verbally discussed.

"Better step on it Lance," shouted Dawson, who had crawled to within a few yards of the wagon. "Or else there won't be any of us attendin' that weddin' tomorrow."

Lance worked feverishly as he began to roll the powder keg back toward the wooded area, the contents pouring out of it, which he intended to use as a fuse that led directly to the open kegs among the crates of rifles.

He issued quick orders to Stenton who blasted at the enemy, furiously covering Lance's retreat. "Call out to the captain and tell him to get back fast."

Drum lost no time as he issued swift orders. He and his men fired continuously at the hidden enemy whose return fire ceased as they huddled low and out of sight to escape the thunderous volley that screamed around them.

From the upper end of the valley, the pounding of hoof beats became more distinct as the nightriders bore down upon them, adding their fury to the raging battle. Hot lead filled the air, screaming madly as the bullets hissed by. Others sang their death note in a higher pitch after ricocheting off some object sailing far out into space. After reaching the rim of the forest, Lance threw himself into a heavy thicket and called out to Drum, who, with his men, moved steadily backward.

"Captain, check your man with the horses; we've got to move out fast."

Drum tore through the brush at the same time, shouting to the men that were with the animals somewhere back in the forest. Not too distant came a voice in answer, assuring him of their location. Lance lit a match and threw it on the powder, which cast off a cloud of smoke as it hissed along toward its destination.

"Hold your fire and let's go," he shouted as he flung his arm in motion.

Before he could take but a few steps, Dawson grabbed Lance by the shoulder and exclaimed, "That Injun is going to bust up the fuse."

Lance spun around and caught sight of the brave who ran wildly toward the powder line in an attempt to smother the blaze. As he snapped his rifle to his shoulder, Dawson was already firing and the brave went down, falling directly across the line of powder. Lance cursed under his breath for he was aware of the fact that the fire would go out just as soon as it reached the body.

"Hold it," shouted Lance to the scrambling men who were making their way back to the rear. "Start firing again and keep me covered."

Dawson took hold of Lance's coat sleeve and at the same time glanced toward the oncoming horsemen shouting, "You can't go out there now. They are too close; you'll get cut to ribbons."

The two scouts were jarred into action as a voice snapped, "Keep me covered."

Before Lance could protest, Turley was already out in the open and zig zagged his way toward the fallen brave.

"Fool boy," hissed Dawson as he opened up once again at the oncoming enemy.

"You two," said Lance quickly, motioning to the soldiers. "Keep them busy over there; the rest of us fire at the ones up here."

Once again the valley echoed with a thunderous roar as the burning rifle barrels spit out their murderous message.

Turley threw himself down next to the dead brave, and his fingers shook as he lit the match and applied it to the fuse. He spun around quickly and started to crawl back toward the others. Wild yells arose as the horsemen pulled to a halt and dismounted in disorderly fashion. They dove in behind trees and boulders and continued the assault. A few yards from safety, Turley suddenly winced, laid still for a moment, and then began to move at a slower pace.

Lance crawled out toward him and took hold of his hand, dragging his friend into the brush.

"Turley, you hit bad?" asked Lance in anxiety.

"Just a knick," said Turley, breathing heavily.

"Everybody," snapped Lance. "Let's go. On the run."

Lance put Turley's arm around his neck, saying, "Hang on, I'll help you to your horse."

The mad scramble back was made in quick order. As they neared the animals, everyone fell to the ground as the blast of the explosion shook the earth about them like an earthquake during its work of destruction. They laid there for several moments, waiting for the debris to cease falling.

Fragments of wagon and cargo along with particles of earth still fell as Lance's voice snapped quick orders: "Let's go, our time's about run out."

Helping the wounded Turley on his horse, Lance mounted his and asked, “Think you can make it?”

“Sure,” replied Turley. “It’s not bad.”

Lance spun his horse around, getting into the lead and said to Dawson, “Watch him, he may need help.”

Lance urged his mount forward, the weary, but anxious detachment following close behind. The whole valley seemed to be on fire, and the once barking rifles that had spit bullets and flame so furiously were now silent. Lance looked back over his shoulder for a moment trying to detect some sign of pursuit, but he observed nothing.

The burning valley, along with the bewildered red men who had again fought savagely for a lost cause, were left behind as the haggard looking detachment disappeared into the darkness.

XVII

The moon was still high in the sky as the weary riders halted near a small stream. They slid off their horses and dropped themselves to the water's edge. The cool water felt like a tonic as they eagerly quenched their thirst. They dunked their heads into the stream, washing off the sticky sweat and dirt that had accumulated during their recent struggle. Just about twenty four hours ago, this same detachment left on a mission, well stimulated with energy, their attire unquestionable; the hand picked detachment could have been the envy of the fort. Under present observation they would hardly be recognized as the same. Their clothing was torn and dust-laden. Buttons were missing, likewise the hats that some of them had worn. Most of them were motionless as they laid in rest, stretched out of the soft earth.

Lance wiped most of the water off his face as he pulled away from the bank of the stream and faced Turley, whose water dripping face shined in the moonlight which added a sparkle to the grin he wore.

Turley spoke first saying, "Do you think that there is enough room for another rancher down by the river? I get to like that idea better every day."

Before Lance could make any comment, Dawson cut in as he walked toward them saying, "You keep runnin' into a hall of bullets like you did back there and you won't be around to keep on likin' the idea of ranchin', let alone goin' on down there. Why in the blazes didn't you crawl out there instead of running exposed like a fool Injun?"

"Can't do much crawling. It tickles my belly."

Dawson's grin was concealed by his heavy beard as he muttered, "Just can't talk sense to this fool boy."

Lance moved closer to Turley saying, "Let me help you with your coat. We'll bandage up that arm wound."

"All Right doc," replied the wounded scout. "And while you are at it, you may as well patch up the rest of them. I feel a few more burns here and there."

Lance stopped pulling on the coat sleeve and asked with concern, "Where else are you hit?"

"No need for alarm doc," assured Turley. "The arm is the worst, and that one is only a minor flesh wound. As a matter of fact, I wouldn't have been hit at all if Dawson could shoot straight."

The young scouts eyed Dawson amusingly as the latter blurted out, "You're sayin' mighty pecular things, young fellar. Must be burnin' with fever, poor boy, and just in case you ain't . . . "

"Pay heed to this you crazy hoot owl."

"If I ever laid ma' sights on you and pulled that trigger, I'd blast that ticklin' belly of yours right on to the next valley and I could watch it go over the mountain top through the hole where your belly once rested peaceful-like."

Drum laughed along with the scouts at Dawson's remark as he pulled out a medical kit from one of the saddlebags and walked over to them.

"How's the arm?" he asked.

"Won't slow him up any," replied Lance.

Drum sighed, remarking, "We've been pretty lucky up 'til now. Perhaps it's because we shoot straighter and faster."

The moon was still high in the sky as the weary riders halted near a small stream. They slid off their horses and dropped themselves to the water's edge. The cool water felt like a tonic as they eagerly quenched their thirst. They dunked their heads into the stream, washing off the sticky sweat and dirt that had accumulated during their recent struggle. Just about twenty four hours ago this same detachment left on a mission, well stimulated with energy, their attire unquestionable; the hand picked detachment could have been the envy of the fort. Under present observation they would hardly be recognized as the same. Their clothing was torn and dust-laden. Buttons were missing, likewise the hats that some of them had worn. Most of them were motionless as they laid in rest, stretched out of the soft earth.

Lance wiped most of the water off his face as he pulled away from the bank of the stream and faced Turley, whose water dripping face shined in the moonlight which added a sparkle to the grin he wore.

Turley spoke first saying, “Do you think that there is enough room for another rancher down by the river? I get to like that idea better every day.”

Before Lance could make any comment, Dawson cut in as he walked toward them saying, “You keep runnin’ into a hall of bullets like you did back there and you won’t be around to keep on likin’ the idea of ranchin’, let alone goin’ on down there. Why in the blazes didn’t you crawl out there instead of running exposed like a fool Injun?”

“Can’t do much crawling. It tickles my belly.”

Dawson’s grin was concealed by his heavy beard as he muttered, “Just can’t talk sense to this fool boy.”

Lance moved closer to Turley saying, “Let me help you with your coat. We’ll bandage up that arm wound.”

“All Right doc,” replied the wounded scout. “And while you are at it, you may as well patch up the rest of them. I feel a few more burns here and there.”

Lance stopped pulling on the coat sleeve and asked with concern, “Where else are you hit?”

“No need for alarm doc,” assured Turley. “The arm is the worst, and that one is only a minor flesh wound. As a matter of fact, I wouldn’t have been hit at all if Dawson could shoot straight.”

The young scouts eyed Dawson amusingly as the latter blurted out, “You’re sayin’ mighty peculiar things, young fellar. Must be burnin’ with fever, poor boy, and just in case you ain’t . . . ”

"Pay heed to this, you crazy hoot owl."

"If I ever laid ma' sights on you and pulled that trigger, I'd blast that ticklin' belly of yours right on to the next valley and I could watch it go over the mountain top through the hole where your belly once rested peaceful-like."

Drum laughed along with the scouts at Dawson's remark as he pulled out a medical kit from one of the saddlebags and walked over to them.

"How's the arm?" he asked.

"Won't slow him up any," replied Lance.

Drum sighed, remarking, "We've been pretty lucky up 'til now. Perhaps it's because we shoot straighter and faster."

"We have that advantage," agreed Lance. "There is no doubt that the Indian has failed to master the rifle up to this point, but they are learning by the day."

"There. How's that?" asked Lance after finishing with the bandage.

"Fine, Doc," replied Turley. "What do I owe you?"

"Show up tonight on time," smiled Lance. "And we'll call it even."

"Near forgot about the wedding," said Drum getting to his feet. "If we're going dancing tonight we'd better get started." Directing his question at Lance, he asked, "How much farther do we have to go? I'm rather lost at this point."

"About a two hour ride, I would judge," replied the scout. "Should make it before sun up."

A night owl, perched high up on a limb of a pine tree, blinked its eyes occasionally, watching in silence as the nightriders vanished into the dark of the night.

Hours later, the haggard looking detachment approached the far end of the camp. News spread quickly of their return. No time was lost preparing warm meals for the returning men.

Hot water for baths and for re-bathing their wounds was over the fire in large vats. Stories of the latest venture flowed freely as those who stayed behind listened with keen interest. On occasions, Lance would steal a glance toward the Bacon's canvas home in hopes that they were aware of their return. He thought of the past twenty four hours. It seemed like a long time since he had seen Naomi last. He put his hand to his face and felt the long slash that was inflicted by White Cloud's blade. *Not the nicest thing to be wearing around on a fellows wedding day,* he mused. A slight smile brushed his lips as he pictured Naomi's face after telling her of his change in plans concerning their marriage. They would get married today rather than when he got back off the next mission. A frown creased his forehead as he thought to himself, *if I ever got back*. Lance wondered at the moment if that possibility was the reason why he wanted to go through with it now.

His thoughts were disrupted as Dawson walked over to him, saying, "You're going to have company soon, the lantern is lit up at Bacon's place."

"Let's go on up there," suggested Lance as he put his shirt back on. "Want to let them know early. I hope they won't mind too much."

Before they could get started, a figure appeared in the semi-darkness and upon recognizing the scouts, greeted them warmly. It was Bacon, whose wide smile vanished as he noticed the slash on Lance's face.

"Looks like you fellows ran into a pack of wild cats," he remarked with concern.

"We did," said Lance. "Some of us failed to get out of their way in time, however, nothing serious."

Lance excused himself during the conversation as he noticed the outline of Naomi. The fading moonlight was slowly making way for the dawn, but the rays still danced about, some of them playing across the faces of the two young people who gazed at each other with hearts full of love and understanding.

She raised her hand slowly to his face and touched the wound lightly. Lance watched her expression change slowly. Her eyes were tinted with sadness and her voice was just above a whisper as she said, "One day, it may be deeper, one day, you may not return."

He placed his hands on her shoulders and smiled down at her, saying, "Now don't you worry your pretty head about it, little one.

Only one more mission, and after that, you and I will be heading for the river, and home."

Her mouth parted slightly as she looked up at him with eyes of approval. At that moment Lance decided to kiss her, despite any one that cared to look, but the attempt was cut short by a familiar voice that remarked, "Now if this isn't a fine time of day to be saying pretty things to a girl."

It was Mrs. Bacon walking toward them with her daughter Mary Lou. Lance whispered to Naomi before greeting the newcomers, "Down by the river there won't be any interruption," and then he winked at her.

He faced the women with a smile, saying, "Good morning. I wish to apologize for arousing you folks so early. We certainly made more noise than I thought."

"Wasn't the noise at all," said Mrs. Bacon. "It was this little girl of ours," and nodded her head toward Naomi. "She can sense when you are in the vicinity."

Lance watched Mary Lou as she glanced about in anticipation. She turned suddenly, facing him, and remarked, "There should be a fellow around here about your size, and I hope still wearing a grin."

Lance pointed in a backwardly direction, saying, "If you walk toward that fire over there, with the vat hanging over it, you may run into him. And if I may add, he could use a nurse."

Her face paled slightly as she asked brokenly, "Is he hurt?"

"Now don't you be alarmed," said Lance quickly. "It's nothing serious, just a slight arm wound."

Mary Lou was off before another word was said. They watched her for a moment as she headed toward the fire pit. Lance applied a little pressure to Naomi's hand that he still held, at the same time directing his remark to the elderly woman, saying, "Mrs. Bacon, you said a day or so ago that you and Mr. Bacon would manage something in the way of a celebration when Naomi and I got married."

"It still goes, Son," cut in Mrs. Bacon. "Just you name the day."

"Today," said Lance without hesitation, and watched the surprised look on Naomi's face. Her look of approval warmed Lance to the depth of his soul, and at the moment could neither do or say anything concerning his feelings other than clasping her hand tightly.

He glanced at Mrs. Bacon, whose wide smile was directed at Naomi, and said, "I know this is short notice."

"Don't you fret about that, Son," she said reassuringly. "We accomplish a lot of things out here on the spur of the moment. Just you get some sleep and ready yourself for the occasion. I'll take care of Naomi here; she'll be ready whenever you and the parson are."

"Thanks," said Lance. "Perhaps one day we can return the favor."

"Peers to me like it's going to be an exciting day," said a voice from a short distance away. It was Dawson, who walked slowly toward them.

"Thought you'd be sleeping by now," said Lance with a smile.

"Not 'afore I talked to some of the pretty women that are running around here this morning," remarked the old scout.

"You're certainly dressed for it," grinned Lance and with the two women, looked over the torn, mud-caked clothes that Dawson was sporting at the moment.

"Little shabby in spots," said Dawson, "but ain't too noticeable in the dark. For the occasion, Bacon had already promised me a new fit of clothes."

"When are you leaving for the river?" asked Lance, changing the subject.

"Right after dark, I 'spect," replied the other. "Want to get in a step or two 'afore I leave." Dawson placed an arm around Naomi's shoulder, saying, "As a matter of fact, I aim to be the first to dance with the bride. It's all right with you, ma' little flower, isn't it?" he asked.

Naomi looked up at him with warmth in her eyes and a smile that only a few men ever had the pleasure of receiving from the Apache girl, then said softly, "I can't dance very well."

He gave her a slight hug and remarked, "Don't you fret none at all. I'm the best two step dancer in this here country, as a matter of fact. Did I ever tell you the time I won first prize over that eastern feller back in Missouri, why . . . "

"You tell us about that tonight," cut in Mrs. Bacon laughingly. "Right now I think that you fellows ought to get some needed rest.

Wonder how the patient is making out," she remarked looking toward the fire pit.

"He's in good hands," said Lance; then he added, "Let's go over and check with the nurse."

Turley and Mary Lou seemed to be lost in deep conversation as the others walked up to them.

"Can't be in too bad a shape," remarked Dawson. "He hasn't lost any of his chatter."

Upon hearing the old scout's voice, they got up from their sitting position and faced the intruders smiling.

Turley greeted Mrs. Bacon and Naomi, saying, "This must be my lucky day, three of the prettiest ladies of the Big Horn country, and all within talking distance."

"There's nothing wrong with this boy," said Mrs. Bacon, smiling broadly.

"Son," cut in Dawson, placing an arm around Turley's shoulder, "you seem to be a might shaky to me. You're going to look a poor sight as best man hobbling about leaning on a hickory stick. Might help you out if I took your place and let you rest."

Dawson's eyes twinkled as he waited for an answer, while the others smiled in amusement.

"Tell you what I'll do," said Turley. "You shave off that overgrown fuzz that's weighing down your chin, and you can go ahead as best man for Lance."

"You been wantin' me to get rid of it for a long time now, haven't you?" chuckled the old scout.

"Well," said Turley, "I thought that it would be proper to see you attending the occasion without that disguise for a change. After all, we really don't know what you really look like, you know."

Dawson grinned as he took his arm away from the young scout's shoulder and took a step or two backward toward the open fire, whereupon he spit a stream of tobacco juice that caused the sudden gush of steam shooting skyward as it came in contact with the hot coals. Facing the young scout again, Dawson remarked, "Son, I ain't aimin' to do any bragging, but I'll tell you this much. Once back in

Missouri I had myself a clean shave, and for a week I had more invites to dinners by eligible women than there are trees on that mountain over yonder, and I'll be danged if I get rid of this here crow's nest again and rile up the womenfolk around here."

The others chuckled gleefully at the old scout's boast.

Mrs. Bacon was still laughing as she spoke, "I think we'd better leave and let the menfolk get some rest."

Lance spoke a few words to Naomi, as did Turley to Mary Lou. Shortly afterwards, the women strolled away, Mrs. Bacon chatting excitingly.

Mid afternoon found the settlers' camp in a gay mood as the usual trend of activates continued, for the evening had something to offer that was familiar but not too frequent: music and dancing at a wedding.

The Bacons had taken care of the arrangements for Lance, and at the moment the latter was conversing with the wagon master.

"Well, Son, you be ready to walk up the aisle at six o'clock. I talked with the parson, and he suggested the time. Said the wildflowers look the prettiest about then. Turley here looks to be in good shape. Dawson insists on giving the bride away, and Ma' and Mary Lou will be ready to cry at the proper time. I'll be at the head of the line to give you the first handshake."

"Thanks," said Lance, smiling. "I certainly appreciate all that you folks are doing for Naomi and me."

"Don't mention it," said Bacon. "Oh before I forget, you take care of this." He handed Turley a ring. "It was given to my wife by her Ma'."

Drum, who seemed to be smiling like a schoolboy, addressed the group. "Let's walk over to the edge of the camp and show Lance the new home that the boys have put up for him and the future wife."

At the far end of the camp, a large tent was erected underneath a tall pine tree. Stakes were driven into the ground, encircling the canvas home with rope attached to each, resembling a picket fence. Lance smiled warmly as he glanced about and then chuckled as his eyes fell on two signs that were placed near the entrance. One read: *Residence of Mr. and Mrs. Lance Winsor*, and on the other, *Please, no visitors tonight.*

Stenton, who was in charge of the construction, remarked to Lance with a smile, "Any time you and the Mrs. want an addition to this masterpiece, just you look me up. I'm the new building engineer in camp."

"Thanks," said Lance chuckling. Then he added as he glanced at the others, "I want to thank all of you for everything. Perhaps one day I can return the favor."

"Well looks like everything is taken care of," said Bacon.

"In that case," remarked Drum, "I'd like all you gentlemen to be my guests. Coffee is being served at my quarters at the moment. Shall we indulge?"

The invitation was met with approval and in short order the men headed toward the captain's quarters. Dawson said to Lance before reaching their destination, "I'd like to have a word with you for a minute, Son."

"Certainly, Will," said Lance, and waited for the other to continue.

"Well, I guess that this is going to seem sentimental to you," said the old scout as he reached into his pocket and pulled out a braided headband. The old scout looked at the band for a long moment, fingering it softly.

Lance was aware of the saddened expression on Dawson's face and chose to remain silent.

"This belonged to my wife," he said rather softly. "She wore it when we got married." He smiled slightly as he looked up at Lance and said, "I wonder if you would mind if I asked Naomi to wear this when you two get married? As a matter of fact, I would like her to keep it. Sort of a remembrance of 'ole Uncle Dawson."

"I'd like that fine," said Lance, "and I'm sure that Naomi will be very happy about it."

"Thanks, Son." said Dawson, his face brightening. "I'll mosey up to the Bacon's and give it to her. I'll be back in a few minutes and join you for a coffee or two."

Lance watched him until he disappeared behind one of the wagons and then he went on into the captain's quarters.

Nightfall had descended upon the camp, and at that moment, the occasion was in full swing. Singing, dancing, and laughter rang out over the brightly lit area. Lance, who was seated at the Bacon's fire pit, smiled as he glanced out over the hot coals toward the many dancers that were at the moment trying to keep in step with the three piece band that had recently returned from behind a large oak, where the bottle was passed around for a quick nip or two. At the moment, Turley was dancing with Naomi, the latter feeling more at ease doing the white man's dance since receiving simple instructions from Dawson. Lance caught Naomi's eye and flashed a quick wink.

"She certainly learns fast," he said, directing the remark to the old scout.

"They all learn fast when taught by the old master," said Dawson with a grin. "Wall now," he remarked, getting to his feet. "Guess it's about time I got started. Didn't aim to stay at the weddin' this long."

"You ought to have a little more to eat before leaving," suggested Mrs. Bacon.

"Well, now ma'am," replied Dawson as he patted his stomach. "The only place there is room left for any more of this good tastin' food is in my saddle bag."

"That, Mrs. Bacon," said Lance, "is a well placed hint," and laughed as he placed an arm around his old friend's shoulder.

A short time later, Dawson was bidding farewell to his close friends. He placed his arm around Naomi's shoulder and smiled down at her saying, "Your old Uncle Dawson will pay you and Lance here a visit one day down along the Big Horn, and I'm going to give you a hint now, I ain't never going to leave."

"You are always welcome," she said softly.

He looked about her lovely face for a moment, then glanced at the braided head band that he had given her. Those about him knew that the old scout's thoughts were of the far-away past, for the girl near his side always reminded him of another woman who was just as beautiful: his Cheyenne wife.

He gave her a quick hug, then lost no time in mounting his horse. Waving his hand in farewell, the veteran Indian fighter urged his mount forward, and man and animal soon disappeared into the darkness of the night.

The camp had quieted down to a laughter here and there as the settlers thinned out with the approach of the late hours. Lance held Naomi's hand as they stood near each other, conversing with the Bacons and Captain Drum. The topic of conversation concerned the many gifts that were given to the young couple.

"Yes sir, Lance," remarked Bacon. "You sure got enough here to start that ranch with. Wagon, horses, steers, and all the implements."

"Certainly didn't expect anything like this," said Lance, his voice well tinted with appreciation.

"Why don't we forget about ranching tonight and let these two young ones be alone for a change," cut in Mrs. Bacon as she circled Naomi's shoulder with her arm. "And dear, you and Lance come up here for breakfast. The invitation goes for you too, Captain," she said, smiling at the military man.

"Thank you," said Drum with an air of approval. "I'd like nothing better than attending a wedding breakfast."

"Whenever you two are ready, I'll walk along as far as my quarters, if I may," he said, addressing the newlyweds.

"It will be a pleasure having a military escort," smiled Lance.

"Need a good scout to lead the way?" asked a voice that came from a short distance away. It was Turley, who now walked toward them with Mary Lou, where they had been engaged in low tone conversation. Lance was about to make a remark, but it died on his lips along with the smile that he wore a moment before, for the cry of a wolf echoed down from the mountainside.

Naomi looked up at him and her hand tightened about his arm. He smiled at her reassuringly but was aware of the fact that she knew that noise was something other than the wolf lurking beneath the darkened pines of the forest, penetrating the stillness with the bone-chilling howl.

He glanced at the others in silence, expecting the call to repeat, but was suddenly jarred out of his silent thoughts along with the others as a fire arrow appeared from out of the dark and smashed into the tent that was erected especially for him and Naomi by his friends.

"White Cloud paying his respects," uttered Turley quickly.

"Mrs. Bacon, you still have a guest," said Lance swiftly as he half shoved Naomi toward the elderly woman.

"Darn those intruders," said Mrs. Bacon as she put her arm around Naomi sympathetically.

Drum was already on the run, shouting orders. The two scouts and the wagon boss dashed for their rifles and lost no time getting over to Drum's quarters.

Fire arrows hissed through the air as they sailed toward their targets. The once-potential home of the Winsors burned brightly, and a pair of saddened eyes watched in silence from the doorway of the Bacon home for a few moments, and then disappeared into the tent. The sudden attack sobered most of the settlers, who but a short time ago enjoyed a night cap that ended the highlights of the day. They dashed about in all directions, shouting and cursing the red man for paying them a visit at such an unearthly hour. Barking rifles added to the already mounting noise, as bullets sped in the direction of the oncoming fire arrows. Several lines of bucket brigades were working feverishly to extinguish the fires. The noonday sun couldn't brighten up the camp anymore than it was at the moment. Those who had to be exposed were easy targets under the circumstances and several of the settlers lay wounded and others dead as they lay on the blood soaked ground. Outside of Drum's quarters the matter was being discussed soberly as the men lay on the ground behind fallen logs.

"Can't be to many of them if it's White Cloud and his men," remarked Drum. "Wouldn't take much to drive them back up into the mountain and out of range."

"That would be best for now," said Lance with approval. He glanced towards the Bacons' tent where his wife of only a few hours huddled in concealment, once again being harassed by the Sioux renegades. The blood drained out of his fingers as they tightened around the trigger guard, for at the moment he was blaming himself bitterly for not plunging his knife thru the chief's heart when he had the chance back at Big Bear's camp.

His thoughts where disrupted as Bacon suggested, "Why don't we circle the upper part of the mountain. Come dawn, we could pick most of them off 'afore they get away easy."

"The idea is appealing," said Drum. "However we don't have the time. We are scheduled to move out of here tomorrow night." Suddenly a bloodcurdling scream caused the men to snap into action. From out of a thicket ran a brave wielding a knife high above his head, yelling madly as he sped forward toward his nearest target. The scouts were the first to open fire on the savage charger, whose knife went flying through space as the impact of bullets tore through his body. The dust flew around him wildly as his body hit the ground with a thud.

Drum lost no time in issuing orders as he snapped, "Bacon, alert your riflemen. There may be more breaking through. Make sure you have every inch of the camp covered. Turley, you take the left flank. Lance, you take the right. Relate to the men that we are taking the offensive. Watch for my signal, then push forward."

Shortly after, the battle with the unseen enemy began as Drum's arm waved in a forward motion, indicating the awaited signal. Every now and then a rifle would bark. An arrow would swish through the thicket searching in frenzy for a human target.

Rifle fire by the Indians was light, indicating the fact that they were either low on ammo

or were being cautious not to reveal their exact location.

Near the mountaintop, a solitary figure stood motionless as he gazed down upon the settlers' camp that was slowly blending in contrast with the dark of the night as the dying flames slowly flickered out. His thoughts at the moment were far from the smoking of the peace pipe. The bitter sneer on his lips added to the gruesomeness of his painted face. Somewhere down below lay his destiny, a girl that was taken from him by the white scouts, and up 'til now he had failed to get her back. The muscles in his face tightened and he began to breathe sharply, for the thought of getting her back one day lingered constantly in his mind, and at the moment he vowed that he would make it a future reality.

His body relaxed slowly as he brought his hands to his mouth and let out a long eerie wolf call. White Cloud, Sioux chief, had decided to pay a visit again at another time, for now he must go back to his people and join them in the great battle that was planned against the white man. A sneer, rather than a smile of satisfaction creased his lips as he waited for his braves to join him.

Once again the night quieted down to a peaceful silence, but the piercing eyes of the defenders kept a vigilant watch toward the darkened forest that concealed the ruthless enemy. As time went by, Lance moved cautiously toward Drum to discuss the situation.

He called out softly, "Captain."

"Over here," beckoned Drum, his voice coming from a short distance below him.

Upon reaching the military man, Drum asked, "Do you think they've pulled out"

"I would say yes," answered Lance. "However, it would be best to keep the guard doubled since the Indian can't be taken for granted. Especially White Cloud; he's about the worst of the lot right now."

"White Cloud," muttered Drum slowly as he stared into space for a few moments then turned facing Lance saying, "I think that we should pay special attention to this renegade when we go up there to fight the Sioux. Should the opportunity prevail, we'll cut his activities short once and for all." Drum let out a sigh as he continued. "Among other things, he's getting into my hair."

"Whether or not we get the chance up there remains to be seen," said Lance. "I think that he anticipates our move up into that country along with the other forces and may take advantage of our absence here and continue his attacks in hopes of getting Naomi."

Lance gazed toward the Bacons' tent and knew rather than felt that she was laying there wide eyed, her face saddened by the turn of events. He also knew that at the moment, she wondered if the day would ever come when they could go toward their planned destiny without having to look over their shoulders every now and then for the foe whose desire was to separate them with certain death. The bitterness that he felt vanished at the sound of Drum's voice.

"Seems to me that he would be expected to join his people in the coming conflict."

"Perhaps you're right there," agreed Lance.

New hope swept over him as the thought of White Cloud being out of the territory during his absence encouraged his feelings of despair.

"Should we fail to meet up with him," said Drum, "we'll hunt him down when we get back here. That Indian will be back in this area again and it won't be hard to find him."

"That's for certain, Captain. He'll be back," said the other thoughtfully.

"Well, for now it would be best to set up the guard for tonight. Let's slip back into camp."

They were soon joined by Bacon, who had been busy stationing his men during the attack.

"Kind of quiet up there," remarked the wagon master. "Do you think they're gone?"

"We've come to that conclusion," answered Lance looking up toward the mountain. "But you can't be sure."

"Bacon," said Drum, "we're going to use your men to stand guard with, with the exception of a few of mine that won't be going with us tomorrow. The rest of us will be needing all the sleep we can get."

"I've got the men and the rifles," said Bacon, "and I believe that we can manage until you fellows get back, but we're a little short on ammo."

"I'll see that you get plenty of it come morning," said Drum with assurance.

"If you fellows are ready to make the rounds we'll get organized."

As an after thought, Bacon spoke to Lance, saying, "You and Turley can bunk in my quarters tonight."

"Thanks," said Lance, looking toward the empty space where just a short time ago stood his newly erected home. He sighed softly, then turned abruptly and followed the others who were already on their way.

XVIII

The first light of dawn brought into view the silhouette of the high mountaintops.

The morning was cool, the sky cloudless. The setting was a peaceful one, a far cry from the night before. The day of departure for the patrol in full force had arrived. For some of them, their venture up north had been a busy one. From here on, until the Sioux were reckoned with, the danger would become more intense, for behind the tall pines along the way, on the other side of the mountains will lay in wait the red man, ready to deal with cunning, treachery, and deliverance of sudden death to his bitter enemy: the white man.

The sound of the bugle split the early morning silence, drawing moans and groans from the slumberers, whose comments directed at the noise maker would certainly be unfit to print. Sleepy-eyed men staggered out of their tents, heading for some source of water. The clanking of metal basins and pans rang through the area as they busied themselves in washing. Most of them were barefooted, without shirts, and with suspenders dangling down over their trousers. The day had begun perhaps like any other but for some it may be the beginning of the end, for a screaming bullet or a hissing arrow may find their mark before another dawn, and their road to destiny may be suddenly reached.

Time went quickly, especially for the outgoing patrol as they readied themselves for the hour of departure. During the course of the afternoon, two riders rode a short distance from camp and dismounted underneath the shade of the tall trees. Lance Winsor tied the reins to an outstretched limb, then turned and looked down at his companion, his wife.

A faint smile creased his lips as they looked at each other in silence, each lost in their thoughts, patterns that were surely identical. He brushed her face with his fingers, then brought them up to the side of her head letting them rest there for a moment as he slowly bent down and kissed her mouth slightly. Lance spoke for the first time since dismounting. His voice was soft and assuring.

"I know that you felt the same way I did last night, but don't you worry none about it. It's not always going to be like this. One day soon I'll build you a house down by the river and there won't be anyone to bother us. The campaign ahead of us should clear the way." His smile faded slowly as he stared out over the valley, for within himself he could feel the question prowling around in his mind. *But will the campaign add White Cloud's passage to the happy hunting grounds?* Naomi sensed his thoughts as she watched his troubled eyes. Lance faced her again upon hearing her soft voice.

"You think about White Cloud, I know."

"Yes," said Lance after hesitating for a few moments. "If I fail to get him on this trip, then I'll have to hunt him down at another time." *If I'm lucky enough to get back*, he said to himself.

The thought of not coming back caused him to become tense as he visualized Naomi facing the white man's world alone. He gazed down at her, his body slowly relaxing, casting the unpleasant thought from his mind, for the girl before him, like many times before, inspired him to the heights of a victorious conqueror.

"Don't you worry none, little one. One day we will be free of the renegade. After all," said Lance with a smile. "We're married now and have a lot of plans, and I don't intend to disappoint you by not making them a reality, why, what would you think of me?"

A smile creased her lips as she placed her hands on his arms and tilted her head forward letting it rest on his chest. His mouth brushed the side of her head and his arms began to tighten about her, but stopped suddenly as a voice rang out loudly by a searcher unaware of their exact location.

"Winsor?"

"Over here," called out Lance. Then he sighed easily as he turned and faced Naomi, saying, rather reluctantly, "I guess the time has come."

They looked up at the horseman who approached them leisurely. It was Stenton, who touched the brim of his hat and at the same time remarked apologetically, "Won't surprise me none if you two get to hate me after a while. Seems like I'm always interrupting."

The latter's remark reminded Lance of the fight that they had back at the fort and he grinned slightly, saying, "I must say that you had good reasons of late."

Stenton laughed heartily, as he too thought of the past, and said, "A teacher needs but one try to get something across to me, and if I remember correctly, it was a right to the jaw." With a smile he added, "I figure it was well worth it. Had fun and excitement, knowing you two since . . . "

"Well," said Lance, "a bit of formality concerning that introduction would have been less painful. I still hear a ringing in my ear once in a while. You don't have a bad right, yourself."

Stenton was flattered by the remark and felt a certain boost added to his prestige.

"By the way," asked Lance changing the subject, "did you want to see me for something in particular?"

"Seems as though I get lost socially at times," grinned Stenton. "The captain sent me out here, he wants to see you. Better be getting back myself," he said placing his hat back on his head, and tugged on his reigns.

"Wait a minute," said Lance. "Ride back with us."

"Thanks," said Stenton as he waited for them to mount. "Don't often get the pleasure to ride with the Winsors."

The sun seemed to be impatient to get a glimpse of what was going on

below, as it appeared every now and then from behind one of the passing clouds. At the moment, its interest was held by the activities within the settlers' camp. A military patrol was in formation, this time in full force, ready to move out across the mountains to seek out the forever hunted. So relentlessly they practiced aggression, which perhaps could be justified by reasons that would be accepted by the white man, though, no doubt, the acceptance would be tinted with reluctance.

In front of the patrol, Captain Drum conversed with Bacon and some of his men. The two scouts were near them but paid little or no attention to the discussion. Their thoughts were elsewhere at the moment. Lance turned in his saddle and glanced at Naomi who stood motionless as she listened to Mrs. Bacon near the latter's tent. A slight trace of a smile brushed her lips as she met Lance's gaze, but otherwise she betrayed no emotion. Upon facing the others again, he noticed Turley in deep thought. Whatever happened between his friend and Mary Lou could be the cause of his sullen mood. Turley wore a deep frown and looked rather disappointed as his eyes bore down into the ground below. Lance chose to disturb his friend at the moment and try to encourage him, unless the troubled look that was quite obvious was a misrepresentation of expression.

He remarked in low tones, "Looks like the two of you won't agree on burying the hatchet."

Turley brought his head up and directed his gaze at Lance. He smiled saying, "The hatchet gets buried all right, but it's always in my head. I guess I blundered in the very beginning. Used the wrong approach or something." He sighed rather hard then added, "Must have teased her too much."

"Perhaps you should have mixed it up a bit," said Lance. "I think it would have softened her attitude toward you."

"I hate to admit this," said Turley with a frown, "but I think that it has come to the point where she really dislikes me."

The bugle sounded off suddenly as Drum gave the order. The animals became excited as their riders pulled hard on the reins and the mounts danced about wildly as the scouts glanced in the direction of the women. Lance turned toward Turley for a moment and said quickly, "She's in love with you fella, bet my prize heifer."

"You wouldn't make that statement if you would have heard her parting words," said Turley still struggling with his rearing mount.

Lance said no more as he looked at Naomi and waved his hand in farewell, for Drum had given the order to move out. She raised her small hand then let it slowly drop to her side.

Her thoughts at the moment could well be described by her crying heart. As the patrol neared the edge of camp, a horse galloped up from behind and headed up toward the head of the patrol. The rider pulled along side of Turley. The latter betrayed a slight surprise upon facing Mary Lou and felt the blood rush up to his face.

He checked his emotions, not wanting it to become too obvious, for her presence at the moment was his most wanted desire, but the least expected up to now. Her face appeared relaxed, and her mouth held a faint trace of a smile as she spoke softly, "I'd like you to have this if you still want it," and she held out her hand, displaying the locket.

Turley's heart seemed to be jumping in all directions as he reached the outstretched hand and squeezed it tightly. He took the locket from her palm saying, "Don't leave the country, fair lady. We've got a lot to discuss. I'll be coming back."

"You'll find me waiting," replied Mary Lou, her eyes growing misty.

With a wink and a wave of his hand he was off toward the front of the patrol. As he pulled along side of Lance, the latter remarked with a grin, "You would have lost if I would have taken that bet."

"Would have been worth losing," replied the other, grinning like a fellow on his first date at a Sunday picnic. From the corner of his eye, Drum watched the scout as the latter placed the chain, attached to the locket, around his neck and proceeded to interlock the ends.

The captain winked at Lance, then turned facing the terrain ahead. The outfit moved on slowly, finally disappearing from the sight of the settlers as they swung in toward the forest, the home of the tall pines.

Mother Nature's wonderland awaited the approach of sundown, and the already creeping shadows warmed their way into their usual playgrounds silently. At the head of the patrol a hand was raised, halting the riders as they came upon the first stream that crossed the planned trail. Captain Drum turned in his saddle and glanced back at his men whose verbal expressions of approval were mixed with wild chatter and laughter.

Animals and men alike welcomed the break, losing no time getting to the cool mountain water. Lance dismounted and followed Drum to the water edge. After satisfying his thirst, he asked, "How much farther do you want to go before setting up camp?"

Drum gazed out over the water, and after a moment of silence remarked, "I'd like to get as far as the base of the ravine that leads to Big Bear's camp."

"We're in for some night riding then," said Lance. "Can't make it before dark."

The other agreed with the nod of his head still gazing out into the empty space ahead. After a few moments of silence, he spoke: "I'm going to split up the patrol at that point. I know that the intended procedure is contrary to our plans, however, more of the territory should be covered. By sending out small patrols as we go along just won't cover too much of it."

It appeared to Lance that the military man has been pondering on the change and had come to a decision but a minute before. Drum faced the scout, who up to the moment hadn't expressed an opinion regarding the matter, and continued. "Wouldn't want to go on past a large force that may be in hiding to strike from the rear when least expected. As you already know, such a move by the Sioux had been thought of as a possibility back at the fort."

He looked at the scout for some sign of approval. Lance was aware of the fact and spoke with concern. "You realize, of course, the consequences should one of our split forces run into a sizeable band of Sioux up here in the mountains. They wouldn't stand much of a chance."

"Then again," said Drum quickly, "if we should slip by a force up here and later be hit from the rear in the heat of battle would be disastrous. We've got to cover as much area as possible from here to the river. Should we encounter trouble, some of us can get through to the river in time with the warning."

Lance realized that Drum was trying to cover every angle and taking nothing for granted. He looked with admiration at Drum and said, smiling, "Captain, for a novice, you sure got the foresight of a veteran general Indian fighter."

"Well," said Drum with a grin that appeared after the scout's flattering remark, "Like I said in the past, and again I repeat, I have excellent teachers."

He got to his feet and glanced around then let his gaze rest on a figure that sat with his back against a tree, looking far out over the horizon. Lance was up beside the military man and he too spotted the silent, thoughtful Turley.

"She sure has him daydreaming," he remarked with a grin. "Certainly has forgotten about St. Louie since coming up into this country."

"You may have neighbors when you and the Mrs. go down to the river," said Drum.

"You could be right, Captain. He's got that blue water look in his eyes right now."

They walked toward their mounts chuckling, but Turley, unaware, was far away, mentally building his castle somewhere in the Big Horn.

Minutes later, Drum gave the order to move out, and the refreshed patrol lost no time in getting underway. Curious creatures of the wilds watched from their hiding places as the horsemen passed by. Once in a while a night bird would cry out as if demanding the reason for the intruders' presence, then would fly away swiftly to a more peaceful haven. As darkness closed in, the patrol set a slower pace. The going became more difficult as time wore on. Upon entering a small clearing, Drum pulled to a halt, asking, "How much farther would you say?"

Lance looked toward the mountain peaks, the silhouette outlined clearly against the background of semi darkened skies. "Not more than a mile or two," was the reply.

"In that case we'll make camp here," said Drum. "Another mile or two won't make much difference. By the way, how does this particular area suit you?"

"A likely spot, plenty of cover and as for stopping a little ahead of time. I'm sure, Captain, that if you were running for sheriff right now, you'd get every vote."

Drum chuckled as he dismounted saying, "There are times when I wouldn't get any."

"You're wrong there, Captain," said a familiar voice.

"Well, well," exclaimed Lance as he faced the scout. "Sure nice to have you back with us."

"Does seem as though I've been away," grinned Turley, rubbing his chin. "Been thinking a lot."

"Dreaming is a better word for it," chuckled Lance.

Utter silence mastered the area suddenly, for somewhere out in the darkness the forlorn cry of a lobo wolf penetrated the stillness. Drum looked at Lance with a frown. His expression was that of uncertainty as he waited for the scout to make some remark concerning the howl.

He barely had time to give his patience a try, for Lance said, "That one isn't wearing feathers, Captain. We can go about our business."

The early morning dawn brightened the cloudless sky as it crept up lazily over the horizon. A bob cat, perched on a limb of an oak tree nearly hidden from view by the trunk, peered cautiously at the human disturbance that had awakened him a bit too early for him to appreciate his morning snack. Apparently, the feline had no desire to press his curiosity, for the nearness of the common enemy was a bit too close for comfort. He descended slowly to within several yards of the base of the tree, then sprang to the ground with all the grace and sure footedness of a thoroughbred of the wilds that he was. The animal stopped dead in his tracks. His body was tense and in a crouch-like position as if ready for a quick take off. He turned his head in the direction of the awakened camp, stared blankly for a moment, than beat a hasty retreat to some distant lair.

Within the second hour of daylight, the patrol reached the foot of the ravine. Drum lost no time informing his men of the temporary change in plans. They had little time to ponder over the dangers that may be encountered by a split force, for Drum was already forming three groups, the matter diverting unpleasant thoughts which were surely running through the minds of the men.

"Stenton, you will take your men through the ravine."

"Turley, you will take your patrol and cross over the range at about the center. We'll decide on the exact spot as we ride on up the valley."

"The rest of us are going to circle the range at the far end, using the same trail on which we blew up the rifle wagons. Our meeting point will be Big Bear's camp. Should all of us meet with a bit of luck, we should make it before sundown. Any questions?"

There were none, and after a brief silence, Drum spoke again. "All Right, Stenton, keep a sharp look and don't take any unnecessary chances. Lots of luck."

"Thank you, sir." With a sharp salute to his superior, Stenton rode to the front of his men and waved them on as he headed into the ravine. Turning in his saddle, he glanced back and raised his hand in farewell, the gesture being returned by the remaining patrol.

Moments later, the journey up the valley continued. The morning was calm and peaceful. Mother Nature was certainly at her best in displaying the glorious beauty that existed in the land of her creations, which forever offer, among other things, mystery and intrigue.

Most of the riders rode in silence and seemed to be lost in thought, for the day was yet cool and refreshing and they took advantage of the pleasantries while they were available. How well they knew that at any moment the smile on Mother Nature's face could fade away at the sudden approach of violence thundering in maddened frenzy, for this was the frontier, the land of the lurking enemy: the red man.

At the head of the patrol, thoughts were expressed verbally. The topic of conversation varied and on one occasion Drum remarked, "Wonder how Dawson is making out at the river."

"Should be getting a good rest for himself," said Lance.

"And spitting that tobacco juice all over the river," added Turley. "I bet many a fish left their happy home and beat it in the opposite direction when he got near the waters. He sprays more of that stuff around than any six men I know. Must have a reserve tank hidden under his coat somewhere."

Turley's amusing remarks drew chuckles from the others as he continued the subject of the old scout's vice. "Did he ever tell you the one about the rattler that was coiled within a few feet of him when he got up one morning and caused the snake to retreat into the brush after splattering its face with a mouthful of tobacco juice?"

"I'm inclined to believe that," laughed Drum. "I've noticed on occasions that there is always some kind of a target at the other end of the stream. I have yet to see him miss."

"This one I've seen myself," said Turley again. "He spat at a squirrel that sat on a log about ten feet from him and caught the animal square in the face. The poor creature toppled off backwards then started to dash around every which way like a half crazed fox."

The amusing conversation ended with laughter as the riders were forced to ride single file through a narrow opening among the large boulders that infested the immediate area.

A short time later, Lance pointed to a low spot in the mountain, saying, "About there would be the best for Turley and the boys to cross over, Captain."

Drum nodded his head in approval, his eyes still scanning the area mentioned.

Shortly, he addressed Turley saying, "You'll be on your own until we get to Big Bear's camp. Anything else you'd like to know before you start on over?"

"Guess not, Captain. Got everything down pat."

"Well then, you can cut in here anywhere now. Lot of luck to you and the men."

"Thanks, Captain," said Turley and pulled his mount over to one side, whereupon he called out to his men. "Those of you who have been assigned to the second patrol, fall out."

He looked over the riders as they gathered around him, and the usual grin that he wore widened slightly as he addressed them. "The second patrol may well go down in the pages of history, for in a moment we will continue where the Lewis and Clark expedition left off."

Drum and Lance eyed each other with a chuckle while Turley's men seemed to be amused by the remark, that is, by those that knew something about the two explorers. Turley's grin was still wide as he glanced at Drum and Lance saying, "We'll be seeing you."

"Don't forget to duck low," said Lance.

"I won't," replied Turley, and with the wave of his hand was off on the assigned mission. One of Turley's men, an old veteran military man with a drooping mustache, was still scratching his head as he rode up to Drum.

"Pardon me, Captain Drum, sir, but this here feller Turkey is plumb loco about this bein' the place where Lewis and Clark left off. Why, I have a book back at the fort about those two men and it don't mention anything about this place at all." The old military man leaned forward in his saddle, stroked his mustache slightly, and with squinted eyes remarked in low tones, "Captain, sir, do you think this man Turkey can lead us over these hills without gettin our selves lost? Why, right now the boy thinks he is where he ain't."

Drum found it difficult to hold back a chuckle, and before he could answer, Lance leaned forward and said in low tones, "I'm sort of glad you're going along with that patrol; you can sort of keep him in line should he stray in one direction too much."

"Oh, and one more thing, he gets awful mad when people don't call him by his right name. His name is Turley, not Turkey."

"Thanks, Mr. Winster, I'll remember that."

At this point, Drum put his gloved hand up over his mouth in aid of holding back a laugh. Lance was more successful. Although he was amused immensely, the scout managed to hold his original expression.

"Well," said the old military man as he straightened up in the saddle, "This is where Mr. Lewis is a gonna straighten out Mr. Clark as to his whereabouts 'afore he leads us right plumb into some Indian village."

With a sharp salute to his superior, he dug his spurs into the animal's flank and galloped toward the rear of the disappearing patrol.

Although the incident was amusing, they both felt a sense of respect as they watched the oldster ride away.

"Don't recall hearing much of his voice 'til now," said Lance without turning his head.

"He is rather quiet," remarked Drum. "Seems to be lost in thought most of the time."

"I've often wondered, when I'd spot him sitting with his back against a tree and smoking that forever lit pipe of his, if it could be his past that he relives during his periods of relaxation."

"Probably," said Lance. "He's come a long way. Must be nearing his sixties."

"I imagine he could tell many a stories of his escapades," said Drum. "As a matter of fact, between him and Dawson, we could be kept entertained for a month of Sundays."

"I'm inclined to agree with you there, Captain," laughed Lance as his thoughts recalled some of the tall ones that he heard the old scout relate.

Hours later, the patrol pulled up to a stream that trickled invitingly under the heat of the noonday sun. The morning went without incident; however, caution was forever present in the land of the Big Horn. The scanning eyes of the men forever roamed around the immediate area. They never relaxed to the point where caution was disregarded completely. Lance dunked his head into the water several times then sat upright letting the trickling water run over his neck and on down to his shoulders. He whipped out a large handkerchief and began to dab it about his head. Upon noticing Drum staring out over the mountains, he asked, "Going to join me in some of this mountain dew, Captain? It certainly is at its best today."

It seemed as though Drum was on the verge of doing just that for he turned his head at the sound of Lance's voice and advanced toward the latter. He smiled slightly, saying, "I could think of nothing better that would blend in with my thoughts at the moment."

Drum sat down beside Lance and hesitated for a moment before dunking his head in the cool of the stream. He cupped a handful of water, then let it trickle through his fingers slowly. The smile still creased his lips and he spoke rather reminiscently. "Sweet, cool and refreshing."

"I sort of sensed that," said Lance, his eyes twinkling with a bit of amusement as he watched the other stare blankly at him for a moment, then submerge his head slowly into the water.

Drum knew that Lance had read his thoughts and at the moment was a little embarrassed, for he was wondering now just how foolish his facial expression was at the time, or how obvious. His head came up out of the stream and he snapped it back and forth several times throwing off some of the water.

Without looking at Lance he asked, "You sensed what?"

"Well," said Lance whose amusement grew as he realized the captain's shyness, "it couldn't have been anything west of the river that occupied your mind."

"Why not?" asked Drum from underneath a large scarf-like handkerchief he was using to dry his face and head.

"For one thing, you were without the usual frown. Your face seemed relaxed and sort of lit up. Should I go on?" continued Lance with a grin.

"No, I feel foolish enough at this point," answered Drum.

"I don't see why," said Lance without a smile now. "You've seen me with that expression more than once."

They eyed each other understandingly for a moment, then Drum slapped Lance on the shoulder and said as he stood up, "Let's get going or we'll be late for supper at Big Bear's camp."

Lance hesitated for a moment and called out, "Captain."

Drum turned around and faced the scout who was still in a sitting position, from which he asked, "What's her name?"

Lance wondered at the moment if he had gone too far by pressing the subject that his friend seemed rather reluctant to talk about, as the latter stared down at him with a blank expression. Lance began to get to his feet and felt a bit relieved as he noticed a smile appear on Drum's lips. In any event, Lance thought that an apology was due for pressing a subject that the other should have if it were to be talked of at all.

"Captain, I'm sorry if I . . ."

Drum cut in on Lance's attempted apology saying, "Her name is Diana, she lives in Boston and she's waiting. And you were right; my thoughts were east of the Big Horn. Now then, want to hear the whole story? I'd like to talk about it."

Lance knew that Drum felt like a little boy who was eager to reveal his most cherished secrets but had to find first someone who would sincerely share his emotions.

"Captain, you've got an ardent listener."

"All right," said Drum. "We'll move out and I'll take you on an eastern excursion as we ride along."

"I'm your passenger," laughed Lance as they walked toward their mounts. Minutes later the patrol moved out.

Although the conversation between Lance and Captain Drum pertained to the east, in reality, they and the patrol headed west.

XIX

Many miles had been covered since their last stop and the most recent ones in near silence. The lack of conversation within the past half hour or so was undoubtedly credited to the specks observed high up in the sky. They seemed to be swaying back and forth lazily and at intervals sweeping around in a large circle. The progress of the flying specks was deliberately slow.

For some time now Lance was aware of the fact that Drum sighted the birds, but the military man held his silence, perhaps for the same reason as his, hoping that the birds would discontinue their present course and fly off in another direction, before mentioning the fact.

It was a known fact that when those birds were around, something had already happened or was going to happen, and after the occurrence, the birds were known to cash in on the remnants.

Lance wondered at the moment as he glanced at the frowning Drum, who was staring rather than watching the high flying birds, if the military man's conscience was bothering him because of his decision which brought about the three way split of the patrol. Although they expected little resistance, if any, on their way to Big Bear's camp, the unexpected still lingered in the minds of the men, especially Drum's, for it was obvious now that he was riding along with a troubled mind.

On one occasion Drum dug into his pockets and took out a cigarette that was partially smoked some time in the past and applied it to his lips. He lit it and inhaled deeply. Letting out a stream of smoke, he kept his eyes on the trail ahead and remarked casually, which was indeed quite contrary to his feelings. "Large birds, those vultures?"

"Yeah," said Lance with equal calmness.

They both glanced upward automatically and after a moment, Drum continued, "Won't be long before they'll be directly above us. Do you think they're on a routine flight?"

"Well," said Lance with the lack of optimism, "they seem to be on a set course."

"In that case," said Drum, "they might be expecting something that might end up in their favor."

"I think that they've already seen it, Captain," said Lance as he turned his head facing Drum who looked at him questioningly. "Could be following a wounded animal."

Drum looked straight ahead searching the area, as if in hope of spotting something that might throw a light on the vulture's objective. After a brief silence he uttered his fears that materialized rapidly since first detecting the vultures. "I've been thinking about our patrols back there. May have run into trouble, Lance."

It was quite obvious to Lance that the presence of the birds had exaggerated the captain's fears and decided to caution the military man of their near unimportance, for at the moment he felt that Drum was contemplating on the idea of back tracking in pursuit of his two patrols, thus defeating the purpose.

"Captain, don't let those critters there throw you off balance. After all they're in such flights every day and not always ending up with their bellies full. I could be wrong about them following anything, you know."

Drum glanced at Lance and let out a deep sigh at the same time pulling on the reins bringing his mount to a halt.

Lance wondered at the moment if the time had come whereupon he would have to object, bitterly if necessary, to any reverse decision that the captain may have on his mind, for the territory up ahead to Big Bear's camp must be cleared. That was the plan, the purpose, and there was no other way.

He was aware of the fact that the captain was on the spot because of the split patrol and was quite concerned over the safety of his men, but he knew, as well as Drum did at the time of his decision, what existed of the possible consequences. Lance was in the process of making a cigarette and spoke without looking at Drum. "Are you thinking about back tracking in search of the other patrols?"

Drum showed no surprise that the other was aware of his thoughts and remarked, "You certainly can read minds. I'd hate to plot against you. It would be a lost cause from the very beginning."

"It would be a lost cause not to continue as planned," remarked Lance presenting his question in another manner.

"Or turn out to be a military blunder on the part of Captain Drum," said Drum rather thoughtfully.

Lance eased out a sigh of relief for any possible disagreement concerning the matter was eliminated with the military man's last remark.

Drum frowned as he looked toward the sky again, saying, "Can't explain why those creatures should make me jittery. They're almost over head now." He dropped his gaze and turned toward the scout saying, "We'll stop here for a while and rest up. After those birds fly over, I, for one, will forget about them."

"They certainly seem to have quite an affect on you today," said Lance dismounting.

"I think it would be safe to say that they stirred your thoughts to a certain extent," said Drum whose lips were parted in a smile for the first time since the vultures appeared on the scene.

"After all, Captain," said Lance with a bit of humor, "my responsibilities include you, too."

Drum was about to carry on the conversation but held back whatever he was about to say for he noticed the smile on the scout's face slowly fade away as the latter cocked his head slightly and listened, his eyes being focused on the dense trail ahead. The captain motioned to his men for complete silence then turned his attention toward Lance's piercing gaze.

The incident added to his already troubled mind, and the anxiety that engulfed him at the moment hastened his impatience to the extent of disturbing the still-wary scout who stood there in a slight crouch as if expecting something to bolt at them from the thick of the greens.

"Did you hear something," asked Drum in a whisper.

"Thought I did," replied Lance thoughtfully, his stare remaining transfixed.

Once again Drum listened intensively, but after a short pause detected nothing and his voice came in a whisper again. "What did it sound like, could you make it out?"

"Kind of a sound a horse would make when stepping on rock," answered Lance in low tones.

Whatever Drum was about to say, Lance cut short as he thrust his hand upward indicating silence. The military man snapped his head around and held his breath as he stared again in the direction that had held their attention within the past few minutes, for his ears had picked up the type of sound that the scout had described but a moment before.

The clanking of metal against rock came at intervals and became more distinctive as the unknown came nearer to the dead silent patrol.

"The animal is in no hurry," remarked Lance in low tones.

"Or the rider, if it has one," put in Drum quickly.

"We'd better get into hiding," said Lance as he glanced about swiftly. "Have your men scatter on both sides of the trail."

Drum lost no time in issuing orders, and in a short time, the trail that was alive with men and horses looked still and deserted. Tense men, ready for battle, lay concealed behind boulders, trees and brush in waiting as the slowly prodding animal made its way toward the ambush. The troubled look on Lance's face took on the expression of curiosity as he caught glimpses of the oncoming approach.

"Over there," said Lance pointing a finger in the direction. "There's a rider on that animal."

Drum spied the intruders, and after closer observation remarked, "He's sure slumped forward in that saddle."

"I've noticed that," said Lance. "Must be hurt or sick."

"We'll wait until he pulls up into the clearing ahead of us and then jump him."

Drum agreed to the idea with the nod of his head. The tension that held the men taut seemed to have diminished to a certain degree, for it became obvious that the rider was alone. Moments later they appeared in full view, and the animal stopped as if commanded upon hearing Lance's voice.

"Hold it, fellow." The animal seemed unconcerned as it stared blankly at Lance and Drum who were advancing out of the thicket cautiously with their rifles at hip level, cocked and ready. The animal was caked with dust and looked tired and haggard. The rider was motionless and held the original position, slumped forward in the saddle. The wide brim of the hat he wore covered his face and he too carried his share of dust and mud.

"Keep me covered from here," said Lance, "and be careful, this boy may be playing possum and suddenly spring into action."

Lance advanced cautiously calling out again to the unsociable rider, "You hurt fella?"

Upon closer observation he noticed for the first time the blood splattered shirt that was unnoticeable from a distance because of the mud and dust that clung to it, and called out to Drum, "Captain."

The animal moved for the first time since coming to a halt, backing away a few paces, and during the slight shuffle the rider slid slowly out of the saddle and fell face down to the ground causing a cloud of dust to shoot upward. Lance made an attempt to catch the falling man but was unable to reach him in time and at the moment stood over the silent form, motionless as he stared down at a broken arrow, its sharp head driven deep into the victim's shoulder.

Drum raced over and helped Lance lift the limp form to a sitting position. Although the man's face was caked with dried blood and dust he was immediately recognized.

"One of the gunrunners," said Lance without showing any surprise. The wounded man showed signs of consciousness for the first time as his parched lips moved feebly in a broken whisper, "Water."

His heavy breathing stopped momentarily as the scout applied the spout of his canteen to the thirst-riddled lips. The victim's eyes opened slowly and wandered from one man to another, but gave no sign of recognition. He wet his mouth with a feverish tongue and attempted to utter something but was interrupted by a series of coughs. The pain that he was enduring at the moment was well indicated by the twisted facial expression. In addition to the arrow wound, a deep slash across the face had added to his grief.

After quieting down, Lance spoke to the gunrunner, asking him, "What happened?"

Between deep breaths, the answer came brokenly. "White Cloud mad I failed to . . . "

He broke off with another series of coughs then settled back against Lance's arm. After a moment, he continued, "Failed to deliver guns." At this point, the gunrunner's eyes lingered on Lance, and the scout wondered if the man was cursing him and the military under his breath for interfering with his business a night or so ago, or if he was searching Lance's face for some sign of pardon for his intended illegal weapon transactions.

As he spoke again, the answer seemed to justify the latter. "I'm glad they didn't get them."

"Have you brought loads of guns up here previously?" asked Lance.

"No," he answered. "But my boss did."

Lance and Drum eyed each other for a moment then the scout asked, "Was his name Barton?"

The gunrunner glanced at the men knowingly, for the mention of his boss' name made it obvious that these men probably knew of his whereabouts. He asked, "Do you know where . . . "

Lance cut in at this point, for he was aware of the forthcoming question. "He's dead, and so are the men that were with him."

If the man showed any surprise it was hidden within the pain wrinkled face. On the other hand he already knew that something was amiss because of his failure to make connections with his former boss since arriving here in the Big Horn. His heavy breathing was uneven now and he closed his eyes as if to shut out any additional pain.

"Let's get him over to a softer spot," said Lance quickly. "I'm going to cut the arrow out of his shoulder. He may be able to hang on a little while longer and it'll lessen the pain.

They carried him over to a layer of leaves and laid the wounded man on his stomach.

"Tear the shirt away from the wound," said Lance as he whipped his knife from its sheath. "I'll try to sterilize this blade a bit."

"He's not going to last much longer," remarked Drum, who winced at the sight of the ugly wound as he tore away the blood-drenched shirt. "As a matter of fact I don't see how he made it this far. I don't think he has any more blood left to lose."

The wounded man began to utter something in a near whisper, which Drum was unable to make out. The military man bent down low and placed his ear near the feeble moving lips in an attempt to make out whatever was being said. Lance, who was down on one knee holding a burning twig under the point of the knife a short distance away, noticed Drum's action and asked quickly, "What is it, Captain?"

He didn't answer right away and his position remained the same for a few moments longer before he drew back slightly and took a hold of the renegade's wrist. Finally he looked at Lance, saying, "He kept repeating, *big Indian tribes*."

Lance sprang to his feet with the original intent of performing an operation that had confronted him on occasions before, but advanced no farther as Drum pointed to the knife saying, "You won't be needing that Doc; he's dead."

Lance pressed his lips together and stared at the dead man thoughtfully for a few moments, then remarked, "He was probably trying to tell us of the gathering of the tribes, a fact that we already know of, however, there were questions in my mind that I'm sure he could have answered."

Lance inhaled deeply and let out a sigh that was well tinted with disappointment, and walked over to the deceased, whereupon observing the motionless form more closely, agreed silently to himself that the captain had made no mistake.

"Well," said Lance as he looked around for a likely burial spot. "He's the last of the gunrunning outfit, or at least of the ones we know of up here."

Drum nodded his head in agreement then remarked thoughtfully. "It seems to me that one's days are numbered when dealing with the Sioux. I was thinking about the trappers who brought Naomi up here. They didn't fail, but they died anyway."

At the mention of his wife, Lance gazed eastward for a long moment and wondered when he would see her again, if he would be lucky enough to get back. Quickly, he discarded the unpleasant thought of not returning to her by continuing the conversation with Drum. "There are some who use diplomacy and get along in their dealings with the Indian for a while. Then when things have reached their peak they pull out, but this fella here and the trappers, they were dealing with a mad man unfortunately. White Cloud."

"Do you think that the guns we blew up were for White Cloud alone?" asked Drum curiously.

"No," said Lance. "He was acting under orders. Probably sent out by Sitting Bull to make contact and convoy the wagon to the village. However, in either case, White Cloud was the executioner."

Lance changed the subject as he got to his feet, saying, "Better have your men dig a shallow grave, Captain."

Drum was on the move before Lance finished and issued orders hastily. Before too many minutes passed, the last stone was placed upon the grave by Lance and again he whipped out the large handkerchief and wiped the sweat and dirt off his hands.

Drum ordered his men to mount and then scanned the skies with a frown, remarking, "Looks like those high flying renegades have gone."

Lance mounted his horse, then looked at Drum and pointed a finger in a direction that the military man was quick to follow. He caught sight of the vultures perched on the dried limbs of a dead tree and remarked, "I didn't see them come down."

"Saw them swoop down a little while back," said Lance.

"Wonder what they're thinking up there now that we've buried their support?"

"I probably could put together their thoughts and express them verbally, Captain," said Lance with a faint grin. "However, being a man with a careful vocabulary I'd rather not exceed my limits."

"I have a good idea," said Drum smiling slightly for the first time since the incident occurred.

"Please, Captain," cautioned Lance amusingly as he raised a finger. "Not out loud." Then he added, "Shall we move out?"

As the head of the patrol was disappearing out of view, Lance, backing up the rear, turned in his saddle and gazed back at the lonely looking grave that would forever be lay beneath the shadows of solitude, and soon to be forgotten by mankind.

Beads of perspiration stood out on his face and his thoughts could have been of an unpleasant nature. He reached up and wiped his face with the sleeve of his coat. The scout's body shuddered for a moment as he took a long last stare and then turned in the saddle facing the forward part of the patrol that led the way through the mountainous green toward the unknown— fatė and destiny.

Time prods along in its leisurely manner, always forward with the same steady pace, but there are many who race against it for countless reasons. Lance Winsor, leading Captain Drum and his military patrol, must have discussed the matter of time along the way, for it was obvious by the look of the sweating and hard breathing mounts, that hard riding had occurred within the past few hours. A minute before, Lance pulled to a stop, halting the patrols as they came upon the large clearing where the attack on the gun wagon took place several nights ago.

At the moment they were staring down at a skeleton of a human being that had not too long ago been molded with living flesh.

It was Drum who spoke first, breaking the silence. "Vultures don't leave anything behind, do they?"

"Nothing but the bones," said Lance. "If they could bite through that, the framework wouldn't be here either."

"Less fortunate then his friend back there," he said, referring to the one he helped bury during the earlier part of the day.

"His scalp should be here," said Drum. "Or at least the hair. I . . . "

Lance cut him short saying, "It'll be hanging, with others like it in White Cloud's tepee. If you're curious about the braves we killed the other night . . . "

Drum cut in this time, saying, "I know, they take the dead back with them and hold some kind of a ceremony that assures them of a safe trip to the happy hunting grounds, or something of the like."

"You know more about Indians than I thought," grinned Lance.

"I studied Indian warfare, the ways of the red man and whatnot before being sent up into this country," said Drum returning the grin. "And I added greatly to my knowledge since knowing you."

"All Right," said Lance, flashing a wide smile. "Today you face the test. When we reach Big Bear's camp, Indian scout Drum will do the pow-wowing."

Drum raised his gloved hand amusingly and remarked amusingly, "How."

Lance chuckled lightly as he glanced at the amused military man for a second, then dug in his heels and urged the mount forward, the others following suit. Shortly the riders disappeared in a cloud of dust.

The heat of day seemed to be following the sun, and in the matter of a few hours, both would be roaming over distant lands leaving the Big Horn country to rest in the cool dark night under the watchful eye of the moon.

XX

High upon the crest of a mountain, the courageous patrol and their mounts stood silhouetted against the blue and gold of the evening sky. From a distance, they appeared motionless as they gazed down at Big Bear's camp in the valley below; however, upon closer observation, it became evident that the lack of movement now was subject to contradiction. Each time a horse would shuffle, or a rider stir in his saddle, a small cloud of dust would puff into the air. If by chance, someone would come upon the horsemen accidentally, their hat would fly into the air without the aid of the elements, for the group certainly could pass as the ghostrider's creepy hollow.

Captain Drum's patrol was in no way presentable for military inspection at the moment and that could have been indeed the farthest from his mind, and probably would be for quite a spell. The scene below had stirred up a mixture of thoughts, and the silence indicated the fact, that each of the men was trying to find a logical answer to account for the change that had taken place at Big Bear's camp since their last visit. The camp was less than half the size in dwellings and inhabitance. Black spots around the area were the remnants of tepees that not too long ago stood erect. Something grave and sinister had occurred recently, which was quite obvious to the viewers.

Drum made no attempt to offer a possible explanation as to his personal opinion concerning the matter, and chose instead to ask the scout for a likely reason to the situation now existing in the valley.

"What do you make or it?"

"It certainly bears the ear marks of a recent battle," said Lance thoughtfully.

"Fighting among themselves at this point don't make sense," said Drum. "Especially Big Bear's tribe. He brought his people to this side of the river to avert . . . "

"I know," said Lance cutting in. "However, he could have been forced in to some kind of a fight."

Lance hesitated for a moment, then glanced at Drum whose forehead was creased with wrinkles as he stared questioningly at the scout. He spoke with a slight uncertainty, for he realized that there were several possibilities as to Big Bear's opponents that waged battle against the peaceful chief.

"White Cloud was in the vicinity. He probably came back this way after we blew up the wagon. No doubt the renegade was raging mad and took it out on the old chief. They were bitter enemies, you know."

Lance became silent again as he cast his glance to the valley below in search of a sign that would prove or disprove the grave possibility that had lingered aggressively in his troubled mind. At the moment, Drum's expression was that of a man whose decision on a certain important matter resulted in catastrophe, for he was aware now of just what the scout was trying to detect: Chief Big Bear's opponents, other than the renegade White Cloud. Reluctantly, his gaze fell to the area below, and after a brief observation, came to the conclusion that he could add nothing to what he had already seen before. He turned toward the scout and remarked rather slowly, "Want me to finish where you left off?"

Lance inhaled deeply and before he could answer one way or another. Drum spoke as if beckoned to do so. "White Cloud and his men over-powered the old chief and his braves, took over the village during his short stay. At least I see no indication down there that could tie in with his band. To cut the story short, the renegade was still in the village when my men rode in unsuspectingly."

Drum hesitated briefly, and then said in conclusion, "If that were the case, I need to say no more."

"Captain," said Lance with a voice tinted with encouragement. "Our thoughts rambled along the same line, but you've noticed that there are no signs of our men down there either."

"They could have been disposed of more ways than one, knowing the Indian and his methods. The point that makes me feel feverish is that both patrols were expected to reach the village several hours ahead of us."

"Our imaginations are running about too loosely," said Lance as he yanked his rifle from its sheath. He examined the weapon closely at the same time remarking, "We'll go on down to the village, won't take long to find answers to some of our questions."

Drum agreed, nodding his head in the affirmative, and then spun his horse around to face the men and quickly issue orders regarding the weapons. Drum rode back to Lance's side in short order and asked, "Any particular approach?"

"Not from this point," answered Lance. "However, when we reach the near edge of the forest, you and I will scout around a bit before riding out in the open. No more was said as Lance urged his mount forward and headed toward a deer trail that wound its way down the side of the mountain. Puffs of dust arose as the others followed suit, and soon, the only sign of life that remained was a rattle snake that laid coiled beneath the rocks, its tongue darting in and out of its mouth as it stared with a pair of cold beady eyes at the disappearing patrol.

A few days ago, Chief Big Bear's camp was alive with activity, but whatever the occurrence since, it left behind traces of grief and disaster. Only the ashes remained of more than half the camp's dwellings, which once housed a full tribe of the Sioux. Teepees and wigwams that had escaped the wrath of fire but disfigured by another source were being mended by some of the members of the tribesmen. A few sat around by themselves staring into space, lost in silent thought. Most of the inhabitants were huddled together at one end of the small wooded area that supplied the only shade for the otherwise barren camp. Their low moans and wails were eerie in tone, and to add to the spine-chilling incident, a brave would tear away from the group, throw his hands into the air, shouting loudly as he danced madly about.

At the edge of the forest, two pairs of eyes were focused on the weird singers whose attraction was near sinister.

It was Drum again who broke the silence. “A man alone could die of fright listening to that singing. What is the occasion?”

“It’s a ritual,” answered Lance soberly.

“It wouldn’t grieve me none if White Cloud was among the deceased,” remarked Drum.

“I doubt that he is,” said Lance. “Got the luck of a cat.”

The scout changed the subject, remarking, “Lets ride on in, don’t seem to be any one around dressed for battle.”

“There sure don’t,” agreed Drum as he cast a glance over his shoulder and proceeded to follow the scout, who was already on his way back to where the patrol was in waiting.

In short order, the patrol was in motion, and riding parallel with the edge of the forest. Lance stood up in his stirrups looking for an area through which he could lead the men and animals without too much difficulty. He sat back in his saddle and his body tensed along with the slight pull on the reins. His head remained in a forward position, but his eyes roamed the area in front of him, to the left then to the right. Lance Winsor wasn’t looking for a way out of the dense forest now, for his sense of danger had been aroused to the extent of sheer caution, and it became quite obvious as he slackened the pace to a near halt.

Drum tugged on his reins rather tightly, causing the animal to prance about nervously. He tried to check the animal, patting it on the neck, at the same time calling out to Lance in a whisper, “What is it Winsor?”

“Somebody else in these woods besides us, Captain,” remarked Lance without turning his head. “Excellent spot for an amb . . . ”

The word died on his lips with the sudden appearance of a death dealing lance that sped across the trail and embedding its sharp blade in a tree to his left. Lance’s horse reared high up on its hind legs and backed into Drum’s mount roughly, near knocking the military man to the ground.

Rifles appeared with the speed of lightning and just as fast a command, shouted by Lance, "Hold your fire."

Drum looked bewildered as he flashed a glance at the scout whose piercing eyes were trying to detect the hidden menace as he struggled to get his prancing animal under control. He looked wildly about, but the hissing arrows that he had expected to come tearing out at them failed to materialize, and the only weapon that had been exposed by the enemy was the menacing lance that still vibrated slightly as it protruded across the trail in defiance.

Lance quickly clarified the situation to the extent whereupon nervous trigger fingers relaxed slightly, for it was imperative that they show no resistance.

"It's a warning to hold on, Captain. They could have pinned me to that tree if they wanted to."

Their eyes searched the dense growth for some sign for the welcoming committee and it was obvious that caution was exercised to the hilt when Drum remarked, "They're not in too much of a hurry."

"They'll show soon, Captain," said Lance, then added, "It'll probably be an invitation to supper."

"I rather we dine alone tonight," said Drum without the usual mirth.

"Hold it," whispered Lance under his breath as he raised his hand slightly, for he had noticed the outline of a brave advancing toward them as the latter circled a growth of laurel about twenty yards distant. With each step, the features of the brave became more distinctive, and only when he stepped into full view it became obvious that he bore no weapons. Walking to within several yards of the rugged-looking patrol, he stopped and eyed them curiously for a long moment then reached over, taking hold of the lance and yanked the weapon from the tree.

"Talkative fellow, isn't he," said Drum from the corner of his mouth. "Must have forgotten his speech."

Lance made no comment. Instead he spoke to the brave, saying, "Big Bear our friend. Big Bear's people our friend."

The brave made no reply, but instead, motioned to Lance to follow him. He turned in his tracks with a backward glance and proceeded forward. Lance beckoned to Drum with a motion of his hand, at the same time urging his mount into motion.

"Trusting fellow," remarked Drum as he placed his hat covering a mop of disheveled hair.

"No doubt he recognized us as the ones that had visited the camp recently, however, he's much more cautious than you think, Captain. If all the arrows that are being pointed at us at this moment were released, we would contain more holes than there are in a soup strainer."

Drum's eyes shifted from side to side in search of other members of the welcoming committee, but it was in vain. He remarked more to himself, "I'm learning the finer points on how to stay alive as we go along."

Lance grinned slightly as he looked back over his shoulder at Drum, saying, "You're well on your way in getting that diploma when this is all over."

"I must double my homework," remarked Drum. "Or I may not be on hand when they hand them out."

Lance chuckled as he resumed his original position in the saddle and the remainder of the trip to the edge of the woods was made without further conversation.

Once out in the open, the brave gave a backward glance without slowing his pace, and continued up in the direction of the tepees. Work stopped as if by command with the appearance of the patrol. A few of the inhabitants began to move in the direction in which they were riding. Others stared blankly for a time, then continued with their tasks. Drum noticed the lack of enthusiasm and expressed his thoughts verbally. "They don't seem to be too concerned with our presence."

"We've lost our drawing power, Captain. However, we still have a few followers. Take a look over your shoulder."

Drum's eyebrows moved upward along with curiosity as he turned in the saddle and felt the blood rush to his ears upon seeing several dozed braves in slow pursuit. The military man's surprised features amused the scout, but he managed to keep a sober face. Drum's glance was brief, and he spoke rather casually, which was quite contrary to the surprised expression that still lingered, saying, "Must be twenty five or thirty of them. Could it be that we're slipping, walking into something like that?" Then as an afterthought, he added, "Are you sure you received your diploma, Winsor?"

The remark tickled the scout to the extent of a wide smile. Even under the circumstances Drum managed a bit of humor, though Lance knew well that the captain's mind was grinding with anxiety as to the whereabouts of his overdue patrols, and knew too, that shortly, he may be informed concerning the fate of his men, which would enlighten his very being or leave a scar that would remain with him 'til the end of his days.

"Captain," said Lance as he cast the unpleasant thought from his mind. "We haven't thrown caution to the wind. An ambush is a difficult thing to detect." The conversation ceased automatically upon noticing several braves appear at the entrance of a large tepee. One of them wore the attire of a chief. Moments later Lance broke the short silence saying, "Looks like they changed chiefs along with the scenery. Or else Big Bear went on a drastic diet since we've seen him last."

Drum glanced at the scout briefly, then cast his attention at the one that seemed to be the new head of the camp.

The brave that led the patrol into camp stopped within a few yards of the chief, spoke a few words, then watched with the others as the visitors pulled to a stop. Only then did Lance recognize that the brave under the feathers was Big Bear's son.

The scout raised his hand in greeting, the gesture being returned by the chief.

It was he who spoke first, saying, "My father's friend, my friend."

Lance was on the verge of asking a question concerning the whereabouts of the old chief but refrained from doing so, as the new head of the tribe raised his hand and pointed toward the mourning tribe-men and spoke with concern. "Chief Big Bear . . . go . . . to happy ground."

Lance and Drum eyed each other as it came to light that the peaceful chief was among the dead. Lance dismounted and strode over to the young chief, placing a hand on the latter's shoulders saying, "I'm sorry about your father, Deer Foot. He was a great chief."

Lance's features indicated sincere sadness, for the old chief had always treated him with respect. Lance waited in anxiety for the other to continue and all indications were that he would, which in turn would probably clear up more of the remaining unanswered questions. The scout waited for the chief to have his say before asking directly anything that went unanswered. The stone-like features of the young brave took on an added hardness as he faced Lance and remarked, "White Cloud will die." He swung his arm in an arc indicating the area of the camp and continued with bitterness. "When moon . . . high . . . White Cloud come. Want braves from Big Bear tribe . . . want many pony. Big Bear mad . . . no give. White Cloud start fight. Kill many braves . . . burn tepee . . . take many pony."

He hesitated briefly, then added, "Kill . . . my father."

A series of chills swept up and down Lance's spine as it occurred to him that the renegade may have sneaked by the patrols in an attempt to take another crack at the settlers. His lips moved, pronouncing a name so softly, that he himself couldn't hear. "Naomi."

"Where White Cloud go from here?" asked Lance, whose voice near died out at the end of the question, like someone realizing that he erred in doing asking it.

The chief turned slowly and pointed out over the western horizon, and he remarked, "Soon . . . Deer Foot find trail . . . Deer Foot kill White Cloud before many moon."

Lance's frame relaxed noticeably upon being informed of the renegade's whereabouts, but he was rather doubtful as to the young chief's intention to track down and do away with the cunning Sioux chief. Lance changed the subject as the impatient Drum dismounted and walked to his side.

"Chief, did you . . . "

Lance got no farther with whatever he wanted to say, as one of the braves spoke suddenly to the chief and pointed toward a small cloud of dust about a mile from camp.

Drum looked at Lance with a tint of hope, and they both turned their attention to the chief, who remarked, “Braves come. We go see.” With the wave of a hand he beckoned them to follow.

“The boys out there are riding kind a hard,” remarked Lance. “Must be on to something.”

Drum waited with apprehension for the scout to make some verbal comment as to what the oncoming riders may have encountered, but the latter remained silent. As did the military man, for his mind was churning with troubled thoughts and chose not to press the issue until facts, not opinions, were finally known.

Tense bodies and anxious faces braced themselves as the riders rode up in a cloud of dust, for it was obvious that something other than the noisy crows flying above was in the air. One of the braves sprang off his pony while the animal was still in motion, glanced briefly at the patrol, and then spoke to the chief excitedly in the Sioux dialect.

Drum snapped his head around, facing Lance with anticipation, for the latter spoke and understood the dialect to a certain extent, and noticed a slight smile appear on the scout’s lips at the same time noticing the scout reach into his pocket and come up with the familiar tobacco pouch.

“What did he say?” asked Drum in a steady voice that lacked obvious anxiety, for Lance’s action indicated the fact that the brave’s statement was in their favor.

“He told the chief that other soldiers are coming this way.”

Lance watched the creases on Drum’s face disappear and the corners of his mouth lift slightly. The joy that they felt at the moment was expressed in silence as the two men eyed each other. Drum reached into his pocket casually and came up with two previously rolled cigarettes. One of them he offered to Lance, saying, “You needn’t bother making one, Winsor. Have one on the captain.”

“Thanks,” said Lance placing the cigarette between his lips and accepting the light that Drum held with an extended hand.

The brave drew the attention of the men as he raised an arm, pointing in one direction, then another.

"Can you make out what he is referring to?" asked Drum, as he watched the Indian curiously.

"Something about smoke signals on the other side of the river," answered Lance, and he changed the subject at hand, for in the distance, another dust cloud appeared that caught his attention.

"Take a look out there, Captain. Should be your men."

The chief verified the fact as he turned toward the men saying, "Soldiers come."

Lance and Drum both agreed by nodding their heads in the affirmative, then focused their attention on the distant riders.

Drum stroked his chin slowly and the sparks in his eyes indicated amusement, credited to the third rider in lead of the patrol, which was bearing down on them at a causal pace.

Lance also recognized the third rider who rode in between Turley and Stenton. It was the old man, Harper. From the corner of his eye, he noticed the captain trying to keep a grin from waning into a smile, whereupon he remarked, "Seems to me that you put two men in charge of the patrols a while back, Captain. Darn if it don't look like three of them leading the way out there."

Drum faced the chuckling scout, saying, "Could be that Mr. Lewis straightened out Mr. Clark and ended up with some kind of a promotion."

Any further thoughts concerning the amusing incident went unsaid and the men waited in silence as the overdue patrol finally pulled to a halt in orderly fashion.

Turley and Stenton dismounted, the latter faced his superior with a salute. Then reported saying, "Speaking in behalf of Mr. Turley and myself sir, I wish to report that all men are present and accounted for."

"That's good news indeed, sergeant. We were quite concerned."

"Well sir, we did a bit of checking our way in and got a glimpse of a band of . . . of the opposition as they high tailed it toward the river."

Stenton's choice in describing the enemy was obvious as he glanced at the unfamiliar face of the chief.

"What prompted the additional scouting?" asked Drum curiously.

"Smoke signals, sir."

An angry voice filled with bitterness caused the discussion to end briefly as heads turned in the direction from which it came. "White Cloud."

Chief Deer Foot's expression matched the tone of his voice as he uttered the name of the renegade, but added no more to the sudden outburst as he stared out over the valley in silent thought.

Turley looked at Lance questioningly, the latter aware of the fact that the returning scout had observed the changes that had taken place, including the strange chief, and said quickly, "I'll tell you. There's been some changes since you've been here last. I'll tell you about later."

Beckoning to Stenton he urged, "As you were saying, sergeant." Stenton's curiosity was already in high gear but he managed to continue the subject without any explanation concerning the noticeable changes. "Well, that's about it, with the exception of three or four more smoke signals at various points across the river."

"Don't sound so good," remarked Drum, looking at Lance.

The military man gazed thoughtfully over the horizon for a moment and then asked, "Do you think they're pushing back toward the river?"

Lance hesitated in answering immediately, and asked a question directed at Turley instead. "How far in would you say those signals were?"

"I judged them to be near the vicinity of Sitting Bull's village," came the quick reply.

Lance faced Drum once more and answered the delayed question. "If they were to change their base of operations, Captain, I hardly think that it would be in an easterly direction. I'm certain that it would be the opposite. They would rather wage warfare in a territory unfamiliar to the enemy."

Drum made no comment regarding the issue, deliberately avoiding any further discussion because of the presence of the chief and his braves. Friendly or otherwise, his trust in the red man was limited.

"Well," remarked Drum as he glanced about. "We can reopen the session later. Right now we ought to get situated and cleaned up a bit."

"Your suggestion will cause no resistance, Captain," said Lance agreeably. He faced Turley, slapping him on the shoulder, causing the dust to fly in all directions, whereupon he remarked after a chuckle, "You need a bath, fella."

"I'm quite used to it now," laughed Turley. "I've spent half my time in water since meeting up with you. And near drowned on some of the occasions."

The grin on Lance's mouth remained as he spoke to Drum saying, "The open area just beyond the chief's tepee will do for tonight, Captain. Have the men move up there while we have a few words with the chief here."

"Mind if I join the counsel?" asked Turley with a grin.

"Well," said Lance amusingly, "it all depends on what you can offer as proof on your background of education concerning the rugged western frontier."

Turley's eyes flashed and the grin he usually wore widened as his right hand slid slowly to the handle of his knife. His fingers slowly encircled the butt end of the weapon, letting them rest there. Lance dropped his eyes briefly to Turley's side, the latter's hand still resting on the knife butt, and remarked as he looked upward again, "Yeah, well, you need show no other references."

They both chuckled lightly. Drum, who took in the amusing incident, smiled broadly as the scouts turned their attention to him, where upon he glanced at one, then the other, before remarking, "I'll be with you in a few moments gentlemen."

Walking over to Stenton, he gave a few orders.

In short order, the patrol rode in the direction of their campsite. The smooth and gentle south wind seemed to caress the scars, as it flowed softly over the wounded Indian camp. The large June moon, orange in color, added its lustrous light to the blazing campfires below. Guards, made up of military personnel, lurked in the shadows overlooking the village as they stood their posts in silent thought. Though the evening was in its infancy, the greater part of the weary patrol had departed to the wonderlands of slumber.

Near the patch of pines where the ritual had taken place, a bright fire cast its light exposing the scaffolds that held the remains of the departed. A solitary figure, with his arms folded across his chest, was motionless as he stood there staring up at one of them.

Flickering shadows danced across the painted face, revealing an expression that betrayed none of his inner emotions. Vows of revenge could have been running through his mind at the moment, for Chief Deer Foot was paying his last respects to his father before leaving to follow the trail of the renegade White Cloud, who had so ruthlessly plundered the camp, and among others, fatally wounded the philosopher of wisdom, Chief Big Bear.

At another fire, the dance of revenge was taking place. The medicine man was a gruesome figure as he pounced about the dancers in his mood of mythical creations.

There were those who sat around another campfire and would shudder occasionally, as the eerie moans of the singers floated by them like a menacing threat before a sharpened blade is plunged, snuffing out the life of an intended victim.

Half a dozen men of the patrol sat around a small blaze in Indian fashion. Conversation in low tones had been flowing freely in regard to the campaign that was scheduled to enter a new phase during the early hours of the following day. At the moment, their attention was focused on the solitary figure that stood erect, with folded arms, looking up at one of the scaffolds bearing the body of Chief Big Bear.

Whatever thoughts roamed the minds of the men was expressed verbally first by Drum, who remarked casually, "Wonder what his chances are in fulfilling the promise he is making at the moment."

Turley's answer was voluntary, and he spoke rather slowly as if weighing his opinion with each word that he uttered. "I would say, that his chances of riding in an easterly direction again are mighty slim. But a lot depends on how ruthless a method he would expose himself to."

"I'm inclined to agree with Turley," said Lance. "Knowing White Cloud the way I do, he wouldn't take the chance of fighting Deer Foot fairly under the circumstances."

The scout's brief hesitation before concluding the sentence caused Drum to become curious as to its actual significance, whereupon he asked, "What circumstances are you referring to?"

Lance sighed heavily, for once again, he knew that the trend of the conversation was slowly leading back to the settler's camp, thus arousing the unpleasant reality that he would carry with him until one day, he or the renegade, would be among the departed. Although he replied in reluctance, the scout showed no outward emotion to that effect.

"White Cloud carries the scars of humiliation. To retain his former prestige with the people he has to live with, the man must redeem himself, and that can be accomplished by defeating the source that had placed him in the category of the shamed."

Lance looked at Drum and noticed the latter's embarrassment due to the fact that he suddenly realized the answer in full at this point. The scout refrained from further continuing the incomplete answer as he remarked in conclusion, "You're familiar with the rest of the story, Captain?"

"Yeah," said Drum as he crushed the remains of a cigarette between his fingers and cast the remains into the embers.

Suddenly a needle like sensation shot through the bodies of the men as a knife flashed gleaming as it sailed over the top of the fire and sank with a thud into a near by log. Harper's pipe fell out of his mouth and he made a quick stab at it as it fell to the ground. Looking up at Stenton, who was now on his feet, the old man remarked rather casually, "Queer time to be practicing, Mr. Stenton. You near took my ear off."

Stenton's grin was sarcastic, for his thoughts still lingered on the previous discussion of White Cloud. The others looked at him questioningly in regard to his strange act and he was quick to comment. "I'm sharing Mr. Winsor's feelings, Mr. Harper. Him and I think alike since our school days."

The old man reached over and pulled the knife out of the log, then tossed it to Stenton saying, "Acting like this, I don't figure you spent much time in school."

"Didn't like classes too much," remarked Stenton laughingly. "For some odd reason it seemed to bruise my skin a lot."

Harper looked curiously at Stenton and Lance as the two men eyed each other smiling. The chilled feeling that had overcome Lance several minutes earlier was slowly being replaced by one far more pleasant as he returned Stenton's warm smile. The understanding between the men was certainly a strange one, for their opinions back at the fort had been quite conflicting.

Turley's voice broke the brief silence, saying, "I think that we are going to be honored by the chief's presence."

All eyes shifted to an outwardly direction, resting on the chief and some braves as they walked toward them. Lance arose, the others following suit. They waited in thoughtful silence for the visitors, whose ashen faces revealed nothing, other than the remorse that was in existence since the raid. As the red men chief to leave his people. Many moons will pass before return of Deer Foot."

The chief motioned to them with his hand and said, "You, my father's friends, you my friends. Always you are welcome to Deer Foot's camp." He turned abruptly and spoke quickly to one of the braves. Facing the others again, the chief glanced about them slowly as if he wanted to remember their faces should their trail cross some time in the future.

Without another word he raised his hand in farewell, turned about face and headed toward the dancers, whose war-like tempo increased with the approach of the chief.

Drum raised the front of his hat and scratched his forehead at the hairline, remarking, "Didn't give us much of a chance to wish him well, did he?"

"Maybe he don't like goodbyes," said Turley with a frown, his eyes still on the chief. Then he added, "It may have been his last."

Lance's gaze was in the same direction and he seemed to be lost in thought as he stood there silently.

Drum disrupted him, however, by directing his remark at the scout who turned quickly, like a little boy caught in an attempt to raid the cookie jar. "Deer Foot may get to White Cloud before you have an opportunity to settle accounts with the renegade yourself."

"Well," said Lance with a sigh, "to avenge his father's death certainly means a great deal to him and I sincerely hope that he is successful. As much as I'd dislike to beat the chief out on that point, I'd grasp the opportunity to tangle with White Cloud again faster than a cougar can jump a deer."

Turley's voice cut in at this point of the conversation as he said slowly, "The hunter will now be the hunted." He looked at Lance, continuing, "Wonder how many moons will rise and fall, how many hunters will go down in the attempt before the enemy's lifeless form is laid to rest under the cool earth of the Big Horn."

Lance understood Turley's remark and shrugged it off with a smile saying, "Under any circumstances, make sure that you're on hand to pick out a soft shady spot for me somewhere down along the river."

The conversation seemed to have vanished with the abrupt silence that over took the camp as the activity ceased. From atop his horse, Deer Foot looked down upon his people and spoke briefly. There was no out cry of any sort as the one-man war party urged his mount forward and headed into the darkness of the night. Chief Deer Foot, son of the great Chief Big Bear, was off in an attempt to avenge his father's death. Somewhere in the darkness a hoot owl gave away his presence, as its mellow call echoed over the silent camp. A short time later, man and animal disappeared into the blackness of the night.

XXI

The sign of dawn was obvious as the ray of light appeared over the eastern horizons. A few braves, scattered about the outskirts of camp, stood their posts in utter silence and in transfixed stillness, watching a group of horsemen slowly riding away. From somewhere in the wilderness, the uncanny scream of a wildcat marred the near-silence of the graying dawn, causing the horses to become a bit nervous as they hastened their pace without any prompting by their riders. The disturbance had little to no effect on the men as they rode on behind Captain Drum and his scouts. The day of major importance had finally arrived, and undoubtedly all thoughts credited to that effect, for the conversation up to this point was near non-existent.

Lance's forehead was wrinkled in thought, and his sharp eyes penetrated the semi-darkness ahead of him for some sign of the enemy or perhaps the chief, who so gallantly rode out of camp the night before. His thoughts were of the latter, for he remarked, "Wonder how far the chief progressed."

It was Turley who spoke in answer. "I don't think that I could make a good guess; however, I don't think that he was in much of a hurry."

"Time means little, if any, in his case," said Lance, and at the same time casting an eye toward the captain, who seemed to be lost in silent thought, riding along like a man alone. Lance had a suggestion to make at this point but refrained from doing so by asking— instead of guessing– the nature of the military mans thoughts. "How are things in Boston this morning Captain?"

Drum was aware of the fact that he had been spoken to, for a slight smile creased his lips as he slowly turned his gaze on the scout saying, "And here I thought that I finally escaped you."

"You still leave an easy trail, Captain," said Lance with a smile.

Drum's smile widened at the same time remarking, "From here on in I'll be wearing a poker face. You followed me to Boston for the last time."

"Didn't mean to intrude," apologized Lance with a chuckle, "but I have a suggestion to make at the moment, however," continued Lance as he raised a hand slightly. "I've considered every angle before arousing you, and came to the conclusion that by making known to you the nature of my suggestion by the way of the pony express would involve too much time."

Lance chuckled amusingly while the smile on Drum's lips turned into a grin.

"Gentlemen," cut in Turley, his facial expression tinted with amusement credited to the conversation between Lance and Drum. "I'm sure after your long journey back from the east, a good hearty breakfast would be just the thing. If you happen to look in a north westerly direction, just right of the highest ridge there, you'll notice smoke signals. Could be an invitation for roast pheasant."

Drum's hand shot upward and the patrol stopped automatically.

"Smoke signals all right," agreed Lance as he peered at the faint puffs of smoke that shot skyward at intervals.

Drum took off his hat and ran a gloved hand through his hair at the same time, asking, "How far away from our point of meeting would you judge those signals to be?"

"Quite a distance west of the river," answered Lance thoughtfully.

"Could be that Sitting Bull's scouts caught sight of one of our patrols," suggested Drum.

"Could be just that," said Lance, then added rather slowly, "could be a lure too."

"It seems to me at this point," remarked Drum, "that it would be a blunder to give away their position, especially if they are aware of our strength. I'm sure that the Sioux know the consequences if they strike all our forces at once."

"Right you are, Captain," said Lance. "However, as you already know, our patrols are split up and it will be many hours before we're all together at the river. I have a feeling that one of the patrols has already reached the rendezvous."

"That would be Custer," said Drum. "As we all know, the General was assigned to lead position."

Placing a hand to his chin, Drum looked thoughtfully at Lance for a moment, then said, "I see what you could have been referring to. If our patrols were attacked one at a time . . . it would be disastrous. But then again, it's a known fact that the tribes have been gathering. You scouts have given an on-the-spot account of that."

"We're jumping to conclusions, Captain. I suggest we move at a faster pace and find out a few things that may or may not exist. However, it would be wise for a few of us to scout on ahead. If you'll let me have Turley and Stenton, we'll move on ahead."

A slight trace of a smile played about the captain's lips as he spoke. "We always seem to think along the same lines, Winsor."

"Stenton."

"Yes, Sir," came the quick reply.

"You ride along with Lance and Turley., and see that they don't attack Sitting Bull by themselves."

"Yes, Sir," answered Stenton as he eyed the scouts amusingly.

"See you later on, Captain," said Lance flipping a hand in the air, and the trio stirred the still-sleeping dust as they rode away from the patrol.

As the last shade of darkness gave way to the early morning light, a trail left behind by a lone horseman was apparently obvious. After following it a little ways, the three horsemen pulled to a stop. Automatically their hands reached into pockets for items needed for a quick smoke.

"Five or six hours old I would judge," remarked Turley as he bent over to look at the hoof prints.

"The chief rode by here, all right," said Lance. "Guess he figures White Cloud to be west of the river, and so do I. Hope we're right."

"Maybe we've seen the last of that Injun," remarked Stenton as he blew a puff of smoke skyward.

"It wouldn't grieve me any," replied Lance. "But if he stays alive he'll come knocking on our back door again. Should you care to remember, the last time he didn't bother to knock. He burned the place to the ground."

"Yeah," said Stenton as he crushed out his cigarette. "That incident automatically made me the hangman incase we get that Injun alive. The little home to be was erected under my supervision."

Lance's face saddened slightly as he thought of that night for a moment. He glanced at Stenton with a look of appreciation, then urged his mount forward without uttering another word. The trio once again headed for the river. Within the closing minutes of another hour, the horsemen gazed about without verbal comment of any sort from atop a high embankment. The river below flowed along lazily, and only the ripples disturbed the silence that hovered over the point of rendezvous.

The usual noise of creatures inhabiting the area was absent. Even the breeze with a near-perfect presence had vanished, leaving behind their wilderness playground. The pines stood tall and still as they stared down at the motionless horsemen, and held within their branches the secret that was the cause of the silence that existed at this spot along the Big Horn river.

Lance shuddered slightly. Turley noticed the physical distraction and was first to break the silence speaking softly, "I feel the same way, fella. Something's in the air. I smell it."

Lance looked toward Turley for a moment, making no immediate comment, but nodded his head in agreement and then resumed scanning the area for some sign that may clear up the mystifying feeling that had overcome them within the past few minutes.

Stenton, whose uneasiness had become quite obvious, shifted in his saddle like a man with a dozen hours of hard riding behind him. He seemed anxious to say something and was about to, for his lips had already formed the first word, but it was moments later before he finally spoke, deciding to interrupt the thoughts that ran through the mind of the eagle-eyed scout.

"Sitting up here in the open like this is an invitation for some brave to pin my new hat up against some tree."

It was Turley who replied, his voice seemingly agreeable. "For a while now, I thought that I was the only one with a desire to rush behind some tree."

Lance turned slightly, finally facing the men, saying, "If there were any arrows pointed our way, we would have been dodging them before this."

He changed the subject before any of the others could make a comment as he pointed to a spot about a hundred yards down the river, remarking, "The brush in that area is trampled to the ground. It would take a lot of animals to do that." Again the scout cut short any possible remark that may have been made by adding quickly, "You gentlemen pick your trees and keep me covered, just in case. I'm going down there and have a look around."

A frown appeared on Turley's brow as he remarked quickly, "If those animals were carrying Indians, and they are still around, you'll never know the outcome of the next presidential election."

Lance grinned as he dismounted and said, "Under those circumstances the two of you can favor me by voting for my favorite candidate."

Lance led his mount a short distance from the embankment and tied the reins to a small tree, the others following suit. He whipped the rifle out of the sheath and examined it briefly, saying, "I'll wade the water opposite the spot we want to look over. Looks rather shallow." Then he turned, leading the way with Turley close at his heels.

Stenton's head seemed to roam constantly with his frequent backward glances. His forehead perspired freely, caused by something other than the heat of day. The military man muttered to himself as he whipped the sweat off his brow with the sleeve of his coat. "Can't see for the life of me how these guys can stay alive so long. Always sneaking along in Injun territory by themselves."

Turley heard the jumble of words and turned and glanced over his shoulder asking, with a wide grin, "What are you reciting? Poetry?"

"Damned if it didn't sound like it," came the reply.

Nothing more was said as Lance slowed his pace, trying to spot the location. After a few more yards he came to a halt. After a look around, the trio moved to the edge of the clearing. Again Lance looked cautiously around. The muscles in his face tightened, for he realized that if his previous remark a short time ago proved to be untrue, then there wouldn't be enough of him to hold all the arrows that would come sailing at him once he stepped into the water. His voice was quite contrary to his feelings as he spoke rather casually. "I'll be right back."

Without a backward glance, the scout slid down the embankment and plunged into the water. He hesitated only for a moment as his eyes darted around swiftly, then proceeded to cross the water in a crouching position. Up on the bank, the two riflemen waited with anticipation. Stenton was weighed down with tension and made no effort to conceal it. "I don't aim to breathe none 'til he gets back up here," he said, his voice toned down to a whisper.

Turley had sensed the military man's discomfort since arriving at the river and it amused him a little, even under the circumstances. Adding a bit more to the already climbing heat, the scout asked without taking his eyes off of the still crouching Lance: "Where do you want the body sent?"

Stenton became conscious of the fact that his uneasiness was known beyond the stage he would have cared to show, and he replied with a touch of indifference. "Didn't know that you had that service out here. Makes me feel better to know that I won't be buried in some Indian's back yard."

Turley's lips twitched lightly, holding back what could have been one of his easy grins, but remained silent, as did the less tense Stenton, for Lance had reached the other side and at the moment was down on one knee observing the trampled area without interference. In very short order he was backtracking across the river and upon nearing the top of the bank, two pairs of outstretched hands grasped him by the shoulders and yanked him over the top as if a hail of arrows was about to be launched at them from the other side. Before questions could be asked, Lance related his findings. "The tracks were made by shoed horses, about three hours ago, I would judge. One of our patrols."

"They are way ahead of schedule," remarked Turley. "Wonder if there had been a sudden change in plans."

"That I doubt," replied Lance. "Drum would have been notified. Let's ride back and meet the patrol. The captain may want to pursue the matter beyond the river."

Looking at Stenton now, he asked with a grin, "Stenton, how do you go for this scouting business?"

"Well," replied the military man, "I don't mind doing it with a patrol, but this sneaking around with a couple of men— and many times alone among these scalp hunters— well, you might easily get yourself lost."

The scouts chuckled lightly and even Stenton smiled at that one as they headed toward their mounts. Captain Drum and his patrol had set quite a pace, for the scouts sported surprised features on sight of the cavalrymen who at this point were about an hour from the river. The information related to him by the scouts increased his eagerness to reach the destination without delay on his part, and at the moment curiosity had overflowed his mind concerning the patrol that had already reached the rendezvous point. At one point, Lance raised an arm, pointing to several smoke signals as they rode above the tops of the faraway hills, remarking, "Couple more of them, Captain. Looks like they're really talking it up."

Drums eyes narrowed down to a squint as he peered out over the horizon, saying, "I'd feel much better if I knew why that patrol left the river. Although they may have gone in a short ways to have a look around since they were hours ahead of schedule."

"The scouting would have been done by a few men, Captain, not the entire patrol."

The men looked at each other meaningfully, but each refrained to make any further comment that would be strictly on the basis of guesswork.

Within the hour, the sweating, dust-covered patrol had dismounted. Men and animals alike were grouped together in the middle of the cool, refreshing water. Down the river a short ways, four men pondered over the possibilities of the vanishing patrol as they viewed the tracks that led into the heavily wooded section.

"According to plan," said Lance, "the first patrol was in Custer's command and this situation as I see it has the ear marks of the General."

"What do you mean?" asked Drum with a voice of uncertainty.

"I've scouted for Custer a while back," replied the scout. "He's not a man to sit around doing nothing, even for a few hours. It could very well be that the General's adventurous blood had urged him forward to have a look around."

"In that case," remarked Drum, "we could expect him to send back some of his scouts."

Lance looked at the military man and spoke without assurance. "He could."

Drum hesitated for a moment, realizing the double meaning of the scout's previous remark. Then he said, rather slowly, "You mean, he may not?"

"Depends on the circumstances," said Lance with an audible sigh.

"Circumstances or otherwise," said Drum as he raised his voice slightly, "It's plain logic that close contact be maintained, especially at this stage. He could have left a few men behind to inform General Cook of his intentions."

"Perhaps there was a change in plans at that, Captain," offered Turley as a possibility.

"We're jumping to conclusions," cut in Lance mildly. "Some of the questions will have to go unanswered for now."

Lance watched Drum staring blankly toward the hills for a moment, and then he remarked, "A little while back you seemed a bit shaken, Captain. I don't believe that it could have been Custer's failure to leave word behind."

The military man was slow in answering, for he seemed to be far away as his gaze still lingered on the horizons. He faced Lance finally and spoke with a tone of agreement saying, "You're quite right, Winsor. The thought of him plowing into that hornet's nest out there with a mere two hundred and some odd men could prove disastrous. Not that he would engage the enemy deliberately without the direct backing of our patrols, but there remains the possibility of an ambush."

"Which leads us directly to our next move, Captain. I know you'll approve. You've already got it on your mind."

Drum's lips widened slightly as he looked at Lance, asking, "How many men do you want?"

"Well," replied the scout thoughtfully, but he got no farther as Drum called out to Stenton.

"Yes, Sir," came the quick reply.

"Lance and Turley are going to try and contact Custer's patrol. I believe they like your company. As a matter of fact I'm inclined to believe that you have the qualities of making a good scout."

"But a mighty shaky one, Sir," said Stenton as he ran a sleeve across his forehead. The remark was followed by smiles as the men eyed Stenton, whose ambition was certainly not that of being an Indian scout.

Turley flung an arm around his shoulder, saying, "At least you've been living an exciting life of late."

"Why, some day they may even write a book about the adventures of Sergeant Stenton."

"Yeah," said Stenton with a slight grin now. "The title to that book could be 'The Sergeant's Scalp Hung High in Sitting Bull's Tepee.'"

The air of amusement was cut short by a voice calling from up above,

"Captain Drum! Captain Drum!"

Drum and the others turned sharply, facing the patrol, and saw several of his men wading across the river toward the opposite shore where a lone horse with full saddle had appeared on the scene a moment before.

"Let's go," snapped Drum, urging his mount forward. The sudden forward motion of the animals churned the bottom of the river, leaving behind muddy waters in their wake. The scene was a quiet one as they looked over the lone mount. An arrow imbedded in the saddle where a rider had once sat carried the grim message of violence.

Lance reached over and yanked the weapon out which he gazed at briefly then without lifting his eyes said, "Cheyenne."

"Sitting Bull succeeded in getting some of them up here," added Turley.

"I don't think he had a hard time with them," remarked Lance. "Custer was assigned to the Cheyenne campaign and I hardly think that he would have gotten a vote from any of the Cheyenne tribes if the General decided to run for sheriff."

"How would they know that Custer would be in on this deal?" asked Drum.

"Perhaps they didn't know," answered Lance. "But it was an opportunity to strike back at the white man in force. However, by now I would say that the General was spotted."

Drum whipped off his hat and ran the back of his hand across his forehead and asked, "What do you make of this?" He nodded his head toward the near motionless mount that stood there as if his fate was being decided upon.

"Could be one of several things," answered Lance. "We'll give it a try and see if we can come up with an answer. Until then, it would be wise to station the men on the opposite bank just in case something is in the air close by that we don't know anything about."

Drum spoke as he replaced his hat, saying, "In the mean time, I'll send word to General Cook concerning the circumstances. On the other hand, he may be aware of Custer's maneuver and inform me accordingly."

Lance nodded his head in agreement then remarked to Drum, "It would be best that Turley and I go alone."

Before the scout could add to the remark, Stenton cut in rather calmly but with an expression of hurt, saying, "Now look, Winsor. I've may impressed you that at present I wasn't much of an Indian scout and I haven't changed my mind in making a career of it, but I'd like this known before any more is said: I'm ready for any assignment, any time, without exceptions."

"Stenton," said Lance, "get this under your hat: there is no one here that thought otherwise. I made that suggestion to the captain for one reason. The less going along, less are the chances of being detected."

"Now that makes sense," remarked Stanton with a noticeable grin. He faced Drum and continued. "Sir, one day we may be without scouts and you may need a man with good Indian schooling; and furthermore, Turley here is a good tracker along any river. Why, he could get down to General Cook before this part of the river itself."

Drum was aware that the switch would at least preserve Stenton's feelings, for it was obvious that the latter wanted to assure them that the remarks he had made in the presence of the scouts was an opinion and his admitted feelings at the time had no baring as far as his bravery was concerned.

Both of the scouts wore a grin as Drum eyed them, seeking answers to his questionable glances concerning the matter without any comment. Satisfied that the visual messages among them were understood, Lance raised his hand in farewell, his mount already on the move, and shouted back, "See you in a couple of hours."

He advanced about fifty yards before hearing the expected. The mad splashing of water as a horseman tore toward him. Without slowing his pace, the scout turned slightly, taking a quick glance in a backwardly direction and observed the brightened features of the oncoming rider. It was Stenton. The scout's smile widened as Lance faced forward again, and upon reaching the scene of the tracks, turned sharply and headed into the woods, the other rider following close at his heels.

Sunlight met the earth at various points as it penetrated through parts of the heavy timberland. They appeared to the two horsemen as guidance toward that which they sought: the vanishing patrol, perhaps receiving guidance toward a lair where death vengefully awaited those that dare tread farther into the land of the red man. The scouts rode along slowly, ever cautious, watchfully picking their way over the soft moss and other cushioned terrain offered by Mother Nature. They kept clear of the sun rays, circling around them as if averting betrayal.

Stenton followed close behind Lance. His broad brimmed hat kept his face cool as his head turned to the right of him, then to the left, then to the rear. He pressed his vigilance to the limit. Though the day was warm and bright above the tree tops, underneath the shading limbs something sinister seemed to float along with the somewhat cooler air, for on occasions, they had both shrugged as if trying to cast off something that ran up and down their spines. Or again, some unpleasant thought credited to the handiwork of imagination.

Lance eased back on the reins faintly, causing the slow-moving animal to stop. Stenton watched him for a moment and upon noticing nothing eventful that may have caught the scout's eye, resumed his watchful task. A full minute went by before anything was said, for up to then, they sat there silently as if awaiting for the unknown to put in an appearance.

Without turning his head, Lance spoke through the corner of his mouth, his voice a near whisper. "Something smells besides the wild flower. A patrol as large as Custer's should create some disturbance."

Stenton moved to the side of Lance, remarking in low tones. "Sure looks like he's movin' way on in. According to the track signs, he hasn't made any stops yet."

Lance made no remark but nodded his head in agreement, then motioned with his hand to follow as he started forward again. After a ten-minute ride, Lance pulled in behind a large boulder and dismounted. Stenton was soon at his side wearing an expression of uncertainty.

"Keep your eyes peeled. I'm going above here a little ways. I'll be right back."

Stenton nodded his head at the same time reaching into his pocket for his tobacco pouch. Not once did he take his eyes off the terrain as he rolled several cigarettes, and as he began to wet the paper on the last one, his motion froze momentarily. He stood there transfixed, for, from the corner of his eye, he suddenly saw the form of an individual standing to the right of him. It took but another moment to identify that it was indeed Lance, and at the same instant finish dragging the remainder of the dry paper over his tongue. He extended his hand toward Lance and offered the scout one of the cigarettes without turning his head. "You must have Indian blood in you."

"That I can't prove," said the scout as he took the cigarette. "But I do practice a lot of their habits."

Stenton puffed on the cigarette deeply and glanced at Lance with a noticeable grin but added nothing more concerning the incident. Instead, he asked, "What's the next move?"

"Well," replied Lance, his eyes moving slowly in their sockets ceaselessly searching the area. "I'm going to try a few signals just in case Custer is camped somewhere within hearing distance. Dawson will pick it up in that case. What we do from there on depends on what ever takes place, if anything. A short ways up ahead is a knoll. We'll get atop of that and I believe we can get a good look around." Lance took hold of the reins and added, "We'll walk on up to the spot."

Stenton nodded his head and soon, both men and their animals were cautiously treading over soft earth toward their destination. A few minutes were spent carefully observing the terrain from atop the high perch. There were no indications whatsoever of any human life during the visual search; however, the possibilities that there may be never left the minds of the men.

Under these circumstances the scout chose to chance a few signals. Lance's favorite signal, the cry of the whippoorwill, went swiftly, far and wide, echoing repeatedly as it glanced over mountaintops in a mournful cry, trying to attract the disappearing patrol.

Stenton, huddling with one knee on the ground at his observation post, shuddered at the first sound of the call, for if up until now their presence was unknown, the secret no longer existed.

Several more times the signals went along their way. Several more times the echoes carried on in relays, finally disappearing over the far horizons. Tension mounted with the dragging minutes and the hope of a return signal slowly began to fade away. Lance's head was tilted slightly as he knelt on one knee, silently trying to pick up the familiar sound that would surely quicken his pulses, but it was in vain. For some strange reason, the silence became deadlier, the position of the patrol more mystifying. The last inkling of hope faded from the scout's body as he slowly turned toward Stenton, eyeing the military man who returned the gaze in silence. His eyes held a question that he refrained from asking verbally but he didn't have long to wait, for Lance's voice came slowly and sounded like one that was completely without choice. "We'll go on, a little ways more."

Once again Stenton nodded in agreement, as if he were saving his voice for some greater occasion. Nearing the end of an other hour, the men continued their progress forward, always hugging the shadows, disappearing behind the laurel at various times then reappearing again. To watchful eyes from a distance, they would seem like ghost riders seeking someone on the trail of revenge.

Making their way down a slope, Lance spied a small run that he knew had existed in the vicinity, for the terrain along the way was a familiar one. He was aware that Custer's trail led toward Sitting Bull's village, or at least where the village used to be. Dismounting near the water's edge, the men peered around before making any attempt to quench their thirst. The animals automatically bent their heads low and sipped the cool water into their feverish stomachs. Suddenly, one of the horses jerked his head out of the water with a snort, causing Lance to tighten his grip on the reins, for the animal's strange action was beyond normal behavior.

"Something frightened him," he remarked quickly, his voice just above a whisper. His hand patted the horse's mane in an attempt to keep the animal calm. Both animal and man stood there as if trapped and now waiting for the enemy to close in. Their observation was feverish as they scanned in all directions and the feeling that prying eyes lingered within the area hovered in the air. But as the minutes went by without any added disturbance, the scout's voice came again in low tones. "We've come far enough. Before we start back I want to have a look on the other side. There seems to be some tracks crossing over Custer's trail. Could be theirs, but I want to make sure."

Once again, the silent but agreeable Stenton bobbed his head up and down while at the same time yanking his rifle out of the sheath just as Lance did. Taking ahold of both reins, the military man quickly led the animals back out of the water and stood in readiness. Lance checked Stenton with approval after a backwards glance, then proceeded across the run cautiously. He looked at the tracks briefly, then snapped his head around, saying quickly, "Pony tracks. Indians. About an hour old."

The scout spun around quickly and started back. His eyes widened as he caught sight of two forms lying in the water underneath some heavy brush, which up til now hid their lifeless forms from view.

Stenton was aware of the scout's expression and called out before the now-rushing scout could make any comment, "What's wrong?"

"Couple of dead men lying there. Stripped almost naked. Let's get out of here fast."

Just as Stenton dashed from his position, the angry hiss of an arrow swished through the air, parting the military man's hair and pinning his hat to a tree. The near-miss caused him to hit the ground, but he spun around quickly, shooting in the direction from which the arrow came. Lance automatically went to his knees and opened up as the first target appeared into view. The slug caught the Indian square on the forehead, shearing off the top of his head. He crumpled into the bushes without uttering a sound. The screaming arrows swished by, some striking with a thud as they buried themselves into solid wood, while others tore through brush and leaves, blazing a thin trail through the thicket.

Lance's voice was loud now as he shouted to Stenton. "Get on your horse and move out fast. They'll surround us in short order."

"Look out," came Stenton's sharp warning as a brave appeared over a ledge nearby, aiming his deadly weapon at Lance. But before he could fire, the arrow was already on its way and sliced a deep gash across the scout's shoulder and tore through the fleshy part of Stenton's arm causing him to drop his rifle momentarily as he braced himself with his good arm.

The men refrained from asking the welfare of the other at the moment, for they both scampered for their mounts under their own power. Once on their mounts, the hasty retreat was geared into high speed. Occasionally, Lance would take a quick look to the rear, and each time noticed that Stenton seemed quite capable of continuing the wild pace despite his wound, and too, there was no pursuit as far as he could gather. Although both men bled freely, agitated by the rough ride, they continued without faltering, for rushing through their minds was the scene of death, where they too, could have been added to the list of the grim reaper who many times before had attempted to close the cover, thus ending the final chapters of their lives. Not before several more miles was left behind them did Lance pull to a quick halt.

"How's the arm," he asked quickly, at the same time working the military man's coat down over his shoulder and pulling the sleeve away from the wounded arm.

"Near got the both of us with one arrow, that damned Injun," said Stenton, evading the question for no apparent reason other then that the wound was incidental at the moment.

"Guess we're lucky at that," remarked the scout, ripping a piece of the large bandana he whipped out of his pocket and tying it tightly around Stenton's arm. The rest of the material he folded and handed to the scowling Stenton, who at the moment was mad at all Indian nations.

"Shove this down on the wound inside the shirt," Stenton remarked.

The scout winced slightly as the cloth slid over the torn flesh. Once in place, he quickly helped Stenton on with the coat, then glanced at the back trail briefly. Yanking roughly on the reins, he brought the animal around sharply and started forward again in a mad dash, the other following close behind.

Stenton looked back over his shoulder, muttering something that could have caused the wildest of flowers to turn to a crimson red should they have heard the phrase that could never be written in the book of famous sayings.

Several miles from the river, Lance caught sight of what he thought were moving figures, and without further observation pulled hard on the reins, causing the animal to rear high as they came to a shaky halt.

The sudden halt caught Stenton unaware and as he veered to the left to avoid crashing into the scout and his horse The animal lost balance, stumbling uncontrollably and sending Stenton flying through the air, headlong into a growth of laurel. Nothing more than a shake up occurred as he charged roughly out of the thicket, asking in amazement, as Lance came rushing to his aid, "What happened?"

"You all right?" Asked the scout quickly.

"Yeah."

"Saw something moving out there. Come on."

Lance ran over to Stenton's mount and yanked out the rifle, throwing it at Stenton, who grabbed it in mid air. Half-running, and in a crouch, the men advanced a few yards and took positions behind large trees. They hastily reloaded the weapons and peered ahead cautiously, waiting for whatever had distracted the scout to appear. After a full minute, Lance began to wonder if he really did see something. His eyes squinted as he looked steadily past the bark of the tree, trying to detect what he thought should be in view by now.

Suddenly it occurred to him that at the time he was atop his horse and could see beyond the rise of ground up ahead. Further analysis left him quickly as the faint sound of hoofs reached his ears. Stenton picked it up about the same time and glanced at the scout, who nodded his head in silence understandingly. Tension had already reached its peak at another point during this mission. Although it still lingered at the moment, the men seemed rather calm compared with their recent brush with the enemy. Perhaps it was because of the metal striking against stone as the horses crossed solid ground that relaxed their nerves somewhat. However, the thought that the animals were stolen and now being ridden by Indians still kept the men cautious to a point.

Lance's trigger finger slid slowly away from the guard, finally resting on the stock upon noticing military hats bobbing up and down as the riders started up the small knoll on the opposite side.

"Men from one of the patrols," remarked Lance as if it were what he had expected.

Stenton showed no emotion, but he did relax for the first time since entering the woods with the scout, sucking in a lungful of air and easing it out unnoticeably.

"I'll try to attract their attention," remarked Lance, as the lead riders rode over the top of the rise. "Keep under cover just in case they get jumpy and start firing."

The scout took a slow step away from the tree, exposing himself, and gave a sharp whistle. Upon hearing it, the horsemen came to a sudden halt. They peered around in confusion trying to locate its origin and the scout whistled again, waving his one arm and shouting: "It's Winsor and Stenton. Over here."

The two lead horsemen saw the scout's motion as they looked past trees and overhanging limbs in the distance. It appeared to Lance that they were cautious concerning his identity, for only two of them rode forward, the rest remaining behind. Their pace was slow, riding in a crouched position, ready for action.

As Stenton stepped out into view, recognition was obvious, at least as far as the uniform was concerned, though battered and torn and far from being in top shape for military inspection.

The riders thundered forward and upon reaching the spot where the scout and Stenton were already mounting their horses, pulled to a noisy stop.

"Seems like we come a mite late." The voice was that of an old timer. "Heard the shots a spell back. Kinda faint, they were. The captain sent us on in to check on you boys. I speck you fellows did the shooting."

"Yeah," answered Lance. "Met up with a few of them back there aways."

"Got sliced up a bit I see," remarked the old timer, "Hit bad?"

"Just enough to open up the spigot," said Stenton.

"I recon we ought to get going then 'afora you drain yourselves dry." Urging his mount around, the old timer threw a glance backwards, saying, "I'll have you all out of these woods pronto. Just you follow close by."

"Wouldn't have more faith in Daniel Boone," remarked Stenton, winking at Lance.

In short order, the partial patrol disappeared behind the knoll led by the old military man, who rode like a general leading his man into an important battle. Perhaps he was reliving part of the past– one of his glorious and daring escapades that he undoubtedly cherished with pride, forever tucked away in his book of memories.

An hour or so later, Drum, pacing back and forth on the riverbank impatiently, was attracted by one of his observers who rode out of the thicket and into the river with a wild splash, calling out, "They're coming back, Sir."

Drum stopped pacing and looked with anxiety toward the spot where the riders would first appear. His fears mounted concerning the two men he had sent in on the mission, for as the riders rode on out in single file, they were not among the leaders. He was about to shout out a question but choked up momentarily.

The old timer called out from mid-stream, "Brought 'em back out like I said I would, Captain."

The military leader's eyes brightened, for the remark caused him to glance quickly toward the back whereupon he caught sight of Lance and Stenton riding the rear of the patrol. They rode across the water to the opposite shore where upon Drum remarked, "Seems like you boys have been demoted."

"Just following orders, Captain," said Lance as he looked over towards the old timer who, with the others, was riding up over the bank.

"This sure must have been his day," said Drum. Then he exclaimed as he noticed the blood spot on the scout's back, "What's this? You hit bad?"

"We both got nicked a little," replied Lance.

In short order, the wounded men were aided in removing their upper clothing, and bandages were being hurried to them at the captain's request.

"It's needless to ask the question," remarked Drum as if he knew it to be a fact.

"We saw nothing of the patrol, Captain. But we did see two dead bodies that could have been part of Custer's men . . . back at a small stream where we were jumped by a few of the Indians."

Drum frowned thoughtfully for a moment, then remarked, "The animal we checked before you left was probably ridden by one of them. The other is still roaming about or else was caught by the Indians. What isn't clear at the moment is who are the two dead men and just what were they doing away from the patrol."

"Well," said Lance, "I've given that a lot of thought since, and the only thing that I could figure out was that Custer was sending them back here with a message of some sort."

"Could very well be," agreed Drum.

From among the men, a voice called out suddenly, "Captain, sir, the patrols are in sight."

All eyes turned downriver to where riders were rounding a bend.

"Might get some answers now, Captain," remarked Lance.

Drum glanced at the scout, nodding in agreement but remaining silent as he stroked his chin thoughtfully. A short time later Drum saluted his superior, General Terry, whose features seemed bright and alert despite the long journey just completed.

"Welcome to the Big Horn country, Sir," said Drum in greeting.

"Thank you, Captain. I'll feast on that a while. I hardly think that I'll receive the same courtesy from here on in." His facial expression was that of curiosity as he changed the subject, remarking, "Strange that Custer wasn't in on the welcoming committee. Resting with his men in the foreground, I presume?"

His voice died down to a near whisper at the end of the remark for he knew well that Custer would have been at his side if he were close by.

"We haven't seen Custer or his patrol since our arrival and we were ahead of schedule."

Terry's brows narrowed as a thought suddenly occurred to him but he failed to reveal its identity as he remarked instead, "Why, we followed his tracks all the way up here. There were no cut offs."

"There is up ahead, sir," said Drum quickly.

"We'll have a look at them," said Terry with a tint of disbelief in his voice.

At the scene, the General was quick to agree. "They went in here all right. I assume you had the trail followed?"

"Partially, Sir," came Drum's reply.

Terry looked at Drum expecting details and it came without further request.

"Winsor went in with one of my men and followed the trail for two hours. Saw nothing of Custer or his patrol, although he tried signaling but to no avail. However, they came across two men that were ambushed at that point and we assume that they were part of Custer's patrol."

Terry looked at Lance and asked, "Assumed? Couldn't you make positive identification?"

"They were stripped of their clothing, General," came the quick reply.

"I see," said Terry slowly.

"We thought that they may have been on their way back here with word from Custer," said Drum.

Terry nodded understandingly as he gazed out over the wilderness and then directed his remark at the scout again. "You buried the men, of course?"

"Didn't have time General. Unfortunately, we were victims of an ambush at that point and were forced back."

"Any size to the Indian pack?" asked Terry with a touch of anxiety in his voice.

"Perhaps a half a dozen, no more."

"Lookouts," commented Terry. "No doubt they had them spotted all along the way."

"In that case, Custer's presence and strength remains no secret to the Indians," remarked Lance, adding to the possibilities.

"A damaging thought, Winsor, a damaging thought." Terry eased out a sigh, for he realized that the scout's remark was indeed more than a possibility. His next words came quick as if suddenly coming to a decision. "We've got to move out fast, Captain."

"Yes, sir," answered Drum quickly.

"You will take your patrol and head north for approximately ten miles. At that point you will head west toward the village. We'll plan to meet there, unless the Sioux interfere before hand. Should that occur, we could come to each other's aid upon hearing gun fire." With a glance at the scouts he continued, "You will continue with Winsor and Turley. It'll be a return visit for them. At least you gentlemen will have a little more backing this time.

"Wouldn't think of shaking hands with Sitting Bull otherwise under the circumstances," laughed Lance.

"Sir," said Drum, "what have you in mind for Major Reno's patrol?"

"Was just about to familiarize you with the slight change in plans. Major Reno is already on his way toward the village. Started inward about ten miles down the river. Custer was to have taken your present position and you were to go up above him; however, we'll move in as already mentioned. That's it gentlemen. Unless something occurs where we will be forced to alter plans, we'll be seeing you at the village. Or at least somewhere near it. Personally, I think that it will be deserted. At least as far as the fighting forces are concerned. Any questions, gentlemen?"

"According to Winsor's report, the distance from this point to our destination should be covered in a little over a day. That would be late tomorrow afternoon. Any further comment on that, Winsor?"

"Your calculations should be near correct, sir," replied the scout.

"Alight then, Captain, get your patrol in order and we'll continue as planned immediately."

"Yes, sir," said Drum with a salute, and issued orders to Stenton as they rode upstream, splashing water in all directions.

As the scouts were about to follow, Cook called out. "Winsor."

"Yes, sir," replied the scout as he turned his mount around, facing the General.

"You've been with Custer for a while, and I would say are aware of some of his methods. What do you make of his procedure, contrary to plans as you well know."

"Anything I would say would be but a guess, General. I would like to believe that his intention was to locate the enemy and then send word as to their whereabouts. The two men we found ambushed were an indication that they were carrying some message; however, like I've stated, that too is only a guess."

"Well," said Cook, his voice filled with concern, "no doubt that the General's move could be explained satisfactorily; however, at the moment I'm quite disturbed, quite disturbed."

Nothing more was said concerning the issue as Drum rode up saying, "All set to move on out, General."

"That's it then, gentlemen," said Cook with a deep sigh. "Until tomorrow." He nodded his head in agreement.

Drum saluted his superior. The scouts waved their hand in farewell, and the trio rode up river to the waiting patrol.

A short time later the rendezvous was deserted. If there was any animal life in the near by vicinity, they stayed hidden, for none appeared to have a look around the area that minutes before harbored life and excitement. Only the river was on the move, as it carried off the muddy waters churned up by the animals of the patrols. Before long, it settled back to normal whereupon the many ripples seemed to come to life, singing their rhythmic tunes as they danced about in the noonday sun.

XXII

Nightfall slowly blended its way into the Big Horn country, blanketing Mother Nature's wonderland and those within. The cry of the whippoorwill echoed repeatedly in the distance and sounded rather mournful as they went unanswered.

Lying around underneath the pines was most of Captain Drum's patrol. The missing were at their posts guarding the area. Near one of the trees sat three men. They were listening to the birds cry, perhaps in hope of hearing a return call from somewhere in the distance, but it was in vain, as none came. It was Drum who spoke first, referring to the incident. "The little fellow seems to be without friends."

It was Lance who added a comment, saying, "They've probably took off seeking more peaceful terrain. Been disturbed quite a bit lately."

"I'll be dammed if I didn't think it was Dawson," cut in Turley. "Still can't tell the difference."

"I bet ole Will is sure talking to himself lately," remarked Lance at the mention of his friend's name. "Custer's plan would hardly have met his approval. I could see Dawson's eyes glistening as he starts throwing some of the tall stories of his recent escapades around a campfire some night."

This drew a chuckle. For all of them had heard some of the old scout's stories in the past and no doubt were looking forward to some more of it in the future, perhaps under better circumstances.

Continuing the subject, Drum remarked casually, "Wonder if he's serious about quitting the scouting business?"

"I think he is," replied Lance. "As a matter of fact he already told me that I'm going to need a foreman and he was it."

Turley casually broke off a small birch twig and placed it between his teeth, saying, "Luck rode the saddle with Dawson for a long time. I'd like to see him ranchin' alone the river with Naomi and Lance."

"How about you Turley?" remarked Drum.

"Don't know just what I'll do after this is all over," replied the scout.

Lance looked slyly at Turley saying, "We could help you find out right away if you care to give us a lead."

Turley eyed Lance with a curious grin as the latter continued, "Like telling us what Mary Lou whispered in your ear the day we left camp."

Turley's grin widened as he folded his arms, placing them behind his head. Then he said, as he gazed up into the trees, "Now darn it if it didn't slip my mind. Never could remember anything that woman tell me."

"You don't have to remember this time," said Lance. "You've been living with it since."

"No comment, gentlemen," said Turley as he laughed softly.

Drum sprang to his feet, saying, "Well, I'll do a little checking around and turn in. I leave you with pleasant thoughts, Romeo."

"I'll keep you company, Captain," said Lance, who arose without much effort. Reaching over to a clump of bushes, he plucked off a small flower and handed it to Turley saying, "From Juliet."

Three men smiled momentarily, then two of them walked off into the night, leaving the last one alone with his thoughts.

Darkness came and went without incident. It was hours after daybreak but nothing could be added that could be referred to as a disturbance.

Lance and Turley, scouting ahead of the patrol, had reached the outskirts of the village and looked about without too much concern. General Cook's patrol was in clear view at the one end of the village.

Women, children and elderly men inhabited the area below. The fighting men were gone. Visually sweeping the area once more as if he might have missed some sign that would indicate the fact that the presence of others was in the near by vicinity, Lance spoke with a touch of curiosity. "Wonder what became of Major Reno's patrol? I expected to find an assembly of forces, including Custer's."

"Change in plans again, maybe," said Turley.

"I have a strange feeling that all is not well somewhere along the line," remarked Lance. "First we have a vanishing patrol and now the Major's ghost patrol. He should have been here by now but I see no signs of them."

Turley's gaze went far beyond the camp, his thoughts becoming verbal as he uttered with a tint of amusement, "Mystery, intrigue, the call of the wilderness."

"Yeah," said Lance rather casually. "One more thing you should mention. The lurking Sioux, and I might add, there's quite a bunch of them."

Turley inhaled deeply then said with a sigh, "It's not too colorful at that, Captain."

Lance eyed Turley for a moment, then remarked, "Perhaps I shouldn't have mentioned the Sioux. You had something more pleasant in mind."

"Much more pleasant, Captain. But it'll keep," replied Turley with a smile.

"In that case, we'll ride back to the patrol," said Lance, as he urged his mount around. Looking back over his shoulder, he added, "It would be nice to have neighbors once Naomi and me get down to the river."

"I'll consider it, providing you make me sheriff," grinned Turley.

"You won't have any business. My wife and me expect to be quite orderly."

"I'll keep in practice 'til the town grows up," said Turley amusingly.

"What do you expect to do, Sheriff?"

Turley's grin widened as he remarked, "I'll keep tossing Dawson in and out of jail."

The scouts chuckled heartily as they pictured just such an occurrence and the old scout continued to be the topic of conversation as they disappeared from the edge of camp.

Some time later, General Cook waited impatiently for the patrol that rode in at the far end of the camp. As if knowing his anxiety, four horsemen broke away from the patrol and rode in his direction at a fast gallop. As they pulled up within yards of the military leader, they dismounted. Formality was brief, and before any report could be made Cook asked, "Any occurrence, Captain?"

"None, sir," was the quick reply.

"I rather assumed that," said Cook. "As a matter of fact, the Major and I offer the same report."

"Then the Major is in the vicinity," said Drum assumingly.

"He was," replied Cook. "I had to act accordingly under the circumstances. Custer has been here and gone right on through early this morning. My scouts returned but a short time ago, finding nothing but the trail of the patrol heading northwest.

"He sure must be pushing forward at a fast pace and without much rest to be that far ahead of us," said Drum thoughtfully.

"There were a lot of Sioux here once," spoke Lance for the first time since his arrival. "Sure must have made a lot of tracks when they left."

"That's right," agreed Cook. "As a matter of fact it must have fired Custer to a high pitch, for it's the pony trail he's following, and my scouts report that they've never seen quite so many in any particular area."

Looking toward the trail, the General whipped his hat off and ran a hand across his sweating brow, remarking, "Custer's strange tactic in this case sure has us on the move too, gentlemen. It is logical to assume that the patrol is in peril. Much more than the General anticipates. Otherwise, he would have waited for the rest of us at this point, to say the least. I had no alternative but to send Reno forward, flanking Custer to the left. And we, gentlemen, will continue our advance, following the same pattern we previously exercised."

Cook reached into his pocket and brought forth the map that had already been displayed much more than ones under ordinary circumstances, at the same time continuing the subject. "Gather 'round, gentlemen, while I brief you on the next move. Like I've stated previously, the Major is continuing forward, left of the trail. His patrol will be about five miles off the trail." He directed his next statement at Drum. "You will angle off from here approximately five miles and continue on up to the right. I will again follow the direct trail. Now then, should the trail continue without veering sharply to the left or right, it will lead to the Little Big Horn River. That is, if it goes that far up. I will make constant contact with both of your patrols by sending riders back and forth. That way neither of the patrols will stray off the course. We'll meet once more, if the entire distance must be covered, at the Little Big Horn."

Cook paused as if waiting for some comments. He placed an already made cigarette between his lips and lit it. If such were the case, the waiting was brief. Drum stroked his chin as he stood there rather thoughtfully and spoke before the General could continue the subject. "For some reason I expected a full scale attack to take place somewhere between the river and the village. Seems strange that Custer should have gotten this far without resistance."

Cook blew out a stream of smoke, saying, "There is no doubt now that Sitting Bull's scouts spotted the patrol on its inward march. That takes us back to the story of the spider and the fly, Captain. The old chief is luring him deep into territory unfamiliar to the General. I only hope that we can be on hand when either one or the other starts an attack."

He drew in a deep breath and looked at Lance soberly for a moment, then asked, "Winsor, what are the General's chances of holding out until help arrives in case of an attack?"

The scout's reply was more of a fact rather than an opinion, as indicated by the tone of his voice." Assuming that the General is continuing the same pace, the nearest patrol is still hours from him. Should an attack occur under those circumstances, I would say that Custer used up his last chance the minute he left the river."

Cook eyed Lance curiously, for he sensed that the scout's answer was based not alone on the faith that Custer would be outnumbered.

He asked, "Would your answer be the same if I were at the head of the patrol in question?"

"Yes, it would," came the quick reply. "However, I do believe that you would have gotten a less fiery reception than would Custer." Lance paused briefly and was quite conscious of Cook's interest, as the latter waited for the scout to explain the difference in opinion regarding his previous statement.

"General, I'm not aware of how much you know of Custer's exploits but I'm sure you do know that they brought him fame through the nation. He's famous in the Indian nation too, however, not in a flattering sort of way. He is despised by the Indians as much as Colonel Chivington was, should you care to recall the final chapter of the Sand Creek massacre."

Cook's face took on a deep shade of red as he clearly indicated resentment and immediately defended his colleague with an even, but stern, voice. "Are you implying that Custer is of the same caliber as Chivington?"

"I am impling nothing to that effect, General. Just merely pointing out that Custer's scalp is as great a prize as Chivington's would have been around the time of the incident."

Cook slowly nodded his head understandingly and after inhaling deeply, said, "I see what you mean. Sorry that I misunderstood you."

"Well, gentlemen, we've toyed with the possibilities off and on since leaving the river and this fact still remains: if Custer goes into battle without us, he will face the greatest odds of his career. When I questioned you concerning his chances, I was probing for a likely chance that would enable the General to escape the lingering disaster that has been running through our minds for the past few days. At this point there remains but one consolation, and that is that we can join his forces in time. Captain Drum."

"Yes, sir."

"Ready your men. We'll move on out at once."

"Yes, sir," snapped Drum with a sharp salute. Without another word, the four horsemen mounted their horses and galloped back toward their patrol.

Like so many times in the past, it was the ordinary routine for old father time to call upon nightfall. The sky was cloudless and in contrast, along the western horizons, a reddish tint cast its beams down over the Big Horn. Slumber time in a beautiful but tense territory. In addition to the colorful setting, father time had engaged the services of the gentle south wind to help the mysteries of sleep overcome the tall timber and the creatures that roam among them.

Too, there are others that are confronted with routine matters, and at the moment, like on many occasions, Captain Drum scanned the area ahead of him for a likely spot to set up camp. He had been relentless in his efforts to keep the patrol moving at a fast pace, hoping that luck would be with him in making contact with General Custer before darkness. Undoubtedly, Cook's parting words were still fresh in his mind. But all in vain up to this point, for he realized that the last flickering light of day would soon be over-powered by darkness.

The patrol came to a sudden halt as a gloved hand appeared into view at the head of the riders, waving the familiar signal. Sighs of relief were quite noticeable as the weary men dismounted. They busied themselves in bedding down the animals and in turn a place for their tired bodies. Not too long afterwards, the well-guarded but fireless camp was ready for the usual visit by the sand man. Some of the men still chewed on the remaining eatables, reluctantly hoisted out of saddlebags, which would have been frowned upon by all but the hungry. Imagination worked feverishly, causing mouths to water as beef was masterfully roasted in their minds every time their teeth sank into a raw potato.

Drum, seated with his back against a tree, was aroused from a thoughtful silence as the scouts walked toward him.

"Are we intruding, Captain?" It was Lance who asked casually.

"Certainly not. Pull up a tree trunk and sit down," laughed Drum.

"Thought perhaps you wanted to reminisce a bit, alone," said Lance.

"Just don't have time for that sort of thing of late," smiled the military man.

"I agree with you there, Captain," said Turley, as he whipped out several apples from his coat pocket, offering them to Drum and Lance. "But we can still have desert."

"I see you gathered more than the others when we come upon that tree back there," grinned Lance.

"Hardly," smiled Turley, "I saved them for this occasion."

"What's the occasion?" asked Lance as he bit into the apple.

"Oh, one of our occasional powwows," replied Turley.

"Needless to say that you have the subject already in tow," remarked Lance. "Which is it, women, woman, or St. Louis?"

"You shouldn't have mentioned anything so close to my heart," said Turley slowly and acting sentimental. "Now I'm apt to wander into the darkness for a bit of reminiscing."

Lance smiled as he continued gnawing the fruit beyond the core, but made no comment. Drum's voice appeared before Turley could go on. "I would say that the next best thing would be a nice thick slice of venison."

"Gentlemen, it's obvious that provisions are low, and the smell of venison lingered at our nostrils all day," remarked Turley.

The two men eyed Turley in silence, waiting for him to continue as they sat there quite relaxed, for they had a suspicion concerning Turley's next remark that he needed no prompting.

"I know that we must refrain from doing any shooting at this particular stage, however, I've already brought down deer with this." A knife appeared in his hand as if by magic, causing Drum to frown slightly, for he definitely didn't notice the scout pull the weapon out of its sheath.

He was about to ask the scout how he maneuvered without being detected, at least not by him, but Turley's spoke again with a tone that could belong to a man trying to regain his credit. "I talked to a couple of Indians once that couldn't understand a word of English, and I got the same blank stare. At least they waved their hands and gave me a sign."

He waited for some sort of comment but got nothing more than slight widening of smiles and after a moment of returning one of his flashy ones, he resumed speaking. "I could leave camp before dawn and wait for the patrol up ahead. In the meantime, from my lair near a deer trail I'll wait for the potential roast to come by. I could be lucky, you know."

Lance slowly shook his head from side indicating a silent no.

"Well, that's one vote shot to hell," said Turley, grinning. "But let me caution you, silent one, we may run out of apple trees. Anyway, there still remains the final word," he said with emphasis, amusingly shaking a finger in the air. "Captain, before you answer, may I remind you that your belt is two notches past home base already and . . . " Turley stopped talking abruptly upon seeing Drum's head moving from side to side with a facial expression obvious with amusement. The scout peered back at the two non-supporters, at the same time ran his coat sleeve over an apple that he held in the one hand. He brought the fruit within a short distance of his mouth and hesitated for a moment before biting into it, deciding to ask a question first. "Why?"

It was Lance who replied casually. "First of all, the captain and me rate you the patrol's number one deer slayer. Don't we, Captain?" asked Lance without turning his head.

"But definitely," came the quick reply.

Turley bit into the apple, hiding most of the wide grin that was quickly forming, for he knew that collaboration was silently taking place to rib him a bit.

"However," continued Lance, "out there alone, you would be hotter than a tin roof on a half burnt house in the middle of a forest fire. Just as soon as those Injuns caught sight of the fine deerhide outfit you are wearing, they'd be on the run, sharpening their tomahawks on their teeth in pursuit of one Blade Turley. We realize, the captain and me, though your buckskin suit is in a shabby state and has long since been ready for display at some antique gallery back east, it would still bring some Injun a good price at a trading post. Isn't that so, Captain?"

Drum could make no answer, for he was engaged in near silent laughter as he covered his mouth and eyes partially with the palm of his hand.

"Then too, dear friend, the captain and me would deeply dislike if some Injun would comb your hair instead of you, as it hung high in the air, drying in the sun as it rests on the branches of a willow tree. Captain . . ."

Lance got no farther as he burst into laughter along with Drum, who still tried to hold back, but was unsuccessful.

Turley took it all in stride, and more so, for he seemed quite amused by it all. The military man was first to recompose himself and he said apoplectically, "We are aware of the fact that you knew the possible hazards in connection with your suggestion and I am grateful that you are willing to buck the risks, but as Lance pointed out, that is, in a humorous sort of way . . ."

"Yeah," cut in Turley. "He gave me the answer just like Dawson would have."

"Thought you might be lonesome for some of Will's remarks," said Lance.

"Sure would like to see that tobacco-sprouting spigot of his in action again," commented Turley.

Frowns appeared on foreheads, and faces became sober as the discussion of their old friend continued. Shortly afterwards, the conversation faded away into silence with Drum's last remark, "I often heard him say, no blasted Injun will ever cut off his beard. We all have the same thought, to hear that remark again."

XXIII

From a distance, nothing seemed unusual at Bacon's camp on this bright June morning; however, upon closer examination, one would notice a quick reaction by most of the inhabitants when a shout was heard at the far end of camp by one of the men at work who heard approaching hoof beats as riders entered the temporary settlement. No one reacted more quickly to the noises than the girl standing in the doorway of a newly erected tent. Her thoughts were far beyond the imaginary line where the mountains met the sky, as she stood there still and silent with the exception of an occasional glance in the direction of the sudden disturbance. Reminiscing was over for the time being as a voice called out, "Naomi."

It was Mary Lou, who added quickly upon catching sight of the Indian girl, "Wait for me there, I'll be right up."

In less than a minute, Mary Lou appeared with an armful of articles and hustled toward the girl in waiting. Naomi held back the flaps, as her companion squeezed through the doorway, commenting, "Well, Mrs. Winsor, shall we decorate the interior with the newly gathered furnishings?"

A close study of the Indian girl's facial expression would detect a slight blush, which was credited to Mary Lou's formality. Naomi picked out three blankets at the same time saying, "We owe you and your people much. Again we are given many things."

"You never did get to use any thing the first time," said Mary Lou. "I could wring that White Cloud's neck. And of all times to come a calling. Why, if it were me that it happened to I would still be broken-hearted. Just like I know you still are." She looked at the Indian girl understandingly and added, "Well, don't you worry none. That renegade won't harm this new set up. I don't think he'll be around after the campaign is over with. At least I hope not."

A voice called out from just beyond the doorway. "Hello in there. Are gentlemen allowed in or is this ladies day?"

"Come right in Dad," beckoned Mary Lou.

Bacon stepped in, brushing through the flap, his face beaming like a little boy who was object of flattery at a surprise party. "Well now, if this doesn't look exactly like the first one the boys put up. Inside and out. This new location should be much better. Don't think they can shoot in fire arrows this far into camp."

"Father, please," exclaimed Mary Lou. "I was just telling Naomi that the campaign should put a stop to any more raids. At least in this area."

"Could simmer it down quite a bit," drawled Bacon. "But only time will tell what's still in store." He squinted his eyes and rubbed a three-day growth of whiskers with the back of his hand as he remarked soberly, "I was hoping for some news by now. The men I sent to the river haven't returned yet. The folks in camp are mighty anxious to hear what's happening down there."

"Father, what will happen if we are told that it still won't be safe to go on further west?"

"Well, we're all anxious to get our own land and start the settlement. If it can't be west of here, then it will be somewhere in these parts." Bacon sighed noisily, remarking, "We have some time left for waiting, or for a little traveling if we get the word, but we'll have to start building sometime in the near future if we are to be set enough 'afore the snow comes. I know it's only June now but time catches up fast when nothing is being accomplished." Bacon smiled at Naomi and changed the subject, remarking, "Guess you'll have everything all fixed up here by the time Lance gets back."

Her reply was already formed on her lips but failed to materialize, for the sudden shouting in camp caused the occupants of the tent to move quickly toward the entrance.

Bacon rushed through the doorway pursued by the women just as a member of camp approached them at a faster-than-normal speed, near shouting. "They're back. They're ridin in back yonder," and pointed in the direction of the mountains.

A cloud of dust indicated the fact that several riders were galloping toward the heart of camp. In short order, the settlers gathered around the wagon boss, whose uplifted arm was quickly noticed by the oncoming horsemen. They pulled to a halt within feet of Bacon, the latter calling out, "Well boys, what are the tidings?"

"Aint seen hide nor hair of 'em, Bacon," answered the spokesman with a voice mixed with bewilderment and excitement.

A deep frown appeared upon the wagonmaster's forehead, for the answer was far from being expected. The next question was directed at all four of the riders as he gave them a sweeping glance. "Did you boys go all the way to the river?"

It was the same spokesman who answered quickly. "Right down to the river and a few miles beyond."

"And you seen no one at all," remarked Bacon in dismay.

"No sir, 'nary a one of em. The whole military seemed to have vanished."

Naomi and Mary Lou glanced at each other in silence but only the latter displayed her feelings of disappointment. Bacon whipped off his hat and ran a rough hand along the side of his head at the same time remarking, "That sure is strange. Seems to me that some one would have been left back at the waters. Did you hear any shooting of any kind?"

The rider that had given the answers so far was unable to speak because of a mouth full of tobacco juice that was long since over due to shoot through the air. He looked about for a spot to spit, for the settlers milling about left him limited openings. Bending down low, he let go a Dawson dandy that caught his animal behind the front hoof, causing the horse to stamp its food several times in an attempt to shake off the annoying streamer. Before he could upright himself, another one of the riders replied. "Didn't hear a thing, either. Not even the rustle of a leaf. We listened in silence for about ten minutes and it seemed as if the whole world had gone off and left us. I've been around a lot of country in ma' time but never afore have I felt like no one else existed but the four of us just then."

"Guess I would have felt the same if I expected to see at least part of all those military men up there," said Bacon. "But then again, there may have been a change in plans."

He rubbed his chin in thoughtful silence for a moment, pondering over the matter, but discarded any further thought as the voice of the first spokesman appeared again.

"I would say that most of the patrols were there. Mighty lot of tracks. As a matter of fact, it was the trail with the most hoof prints that we followed there for a while."

Suddenly a voice from the thick of the crowd called out. "Well Bacon, what do we do now?"

"We're going to wait here 'til further orders from the military," came the quick reply.

Another voice spoke up sharply. "Seems to me if the Indians are west of the river it'd be safe to move up that far."

"I'm for moving up," came an outcry that was followed by shouts in favor and against. Bacon's arms waved frantically as he shouted in anger, trying to ease the tension that had gripped the confused settlers. It took little time for the well-respected wagon boss to calm the camp down to a peaceful situation. His elbow came to rest on his knee after placing his leg on a tree stump. From that position he glanced at the settlers with squinted eyes, finally resting on a member of the wagon train that seemed to have more than his say. With a curved finger in motion, he beckoned the man to step forward.

"Mr. Sutton, I would like to have a few words with you. That is if you don't mind," he added rather dryly.

The man stepped forward, pushing by others until he stood facing Bacon. With his thumbs hooked in his belt, he stood there with an ashen face while the other looked at him for a long moment. Bacon talked quite loud, for whatever he was about to say was intended for everyone.

"Mr. Sutton, I am well aware of the fact that you are anxious to get moving."

"Then I say let's get going and quit fiddling around here," cut in Sutton rather loudly. He glanced about the crowd inviting some verbal backing, which he got, but it was very weak.

Bacon shook his head from side to side and his tongue ticking noisily indicated shame. Then he said, "You were rude, Mr. Sutton. I wasn't finished talking." The manner in which he spoke caused the blood to drain from the settler's face and it was obvious that he was annoyed and embarrassed. Bacon's voice took on the original tone as he continued. "All of us are eager to move up but we will not make the start until we get the word. Everyone knows that as well as I do. We've had hardships along the way and with the grace of God made it up this far. We cannot go ahead blindly and against orders. That could prove to be disastrous. If one day we get to go where we're headed we'll know then that the chances for survival are good and the chances of being harassed by attackers are limited."

A slight sneer appeared on Sutton's lips as he remarked sarcastically, "Naturally, the attacks will be made by Injuns. Her kind of people." He refrained from pointing but glanced at Naomi while making the remark.

Bacon's facial features remained the same and held the same expression upon hearing the next remark.

'I fear no Injun and I don't aim to live in the same camp with one any longer. And I'm moving on out. There is no law saying we can't leave here, only verbal orders which we can take or leave."

Once again the speaker turned to the crowd anticipating support. Again he got it, but as before, it was very weak.

"All Right then," spoke Bacon loudly. "But remember this, once any of you leave this wagon train, you concede any support, any protection, of which you now have the privilege."

With that, the outspoken settler turned with the intention of going about his business when he suddenly spun around as if by force at the sound of Bacon's voice calling out his name. "Sutton."

The latter eyed the wagonmaster curiously but made no comment of any

sort as he quickly noticed the cool look directed at him. Bacon spoke slowly saying, "Most of us here are religious people. We hold no prejudice against color or creed. We'll fight any aggressor that tends to harm us in any way, be he red man, white, or otherwise, but we'll also share and help protect those that are law-abiding and have peaceful intentions. You have insulted one of our women folk, which leaves you with just one choice. An apology. Under other circumstances you would still be picking your teeth out of the dust if you were able. Consider this an easy way out."

Sutton glanced at Naomi for a moment and said, "Sorry ma'am, I meant no offense against you."

Once again he turned facing the crowd and spoke sharply. "Those of you who are going with me, make your selves ready. We're pulling out today."

Bacon's arm flew up into the air causing all to heed attention as he shouted above his listeners. "Just one more thing. For you who are about to leave us, please make yourselves a nameplate. Brand your name on a small piece of wood or stamp it on a piece of metal and keep it hung around your neck. Later on when we all move westward, I for one, will want to know who I'll be tipping my hat to as I gaze down upon the bones left behind by the buzzards."

Bacon discarded the matter abruptly as he placed one arm around his daughter's shoulder, and the other around Naomi's, saying, "By the looks of you two pretty ones, it's going to take a lot more than a good hot supper to bring the smile back on your faces. So for a starter, I'm going to escort the two of you on a ride around the area. The fresh winds will clear the minds of ill thoughts and allow the pleasant ones to get their chance. Jus' you wait for me at the wagon, I'll have the horses saddled in a few minutes."

He threw a wink at the girls as he departed then focused his attention on his wife upon noticing her in waiting a short distance away.

"Looks like the news and all the heavy talk around here this morning got a hold on you, too," remarked Bacon as he placed an arm around the shoulders of a third woman in just about as many minutes, this time his wife's.

"I've been wondering Dan," said Mrs. Bacon with a tone of curiosity. "You know more about things, like the river incident. What do you really think happened out there?"

"Something did happen," said Bacon with a frown. "Something that perhaps wasn't anticipated. Then again, any change in plans might occur during a campaign of that type." He sighed slightly before continuing, then said, "We'll just carry on here until word arrives, and hope for the best."

Mrs. Bacon smiled at her husband understandingly, then changed the subject. "There are two beautiful ladies in waiting."

"That they are," said Bacon. "But not quite like you are."

Flashing a quick wink at his wife, he then hastened toward the horses.

The time of night continued on it's way, encountering nothing more than a few greetings from an occasional hoot owl. Though the inhabitants of the area were geared for war, and the silent vicinity a potential battle ground, it could well have been named peaceful valley based on the pleasant outcome of the night.

Several hours after daylight found Drum's patrol moving along, steadily eager eyes searching the terrain ahead for some sign of the vanishing patrol or the enemy. Within the last mile or so, Lance commented only when spoken to. His interest was absorbed by a set of hoof prints which he caught sight of occasionally as they reappeared on the trail being used at present. At intervals, the tracks would veer sharply to the left then come back out to the open trail. It seemed to the scout that the rider could have been an advanced scout or riding the flank of a party of Indians. Lance lifted his gaze and glanced over to the right as it occurred to him, if such were the case, then there would be numerous tracks some where in that direction. He was about to inform Drum of the possibilities, when he focused his gaze on the trail ahead of him and observed the prints as they reappeared again. But his silence was credited to the second set of prints that showed up to the right as they emerged out into the open. Before he could give the matter any additional thought, Turley pointed to the ground saying quickly, "Here's another set coming out from my right."

Lance looked at Turley remarking, "I didn't know that you knew about the ones on my left. They're kind of faint."

"I didn't for a while," said Turley. "But when I saw you straining your eyes, I looked a little closer."

A tint of bewilderment fell over Drum's face as he scanned the growth to the left for the prints in question, then said with a grin, "Gentlemen, I need more time on the trail."

Both of the scouts grinned slightly as they cast a glance at the captain.

"Let's ride up a little ways and have a look around," suggested Lance.

The three horsemen pulled away from the patrol and rode about a hundred yards where upon they came to an abrupt halt.

"Just as I thought," said Lance as he looked down at the numerous tracks that led out to the open trail.

Drum shoved his had upward and with the same sweep of his hand wiped his forehead then asked, "What do you make of it?"

"I figured who ever made those tracks back there to my left could have been riding the flank of a band of Indians."

"How long ago were these made would you say?" asked Drum.

"Better than a day. Maybe two," replied Lance.

"By the indication of the prints, I would say that it was a sizeable band," remarked Turley, then asked quickly, "Do you think that they are part of the bunch Custer was following?"

"Don't think so," replied Lance. "Probably one of the war parties on their way down to join the Sioux. Chippewa's more than likely."

"Let's move on, Captain," suggested Lance.

Drum nodded his head in agreement, and with a backward glance at the on coming patrol, which was but a few yards away now, he uttered satisfaction and urged his mount forward, pulling abreast of the scouts.

The pace was exceptionally fast. Anxiety now continued to be a constant visitor due to several near future possibilities. Meeting up with Custer's patrol, eating again the meat of wild game, and getting the campaign over with one way or another. The already-quickened pulses were increased to a faster tempo as the familiar cry of the whippoorwill sounded clear and sharp, coming from a point on the trail ahead. Drum's gloved hand seemed to fly into the air automatically bringing the patrol to a sudden halt. They listened to the call in silence once more, then as it broke off a question on the lips of others but asked verbally by Drum, "Dawson?"

Lance shook his head with a slight trace of disappointment, and then replied, :No."

"I kinda thought that He'd shuffle in on this deal somehow."

"I'll signal back, then we'll ride on up and see what news the General's rider has to offer." Lance gave out with two sharp calls. After a visual confirmation by the scout, Drum motioned the patrol forward at the same time saying, "I hope it's good."

"No news is good news, Captain," remarked Turley.

Drum faced the speaker and said, "There are always exceptions to any rule."

"You sound like a professor, Captain," said Turley with an indication of a grin.

"I was told that many times," said Drum, "and most recently by a great scholar of the west."

"You don't say," exclaimed the scout with a suspicious frown. "And who might that be?"

"Dawson."

Lance listened without making any comment and a slight smile creased his lips at the mention of his old friend's name. After a few minutes of riding, Cook's messenger appeared into full view.

The horseman urged his mount forward and rode up to the patrol. He snapped a salute, and then thrust the note forward with his hand saying, "Message for you sir, from General Cook."

Drum read the contents of the message openly, bypassing the formalities. "Unless something has occurred where you would need my personal and immediate attention, continue on as planned. I offer nothing new in developments and will adhere to plans accordingly. Good luck."

Disappointment was obvious, for the lack of any contact with the Custer forces now prolonged their anxieties. There came no comment. Each seemed to be lost in momentary thought.

Drum spoke shortly, addressing Cook's messenger. "How long did it take you men to contact us?"

"A little over an hour, Sir, I would judge," came the quick reply. "We cut across after leaving our patrol until we thought the five miles was reached. Not seeing any of your signs we continued north and ran into these Injun tracks. I stayed here and sent the other fellers on up for a distance thinking that you might be up there a might deeper but they came steemin' back here in short order and said that they had spotted the patrol when they reached the top of the ridge there, and sure enough, Sir."

"You gentlemen did very well," smiled Drum.

"Thank you sir," said the spokesman with an air of one who had just been presented with a citation.

"Will there be a return message sir?"

"No," replied Drum. "Just report that you've made the contact."

"Yes, Sir."

With that and the quick formality of saluting, the three horsemen headed toward the assumed direction of Cook's patrol.

"Well, gentlemen," said Drum. "We continue toward the unknown."

Lance agreed with the shake of his head but made no comment. Once more the patrol continued the westerly direction and in their minds lingered the fact that unless something occurred in a very short time, they would quench their thirst on the waters of the Little

Big Horn before the end of day. A probability considered very unlikely when starting the pursuit of Custer.

As they rode deeper into the unknown territory, reaction to noises, familiar or other wise, was obviously noticeable whenever the occurrence presented itself. No small wonder the mounting tension with the exception of hoof prints, Custer's patrol, and the war-painted Indian tribes seemed to have vanished completely from the land of the Big Horn. At one time or another, from Drum on back to the rear guard, the thought of fate and what it had carved out for them on this mystifying journey to the Little Big Horn brought on many answers, but none that could qualify as a basis for a wager. As the hours wore by, General Cook's position could have been located literally without difficulty if need be, for Drum and his scouts watched the departure of the fourth set of riders that Cook had sent to make contact since leaving the village.

The latest message to Drum indicated nothing more than the three previously sent. However, the number of contacts made did signify that Cook, too, was riding forward in anxiety and bewilderment. As the patrol started out again, Lance remarked casually, "The General is sure trying to get something solid to go on."

"The feeling is certainly mutual," said Drum with a deep frown.

After a few moments of silence, Turley, who seemed to be riding along as if no one else were about, which was quite contrary, for the glint in his eyes indicated the fact that his forth coming comment would be picked up by several pairs of sharp ears, spoke with an air of wisdom. "We follow the great rainbow toward the clear waters of the Little Big Horn. Mother Nature has been kind indeed to provide us with a guide to intercept our destiny." Turley paused briefly and from the corner of his eye noticed Drum and Lance look at each other understandingly. A slight grin touched his lips as he continued. "As you know, the storybook of the rainbow always favors the weary traveler with a pot of gold at journey's end. Gentlemen, fear not, for we, too, will be favored with some sort of a pot, or if I may change it to a keg, a powder keg. An old master of the wars am I and I implore you to be cautious to the bitter end, for the price of hats are sky high back at the trading post."

"Mr. Turley," said Drum with an air of satisfaction and continuing the acting roll, "You have strayed from the category of humor to the more serious lines of philosophy, and I must say that you have spoken words of wisdom."

"Far be it that I change my brand now," cut in Turley with a grin. "Allow me to rephrase the whole thing."

"Never mind," snapped Lance with a smile. "Don't spoil the speech. It just bares out what I've known right along. You have the qualification of a deacon."

"A deacon," exclaimed Turley as he bent forward on the saddle trying to get Lance's eye. The latter sported a smile but deliberately avoided the others gaze.

"A knife-throwing deacon," muttered Turley as he sat back to his original position. "I'm afraid that the congregation would frown upon one Blade Turley relating to them the words of gospel."

Once again silence befell them for thoughts of what lay ahead over-powered all other matters that could have otherwise led to continued conversation.

Hours later, the patrol stood near-motionless as they gazed down upon the Little Big Horn River. The expression on the men's faces was more than tinted with bewilderment as they gazed about for some sign of life, which for some reason seemed to be expected at the now-reached destination. Perhaps it was because the latest plan included nothing beyond the Little Big Horn.

It was Drum who spoke first and his voice carried the tone of concern. "Have you gentlemen observed anything that I may have missed?"

"I don't think that there is any one in the immediate vicinity, Captain," said Lance bypassing a direct answer.

Drum looked at the scout questioningly but the latter was already with an answer as he pointed beyond the river saying, "If you look close between those two oak trees where the brush stands high, you will notice the antlers of elk bobbing up and down occasionally. Can't tell how many there are but they are feeding. Couldn't have bean any disturbance of late or else they wouldn't be there."

Drum shook his head, either indicating the fact that he agreed with the scout's last remark or had actually noticed now the animals in question and said instead, "Let's ride on down to the waters and have a look around."

As they started down the small grade, Turley's lips were pressed together forming a white line and he shook his head as if at loss to come up with a logical answer concerning the situation. Lance noticed the scout's silent action and asked, "How do you figure it fella?"

Turley glanced at Lance who was watching him and only then did he assume that the question had been directed at him. He replied by saying, "All I could say at this point that would make sense is that we're still riding through God's country."

"Least we forget that it is being leased by the Indians," said Lance casually.

Turley squinted at Lance and said, "That I'm aware of. I just thought I'd mention who the owner was."

Drum and Lance eyed each other for a moment with a trace of amusement and the remainder of the trip to the water was made without added comment.

Drum lost no time having the area searched. Riders were ordered to look about and sent in various directions. A radius of several hundred yards was covered in short order but the cause failed in the attempt to uncover any sign of a human being or the animal that may have rode, if such were the case in the not too distant past.

The two scouts were the last to report. It was Lance who spoke as they rode up to Drum and the waiting patrol. "Looks like we're the only ones that dare tread this area, Captain. Not a sign of any kind."

Drum shook his head acknowledging the fact then said with a faraway look in his eyes, "We can't find any and on the other hand I'll wager that General Cook can't get rid of them."

The mention of Cook's name seemed to hasten Drum's next move, for he followed his previous remark with an order directed at Stenton. "Sergeant."

"Yes, Sir."

"Place some men around the area, then report back to me immediately."

"Yes, Sir."

As Stenton galloped toward the bulk of the patrol a short distance away,

Drum spoke to the scouts. "We're going to camp here indefinitely. Let's move over to the other side of the stream and ponder briefly over the matter at hand."

There were no speed records broken as they rode through the shallow waters. Once on the other side, the journey's end was evident, at least for the time being. The scouts were silent, for they were aware that the question on their minds would soon be answered. Extreme patience wasn't necessary, for Drum spoke at the same time he started to dismount.

"At this point, we are to wait until word reaches us from the General. If I were to send some riders down the river, they could meet them along the way and then get back here with the message in short order and in turn Cook's riders would pick up my report. It would save time, which would prove to be vital, depending on the circumstances. Should my riders have to ride all the way to Cook's patrol, the time element would have the same hearing."

Drum looked at the scouts waiting for comment, which came from Lance with a ring of approval. "As far as I could see it, Captain, we seem to have but one choice that could be termed logical as it stands now and you picked it right out of the bag."

"You have a fast-riding volunteer at your service, Captain," said Turley who seemed to have listened in thoughtful silence up to now. "I'd like to make the trip down the river."

Drum eyed Turley with a twinkle in his eye as he walked over to the scout and pulled the latter's long knife out of its sheath. He ran a finger along the cutting edge to the point of the blade and after another moment of inspection said, "I consider you the deer slayer of the outfit, Mr. Turley. Of course I base that remark on the stories that I heard you tell on occasions."

Lance noticed a sly grin appear on Turley's lips as the captain continued. "In as much as the food situation is an immediate matter to be considered, I now have the opportunity to allow you to test your skill on behalf of the near-starving patrol, which of course is very near correct. I might add, Mr. Turley," said Drum as he swept off his hat and slapped it against his leg loosening most of the dust, "that the ones we spotted a short time ago might still be lingering in the vicinity."

"At least the tracks are," grinned Turley.

Drum slipped the knife back into the scout's sheath and with a word of caution said, "Stay within signal reach. We may have to move out of here sudden-like."

Turley mounted his animal, then looked down at the two men briefly with a grin. He flipped his hand into the air in farewell, at the same time urging his mount forward and riding slowly away in silence. A short distance farther, the scout pulled to a halt as two horsemen tore through the brush. It was Stenton on his way back after carrying out his orders, and the oldster Hargerty.

It was Hargerty who spoke first as they stopped with in a few feet of Turley. "Where you headin', Mr. Turley?"

The scout flashed a quick wink at Stenton then looked about in cloak and dagger style, shifting his eyes from side to side as if wanting to be sure that no one else was within ear shot. He hunched his shoulders and leaned toward the oldster saying just above a whisper, "The captain is sending me on a secret mission."

"Is that so," whispered Hargerty with keen interest. It was the old military man who glanced over his shoulder at Stenton, this time in a secretive manner. He turned slowly back and faced the scout, then shifted his eyes toward Stenton indicating the fact that the latter was listening.

"He's all right," said Turley assuringly, and at the same time nodded his head and an gave upward twist to the corner of his mouth further indicating approval.

"What's this mission about, Son?" The question was asked impatiently and with a tone of eagerness.

Once more Turley looked about in a sly fashion, then replied, "The captain is sending me on out to capture and bring back Sitting Bull."

Hagarty's eyes squinted as he stared at the scout. From his hunched position, he turned and glanced at Stenton who managed to hold a sober face. Whatever ran through the old man's mind suddenly came to a quick decision, for he reared his mount, backing a few paces and whipping out his rifle from the sheath, training it on the scout. He ordered sharply, "All Right Mr. Turkey, forward. We're going to have a little talk with the captain."

Turley frowned slightly for at the moment he wondered if Hagarty had really taken him seriously or if he was returning a little stunt of his own. Before he could make any comment, Stenton cut in quickly, saying, "Now, Harry, there's no need for gun play."

"There won't be any, Sergeant, if he behaves. I've been watching this lad for a spell now and after the yarn he just told us, it convinces me the man needs attention. Sergeant, I'd like permission to see the matter through by taking Turkey here for a few words with the captain."

"Now look, Harry, all this is . . . "

Stenton said no more as he caught the scout's eye indicating that they make the short ride.

"All Right then," agreed Stenton. "If you think you're on the right track."

"Thank you, Sir."

Turley moved forward without prompting, the others following close behind. Drum and Lance's eye brows shot upward as they discontinued conversation upon noticing the strange procession moving out of the brush toward them. They assumed that Turley was behind whatever was taking place, for he rode toward them obviously chuckling.

"Can't figure this one out," said Lance in low tones. "Hagarty got his rifle out as an inducer."

"We'll soon find out," said Drum.

"Sergeant, what's the meaning of this?"

"Sir," replied Stenton quickly, "Doc Hagarty here seems to have a case he'd like to discuss with you."

"Well, Hagarty?" The captain's voice was tinted with curiosity. He widened his lower lip showing a row of white teeth but blotted out the forming grin.

"Begging your pardon, Sir," stammered the old military man as he jammed the rifle back in its sheath. "I think that Mr. Turkey here is a sick man and needs your immediate attention."

Drum glanced at Lance but the other had already turned his back to the group for obvious reasons. Drum cleared his throat and remarked, "Seems to me that a sick man needs no prompting with a rifle."

"Well, Sir, didn't want to take any chances." He pointed a finger to his head and remarked, "He's sick up here. It's like I told the sergeant sir, I've been watching him for some time and what he told us a few minutes 'afore shore bore out my suspicions."

"Go on," urged Drum upon noticing the speaker hesitate for probable comment.

"Well, Sir, he said that the captain had sent him on a mission and that was to capture Sitting Bull and fetch him back to camp."

Drum's hand went quickly to his mouth and from the corner of his eyes noticed Lance slowly walking away. Drum brought the incident quickly to a close, as he said, "I think that there has been a slight misunderstanding and any more comment concerning the matter can be discussed at a less crucial time. Mr. Turley was on his way for a try at a bull elk."

"Well, Sir," cut in Hagarty as he looked at Turley with squinted eyes, "I think this young fellar can do it too. With some of the yarns he tells, he could easily stun a bull to a stand still."

"In that case, Mr. Hagarty," said Drum, "My confidence in this young fellow rises a notch or two. It'll be steak for the camp tonight."

Once again Turley flipped his hand without a glance at any one, urged his mount forward and headed for the brush. The grin he wore grew wider as the lingering thought of the incident reoccurred in his mind.

"Sergeant?"

"Yes sir."

"I want you to ride the river. Take Hagarty with you."

"Yes sir."

"Under the assumption that everything materialized according to plan, you should contact the General's patrol, roughly speaking, about five miles from here. Make this report. We have reached the river without incident and now await further orders."

"Yes, Sir. Ready, Mr. Hagarty?" called out Stenton.

"Ready sir," answered the oldster as he reared his mount.

Several hands went to the edge of a pair of hats in a salute to their superior, and in another moment the two riders left a spray of water in their wake as they galloped down stream.

"Seems to me that the old man rode off with a certain amount of pride," remarked Lance as he gazed down stream.

"Yeah," agreed Drum. After a moment of thoughtful silence, he added, "He seems to be a serious-minded fellow. I wonder if he understands our humor. I wouldn't want him to think that we're treating him with disrespect."

"I'm sure he don't, Captain," said Lance.

Drum looked at the scout, waiting for an explanation, which came without prompting.

"Personally, I think that the old man bringing Turley back here at gunpoint was a joke of his own."

The other made no comment, but a sense of satisfaction surged through him upon hearing the scout's opinion.

"Well," said Drum as he let out a heavy sigh, "May as well rest a while in the shade. Will you join me in a smoke?"

"Sure will, Captain. We were thinking along the same lines."

XXIV

They picked themselves an inviting spot and stretched out as if bedded down for the rest of the day. Lance watched a group of soldiers stretch out a piece of canvas, then carry it over to the middle of the river. It was obvious that the men were going to do a bit of seining and at the moment seemed to be in disagreement as to the right approach. They quieted down as one of them either shouted louder than the rest or had come up with a likely strategy. In short order, the men shuffled about, taking hold of three sides of the canvas, and plunged forward into the waist-deep waters. The maneuver met with a certain amount of success, for shouts of glee were uttered as the seine was lifted up out of the water.

"We're going to have fish for supper, Captain," remarked Lance with a chuckle.

"I hardly think that they can scoop up enough to go around," said Drum as he blew out a stream of smoke. "However, a little luck along with Turley's skill and we can lead to an all-out loosening of waist belts."

Suddenly the two men fell into silence as the faint sound of galloping of hoofs through shallow water swept past their ears. They sat upright as it grew louder and glued their eyes on the bend in the river, waiting for the horsemen to come charging around it.

"Probably one of your guards coming off his post," said Lance.

"Could be," agreed Drum. "But he's riding like someone that had something to offer other than an all clear report."

As the rider came into view, the two men sprung to their feet and waited for the charging horseman with more than a shade of curiosity.

"Four horsemen approaching, Sir," came the quick report as the rider came to a splashing halt.

"Recognize any of them?" asked Drum.

"Couldn't make them out at that distance, Sir," came the fast reply. "But they are riding mighty hard, Sir."

Drum faced Lance, saying, "No doubt Stenton and the oldster are among them."

"Perhaps the mystery of the vanishing patrol will finally come to life." As the faint noise of the oncoming riders came within earshot, Lance remarked, "We'll soon find out one way or another, Captain."

Once more, curiosity engulfed the men as they waited for the distant riders to come charging up with news that could be more than the ordinary report of the past few days. The grim expressions on the faces of the men indicated that all was not well as they pulled to a halt. Those in waiting hadn't a chance to test their patience that was crowded by anxiety, as a voice spoke clearly and quickly after a hasty salute.

"I make this report with regret, Sir. General Custer has been wiped out to the last man."

There had been many occasions of silence during their trip to the river, but the one hovering over the immediate area at the moment won the award for the quietest. Even ole sol seemed to want to hide from the shocking news as it slid from sight with the aid of the passing clouds.

At the moment, the spokesman, whose stripes placed him in the category of a lieutenant, had the look of one whose guilt was being determined for cattle rustling. Lance stared straight ahead blankly. The news was sad in itself and to make it a shade grimmer, his old friend Dawson was head scout for Custer. His thoughts flashed back to the settlers' camp. It was right after the wedding that the old scout waved goodbye and headed for the river to join Custer. It was Lance who broke the silence as he spoke automatically. It was a question already answered, but for strange reasons like in many cases, reality, especially when it's bitter, will be questioned as to its sincerity, even though it stands erect a fact. "Was every man accounted for, Lieutenant?"

"Unfortunately, every man. No one escaped," came the reluctant reply. The latter brought an envelope into view and handed it to Drum, saying, "For you, Sir."

Drum took the message, and for the first time faced Lance while they exchanged glances, but neither of them made any comment. Suddenly he faced the lieutenant, apologizing. "Sorry, Leiu. I sort of slipped up on the formalities."

"Quite all right, Sir. This has been a regretful experience for all of us."

Drum tore open the message and read it. "Captain Drum, with the assumption that Lieutenant Attley reported the tragic news verbally, I will now reconfirm it briefly. Gen. Custer and his entire patrol were slain in battle while engaging the enemy. Bypassing details, our intelligence reports that Sitting Bull is headed for the Canadian border with a small sized band. His trail should be clear and not too hard to locate. It leads northward on the west side of the Little Big Horn. You will follow and try to apprehend the Sioux chief. Will put scouts on your trail in a day or so with further orders. Keep a vigilant lookout for them. Should they fail to make contact, you will find messengers at your present location when you return. Under those circumstances, allow ten days for the mission if need be. Good luck, Gen. Cook."

Drum handed the message to Lance, than faced the lieutenant. "I have a verbal message for the General, Lieu."

"Yes, Sir."

"Tell him that I have read the message and will start on the mission immediately."

"That it, Sir?"

"That's it, Lieu," and Drum extended a hand, which the other grasped in a hand shake.

"Should our trails meet again," said Drum, "I certainly hope that it will he under happier circumstances."

"I hope so too, Sir."

Cook's messengers saluted Drum in orderly fashion and then made a hasty getaway down the river.

Drum cast a glance at Lance, the latter lost in silent thought. After a brief pause, he spoke to the scout sympathetically. "This news is certainly bitter to all of us and more so to those closely related to the deceased. I'm sorry about Will."

The scout nodded his head slowly but said nothing. Drum thought it best to let him alone for a minute or so, for he suddenly urged his mount around and said to Stenton, "Round up the men you have out at their posts and I'll get the remainder of the patrol in readiness. We'll be moving out shortly."

"Yes sir," said Stenton, and he rode away in a surge of speed.

"Captain," called out Lance before the military man advanced but a few yards. Drum tugged on the reins, turning his mount and facing the scout who rode toward him, saying, "I'll ride out and round up Turley. We'll wait for you somewhere up ahead."

"Fine," said Drum, then as an afterthought added, "We won't have to keep our guns silenced now. Should there be an opportunity for meat, blast away."

Before any more was said, the two men turned their heads in the direction of a galloping horse that tore through the brush like a frightened rabbit. As the animal and its rider appeared into view, Lance exclaimed upon recognition, "It's Turley. Got something more than a bull moose on his mind."

The rider spotted the men and in a few moments came to a noisy halt. "Didn't get that deer," he said quickly. "But I ran into a trail made by a sizable band. About six or seven hours old I'd say."

Lance and Drum looked at each other understandingly while Turley watched them with curiosity prompting him to ask without hesitation, "Something I missed out on gentlemen? Can't help but feel that you know more about it than I do."

Drum placed a hand on Turley's shoulder saying, "Glad you run across that trail. You've saved us time and trouble. For a short time now we knew it was up ahead somewhere and also who it was made by. Lance will tell you what has taken place since you were gone. See you gentlemen shortly." Drum urged his mount forward and rode slowly away.

Turley's gaze lingered on the departing military man for a long moment. He then turned to face Lance and asked rather reluctantly, "What? What happened?"

Turley lost no time in leading them to the trail. After a brief but close observation, Lance agreed with Turley's calculation, saying, "Like you say, about six or seven hours. Heading for the border and on the run."

"Going to be rather difficult catching up with them," said Drum frowning as he gazed in a northerly direction.

"Got to push hard the rest of the day," said Lance, "and keep wide awake. Wouldn't want to follow these few dozen tracks for a long ways and find about five hundred waiting for us at the other end."

It occurred to Drum at that moment that the scout's remark was based on his theory concerning the massacre of Custer, and to have it confirmed or denied, he asked with a hint of curiosity. "Like Custer?"

"That's the way I have it figured," replied Lance as he glanced at the military man, who quickly agreed silently within himself that the scout's theory was much more logical than the ones he had pondered over since first receiving the tragic news.

"Indian strategy mixed with deceit, gentlemen," said Turley with a soft voice. "We've found it to exist from the very first battles with the red man." Turley sighed deeply as he continued. "General Custer was a noted Indian fighter. It seems to me that he had disregarded some basic rules that had aided him to achieve much success in battling the Indians in the past. I just can't figure out why a man with his experience went on ahead and plunged into . . . "

Lance cut him short, saying, "Some of the answers will never be verified as a fact."

"Nor will his actions be forgiven by many," remarked Turley.

Although Turley maintained the level of his tone, it was obvious now that his remarks held the tint of bitterness. Drum directed his question at the younger scout, asking, "Under the circumstances, if we were engaged by the enemy somewhere along this trail in battle and wiped out to the last man, would your last statement be applied to me also?"

"Certainly not, Captain," came the quick answer. "As long as you were operating with in the jurisdiction of given orders. And as we all know, the general was . . . "

"Hold it." Lance's voice cut in sharply, causing Turley to shift his gaze to his friend, whereupon he was confronted by that familiar grin which was indeed contrary to expectations. Lance paused briefly as he placed his hand on the scout's shoulder, and then said, "You were much closer to Dawson than I thought. I'm glad, fella. For a moment there I thought that you had a personal grudge against the General."

"No," said Turley with a smile. "I just wanted to find out how foolish I can feel arguing a lost cause with the captain."

"I think that the basic reason behind your flowing comments was a stall for a brief rest," said Drum amusingly. "It wasn't necessary though. I was about to call for a five minute break anyway."

"See what I mean gentleman, a lost cause," said Turley. "Captain, I would like to redeem myself and get back into your good graces. I would like to make a suggestion at this point."

"Go right ahead," said Drum. The scout was about to comment but Drum cut in saying, "Or we'll all starve tonight."

Turley looked at Drum saying, "You read me well, Captain."

"Just guessing," laughed Drum, then added, "You go on up ahead but don't wander too far off the trail."

"Stenton."

"Yes, Sir," came the quick reply.

"Ride along with Turley."

"Yes, Sir." The scout whipped his rifle from its sheath and held it in front of Drum, saying, "Much more effective at long range, Captain."

"Approved at this point," said Drum. "And I certainly hope that you gentlemen meet with success." He nodded his head toward the waiting men in his patrol and remarked, "Along with Lance and me, they too will be looking forward with anticipation to some point along the trail where you two lads are waiting with several hundred pounds of choice elk."

Turley eyed Stenton for a moment, then with a wide grin said, "Don't dare come back if we fail."

"In that case," said Stenton, "We just as well pick up the trail where Lewis and Clark left off, and keep on going."

Turley was about to urge his mount forward but hesitated upon hearing Lance's voice, which was obviously directed at the potential hunters, saying, "In that event, the captain and myself will be greatly concerned. Write once in a while and keep us posted. After all, we are all old friends."

Nothing more was said but the smiles lingered as the elk hunters rode off at a fast clip and disappeared from view. The trail bore through the thickest part of the wooded area, however it was easily followed. The tracks left by Turley and Stenton stood out above the others clearly, as their fast-moving mounts dug into the soft earth. The patrol moved along steadily, carrying with them an air of anticipation. Caution and alertness was maintained as usual but the organ of hearing rode the highest on priority, waiting patiently for a familiar rifle shot that would indicate fresh venison on the menu tonight.

Each passing mile drew them closer to darkness. Later, as nightfall slowly appeared on the scene, the taste of roasted meat faded from the lips of the men. Conversation passed among them on occasions expressing little or no hope for the hunters to catch up with their group. There were some that were optimistic and were soon confronted with a wager. The once-alerted ears eased back to normal as the betting gave way to other interests. The activities within the patrol stopped abruptly as Drum shot his arm into the air and called a halt. He took a backward glance, whipping the hat off his head and letting it rest on the forward part of the saddle before remarking. "Turley sure stuck to the trail. He hasn't veered off once."

"I thought that he would make an attempt to track down brother elk before this," said Lance as he gazed around the area with piercing eyes.

"Might be able to contact them by trying a few signals," suggested Drum. "Won't be long before darkness."

Lance shook his head in the affirmative in agreement. He urged his mount forward a few paces, halted the animal then tried his first signal. The human-uttered cry of the whippoorwill echoed far and distant and even the bird with the identical call would find it rather difficult to distinguish. Once again ears were primed to alertness, listening for the return signal, but none came. The scout continued the call several times. The frown on his forehead clearly indicated disappointment. The calls were unanswered.

Drum's thoughts were made verbal and he spoke like a man alone. "Followed another set of tracks mile after mile a few days back. Never did run into the riders who made them. At least we didn't. This situation seems to have the same ear marks."

Lance glanced at Drum, weighing the remark, but refrained from saying anything as a rider rode up from the rear and halted at the side of the military leader, saying, "Beg pardon sir, but this here situation has stirred me up a mite too."

The speaker was Hagarty. He eyed the two men, half expecting reluctance because of his abrupt appearance, but soon went into high speed upon Drum's inviting question. "Have any logical theories, Mr. Hagarty?"

"Thems mighty big words you used thar, Captain, and I can't say that I know one from another, but I know this and I'm shore that you sir and Mr. Winsor here will agree that them there tracks made by horses with shoes belong to Mr. Turkey and Mr. Stenton."

"You'll get no argument on that Mr. Hagarty."

"Well, Sir, and I hope I'm wrong sir, but them boys could be atop their mounts riding with their hands tied in back of them and followed by a half dozen Injuns that had grabbed them in ambush. Else wise they would have appeared afors this." He tore his hat off with the swish of his hand and scratched his head while frowning, then remarked with uncertainty as his listeners sat in silent thought. "I may be all wrong about this here, Captain. Mr. Turkey shore does things in a funny way sometimes."

Drum looked at Lance, saying, "I've been thinking along those lines myself. However, not in the manner Hagarty here spoke of. Have you drawn any conclusions of your own?"

"Well," said Lance, "I find a flaw in Hagarty's theory. There hasn't been any shuffle along the trail indicating confusion that would be plain to see if they have been attacked." To spare the old man's feelings, Lance turned to him now, saying, "Mr. Hagarty, what you say could be true but I only pointed out that such an occurrence was unlikely because I know Mr. Turley pretty well and before he would..." Lance stopped abruptly as a mating call of a bull elk echoed through the valley. A sudden inspiration engulfed him, for some strange reason the presence of the animal made him feel that Turley too lurked somewhere within the green, waiting for just such a chance. But as the calls ceased finally, likewise did their hopes diminish. A full minute went by in silent waiting.

It was Drum who spoke first, saying, "I was almost certain that the crack of a rifle would ring out at the middle of one of those calls."

"I would have bet my last dollar on that, Captain," said Lance as he continued to look in the direction from which the calls came. "Captain, we'd better . . . "

Lance never finished the sentence, for the sudden crack of a rifle some distance ahead was welcomed eagerly as the sharp broken sounds sailed over their heads. The rear of the patrol became quite talkative with optimism staging the attack. That the gunman was Turley or Stenton was taken for granted and that assumption was quite obvious up front as the expression on the faces of the men indicated.

Drum made a remark after letting out a sigh. "Very untimely that Turley, very untimely," to which they both chuckled lightly.

"Just like I said, Sir," cut in Hagarty. "That Mr. Turkey is way out of tune."

"We'll soon find out," grinned Lance, then directed his next remark to Drum."Any time you're ready, Captain."

With his hand in the air, Drum urged his mount forward and the patrol followed in close pursuit. They set a fast pace for about a mile and a half, then slowed down suddenly as a rider loomed out of the brush into full view. As he caught sight of the patrol, an expression of relief appeared on his face followed by a wide smile. Urging his mount forward, he raced toward the approaching patrol. Moments later Stenton made his report after a quick salute.

"Glad to report we've met with success sir."

A howl arose to the rear by winners and losers both, as the thought of fresh venison for supper was now a near reality. Drum glanced to the rear approvingly, then focused his attention on Stenton saying, "This comes as a surprise to us. Lance and I have long since agreed that the two of you had taken off for new trails west of here. Where is Turley located from this point?"

"About a hundred yards off the trail from where I came out," replied the still grinning Stenton. "Should have it cut up by now sir."

"Or eaten," cut in Lance.

"Take a few men with you and pack up the carcass," said Drum. "We'll wait for you at the point you'll cut in off the trail."

"Yes, Sir," replied Stenton, who immediately called out for several men by name and made a hasty departure.

The darkness of the night was penetrated by the flames of a roaring campfire from which the odor of roasted meat was being inhaled vigorously by those seated nearby. Patience wasn't very popular at the moment, for the men of the patrol were eager to accept a portion of venison even though it was still semi raw. Comments such as, "Hand me my piece chef before you burn it to a crisp," proved quite obvious to that effect. Some time later, the men preparing the meat finally cut into the flesh of the once-proud elk, and distributed the first portions to Drum, the two scouts, and Stenton.

It was Hagarty who assumed the responsibilities of a head chef, thus masterminding the lone item on the menu. He had gone about the task as if preparing a seven-course dinner for a banquet on behalf of the president. His pipe was smoking like the stack of a laboring locomotive as he served the men their portions.

"Well now, Hagarty," exclaimed Drum as if in surprise. "If this tastes as well as it smells, your prestige as a cook will soar to utter heights."

"I roasted animal meat for others 'afore sir and I'm mighty proud to say that I ain't had any complaints yet," remarked the oldster.

"Especially from the deceased," cut in Turley forcing back a grin.

Hagarty puffed wildly on his pipe several times, then withdrew the stem of the smoking inferno from his mouth. A smile tickled at the corners of his mouth as he remarked, "Mr. Turkey, if such is the case, come morning I'll be expectin' no complaints from you."

Drum and Lance broke into laughter as they watched the half choked Turley fighting back surprise.

"There's a lot more left. Just call out, Sir," said Hagarty as he walked away with a sense of satisfaction.

"Well I'll be dammed," exclaimed Turley. "Didn't think for a moment he'd be familiar with the word."

Eager comments were forming on the lips of the men but before any one could express one verbally, their interest turned abruptly to one of the guards who approached them quite rapidly indicating the fact that something other than the usual routine was forthcoming in the report. Silence and expressions of curiosity paved the way for the man off his post to make haste with whatever was responsible for his presence, which he did so as he halted in front of Drum saying. "Begging your pardon, Sir, I wish to report a lone rider coming up the trail toward camp."

Drum was up on his feet as if aided by a coil spring, the others following suit.

"Were you able to make the rider out?" asked Drum quickly.

"Yes, Sir. I . . . "

Drum shot another question before the man could finish whatever he intended to say. "Military?"

"No, Sir."

"Are you sure?" asked the captain without any indication of surprise.

"Yes, Sir. Rode right on past me as I huddled off the trail just past my post."

"What? You made no attempt to challenge? Jason, I assume that you have taken upon yourself the responsibility of issuing free passes to the Sioux to join us for a portion of roast elk."

"But, Sir," stammered the bewildered guard but his plea went unheard as Drum issued orders to Stenton.

"Remind me to have a personal chat with Jason should we survive this incident."

"Yes, Sir."

"Alert the men and get under cover."

"Yes, Sir."

The military leader focused his attention on the scouts, saying quickly, "We'll cover the trail and give our guest a rousing welcome."

As they started to advance toward their objective, the guard called out in a tone worthy of attention. "Sir."

The men stopped and swung around facing the guard questioningly.

"Sir, that rider you're going out there to welcome is a lady."

The blood rushed to Lance's face for a moment as he thought of Naomi but quickly discarded any possibility that the rider could be her, especially after listening to the details uttered by the guard as Drum asked, "A woman?"

"Well not exactly, Sir. I got a glimpse of her face in the moonlight and I would say that she was a little lady, about ten or eleven years old."

The men glanced at each other but were at loss for an explanation at the moment, which didn't help the matter any, as Jason, somewhat relieved now, spoke more boldly.

"Sir, I never challenged any one at that age before and I thought it better to make the report to you and let you decide on the matter rather than for me to scare the tar out of her."

"I see," mused Drum as he glanced at the scouts in hope of a suggestion under the strange circumstances. It was Lance who spoke, but not in a way of a suggestion, as he gazed out over Drum's shoulderm saying above a whisper, "Captain, you being a well-bred gentleman from Boston places you in the position to welcome our guest. Take a look over your shoulder."

The men followed Lance's gaze to a spot not more than forty yards from where they stood, and let their eyes rest bewilderingly on the little rider seated on her Indian pony. The animal was motionless as it stood there with its head bent low seemingly in wait for a command from its master. The girl sat on her pony with about as much stillness as a stone statue staring back at the men with an expressionless face. She showed no concern as to her fate, nor showed any indication of her next move; she just appeared to be in waiting for the men to make their move.

A touch of sadness crept to the faces of the men, for the forlorn looking animal and its rider certainly fit into the category of lost souls. It was Drum who broke the awkward silence as he said in a near whisper, "Lance, I suggest we move up a little closer and you talk to her. You speak the Sioux language."

"She's Cheyenne, Captain."

"Cheyenne," exclaimed Drum in surprise. "I know that they are up here in force but this little girl, what would she . . ."

"Don't know myself," cut in Lance. "Let's ease up and find out." The scout got to within a foot of the animal and stopped, as did the others. He reached over and patted the animal's mane gently, at the same time keeping his eyes on the girl for some unexpected reaction. Her dark eyes flashed in the campfire light as she glanced at one man, then another, finally shifting her gaze hack to Drum, staring at him steadily. A slight smile appeared upon her lips, causing the military man to flush slightly. He glanced at the scout urging to do something that would bring to a close the awkward situation.

Lance grinned back, for he was quite aware of Drum's uneasiness and said, not adding to the captain's relief, "You seem to appeal to her captain. Undoubtedly the object of her affections."

"I feel flattered indeed," said Drum trying to hold back a shy grin. "However, at the moment, the object of her visit should be clarified."

"Just dropped in for a social visit to chat with her favorite white leader," cut in Turley, who refrained from meeting the captain's eye least his grin become wider.

Lance spoke to the girl quickly now, for he sensed rather than felt that the ribbing had gone the limit. As he spoke, the girl's gaze shifted to him. Her facial expression now sported the element of surprise. The scout's voice was soft and carried the tone of encouragement. She answered rather shyly, but freely. After several minutes of questioning, Lance turned toward Drum and was met with a question, "What do you make of it?"

"Well, as much as I could gather, she came up here with her father along with a sizable band of Cheyenne. The girl was left in one of the villages. There was quite a bit of disturbance within the past few days and during the shuffle she strayed off and got lost."

"Seems rather odd for her to have wandered off this far," said Drum as he glanced at the visitor from the corner of his eye.

"She didn't come upon us by chance," remarked, Lance. "At least not at this point."

"Spotted us before this then," mused Drum as he calmly rolled a cigarette.

"As we started away from the river," said Lance.

"Come a mighty long ways for a little woman. Did you ask her just why she followed us?"

"Said she was alone and afraid," replied the scout. "And we were company."

"Well," said Drum looking back over his shoulder as if in search of a spot which would be suitable for a guest room. "Having a lady in camp under such circumstances is quite new to me. What would you suggest at this point?"

"First of all," replied Lance, "supper for our guest. I'll escort her to the dining room."

The scout spoke a few words to the girl, at the same time easing his way close to her casually. He reached up and placed his hands around her waist and lifted the girl off the animal. She slid into his arms without comment or resistance and to the scout's amazement, placed her head on his shoulder unafraid, as if the man holding her so gently was next of kin. Lance looked down at the huddling little form sympathetically, then faced Turley, saying, "Boy, take care of the lady's horse."

"Ah," exclaimed Turley, following up with a bit more wit. "My career is starting to shape up. Stable boy at last."

He glanced at the shabby looking animal for a moment and then added, "I don't think that this creature can make it to the stall, General."

Lance, who was already on his way with the others, turned and looked back saying, "Turley, we've got to be big about this. I'm carrying one of our weary guests, you carry the other."

Chuckles burst forth following the comment. Turley himself enjoyed the humor as he gazed at the others for a long moment with a lingering grin, then looked at the animal as he took hold of the reins saying, "Come on fella, show them you can make it."

Stomachs filled to near capacity in addition to their weary bodies, paving the way to early slumber, which was the direct cause for near silence about camp. However, not all were overcome by the magic drug administered by the sand man, for a few remained in lingering conversation as they sat off in the shadows a short distance from the dying embers of the campfire.

Close by was the little guest, who after being fed was bedded down in blankets given up by the scouts. Only her head was visible as she laid there without a stir. She was still awake despite the fact of a very tiring day. Undoubtedly the little lady's mind was filled with curiosity and perhaps mixed with confusion, for the white man's kindness this night certainly was contrary to stories she surely heard at one time or another back home. She glanced from one man to another in deep study as if gathering valuable information from the enemy, or on the other hand, just wondering why these supposed ruthless white men smile so easy and so often. When her gaze fell upon Lance, he gave her a quick wink, which caused no more reaction than if he had scratched his head.

Turley observed the intended flattery in addition to the nonreactive results and remarked, "Now back in St. Louie, you would have probably have gotten a smile, or if you were unlucky, a slap that would have elevated your hat about three feet into the air. I would say that the little lady is in belief that you have a fluttering eye lid and much in need of the tribal medicine man's services."

Lance shrugged that one off with a grin, otherwise making no comment.

Drum took advantage of the silence and asked rather soberly, “How would you gentleman suggest we bid farewell to our lady guest in the morning? That is without crushing her faith in the white man’s hospitality.”

“I don’t think you’d turn her loose to wander around by herself up in this country, Captain,” said Lance as he glanced at the girl in question.

Drum looked at the scout thoughtfully but made no reply, whereupon Lance continued. “If need be, we can leave her at Big Bear’s camp on our way back, unless we encounter some of the elders belonging to one of the tribes before hand.”

Drum let out a sigh indicating he was obviously engrossed in thought as he gazed out into the darkness, and then remarked after a brief silence. “During my training, I studied the numerous situations that one would be apt to find himself in once past the frontier, but this one failed to reach print.” He continued after a moment, changing the subject as he remarked casually, “Mentioning Big Bear’s camp reminded me of Deer Foot. I wonder if the young chief still breathes the pine scented air of the Big Horn?”

“Come to think of it,” said Turley, “we haven’t seen any sign of him since he took off into the dark that night.”

“Keeping under cover pretty well,” cut in Lance. “Rather dangerous country on this side of the river for any of Big Bear’s braves since the old chief refused to join forces with the others.”

Turley placed at cigarette to his lips before remarking. “Personally,” he hesitated long enough to strike a match on a near by pebble and set first to the tobacco before continuing, “I think that Sitting Bull was indirectly responsible for the old Chief’s death.”

“I’ve been thinking along those lines myself,” agreed Lance.

Drum took advantage of the silence and asked, rather soberly, “How would you gentleman suggest we bid farewell to our lady guest in the morning? That is without crushing her fate in the white man’s hospitality.”

"I don't think you'd turn her loose to wander around by herself up in this country, Captain," said Lance as he glanced at the girl in question.

Drum looked at the scout thoughtfully but made no reply, whereupon Lance continued. "If need be, we can leave her at Big Bear's camp on our way back, unless we encounter some of the elders belonging to one of the tribes before hand."

Drum let out a sigh, indicating he was obviously engrossed in thought as he gazed out into the darkness, and then spoke after a brief silence. "During my training, I studied the numerous situations that one would be apt to find himself in once past the frontier, but this one failed to reach print." He continued after a moment, changing the subject as he went on casually. "Mentioning Big Bear's camp reminded me of Deer Foot. I wonder if the young chief still breathes the pine-scented air of the Big Horn?"

"Come to think of it," said Turley, "we haven't seen any sign of him since he took off into the dark that night."

"Keeping under cover pretty well," cut in Lance. "Rather dangerous country on this side of the river for any of Big Bear's braves since the old chief refused to join forces with the others."

Turley placed at cigarette to his lips before remarking. "Personally," he hesitated long enough to strike a match on a nearby pebble and set fire to the tobacco before continuing. "I think that Sitting Bull was indirectly responsible for the old chief's death."

"I've been thinking along those lines myself," agreed Lance.

"Well, in any case," said Drum, as he chewed on a small twig that protruded out of his mouth. "Big Bear hastened his steps toward destiny the day he stopped Lance here from finishing off White Cloud and prolonged the renegade's ruthless activities to continue . . ." Drum took a deep breath, and then in conclusion said as he faced Lance, ". . .in your direction."

Lance observed the remark in silence, nodded his head in agreement, his thoughts remaining unexposed. Drum walked over to the girl and tucked the blanket under her shoulders. She smiled at the military man, uttering a few words in her native tongue. He accepted that as a word of thanks and said casually, "That's quite all right."

Turning quickly toward Lance, who now wore a slight smile, he asked, "What did she say?"

"Her heart is happy," the scout replied.

"You certainly have that fatherly touch, Captain," remarked Turley, as he nodded his head at the same time convincingly.

"Just a way with women, fellas," said Drum with a quick wink to Lance as he walked toward his blankets and saddle. The two men watched the military man in silent thought for a few moments, perhaps wondering about his sense of humor, soft-spoken, well-mannered, and effective leadership. A short wave of the hand, followed by a few words, automatically put the scouts into motion toward their gear as he said, "See you in the morning, gentleman."

XXV

The gray dawn of another morning inched its way over the silent wilderness. At any minute now the camp would go into action, following the same pattern of the early hour routine. One man was already awake but his usual routine failed to take shape, for his attention was focused on a little bundle that lay a yard from Drum. Lance reached over and shook Turley briskly, the latter exclaiming as he bobbed up his head sleepily, "Wassa matter, you lonesome?"

The scout replied with a nod of his head in the direction of the military man. The other braced himself up on his elbows and turned his head. He was quick to notice the little form concealed entirely underneath the covers, and too, the spot she originally held the night before.

Turley uttered a few words that certainly weren't meant for Drum's ears. "Shame, shame on the captain for sleeping near the woman folk under the same pine tree."

"We'd better wake him before any one else gets up," Lance said. "He'll be embarrassed as it is."

Suddenly Drum sprang up into a sitting position probably awakened by the low tone voices, and looked curiously at the scouts who looked and felt quite awkward at the moment. Lance quickly eased the situation at least for the moment, as he flipped a hand into the air and said, "Good morning, Captain."

Turley followed suit. "Top o' the morning to you, Captain."

The manner in which the greetings were presented this morning caused Drum to grin slightly, whereupon he remarked, "This certainly is an unusual . . . " His voice ceased abruptly as he spotted the huddling form in his attempt to get to his feet. If the captain felt embarrassment, it failed to appear on his features. The remark that followed was certainly a casual one. "This little tot sure rolls in her sleep. Must have traveled all of twenty yards."

"You know, I've been thinking, Captain," Turley said. "Maybe she's spying for the tribes and took her present position in hope that you reveal something of importance in your sleep."

"In that case," chuckled Drum, "her breakfast shall be delayed several hours as due punishment."

No more was said, for their attention was aroused by a small dark head that slowly appeared from beneath the blankets. Her eyes seemed to hold a shade of fright. Lance was quick to observe this and said, smiling in her native tongue, "Good morning, little flower. Did you sleep well?"

She answered quite shyly in the affirmative.

"Hello there," greeted Drum as he smiled down at her. Not understanding English, she refrained from verbal comment but gave the captain the usual wide smile that exposed a set of pearly teeth.

"Young woman." Turley's voice caused her to glance in his direction, after which he continued, "Do you realize that you are a suspected spy this morning?"

Although she smiled, it seemed that the pearly ones were reserved for the captain only, who she glanced at for a second and then looked back to the scout as he said, "She sure is a fearless one, or else thinks that I recited a bit of poetry."

The girl got to her feet and quickly folded the blankets. She then walked over to Lance and handed them to him. He tossed one of them over to Turley saying, "It's been neatly folded. Show your gratitude to the little lady by keeping it that way."

"By all means," Turley said with a sly grin.

Drum pulled a field jacket from one of his saddlebags and placed it around the shoulders of the girl. He then buttoned the jacket and rolled up the sleeves. Stepping back a pace, he looked her over, saying, "It hangs down over your knees, but then we won't be going formal for a while."

Glancing at Lance, he asked, "By the way, what is her name?"

The scout spoke to the girl where upon she quickly answered, "Tioga."

"Tioga it is then," remarked Drum before the scout could repeat the name. Facing Lance again he said, "Better brief her about being the guest of the army for the next few days."

Lance nodded his head and walked toward the girl.

A short time later, the camp was wide-awake. Stenton rounded up the guards and made his report to Drum, who was in action shaving away a day-old growth of beard.

"Nothing amiss during the night, Captain. Looks like we're roamin' around in tame country."

Drum halted briefly as he turned and glanced at the sergeant, saying, "It's the quiet, peaceful-looking spots that deal out sudden death, Sergeant."

"Guess you're right, Captain," Stenton said more to himself as he shifted his attention to the little figure emerging from out of the thicket with a canteen slung over her shoulder. "Appears like she's goin' to earn her keep."

Once again, Drum turned away from the mirror he had attached to a tree and immediately caught sight of the girl. A touch of embarrassment shaded his face as he spoke in defending tones, "Now I wonder what prompted her to do that?"

Stenton made no comment. A grin stole across his lips as she appeared in full view. He gave her the once-over as she trudged along in that heavy, over-sized field jacket, and asked when she glanced at him, "Who is your tailor, little girl?"

Surprisingly, the girl answered; however, it was not in response to the question.

"Tioga"

"Is that so," mused Stenton, rubbing his chin curiously. "And who might that be?"

This time he directed the question at Drum, who replied, "Tioga is her name."

He reached over, after jamming his razor-edged knife into the sheath, and relieved the girl of the canteen, saying, "I'm looking forward to return the favor some time." He then turned to face Stenton. "Well, Sergeant, shall we say we'll be heading north with in the next fifteen minutes?"

"I'll have to use the whip sir, but I'll get them ready."

Lance and Turley walked up just as Stenton tore away. They watched the captain dabbing his face with hands full of water for a moment, then Winsor took a would-be towel that hung on a branch nearby and handed it to him.

"Oh, thanks," said Drum. "Must be my lucky day. I'm getting service from all angles. By the way Winsor, would you rush the lady to breakfast?"

"You beat us to it, Captain. We were just going to ask your permission," said Lance.

Drum squinted at the scout briefly, playing along as usual, then said simply, "You have it."

The scout spoke to the girl and clasped her hand. Turley walked over and held on to the other.

"Hold it, my boy," said Drum as he placed a hand on Turley's shoulder. "In this case, you would be an intruder. A lady dining with two men would be frowned upon by the medicine man. Anyhow, I want to ask you a something that I'm sure you are an authority on."

"It's got to be women then. And so early in the day, Captain," said the scout with a slight exclamation.

"I think that the subject would interest you at any hour of the twenty four," laughed Drum.

"It does," said Turley.

They watched Lance and the girl walk toward the center of camp where the one and only dish was still roast elk, then they resumed the conversation. Drum asked, "If you were up at this time of the morning back in St. Louis, just what would you be doing?"

"Undoubtedly, getting ready for bed," was the reply. "Not very interesting, Captain. However," went on the scout with an eager tone and a glint in his eye. "I could tell you what I did and where I've been up to the point of retiring." Drum glanced at the scout slyly, asking, "Did she have light colored hair?"

"No, red," came the quick reply.

"Sounds intriguing," mused Drum. "Why don't you open up the big town while we indulge some of that steaming coffee they're pouring out over there."

"Captain," said Turley as they started forward, "I've seen all types of officers in my time but none like you."

Drum grinned slightly but made no comment.

The rate of speed at which the patrol was now traveling was partially credited to a good night's rest and a full stomach. The high-ranking officers of the military would have come to a sudden halt and looked twice at the new addition up in front with Captain Drum and his scouts, should they have met under the circumstances. Tioga, with a bead-studded band around her head and a long eagle feather tucked in at the side, pointing skyward, rode along on her small pinto like a veteran of many a trail. To the amazement of the men up front, she seemed to be quite enthused by it all and appeared to be having the time of her young life. Obviously, she took to the flattery and attention showered upon her by the men unlike anything that happened to her before.

On one occasion Drum winked at her and to his utter surprise she winked back, causing him to exclaim, "Well now, what do you know."

"Catching on fast or else she'll flirt with no one but the captain," Lance remarked after witnessing the exchange of fluttering eyelids.

The topic of conversation was changed abruptly as Turley's voice called out with a tone of unusual soberness, "Oh, Captain."

"Ah," exclaimed Drum. "Glad to see you're still with us. You seemed to be lost in thought for quite a while."

"As a matter of fact I've been quite observant," said the scout.

Before he could continue, Lance slapped him on the back lightly, saying, "He's wide awake, Captain. I'll bet my future ranch that this boy was goin' to mention somethin' in connection with the tracks along the trail."

Turley eyed Lance with squinted eyes, remarking, "Ole hawk eye himself. I was afraid that you were losing your touch."

Drum halted the patrol, then faced the scouts with a frown, and asked, "What have I missed along the trail now, gentlemen?"

Lance was silent as he placed a cigarette to his lips,which was obviously an invite for Turley to do the briefing, which he did. "First of all, the trail has diminished in size. Riders have been veering off at intervals, some to the right, others to the left."

The scout stared hard at the trail up ahead for a long moment before remarking. "Something has been planned and is taking shape at this point."

Drum looked at Lance, asking, "Same conclusion?"

"Same conclusion," was the reply. "I was going to bring it to light after checking that small rise up ahead there."

A deep frown creased the smooth forehead of the military officer as he scanned the trail ahead. It seemed as though he was trying to detect some sign that would betray the presence of the enemy. His next question obviously in conjunction with his thoughts, "Do you think that they are in hiding and ready for us somewhere nearby?"

It was Turley who offered an answer due to Lance's hesitation, for it appeared that the latter was still weighing the matter thoughtfully. "I wouldn't want to guess at picking the spot, but I'm sure they'll take a crack at us before we reach the border.

Lance came to a conclusion suddenly as he quickly directed his question at Turley. "Why would you say those riders left the trail?"

"To confuse us. Which would slow our forward progress."

"That's possible," agreed Lance. "However, they veered off at intervals, perhaps the strategy being that we fail to detect all of them or if we did notice some, have little cause for suspicion."

Suddenly, Turley turned and looked in a backwardly direction, whereupon Lance

Remarked, "That's right, fella. One of the oldest Indian games in the book."

"There should be about eight of them back there following us," said Turley as he obviously more than realized that such an occurrence had taken place.

Drum was dissatisfied with himself at the moment, for his voice betrayed his feelings. "I'm going to learn that signs are just as important, if not more, than the actual form of the enemy or my career may come to an unsuspecting sudden halt. Stenton."

"Yes, Sir," came the quick reply from the rear. The sergeant was preparing a cigarette, its tobacco flipping into the air at the snappy call by the captain. He threw the pouch back to the man he borrowed it from, muttering something unmentionable under his breath as he urged his mount forward, riding to the head of the patrol like a pony express rider delivering a personal message from the president.

"Alert the men for instant action," said Drum in a voice appearing unusually calm under the stressing circumstances.

"Yes, Sir."

Stenton rode back to the middle of the patrol and relayed the captain's orders with a convincer of his own as he raised his voice above normal. "All right men, you wanted action, you may get it right quick. Stay alert and wide awake or else you may get that elk meat you ate this morning blown against some tree stump along with your stomach."

With that accomplished, he raced his mount to the head of the patrol again.

Drum slipped his gloves off casually as if readying himself for a cup of noonday tea, but in his mind a plot began to take shape that was quite contrary to sipping tea and dunking crumpets at some social gathering.

"Well," said the military leader, hesitating briefly, then continuing, "They are planning to ambush us some place up ahead and attack us from the rear at the same time."

"It stacks up that way, Captain," said Lance.

Drum reached into his pocket and drew out a cigarette, which he placed between his lips at the same time, remarking, "No doubt old

Sitting Bull would frown upon my intentions with a sneer if he knew, but all's fair in war."

"And love," added Turley.

"That, my boy, is debatable," commented Drum, side stepping the matter at hand for a moment. He then continued with revealing his plan.

"We're going to give those braves a reception they're quite familiar with. First, we'll move up to that small rise over there and have a look around. Should it prove to be a likely spot for such a venture, dig in and wait for the enemy. The element of surprise will be in our favor at this point, for we can quickly dispose most of them and remain intact should the others up ahead come running to their aid. Well, gentlemen?" added Drum in conclusion as he waited for comment.

"I know of no other way to lessen the strength of the enemy," said Lance with a tone of agreement. "But I would suggest that we scout ahead a quarter of a mile or so and make sure that the area is clear. Otherwise, they may be near enough to see our every move and crack down on us as originally planned. If they're in waiting like we suspect."

"All Right then, let's move on up there," said Drum as he signaled the patrol forward.

Suddenly his face deepened with concern as he glanced at the girl riding beside him, for during the discussion he had forgotten about her. He smiled at her, saying, "I'll see that you have a special guard in the event Sitting Bull gets nasty. I wouldn't want anything to happen to my coat, that is while you are in it, ma'am." He tipped his hat at the conclusion of the last sentence, at the same time receiving that pearly smile which would be worth tipping a hat under any circumstance, which amused him and the scouts alike.

Once atop the rise, the terrain ahead became thick with heavy timber and saplings. An ideal spot for the patrol to make their stand, or the enemy, and this they were well aware of.

Piercing eyes scanned the area and detected nothing out of the ordinary. Lance's voice drew the attention of the others as he said, "You can see a couple hundred yards in either direction from this point, but beyond that it closes in kind of tight, and as far as I can see, the trail leads right into it. Turley and I will ride on up a ways and have a good look around."

"All Right," agreed Drum. "We'll wait here for your return. Stenton."

"Yes, Sir."

"Have the men ride down off this rise with the exception of two or three. Place those men you pick to remain behind in a position where they can observe the back trail clearly."

"Yes, Sir."

Stenton progressed no further than an intended attempt to carry out his orders, nor did the scouts advance but a few paces, when suddenly a signal from a southerly direction caused automatic inactivity. The cry of the whipoorwill was repeated several times, and then was followed by silence. A disheartening factor for the caller, be it man or bird.

The scouts back-tracked the short distance to where Drum waited, tight lipped and undoubtedly wondering what bearing the signals would have on his intended plan. "What do you think?" he asked as they rode up.

"It's not the little fella with wings," remarked Lance. "The call was made by a human being. By someone I'd swear I've heard before."

"Dawson," said Turley questioningly, for he remembered the scout's praise concerning the near perfect call developed by the old veteran.

Lance hesitated for a few seconds as he slowly discarded his thought then replied rather reluctantly, "Certainly sounded like one of his calls. Guess I'm mistaken this time."

"Would it be wise to answer?" asked Drum cautiously.

Lance wore a deep frown as he glanced in the direction he and Turley had attempted to investigate and replied. "If the enemy is nearby, then he already has us spotted. Should the distance between us be lengthy, then it won't matter to us, but it will matter considerably to the man trying to locate the patrol."

Drum shook his head in agreement at the same time saying, "Go ahead."

The scout signaled twice in succession. A familiar silence prevailed as on other occasions while in wait for a return signal of acknowledgment. The seconds edged their way on toward a full minute without the expected results, causing the men to eye each other understandingly.

"That's strange," uttered Drum in somewhat above a whisper, his facial expression featuring confusion.

"Something happened," offered Lance in dull enlightenment as he squinted thoughtfully in the direction of the back trail.

"Have you ever heard the cry of the bird this time of day?" asked Turley casually.

The scout was quick to reply, "On rare occasions. And I'll answer your next question which you have on your mind and want reconfirmed, but you don't dare ask."

A grin appeared on both their lips after the previous remark. Lance broke off momentarily, and then reassured the scout in conclusion, saying, "It definitely was a signal from one of the men of another detachment."

"Something silenced those men," remarked Drum who was obviously trying to come forth with a logical answer."

"Blazing arrows," cut in Turley as if in answer. "Shot from the bows of the braves that we suspect are following us."

"Could be that they spotted the braves first and are laying low," suggested Lance optimistically.

"Gentlemen," said Drum in a tone of voice that was tinted with determination. "All of our suspicions are based purely on theory. We're facing a stonewall, and up to this point there are several possibilities as to what lies on the other side. The time has come to crash through and find out definitely."

"We go on as planned," cut in Lance, quite aware that he had spoken for the captain, and he did just that as Drum repeated, "We go on as planned."

"We'll be back shortly," said Lance as he urged his mount forward. He glanced at Turley as the latter pulled up beside him, saying, "I think the theory business concerning the signs has the captain troubled. This hide and seek warfare is not his style."

"It will be if he remains out in this territory. Sooner or later he'll learn all the angles. If he can manage to keep breathing."

They rode along in silence to the spot where the growth gradually became more dense. There the scouts stopped and leaned on their saddles as they turned for a look at the patrol that was still visible at this distance.

"They could still see us at about another hundred yards, then we'll be on our own. Well, let's ride on up for a half mile or so and see if we can stir up something educational in Indian warfare for the captain."

"I'm for it," said Turley in agreement, "but let's not give up our scalps as a down payment towards his tuition."

Lance grinned as he urged the animal forward and said a few words of caution, "Follow me fella, ride along, and keep those eyes keen, like that of a hawk."

At a distance of about fifty yards from the spot where they previously stopped, giant timber loomed up as if in defiance, the spreading limbs heavily laden with twigs and needles. Sunlight was limited to a few scattered rays that found their way through, finally resting on Mother Nature's soft earthen floor. Although it was only past midmorning, it appeared to be nightfall underneath the tall trees that grew so densely in this particular part of the vast wilderness.

The scouts rode slowly and in near silence, scanning everything that would harbor a lurking enemy. The hoofs of the animals pounded out a softly rhythmic beat as they dug into the soft forest floor. The riders' glances would meet on occasion and linger momentarily to pick up a visual massage should there be any, then renew their search, scanning the area in all directions. A sudden flash surged through Turley's body as he unexpectedly heard Lance's voice call out softly but sternly. "Hold it. Be casual. Don't look around suspiciously. We've just started classes on behalf of the captain. Now, turn and face me with a grin. I'm goin' to offer you a cigarette. Take it and light it up."

Turley obeyed without flaw. As he faced Lance he lost all conception of danger but for a second, for the latter sported a smile that didn't quite seem to be in alignment with his voice.

"Don't look or act suspicious," cautioned the scout as he handed the other the tobacco.

"I gather we have company," spoke Turley without moving his lips.

"We have," confirmed Lance continuing in a mellow tone of voice.

"Sizable?"

"Can't say. But I'm sure they're all grouped around nearby."

"Did you actually see one or just a sure sign?"

"I saw the form of one."

"Where is he located, just in case?"

"He's up in the trees above you."

Turley's hand stopped automatically in mid air for he was about to take another puff when informed that the sidekick to the grim reaper lurked just above him. He had the urge to take a quick glance at the harboring tree, but decided against it rather than be contrary to Lance's cautious warning. His hand was now in motion as he placed the cigarette to his mouth where he let it dangle as he spoke. "Get us out of this one captain and I'll give you that promotion I promised you. Right up to General. Call the move, I'm ready."

Lance lost no time in briefing Turley. "Turn your mount around facing the patrol but don't move forward. Let's go. Real easy."

The scouts tensed as they made the maneuver, for they half expected to feel the sting of a bullet or the slicing edge of a sharp arrow. They both sighed noiselessly as they exchanged glances. The burning fuse had not reached the point of explosion. However, the scouts were aware that the enemy was being patient in hopes of getting the entire patrol to ride into the trap, and too, they would never make it back to where the captain and his men were waiting, without being shot at.

Drum and Stenton had watched the scouts since their departure and at the moment were freely making comments about what appeared to be somewhat of an unorthodox procedure on the part of the men in question.

"Perhaps they've come across something that failed to be noticed during our discussion," mused Drum as he stroked his chin lightly.

"Can't figure it out, Sir," said Stenton. "Maybe they got a new angle," he added as an afterthought.

"If that were the case, they'd be here right now talking it over with me." He sighed deeply and said at its conclusion, "Something's in the wind, and I don't smell it."

Turley ejected the cigarette from his mouth with out the aid of his hands. He was all ears as Lance continued speaking in a casual manner. "I'll motion to the captain and at the same time call out for him to bring on the patrol. That's just what they're hoping for back here. I'll continue the motion and throw in some words of warning. I don't know how the captain is going to react, nor the enemy. In any event, slide low to the left side of your mount and ride for all your worth when I give you the go sign. It's not too dense to the left of us. Can't be too many of them in hiding there."

No more was said between them as Lance motioned quickly calling out, "All right, Captain. Bring on the patrol."

Curious glances were exchanged by the captain and his aid, whereupon Drum remarked with a tone shaded with anger, not caused directly by the action of the scouts but by the feeling that some unseen existence was evident and he failed to grasp it. "What the hell is going on? They never acted contrary to plans before."

Again Lance motioned and yelled. "Bring on the patrol, Captain, let's go. Got some company."

Drum snapped his head around with the intention of calling out for an explanation but caught himself quickly, for the scout's last sentence sunk in, causing him to act with speed as he uttered, "Good God. They must be sitting there right in the middle of those blasted red skins. Now listen closely," said Drum addressing the men. "There's an ambush awaiting us down there and the scouts are sitting in the middle of it. When I give the order we'll ride in that direction as if nothing is amiss. Be alert at an instant for the signal to attack. In that event, the right column will veer off to the right of the trail, which I will lead. Stenton, you lead the other column to the left of the trail and proceed on down toward the target area."

"Yes, Sir."

"Hagarty," called Drum.

"Yes, Sir," came the quick reply as the oldster rode to the head of the patrol.

"Send those two men guarding the back trail up here in a hurry."

"Yes, Sir," he said urging his mount forward."

"Wait a minute," snapped Drum.

"Yes, Sir."

"I want you to guard the back trail, and take this girl with you."

"But, Sir," uttered Hagarty with a look of disappointment.

"That's an order," said Drum in milder tones. "I know that I can depend upon you to keep her from getting hurt."

"Yes, Sir."

Hagarty grasped the reigns of the Indian pony, whereupon the girl glanced at Drum with frightened eyes. He managed a smile and nodded his head in the affirmative, reassuring her it was all right, then faced in the direction of the scouts, calling out as he lifted one arm into the air to attract them. "We're coming on down."

The scouts still appeared to be calm but within them they were all geared up for what could be the fastest attempt ever undertaken for a hasty exit.

Lance spoke without turning his head. "The captain is going to split up that formation with lightning speed before getting to this point. We've got to move before that happens or . . ."

"That's when the lid blows off," said Turley reading Lance's mind.

"They'll cut us down without a chance," continued Lance. "We've got to make the break first. You all set?"

"I'll be halfway up the line before you finish saying the word go," replied the scout.

"Be careful you don't run me down," said Lance, "I'll be in front of you."

Turley glanced at his friend from the corner of his eye and noticed a faint grin that vanished as he spoke in a near whisper. "Here they come."

Drum's voice was loud and clear as he ordered the patrol forward. His piercing eyes sought for an impatient move by a member of the red clan but it was all in vain. It suddenly occurred to him that he had jumped to conclusions concerning the location of the company referred to by the scout. However, after a brief consultation within himself aided with the former belief, especially since the scouts maintained their solitary position. Tension ran a close race with imagination as the alerted patrol slowly neared the halfway mark. Anxiety was obviously featured and exposed on the faces of the scouts, although not exposing it in the open. They were more than eager to make the break before a death-dealing arrow sped past the arc of the bow.

Lance swallowed hard as Drum led the patrol past the halfway mark and uttered in low tones, "He's coming in too close."

"Any time you're ready, Captain," hinted Turley with a hint of impatience.

Suddenly a volley of rifle shots cracked loudly somewhere along the back trail, drawing the attention of the patrol and the enemy alike.

An instant later Lance's voice called out, "Let's go!" taking advantage of the unsuspected opportunity with lightening speed, and only a few poorly aimed arrows, shot by the confused enemy, followed their hasty retreat.

"There's a bunch of them in there," shouted Lance to Drum as he and Turley sped towards him. Now is the time to take them on, Captain."

The scouts veered off the trail tearing into a growth of laurel where they dismounted in a non-military-like manner. Drum's column was right on their heels and hell bent for action.

"Spread your men out, Captain," said Lance quickly. "Some of them may be in off the trail aways."

Drum issued the orders quickly, then in a crouching position, made his way to where the scouts were already inching their way forward. The three men hit the dirt as a sudden burst of rifle fire roared thunderously to the left of the trail.

"Stenton and his men got them spotted," remarked Drum quickly.

"Captain," shouted a voice from somewhere on the other side. "They're moving back pretty fast. Moving out I believe."

"Lets go," said Lance, springing to a crouch and starting forward.

Drum signaled the column with the wave of his arm, then suddenly bent down low as the scream of a ricocheting bullet sailed within inches of his head but took with it the black hat he wore. It spun crazily in the air, finally hitting the ground where it rolled along for a short distance like a tumbleweed in a wind storm. He paid little as he once again made his way to the side of the scouts.

Lance glanced at the military man momentarily, noticing the missing headwear and remarked, "Getting your hat cleaned, Captain?"

"Reformed. It's a little out of shape," came the quick reply. Just as he uttered the last word, a bullet caught Drum high on the shoulder, ripping open the seam of the sleeve and digging deep enough to draw blood. "And this one goes to the tailor," said the military man in bewilderment as his hand moved quickly to his shoulder.

The scouts dove backward, falling at the wounded man's side, both men asking the question at the same time, "Are you hit hard?"

"Just a graze. Somebody's after me, fellows," he said, the remark obviously meant to be humorous

"Let's see who the unfriendly chap is," said Lance as he got to his feet in a hurry and bounded toward a boulder about twenty yards away. A lone arrow hissed by him and crashed into the brush. Turley and Drum, who were up in a crouching position, spied the brave who now darted out from his place of concealment and blasted away at the running renegade. The brave's speed was increased somewhat as the bullets tore into his body giving him an added boost, but only for a few yards before going down, head-long in a dive that, under other circumstances, would be the envy of all swimming tribesmen.

Drum looked wildly about for another marksman as he covered Turley who bounded toward a large tree like a jackrabbit running down hill, but his rifle remained silent. A moment later, he called out to his men again. "Let's go."

After progressing forward in the vicinity of a hundred yards, the enemy became more numerous and the firing became heavier, but a state of confusion seemed to exist among the red man as they scampered about wildly.

"They must have been routed out from the other side by Stenton and his men," remarked Drum on one occasion as he reloaded his rifle. Before any one could offer comment, a shrill voice called out a warning. "Captain, look out above you."

Three frenzied braves with wild like features jumped off the ledge above just as a barrage of shots from Drum's men screamed up at them. Two of them were dead before they fell partially on Lance and Drum who tried to scurry out of the way. The third, slightly wounded, held onto his knife as he pounced on the alerted Turley and jabbed like a mad man who was aware that his time had come but wanted a white scout along for company. Blood covered the scout's wrists as he struggled with all his strength to keep the Indian from delivering the final blow. Suddenly the brave wrenched his hand free from the scout's bloody grasp and raised the red-stained blade into the air. At that instant, Turley slipped both his feet against the enemy's stomach and shoved furiously, sending the brave sprawling backward and hitting the ground with a thud. Both fighters bounced up like a rubber ball, but Turley's wrath, aided by his stupendous skill, bewildered even the enemy as he suddenly became motionless staring at the knife-thrower for a moment. His own weapon slowly slid from his fingers as he sagged at the knees, finally collapsing in a heap. The scout took a few fast strides, yanked the knife out of the dead brave and threw himself down to rejoin the others.

"Cover us with your men, Captain," said Lance quickly. "Going to doctor this boy up a bit."

"Cut deep?" asked Drum automatically before complying.

It was Lance who answered after a close inspection. "Nothing serious, Captain."

Without another word, Drum motioned the men forward, advancing a short distance before a rifle barked to the rear where he assumed Hagarty and the girl were positioned. He glanced over his shoulder as another shot rang out, then another. His eyes were at straining point and he gazed with anticipation for some movement, but none appeared. His concern showed plainly on his facial features but the matter was obliterated from his mind momentarily by the rapid gunfire triggered by the men around him. He looked over the situation up ahead and after a snappy but thoughtful consideration, shouted to his men. "Keep pressing them and don't leave any stone unturned."

Within another fifty yards the firing ceased considerably. Drum was down on one knee peering over the trunk of a fallen tree. He glanced backward at the sound of running feet and observed the scouts coming toward him in a burst of speed. They came to an abrupt halt, scattering the leaves as if blown about by the wind.

"How does it look?" asked Lance, whose breathing tempo increased along with Turley's during the speedy run.

"Thinning out. Should have them out of here in short order. Whatever is left of them," replied Drum optimistically.

The sound of galloping hoof beats drew their attention and they quickly turned their heads in the direction from which the noise came.

"Got a glimpse of the horse but not the rider," said Drum squinting his eyes as he tried to see through the heavy thicket.

Lance brought his rifle to eye level saying, "We'll soon find out who's heading up the trail when they ride into that clearing over there."

"It may be Hagarty," warned Drum. "There was some shooting up his way a little while back."

"We heard it," said the scout. "Wanted to check it out but . . . "

The sentence went unfinished as the horse and rider darted into view. Drum sprang to his feet like a cat overtaken by surprise. He called out sharply, "Tioga."

XXVI

The girl pulled hard on the reins, obviously confused, as her horse pranced about in circles impatiently. The military man dashed madly in the direction of the girl, who was still trying to spot the man with the voice that had become quite familiar.

Before Drum reached the trail, another rider appeared and pulled up quickly to the side of the girl. He whisked her off her mount. "In here, Hagarty," shouted Drum as the oldster started in the direction from which he came. A hissing arrow cut short any further maneuver as it caught the old military man squarely in the back. The impact of the flying wedge caused him to bend back sharply and momentarily kept him from falling off as he held on to the reins. The animal reared high into the air, throwing the wounded man and the girl to the ground. As the scouts rushed to the fatal spot to assist, Turley caught the girl in his arms as she came flying into the brush after a quick yank by Drum. With the help of Lance, he then dragged the struck man off the open trail.

"He's hit hard," said Lance. "It almost went through him."

Drum was silent as he cradled the old man's head in his arm and reached for his pulse. After a moment he called out in low tones, "Hagarty, Hagarty, can you hear me?"

Several rifles barked in the distance as if in salute to the old veteran, whose stillness, in addition to other factors, was evidence enough that life ceased to exist.

"He's dead," said Drum slowly and with a saddened expression. Their attention was diverted suddenly to the mad pounding of hoof beats, once again coming from the back trail.

The speed at which the riders bore down upon them gave them no time for conversation. They scampered further from the trail and barely turned in time to get a glimpse of the horsemen as they sped past the clearing.

"They're soldiers," said Lance swiftly as he and the others got a glimpse of the uniforms.

The lead rider caught sight of Drum's man and swerved his mount sharply to the right at the same time calling out sharply. "Over in here, men."

The familiar sound of that voice caused Drum and the scouts to stare at each other in disbelief. A moment later they tried to get a glimpse of the new arrivals as they slid off their mounts and dove for cover. They got just that and were unable to identify any one of them. Once again, the observers froze briefly as the voice called out, "Captain, what's those two sneaking scouts of yours hidin'? In the rear?"

"It's Will," uttered Lance in a tone of voice that was far from being convincing.

Turley ran a sleeve across his forehead saying, "If I were a believer in ghosts I would say that Dawson is on a special mission sent down from the great beyond."

"If that's the case, let's find out what it is," remarked Drum as he got up to a crouch and hustled to where his men wore progressing forward against light and scattered resistance.

The scouts were at the captain's heels as the latter drew up behind a large rock and stopped abruptly. He was quick to spot the individual who now silently confirmed their suspicions. It was Dawson in the flesh. He looked curiously at the three men who stared at him blankly without uttering so much as a greeting; he was at a loss concerning their strange behavior.

"Wall," he blurted out. "Who'd you been expectin', General Cook?"

A volley of shots aided the captain to regain his wits for he quickly rushed over to where the scout knelt on his one knee and said, "Welcome home, Will. We'll reminisce a bit later."

With that, Drum rushed forward and waved the others on. Lance and Turley stopped at the old scout's side and each took hold of an arm, yanking him to his feet whereupon he said with a scowl, "What's a matter with you crazy coots? The fightin' too much for you?"

The younger scouts smiled broadly, finally convinced that this was indeed reality and not a trick of fantasy.

"We'll talk about it later," said Lance, and he slapped the scout roughly on the shoulder as he and Turley started forward.

Dawson nearly swallowed his chew, causing him to cough several times before managing to get it back to the usual side of his mouth.

"Fool Injun chasers. Near spoilt my appetite."

Turning to the men he rode with, he remarked, "Let's go on and give them a hand. Haven't seen anything to shoot at yet." He looked about cautiously for a long moment but saw nothing with the exception of the advancing column whose silent guns indicated the fact that the enemy resistance had all but faded away. His lips tightened, then protruded outward, followed by the familiar stream of juice that hit the vegetation nearby with a splatter. It caused a toad to seek other shelter as it leaped frantically into the air, making a complete flip before crashing against a rotten tree trunk and then quickly scampering away and out of view. The old scout shook his head as he moved forward saying, "These fellas must be out on a squirrel hunt."

Drum's column moved fast now and without incident. Minutes later, a figure stole across the trail to where Drum and the scouts conversed on the present situation. It was Stenton.

"Not a sign of a live one any more, Captain. Must have cleared out."

Drum shook his head in agreement as he stared up ahead, probably reassuring himself that he had agreed correctly. The short observance was followed by a remark exposing his thoughts. "We'll go up a ways and make sure." He glanced at Stenton now and asked, "Any casualties?"

"Lost Buckman and Roe. Several others are wounded," came the reply.

Drum sighed heavily, and then spoke before any comment could be offered. "We lost Hagarty. He lays back there a ways." The mention of the deceased oldster reminded him of the girl and he quickly directed his question at Turley. "What happened to Tioga?"

"Hiding in that laurel over there. Guess she stayed put after being briefed by Lance here."

"By the way, Captain," cut in Lance. "The girl told me that she rode down here after Hagarty opened fire on two braves that appeared on the back trail."

"He got both of those Injuns," spoke up Dawson. "They're deader than a field mouse in an owl's nest."

Lance changed the subject directing a question at the old scout. "Did you hear our signal?"

"Shore did. As clear as a mountain brook. And ready to signal back when sudden-like, we caught sight of seven or eight braves sneaking along the trail. Sort of figured they were followin' the patrol, so when we got into a good position, we blasted away at them."

The men seemed to have the same question running through their minds, but up to this point, they just listened to the old scout, eyeing him with a secret sense of curiosity.

As if a powwow was held previously before hand, Drum suddenly asked, "Dawson, there's a slight matter that you could clear up for us, which, under the circumstances, could lead to an embarrassing situation. It'll have to be clarified sooner or later."

"And what might that be, Captain," asked Dawson with a noticeable appearance of curiosity which mounted as he studied the expressionless faces staring at him.

Drum hesitated momentarily as the scout reached into his pocket and pulled out a white form. He handed it to him and said, "Orders from General Cook, Captain. Should have given it to you when I slid in but . . . "

Drum took the folded paper and slapped it against the palm of his hand several times thoughtfully, then looked at Lance and Turley who were also aware that Dawson's presence here with orders from the General certainly made the matter more mystifying; an acceptable explanation was expected concerning him being alive at the moment.

Dawson noticed the glances again and said, "You fellers seemed awful surprised when you saw me and you've been glarin' at each other since as if I might be the rustler ridin' off with your herd."

Drum made no comment concerning the remark but followed with a question instead. "Were you at the scene of the massacre at all before coming up here?"

The muscles on the old scout's neck stood out plainly as he clinched his teeth momentarily, for the mention of the gruesome event still lingered fresh in his memory. His voice lacked the original tone as he answered. "As a matter of fact, 'twas me and two other men who first spotted Custer and his men. All kilt' to the last man. We were scoutin' up ahead apiece when we come upon 'em."

Turley's impatience was obvious as he involuntarily uttered rather than asked, "Scouting? For who?"

"Why you tin eared pony rustler," scowled Dawson. "Only a fool would ask such a question . . . "

"Who was you scouting for?" cut in Drum instantly.

" . . . Or a captain if the matter was serious enough," added the scout as he attempted to justify his last remark. After a rapid recovery he answered, "Why, Major Reno of course, Captain."

"When was that switch made?" asked Lance breaking a brief silence. "We were under the impression that you were with Custer as planned."

"I see," said Dawson as the reason of his friends' behavior dawned on him. "So you all thought that I went down with the General? Wall, I probably would have if things went on accordin' to plan, but the General was way ahead of schedule, for when I got down to the river that mornin' he had long since passed the meetin' place. Of course I didn't know which of the patrols it was 'til the others come up."

"Who was the General's head scout?" asked Lance.

"He borrowed Bajou from Reno until they got to the place of meetin' where I would take over, but as you know, they kept right on going."

"Well, I must say that you jarred us somewhat with your appearance. However, pleasantly," said Drum.

"Don't think it was pleasant for those two there," remarked Dawson. "They keep staring at me as if I might be a ghost. A good shot of this here tobacco juice in their direction should change their minds pronto."

Turley reached over and felt the old scout's arm, then his shoulder, finally slapping him on the back and causing the dust to seek other refuge as it took off in the form of a small cloud. "Darn if it ain't him, alive as ever," exclaimed the young scout.

"I'm convinced beyond a doubt," said Lance. "No ghost can stand chewin' the stuff he does."

Dawson made no comment, for his interest at the moment shifted past the group to the oncoming individual whom he peered at curiously out of the corner of his eye. "Gentlemen," he said suddenly. "Either my eyesight is failing me or there is a coat wandering around back there apiece without legs."

It was the Indian girl, Tioga. She stopped as the man turned in her direction. Drum walked over and took hold of her hand to lead her back toward the men.

"Wall now," remarked Dawson. "At least we are at peace with the tribal women folk."

"This is Tioga," said Drum warmly as if introducing one of his own.

"And this is your uncle Dawson," cut in Turley with a grin, which hadn't faded away after the scowl the old scout made at him.

"Now ain't she the pretty one," said Dawson. "Just how did it happen she joined our forces?"

"Tell you all about it just as soon as we move out," said Drum. He then turned to Stenton and said, "Get a detail to dig out the graves."

"Yes, Sir."

"Lance, you and Turley take a look around up ahead and I hope this time the short ride will be a pleasant one."

As if it were automatic, he unfolded the message that was handed to him previously by Dawson and read it. Shortly he made known its contents. "Nothing more here than we already know. A brief resume of Custer's fate. We go as far as the border if necessary and start right back with or without our reinforcements. Further instruction awaits at the original meeting place on the Big Horn River. That's it gentlemen. We'll go about our task here and move out as soon as possible."

The scouts lost no time in getting their mounts. As they neared the old scout on their way out to the trail, Turley bent down slightly and said, "We're going out to check on the chiefs and the braves. You be sure to take good care of the women folk back here."

The old scout took that one silently but a glint in his eye gave away his inner feelings. The tobacco in his mouth rolled about with speed quite contrary to normal, which indicated the fact that part of it was destined to take flight. Turley winced slightly as a stream of juice streaked past his left ear and came to a sudden stop as it struck a near by tree. Part of the splatter caught his mount squarely on the face, causing the animal to shake its head viciously. The scout grinned widely and rode on as if unaware of the incident.

Lance glanced back over his shoulder and caught Dawson's wink, as the latter stood there, obviously quite amused.

The little stream that looked like any other gleamed in the sunlight and appeared to be full of life as it flowed along swiftly over its permanent path. Here and there a larger stone protruded above the water line, appearing like a watchful eye on behalf of the racing stream that seemed to pay no heed to the new comers who stood silently near her banks staring about.

The center their attention was a Sioux lance that was embedded in a tree on the opposite side of the stream, sticking out partially on the trail menacing as it was meant to be. Obviously, somewhere on the other side lay hidden the scouts of the red man.

The sight confronting the red man was a repeated performance, however, with one exception. His stare is mixed with hate, revenge, and curiosity. Topping the list momentarily was the confusion of the strange presence of one of his kin who sat on her pony very casual like at the head of the patrol. Four of the men were glancing at a map that was spread before them.

Lance fingered a point on the roughly sketched map, saying, "I would say that this is the stream we've come upon."

"In that case, we've reached the border," said Drum. He looked to the other side and remarked, "That lance over there is obviously a reminder."

"Strange that those Injuns would know anything about the border or where it was located," cut in Dawson.

"I couldn't guess as to what they know but Sitting Bull headed north, and as you see, he appeared to know what he was doing," said Lance. "The chief sat at various councils with the white leaders and undoubtedly picked up information concerning border matters while discussing treaties at one time or another."

The old scout took the explanation with out comment but the matter still lingered in his mind as he took his hat off and scratched his head thoughtfully. Suddenly he turned toward the water and let fly a mouthful of juice that splattered in front of a toad sunning himself on a rock. The creature's hind legs shot backwards one at a time in an attempt to shake off some of the stain while the largest portion of it trickled down over its face. The animal was taken by surprise and appeared to come to its senses as it leaped madly into the water, disappearing among the rock bottom of the creek bed.

As the old scout turned, he faced Turley, whose amusement was obvious. Reaching into his pocket and coming out with a plug of tobacco, he offered it to Turley, who grinned back and shook his head in the negative. "Fool boy," uttered Dawson as he replaced the plug.

As the discussion of present matters regained its status as the topic of conversation, Tioga went unnoticed as her mount drifted slowly toward the creek. She dismounted and stood by while the animal sucked in the cool water. Her hand stroked the pony's shoulder, but her thoughts were elsewhere as she gazed at her reflection in the water.

From across the way at a not too far distance, a sinister face with stone-like features was motionless, as were the cold eyes that kept a vigilant watch on the unsuspecting Indian girl. His hands held a bow and arrow that he lifted slowly to eye level. Once it was at the desired height, the Indian picked his target. The deadly arrow was pointed straight at Tioga. Carefully, he applied pressure on the bow but failed to release it immediately, for the branches and twigs swayed back and forth in the breeze. He waited patiently for an opening and then released the arrow, which was deflected by an untimely twig that betrayed his aim. The arrow hissed by the girl and tore into the thicket, causing the entire patrol to go into action.

"Fall on back," shouted Lance as he dug his heels into the animal's flank and rode wildly toward the water where he leaned down and swept the girl up from the ground. He raced back to the rear of the dismounted men but refrained from setting the girl afoot, for as he whipped around, all was still silent. Lance glanced at the crouching men, then to the other side of the stream. A frown appeared on his forehead as he gazed about curiously.

"That arrow was meant for the girl," remarked Drum who glanced up at the scout.

"Who ever it was certainly didn't like her being in our company."

"Do you think there was only one?" asked Drum.

"There would have been a lot more arrows to dodge if there were more," replied the scout. "Better we start back-trackin', Captain."

Drum voiced orders quickly and the patrol was soon heading south without the enemy. However, the mission carried out as ordered.

Daylight had long since lost its luster, as did the patrol's progress forward, for all indications clarified the fact that the campsite for the night was agreed upon. The patrol moved in off the trail a short distance and began the usual routine of settling down. Hours later, the glowing embers of the fire seemed to be full of life and performing on behalf of those seated about as they cast flickering shadows across the men's faces and caused splinters and dirt to spray about lightly as small pebbles and wood burst on occasion. The sight was quite common with the one exception of Tioga. She sat close to Drum, as usual. The military man was the object of her affections from the very beginning. Every once in a while, she would turn her head and look at him as if he were the hero who had ridden through muck and mire to save her from the grief-stricken existence in a battle-torn territory and had transplanted her in a world offering protection, kindness, and affection. Drum's inspiring interest on behalf of her well-being could be credited to pity or fondness. However, in any event, her safety would be guarded to the fullest by the men that presently sat in her midst.

At the moment, Dawson's working jaw was a sign that a potential spray was forthcoming and it came like a whip as he suddenly let fly a stream that headed for the center of the hot embers, causing a gust of steam to shoot upward. Turley looked at him with slanted eyes and said, "Must you use such ill manners in the presence of a lady?"

"'Taint a matter of manners," replied Dawson lightly.

"What would you call it?" asked Turley.

"A little amusement on behalf of the child. Did you notice her eyes widen when I smacked that fire dead center?"

"Sure I did. That was the sign of fright."

Dawson squinted at Turley, saying, "I just don't think that you understand women." The old scout winked at the girl who stared back at him curiously, probably wondering what lay hidden behind that bushy beard.

"What you intend doing with her, Captain?" asked Dawson, for the thought had occurred to him before.

"We plan on leaving her at Big Bear's camp," came the quick reply. "Only he won't be there to greet her."

The oldster's brow wrinkled as he exclaimed with a voice tinted with curiosity, "That so?"

"Yes," said Drum. "He was killed by White Cloud when he raided the village."

"Wall, I'll be . . ." muttered the old scout as he lifted his hat and scratched his head for a long moment. Then he remarked, at the same time shifting his eyes toward Lance, "Big Bear signed his death warrant when he ordered you off from atop that renegade a while back. What happened to his son?"

"Deer Foot vowed revenge," answered Lance. "We were in camp the night he took off after White Cloud. Haven't seen him since."

"Alone?"

"Alone," was the reply.

"'Tain't likely that we're going to see him again under those circumstances," said Dawson slowly as he peered with squinted eyes into the darkness.

"He's Indian. Knows a few tricks of his own," said Lance.

There was a long moment of silence and the dead of the night seemed to creep in and cast about sinister thoughts, for the expression on their faces indicated something other than pleasant ones. The timely cry of a hoot owl caused eyes to shift about in uneasiness as they tried to penetrate the darkness beyond.

Dawson spoke again as if no break in the conversation had taken place. "He's but one man against a band of renegades."

"Deer Foot won't fight the band," said Lance, "Nor do I think that he will fight White Cloud."

"Ambush?" asked Dawson.

"Ambush," was the reply.

"How do you figure that? Indian against Indian? That's unusual."

"Deer Foot would be the one to die under those circumstances and he is quite aware of that I'm sure. White Cloud would see to that. So, during the night the avenger steals softly up to the renegade's camp, picks out the target, lets fly a well-placed arrow, and then vanishes into the night."

The conversation stopped again as the hoot owl chose to cry out from its perch some distance away. Something strange seemed to hover in the air, for they shifted about uneasily from time to time and although they sensed it, no one chose to bring up the subject.

Suddenly, with a startling effect, a hissing arrow sailed between Lance and the girl and crashed into the dying embers, which sprayed about like maddened hornets.

"Get to cover," shouted Lance at the already scampering group.

"Damn blast them night prowlin' injuns," muttered Dawson as he brushed against Drum who had Tioga under his one arm. Then he said, "Pardon me ma'am. Didn't mean to use cussin' words in front of a lady."

"You pick the strangest time to apologize," said Turley as he grabbed the oldster by the shoulders and dragged him over a small embankment.

"You fool boy. You've loosened the buttons on my coat."

"What do you think, Lance?" asked Drum as they gazed out over the dim light of the harassed fire.

"Can't be many of them but they sure slipped by the guards. Better awaken the men. It's all out from here."

Just as Drum was about to shout a warning, a piercing cry like that of a wild cat added more to the tense moment, as the charging form of a brave flashed across the firelight. Lance sprang to his feet quickly and met the full impact of the frenzied red man, both crashing into the brush beyond. Once again the blade of the scout trickled with blood, an assured fact that another member of the Sioux tribe would fail to answer at roll call.

Before Lance could gather his wits, several more braves came charging toward them and it was Drum who was in direct line of charge. The military man crashed to the ground, failing in his attempt to side step the charge as he was handicapped by the Indian girl, who, at the moment clung to his protective arm. There was a mad pile-up as the two scouts and Stenton sprang to Drum's aid. Knives flashed in the dim light, some finding their marks, others just missing theirs. There were grunts and heavy breathing, in addition to some muttering by Dawson, which, if heard by Mother Nature's full blooming violets, would change their color to a crimson red. By now the camp was in an uproar, as the members of the patrol awakened from their slumber and dashed about with alert expressions.

They didn't have long to wait for an answer, as the Lance and the others walked out into the open. Blood dripped down the scout's face from an open wound, as observed by Stenton who quickly called to one of the men to rush out medical supplies. In short order it became known that each man that participated in the recent combat had felt the sting of a slashing blade, however, none hurt seriously; that is, with the exception of Drum, whose absence in the near-darkness went unnoticed briefly and his condition was not known. It was Lance who became conscious of that fact, although he had noticed Drum start walking out into the opening with them.

"Where's the captain?" asked Lance as he looked about quickly. He received no answer, nor did he need to be enlightened by others, as the men about followed his bewildered gaze to the recent scene of the fighting.

Drum stared at the men with a bewildered expression on his face. In his arms he held the limp form of the Indian girl. It was quite obvious to the group that the girl was beyond help and no one chose to ask the question verbally. They waited instead for the captain to speak first and he did, verifying the unpleasant fact with a voice of sorrowful concern. "She's dead."

He walked slowly toward the dim light of the remaining embers of the fire and asked for a blanket.

"Here is one, Sir," called out a voice from among the men, who were all milling about with the exception of the guards.

Lance took the blanket and spread it on the ground whereupon Drum placed the body on it gently, saying, "She must have gone down pretty roughly during the first charge. I tried to hold on to her but . . . "

Whether the military man choked up or just refrained from any more comments concerning the incident was unknown; but he stopped abruptly as his hand slid into his pocket withdrew his handkerchief. He reached down and wiped the trickles of blood off the girl's forehead at the same time calling for his lieutenant.

"Stenton."

"Yes, Sir?"

"Get a detail out to . . . " Drum hesitated for a moment refraining from completing the sentence, then continued with what he chose as a less grief-riddled phrase. "We're going to lay the little lady to rest tonight."

"Yes, Sir."

XXVII

An hour after dawn found the patrol ready to pull out. Eagerness was quite evident, for it meant back to the Fort for most of them, and new adventures for some of the others.

Drum turned in his saddle and glanced in a backwardly direction for a few seconds. His eyes didn't sweep over the riders as usual, but were focused on the little grave that would be soon left alone with the towering trees, which seemed to look down upon the grave in a silent vigil. Drum held an object in his hand that he caressed with his fingers. It was the beaded wristband given to him by Tioga. His thoughts could have wandered to the night before, for his lips suddenly went white as he pressed them together tightly, at the same time flipping the object slightly from his hand, and grabbing it swiftly as if in disgust. He slid it into his pocket. The usual procedure followed quickly and the patrol moved out.

Though most of the day had passed behind them, the patrol bore on with a fair rate of speed. There is no doubt that the campaign had dealt out grief and sorrow; however, that sorrow failed to completely crush out the existing thought that they were traveling the road to home.

There were several breaks up to this point and conversation was more popular during these periods than a belle at a May dance. Then it was back to near-silence after remounting and continuing on their journey.

At the moment, they rode along as if a peace treaty had been just recently been signed with the red man; however, not every one puts their faith in such documents. Nor had the scouts up front cast caution to the winds, for their piercing eyes searched for the enemy, who only the night before proved that the fight was still on. Although their trained eyes kept up a steady watch, not always do they get some opportunity that would give way to lurking danger, and this was one of those cases. The familiar hiss of an arrow sped by Lance's head and ricocheted off a tree, spraying the nearby brush with splintered bark.

"Take cover," shouted Drum as a barrage of rifle shots nearly obliterated his order. The scampering Indian was mowed down quickly by some of the men in the rear upon spotting the fleeing enemy.

The patrol was geared for action as they braced themselves against trees and stone, but the resistance seemed to have died with the death of the bullet-riddled brave.

"Some more of their sniper action," said Lance peering out across the trail.

"Seems to me that they are trying to pick us off one or two at a time," remarked Drum. "They got a little girl last night but failed to get any of us then or at this attempt. We still have a long way to go. They may start getting lucky."

"Better alert the men to a higher pitch," said Lance." It'll help if we could get in the first shot for a change."

Drum shook his head in silent agreement as he took a last scan around the area before saying anything to the men.

Dawson's jaw worked slowly as he ground away on the mouthful of tobacco. He looked curiously at Lance in silence, and whatever his thoughts were, remained unexpressed verbally, at least for the moment, as Drum's voice sounded off sharply.

Several more miles of riding brought the patrol to the rock formation that was ridden through in single file on their trip north previously. Near the entrance of the canyon-like pass, Dawson deliberately cut in front of Lance and took the lead, remarking, "Pardon me, young feller. I don't want to be late for the meetin'."

There was no change in expression on the young scout's face, nor did he make any comment as he followed the oldster through the pass. The sharp clicking of metal against rock echoed like the crack of a whip in an empty barn as the patrol followed in close proximity. Though vigilant were the keenest of eyes, the enemy went undetected thanks to the aid given to him by Mother Nature, whose many offerings she is indeed helpless to privilege.

Several pairs of dark eyes peered out at the unsuspecting riders as they filed by. Their expressionless faces ensured non-betrayal of intention. Nevertheless, the lurking enemy had his strategy planned and waited for the moment to strike. Their position was at one bend in the pass where a rider in the rear at that point was out of view for a few moments to the ones riding ahead. Silent as the dead of night, patient as the pursuing vulture, the red man bid his time. And when it came, he would strike swiftly, merciless and fierce.

One of them moved out suddenly, grasping a long-bladed knife. He rushed noiselessly toward the last rider with a cat-like spring, mounted the flank of the animal, circled his arm around the rider's throat in a vice-like grip, and plunged his knife into the victim's side. The knife still protruded from the side of the human target as the Indian grabbed hold of the reins and skillfully urged the animal in the opposite direction. At that moment, the second brave was going through the same procedure and in short order four men were heading swiftly north, two of them never again to see the comforting sights of Fort Laramie. The act was carried out in deliberate suddenness and with a tint of precision. The animals themselves seemed undisturbed other than that they were now going in another direction and the load was twice as heavy; they were probably thinking that the rider had quickly consumed a heavy meal, that is, if horses can think that deeply.

A distance of nearly a half-mile from the pass was covered before it became apparent that two of the men were no longer with the patrol. An excited voice from the rear caused the captain to turn sharply and bring the patrol to a sudden halt as someone shouted, "Captain, sir, Blake and Nutly ain't caught up yet. They ain't here."

Drum and the scouts sported frowns as they glanced at the riders, then further back up the trail. After a brief glance, Drum urged his mount toward the rear of the patrol and the scouts followed in close pursuit.

"Tobin."

"Yes, Sir."

"You said that Blake and Nutly hadn't caught up yet. What did they decide to do, stop off for an early lunch?"

"I . . . I don't know sir."

"Didn't they say anything to you at all?" asked Drum with a hint of impatience.

"No, Sir."

"Were they struggling at all when you noticed them last?"

"No, Sir. They were right behind us as usual."

"And where was that?"

"Before we entered the pass, Sir."

Before any comment could be made by the now sober-faced scouts, Drum voiced his quickly. "We'll take a few men and ride back to the pass, if it's necessary to go back that far."

"'Tain't no use, the way I figure it, Captain." The voice was Dawson's and so was the tobacco juice that went splattering into the brush as the old scout leaned far to the side.

Drum looked at the scout curiously, waiting for Dawson to explain his remark in detail, but it was Lance who spoke, supporting the scout's theory saying, "I don't think we'll find them along the way or at the pass, Captain."

Drum took off his hat and wiped his sweating brow with the sleeve of his coat, at the same time, saying, "Gentlemen, I'm a man of logic. I gather that I'm being led to believe that two of my men with their mounts have vanished from the ranks of an alert and fast moving patrol."

"Happened on occasions 'afore, Captain," said Dawson, whose working jaws were the nearest to be found in relation to perpetual motion.

"I assume then that the men will be stripped of their clothing and other belongings, including the animals, then cast off along the trail to rot in the sun."

"That's the usual procedure," verified Lance.

Drum bit his lip lightly during a moment of thought, then said, "They won't carry them far before ridding themselves of the burden. The least we can do is to sacrifice a little time and go back and bury the men."

"You may sacrifice a few live men for a few dead ones by attempting that maneuver," said Lance with a tint of reluctance.

Drum made no comment as he turned his head to the back trail and gazed in the northerly direction with a deep frown. Whether or not Lance thought the captain needed additional convincing seemed partial to the matter as he spoke. "That trick back there was carried out for any number of reasons. To lessen the size of the patrol, get the loot the two men were carrying, split the patrol, part of them going back to where the ambush took place right into another. No doubt that the tribes are on the run, but for some reason a feeling that a sizeable band lingers in the vicinity plagues in my mind."

"And led by White Cloud," cut in Dawson.

Drum turned, facing the men for a moment, and then said, "Do you think he's still alive?"

"Didn't see him among the dead back at the massacre," replied the scout. "And these assaults along the way, I'm sure, have been carried out after a briefing to get you first." The old scout eyed Lance as he finished the remark.

"Is that the reason you crowed me at the pass?" asked Lance.

"Just wanted to see who was on the other side first," said Dawson with a bit of modesty.

Lance's eyes lingered on him for a few seconds then shifted to Drum as he spoke. "I'm sure if the chief has a band out there, he'll strike some where along the way. Up to now, they have been hitting us at two and three mile intervals. At this point the next anticipated attack would be several miles from here. I suggest that we move up to that thick area up ahead, then out from the trail and go east."

"They may be spying on us right now," said Drum.

"Maybe, maybe not," said Lance. "Depends on how they have their strategy planned. We know what to expect if we follow the trail. If we get a break here, we'll leave them far behind."

Drum shook his head in the affirmative, for he seemed to be lost in thought as he sat in silence. He asked quickly, "Ready?"

"Ready," replied Lance.

Nightfall was closing in fast. Visibility was limited to about fifty yards. For the past few minutes, Captain Drum's patrol had been at a dead standstill. The ever-roving eyes of the men still skipped about in the semi-darkness, which, for the time being, was credited to the force of habit, for the organs in the limelight at present were the ears. The sudden halt of the patrol was brought upon by the call of the lobo wolf. It seemed that the girly wolves in the area had cast aside the shyness and willpower that guarded their virginity, and they were all out to get their men, paying no heed to their mothers' warnings that only little wolves could come of it. Ole master lobo could have been licking his chops and throwing out his chest in a conceited manner, for the answering calls were several and from various directions. However, in reality, any romantic inclinations being attempted by beasts were ruled out quickly by the scouts, whose glances at each other indicated the fact that they were aware that the red man was on their trail and was signaling the results.

Drum was learning fast, and if he lived long enough, would one day be a master detector on Indian trickery. It was he who broke the silence, remarking, "They're on to us."

"Yeah."

The word was uttered quickly, but broke off sharply as if in reluctance to agree. The voice had been Lance's. The expression on his face was disappointment more than it was worry. Dawson was quick to observe and spoke in defense of the young scout's suggested plan that led to the present predicament, saying, "'Tain't no use pondering over what you're thinking, feller. It would be the same, if not worse, going the other way."

"The suggestion was Lance's," said Drum. "The decision was mine. It's just that our luck has thinned out a little. As a matter of fact, all of us hoped for a little more. Well, it won't be long before it really gets dark, so, after my observations, I find that we don't have much choice but to press forward. As I see it, that ravine up there would be the likely spot to cross through. It'll be quite dark before we get to the foot of it and we'll have to inch our way. Under the circumstances, I believe it would be in our favor to travel through the night and whatever additional time it will take to reach the point of destination. I can't help but feel that a real reception awaits us somewhere along the trail. We lack the force to cope with any thing of size. That fact alone prompts me to this sudden determination to keep moving. Lance, what do you think?"

"I'm for it all the way."

"Best we be movin' then, Captain," cut in Dawson. He quickly placed his hand on Turley's shoulder, saying, "The reason we ain't askin' for your approval, Son, is because you ain't quite old enough to vote."

A grin appeared on the old scout's lips as he urged his mount forward a moment after Drum ordered the patrol to advance.

Total darkness had stolen in on the patrol like the gentle, old south wind, but not fully unaware, especially Lance who led the patrol as he picked his way toward their destination: the ravine.

The signaling was much closer now and came from three distinctive directions. The circumstances under which the men pressed forward were not enlightened by the strange event of signaling. Sweating bodies clashed with cold chills every time the eerie calls echoed through the night. Bodies were already tense and rapidly achieving the point of impatience. Men cursed softly as twigs and branches snapped back at them after being pushed forward by the riders ahead. Glances to the rear were frequent, for the incident at the pass was still fresh in their minds. A camel caravan moving at its slowest pace would overtake and surpass the near bogged-down military patrol. Anxiety to get into the ravine first kept comments from being uttered. During the past five minutes, the outline of the ravine had vanished due to the tall timber that appeared in the area and Lance now relied on his sense of direction in working his way toward the objective.

Chills and sweat were suddenly jolted by a bolt that left stomachs hollow like an empty barrel as the latest signal seemed close enough to have felt the caller's breath. The patrol, in the dead of night, in the dead of nowhere, in the darkness of uncertainity, was at present at an automatic standstill.

Lance's voice came with a snap but with a tone just a shade above a whisper. "Pass the word back. Stay quiet as possible and gear yourself for action." Lance's order reached the rear of the patrol in record time. If honor were to be bestowed upon those by the high brass for such a notable performance, here was a group of men ready for citation.

Dawson's voice appeared puzzled as he asked, "What do you think of it Lance?"

"I thought of several possibilities. They just don't make sense."

There were a few long minutes of silence. Nothing was heard nor seen. Thoughtful minds began to grope for an answer. Has the enemy gone beddy-bye or were they lurking in wait for the kill?

Drum's tightly pressed lips were obviously a sign of anger, which was soon verified verbally as he spoke. "Those three redskins out there got us buffaloed. Let's get to that ravine. All they can do in this situation is to take a few pot-shots at us in the dark. Once we get in there, we can work out something with some foundation."

"All Right," agreed Lance quickly. "Pass the word back again to dismount. We're walking the rest of the way. We're sitting ducks up here."

The rustling of the leaves indicated the fact that Mother Nature had assigned one of her winds to roam the area tonight, and since blowing in a northerly direction, it would obviously be the glamorous south wind. But, it could just as well have been the north wind as far as the patrol was concerned, for it would take more than any of the winds to soothe their inner feelings at the moment.

Five minutes had passed since their last stop and now with each forward step the climax was anticipated, for the red man had since seemed to have vanished. Yet, they knew that the enemy was uncomfortably close, so close that they could feel them breathing down their backs. It could be explained just that way and Lance Winsor was certainly contrary to being indifferent as he suddenly called a halt.

Moments of silence followed. The tension was so high that all hands tightened on their rifles and a sharp pang surged through the bodies of the men as the sharp splat made by forced tobacco juice through the lips splattered against the trunk of a tree. In daylight, one would have noticed the blood drain from Dawson's face, for the noise the act created in the dead silence sounded like a pistol shot, at least it had the same effect under the circumstances.

Turley whispered quickly to Dawson, saying, "Your age keeps you from being hung right now."

"How much farther do you think?" The question was directed to Lance. The voice was Drum's.

"We're at the foot of the mountain now. Shouldn't be more than a hundred yards or so."

"These mountains are cliff like. We'd never get over them with the animals if forced into such a predicament," remarked Drum. Drum's thoughts of an escape route roamed beyond the ravine and now awaited comment as to the scout's course of action in just such a case.

"If we were cut off from the south at this point, we have to head north and around this range," said Lance quickly.

"'Tain't never seen the likes of this," muttered Dawson. "I'm anxious to go in any direction soon as you and the captain are ready. Seems like the point of a blade nicking at the small of my back and I ain't hankerin' to have it shoved any closer."

Lance inhaled deeply then started forward, the others followed suit. As they disappeared from the spot they occupied during the brief stop, with them lingered the morale found in the category of the condemned.

Near the completion of a forty-yard advance, the jittery patrol came to another one of their frequent stops. A sharp signal from somewhere to the rear of the patrol brought about the expected but unscheduled halt. Adding to the already confused situation again was a signal from the right of the huddled men and animals. Then another from somewhat of a distance up ahead. After that, all was quiet again.

Drum was first to speak, offering a possible solution to the uncanny pursuit, saying, "The method they are using, I'd swear they're trying to push us into the ravine deliberately."

"I've been thinking along those lines myself, Captain," said Lance.

"Something is brewing there and if I'm right, then it's a mystery as to their being there ahead of us, unless it's more coincidence."

"'Tain't a mystery to me. If those buzzards are actually there," cut in Dawson.

"If such is the case, then you're on to whatever has taken place," remarked Lance with a voice encouraging the old scout to explain.

Dawson bypassed the acknowledgement referenced in Lance's previous remark and immediately spoke of his theory in a hushed voice, as if the brave nearest to them was a graduate of Boston University, majoring in corrective English. "As I see it, eyes were on us when we left the main trail. The main bunch, which we already figured was around somewhere, must have been pretty close to us at that time. They soon got the word that we left the trail. Whatever they had in store for us was discarded. They plunged out to this here ravine knowing that we would finally end up going through it. I'm sure as, being way over due for a shave, that they know this country. That's just the way it smells to me and the odor is mighty familiar."

"I'm inclined to go along with you on that theory and I see now that they could have gotten here way ahead of us. We were slowed up quite a bit since the first calls. Well, in any event, our move in the direction we choose will be observed, in this darkness or otherwise. We've been climbing a gradual rise within the last few yards. I'll go with Dawson here to the top and have a look around. Should be able to make out the ravine. When we return, a decision will have to be made without hesitation. If it's a trap we're in, our chances will be less in day light," said Lance.

"We were against splitting the patrol back on the trail," remarked Drum.

"I still am," cut in Lance quickly, "but under the new developments we're being forced to alter our actions. The two of us may get to the top without being detected. Move the entire patrol, and the howlers will go into action out there."

"All Right," agreed Drum. "Shall we say approximately five minutes?"

"That should cover the short trip," said Lance. "Ready Dawson?"

"Always," came the hushed answer. The old scout handed his reigns to Turley, saying, "Hang on to this animal. If he gets away, you're going to have to stay behind and join the tribe. See you later, Chief."

The scouts eased their way up the remainder of the incline in a crouched position. At the very top, they dropped to one knee and silently stared unbelievingly through the dense and darkened forest at what appeared to be flickering lights dancing about faintly in the not too far distance. The moon casting its rays on swaying leaves could cause the same affect, but the scouts realized that the shining disc far up in the sky wasn't due to appear for hours. The mystery deepened and Lance's voice verified just that, as he whispered, "Can't be that my eyes are playing tricks on me . . ."

"'Tain't no one down there swingin' a lantern to guide our way. Son, that little bit of light we see is cast off by a campfire."

"Got an answer for this one?" asked Lance.

"Darn if I could think of one off hand," came the reply.

"No turning back now, we've got to have a closer look," said Lance.

Dawson laid a hand on the scout's shoulder, saying with a word of caution, "It may be our last."

"Could be an invitation to smoke the piece pipe," said Lance, trying to lighten the matter.

"Or get rapped over the head with the heavy end of one," added the old scout.

"Hang on to my coat, but don't pull too hard. It's rather weak at the seams," said Lance as he moved forward.

"Fool boy," muttered Dawson. With that, he started ahead and at the same time let go a stream of juice that struck a sizeable sapling inches from his head, which, in turn, splattered back into his face, which caused the old scout to jerk back his head in bewilderment. The unfit vocabulary that followed even startled the old scout and he waited for some comment from up front in regard to the beyond distasteful group of words, but none came.

Minutes later, the scouts' motionless figures hugged the ground as they peered past brush and tree trunks in silent amazement at a campfire whose dancing flames skipped across the faces of eight Indians, including a chief. Their appearance seemed to be quite calm, as if it were a get-together to reminisce of days gone by.

"Nonchalant about our presence, those red skins?" remarked Lance in hushed tones.

"I'm going to agree with you this time," said Dawson, "but from here on, use the smaller words. I just can't figure out those big words at a time like this."

There was no comment from the younger scout concerning the remark, for he was thoughtfully groping for some answer to the dilemma-like situation which was clearly indicated by the wrinkled skin around a pair of squinting eyes. He voiced part of his thoughts as if alone. "They know we're here, yet . . . " He allowed no more time to ponder over the matter as he uttered quickly, "Let's get on back."

Despite his years, Dawson was up like an antelope and followed at the heels of the fast moving scout.

Back at the huddling patrol, Turley was the first to notice activity up ahead as he whispered, "Someone comin', should be them."

Their anxiety was spared to any length, as the two scouts burst in on them. Lance spoke before the expected questions were asked.

"There's a campfire down there all right, with about seven braves and a chief. They seemed no more concerned then if they were engaged in a friendly game of poker."

"Then we are in some kind of a trap," said Drum. It was more of a statement than a question. "What could they be waiting for?"

"I don't know," replied Lance with a voice shaded with defeat as to a solution.

"Have you something in mind in regard to our next move?" asked Drum.

Lance's voice was low but effective as he replied. "Let me outline the possibilities briefly. We could rush them down there and try to fight it out, but there is this fact to recon with. We don't know how many more of them are hiding nearby."

"And," cut in Dawson, "Those at the campfire won't be just sitting there if we decide to charge in."

"That I'm sure of," agreed Lance. "On the other hand, we can wait 'til morning and make a stand."

"The length of time we can hold out will be limited," said Drum. "Our ammo is down to a frightful quantity."

"I'm aware of that also," said Lance. "I want to mention one more, which won't enlighten you any more than the others. We can try to bust out of here and head north. Maybe we can shake them, maybe not."

"Now if that ain't a ticklish group to pick from," remarked Dawson as he slowly scratched his beard thoughtfully.

"Have one that meets your fancy?" asked Drum as a feeler to perhaps enlighten a choice that could lead to his decision.

"I'm for heading north," replied Dawson slowly, as if expecting to be criticized for his opinion.

"Lance?" Drum's voice was low but with a tone of eagerness.

"I'm inclined to favor Will's direction," came the reply.

"How about you, Turley? Which one would you want to wager on?"

"I'll back any move decided by the council, Captain."

"North it is then, gentlemen. Lance, we'll move out in any formation you suggest."

"Grouped close together," came the reply. "If we meet any resistance, orders will follow."

"Stenton, pass the word along to the men."

"Yes, Sir."

Once up front, Lance inhaled deeply as he looked skyward, perhaps in search of the moon, whose light would serve well during a night ride, or maybe just gazing at the faint outline of the tall timber silhouetted against the night sky. Could be that he was trying to picture a face up in the heavens, one that he hadn't seen for many days, but which seemed like many years, the face of Naomi. In any event, he was in waiting for the go sign from Drum, which appeared in a whisper.

"We're ready."

The detachment of General Cook's forces, now on patrol, headed by Captain

Albert Drum, moved forward. The snapping of twigs and the swaying of branches indicated that men and beasts were on the move. Faces would wince when an animals steal shoe would come in contact with stone, for it echoed through the night like the cry of a blacksmith's anvil. The heads of the patrol relied little on silence in their attempt to escape, but depended greatly on the darkness of the night. The strategy at the moment was to break out of the assumed trap. Complete escape from the enemy was hoped for, but the basis of the maneuver was to gain a more suitable position in daylight when the enemy would surely attack.

Dawson was the first to speak since the move got under way. "Wonder how far we're going to get before those buzzards out there start their chatter."

"I expected it before this," replied Lance. "In any event . . . "

The remaining part of the sentence died on the scouts lips, for the familiar sound of an arrow leaving the bow caused him to shout out, but it unheard as the singing arrow sunk deep into his mount's chest, causing the animal to squeal loudly. The animal reared high, causing the rest of the patrol to scatter about, and then collapsed to the ground in a heap. Amidst the screaming arrows, Lance's voice was heavy with anguish as he shouted, "Retreat! Everyone on back!" A mild panic was in the making as men and beast scrambled about in the pitch darkness. Lance was feverishly retrieving some of his belongings from the saddle of his dead mount and in short order joined Drum at the head of the retreating patrol, who was shouting as he led the way. "Keep your heads men and move up fast."

The end of the attack ceased as fast as it had started. Nevertheless, the progress forward continued. Bodies scraped tree trunks, others smashed into them solidly. Scratches and bruises were plentiful, dealt to them in the maddened haste. It didn't take long for them to reach the small incline, which the two scouts had gone over a short time ago.

Lance in the lead, made no effort to stop. Whatever thoughts roamed through the minds of the men up front remained thusly concealed. They assumed that the scout was aware of his position and relied on him, come what may. As they went over the top, Dawson spotted the faint flickering light that he had noticed on his previous trip. He knew that Lance was aware of it and wondered why the scout kept on going. Adding to his dismay was the appearance of three sharp signals, both of which also failed to slow down the leading scout. The light of the campfire was beginning to become quite obvious now, causing Drum to glance at the two scouts, attempting to induce comment, but none came. Anxiety concerning Lance's intention mounted with each forward step. Suddenly, Lance stopped abruptly and turned around. His saddlebags were slung over his shoulder and his rifle held tightly in his hand. The patrol was laboring under the stress, which was well indicated by their fast tempo of breathing. The tired, haggard-looking, disarrayed, and bewildered patrol stood there in silence as they sucked in the cool air.

From the rear of the line, a soldier walked slowly to the front. It was Stenton. Facing his superior, he spoke. "All men and animals are intact, sir. That is, with the exception of Lance's here. I didn't know whose mount was hit until we got into this light here."

Drum acknowledged the fact by shaking his head in the affirmative, then faced Lance and waited for him to speak next. The scout let the saddlebags slip from his shoulder and looked toward the campfire for a moment, then said, "Look at them down there. Still sitting there as if nothin' happened."

"I've noticed them since we've stopped," said Drum. "Thought for a while you were going to walk right in on them."

"Just wanted to get into the light here," said Lance. "Want to see who I'm talking to for a change. If we got the chance and I believe that we are going to get it. They don't seem to be in any hurry down there."

"I've been in many a predicament," remarked Dawson, "but I can't recall any that would top this one."

"The cunningness and trickery used tonight which led us into this trap is all Indian," remarked Lance. "But this," he held out his hand in the direction of the fire and finished the sentence. "I would have to turn the pages of history to find the answer. I doubt that something like this has happened before."

It was the sober-looking Turley who chose to speak at this point as he stared at Lance blankly, saying, "We've all tried to come up with an answer and each one has been slashed out from under us. You have been hoping that one of them would solve the answer one way or the other. Right now, there is one thing left that they could want and you know what it is."

Lance stared back at Turley in silence.

Drum's patience dwindled quickly because of the sudden lull in conversation and asked if the chief down there was White Cloud.

Turley glanced at Drum then held his eyes on Lance as he spoke in reply, "I think that the chief is in the mood for a powwow."

"At this stage of the game," cut in Drum, "what would he want to talk about, graduation day?"

"Captain," said Dawson as he hooked his thumbs on to his belt. "Since things turned out the way they did, the chief down there has the upper hand and finds himself in a good position to make some kind of a deal with Lance here. Remember now, we're assumin' that it's White Cloud sittin' there pickin' his teeth."

Drum's mind had worked desperately within the past hour or so, trying to come up with an answer to the tactics displayed by the Indians, and now finally realized that he had been reaching in the wrong direction as the insinuations made by the scouts began to take shape. Then Naomi appeared in his mind like a flash, and with a slight turn of the head, Drum met Lance's steady gaze. The latter had watched the military man's expression and was aware the he knew now what the yet unspoken subject was to be at the potential pow-wow, if such was the case.

"Well, Captain," said Lance. "Shall we wander down and see what the chief has to offer? I'm sure he don't want to fight us. At least not right now."

Before Drum could reply, the old scout remarked quickly. "I believe the chief is going to be formal tonight and give us an invite. Look down yonder."

Eyes followed the recent indication and were met by the sight of two braves making their way toward them in the dim light. They walked up to the patrol as if they were a part of it rather than the enemy. The men watched them like a group attracted by a magician who had another offering that could elude detection.

The braves lost no time making known the purpose of their visit, as one of them spoke gruffly. "White Cloud. Talk." He pointed in the direction of the campfire without waiting for a reply, then turned and walked in the direction from which they came, leaving the men staring in thoughtful silence.

Lance was the first to make a move. He picked up his saddlebag and slung it over Turley's mount, then pulled the latter's rifle halfway out of the sheath and placed his rifle along side, jamming the two firearms in as far as the one weapon case allowed. Facing Drum, he spoke, seemingly without concern. "Well, Captain, shall we be polite and join them?"

"I feel saturated with curiosity this evening, Winsor. Lead on."

XXVIII

Drum ordered the men forward. The slow moving and suspicious patrol headed toward the Indian camp. Among other existing emotions, curiosity reigned the throne as the patrol moved out of the heavy timber and out onto a clearing. At this point, the Indians got to their feet and faced the oncoming, but reluctant guests, whereupon Dawson confirmed rather than displaying surprise, as he remarked, "It's that buzzard White Cloud all right."

"This is a rattlesnake's den if I ever saw one," said Turley as if talking out loud to himself.

Lance made no comment for his thoughts wandered elsewhere. But as they came within thirty yards of the campfire, he stopped suddenly and likewise the patrol did, as if ordered. He spoke quickly to Drum, saying, "Caution the men to be ready and alert. Revelry will be a little late tonight."

"Stenton."

"Yes, Sir."

"Pass the word to the patrol."

"Yes, Sir."

Directing his question to Lance, Drum asked, "Want the three of us to join you the rest of the way?"

"Sure. I wouldn't want the chief to think that you gentlemen are antisocial." The scout took an undetected deep breath as he stared at the red men, and then spoke as he exhaled slowly, saying, "Dinner is served, men. Be careful of your table manners."

As he started forward, the others followed suit. Moments later, a few yards apart, the quartet came to a stop and faced the chief and his braves. Utter silence befell the groups as the white men stared at the red men. Emotions that stirred within were contrary to the expressionless faces. This certainly was a powder keg situation, but for some odd reason, the fuse seemed to be missing, or at least out of view. For the men of the patrol, the tense situation at present headed the list of strange incidents that happened thus far, and if impatience was headed toward a new high, it was suddenly stopped abruptly as the voice of the chief marred the peaceful-like silence with his eyes focused on Lance. He said, "White Cloud want squaw." The chief's demand had no more affect than if he had asked for some Virginia tobacco, for the opening subject had been anticipated.

Dawson spoke to Lance through the corner of his mouth saying, "This Injun is wasting no words. Right to the point, ain't he?"

The scout made no comment concerning Dawson's remark, but made it known quickly that he too would do no stalling, which was obviously clear as he replied. "White Cloud and his braves come with patrol to village. If girl want Chief, you take. If she no want to go with Chief, she stay."

Optimism gained momentum as the men allowed the slight possibility of hope that such a deal might be accepted by the Indian chief, and they waited with anxiety for a favorable reply to that effect. The pleasant thought was short lived. The Sioux made no indication whatsoever that he so much as heard the offer, as he spoke in turn, saying, "You go with two brave. Bring girl here." Pointing to the patrol, he concluded, "Soldier stay."

Lance decided to push the issue to the hilt with a question, which he had already answered to himself. "And if I don't go?"

A slight sneer formed at the corner of the chief's mouth and lingered there for a few seconds. Finally, with the sweep of his hand arcing over the entire patrol, he said with a louder voice, "All die."

If the chief expected his remark to cause emotional disturbance, he got no returns for his efforts. Instead, the four men stared back coolly in defiance. The dead, but tense, silence was again disturbed by no other but Dawson like on occasions before, as he spit viciously into the fire, which could very well have been in answer to the Indian's threat and might likely be interpreted as an insult.

Lance spoke at this instant just in case there might be retaliation in the making. "We have powwow. I come back."

He then spoke to the others without turning. "Let's go back to the patrol and talk this out." Lance waited for some objection from the enemy but none came. He turned slowly and followed the others to the rear.

Dawson's sense of humor seemed to have left him completely as he blurted out in an angry but guarded tone. "That lousy coyote stood there like a hangman backed up by a mob and handed out a verdict like we were proven horse thieves. Why, a word from the captain here and we could have filled all of them with lead faster than a jack rabbit with a bob cat on his tail."

"He's aware of that," said Lance. "He's aware too, that we know our position is surrounded by his braves. The Indian is banking on that fact to keep us at bay. The Sioux hold the ace."

"I think he's bluffin'. There aren't that many of them out there."

"We may have to call his hand, but only as a last resort," said Lance in a mild tone.

"We've been confronted with a lot of choices tonight," said Drum as he glanced toward the campfire. "However, none seem to be in our favor."

Lance eyed the captain briefly and noticed the strained expression on the face of the military man. He himself was stressed to a point far beyond being grieved, but yet he felt a sense of pity for this man, whose first venture into Indian Territory burdened his responsibilities to utter heights.

The scout sought a way to ease the tension for at least the time being, something indicating a bit of hope. Before he made known anything to that effect, Turley, whose thoughts seemed to have roamed along with the faraway look he had displayed within the last minute or so, suddenly spoke. "What takes place if you accept the chief's terms?"

Lance looked at the younger scout for a long moment, the asked, "Don't you know?"

"I believe I do, but, if you went over it lightly, perhaps we could grab on to something that hasn't been noticed in all this confusion and maybe upset the apple cart."

"I'm for you all the way, fool boy," cut in Dawson. "I personally want a way to upset that renegade over yonder and carve up the supper he ate tonight."

"Well," said Lance. "First of all, they would disarm the patrol and take the mounts. That would be part of the deal I'm sure. When I come back with . . . " The scout hesitated briefly, then reluctantly mentioned his wife's name, " . . . Naomi, the execution of Captain Drum's patrol, including his scouts, would take place. On the other hand, I could escape the braves, who would be cautioned not to be overtaken by myself or any one else. They would stay their distance. The only reason they would be sent along is to report by trail at the very first indication. Even if we do away with the braves and I returned with a sizable group of fighters, the chief wouldn't be here to greet us. In any event, his plan is well formed. He won't get caught napping."

"You're going to have to tell him something pretty soon now. What'cha got on your mind." The voice was Dawson's.

Lance squinted toward the waiting enemy, saying, "I'll tell him that I'll be ready to go in the morning. Whatever is in store for us after that, I can't say, but we'll soon find out. Let's go back there."

Once again, enemy faced enemy. The scout's reply to the deal was brief. "Before the sun arises, I will be ready to go."

The men waited reluctantly for the expected, the surrender of animals and arms at this point. But they knew, too, that there would be no such maneuver, and once again threw their faith in Lance, relying on the scout to induce the chief one way or another to let them stay intact 'til morning.

Suddenly the chief spoke. The Sioux dialect was used and was directed to one of the braves, who soon broke away and headed for the nearby wooded area. The three men looked at Lance for a hint concerning the move. He was aware of their anxiety and replied quickly. "Hold on."

The order of deceit hung low and heavy as if both sides expected a sudden blast of violence during the short but awkward silence. It was disturbed by the sound of hooves as the brave who left a few moments ago emerged from the woods leading a group of horses. Another order from the chief, and the red men mounted the animals.

From atop his mount, the chief stared at Lance for a long moment, and then said, "Long before sun come over mountain, I come back." With the sweep of his hand indicating the immediate area, he said in conclusion, "Soldier sleep here." He then urged his mount forward, and with his braves, headed toward the spot where the patrol had but a short time ago emerged from the heavy timber.

Drum and the scouts watched them ride away in utter disbelief. Their faces held the mixture of surprise, mystery and hope, for the latest incident solved no portion of the red man's strategy. Whatever thoughts raced through the minds of the men stayed unexpressed for the time being, with the exception of Dawson who blurted out, exclaiming, "Did you ever see? Damn that Injun, he's got me wound up so tight that my stomach is accusing my liver or trying to choke it to death."

"No doubt we all have something similar to that effect," said Drum as he kept his eye on the disappearing riders.

"Gentlemen, this could be what is known as psychological warfare."

"It certainly appears to be."

"In that case," said Lance as he faced Drum now, "he's waiting for us to crack, pull the wrong move, then hit us when we are at our weakest."

"Which backs up what I said before," cut in Dawson quickly. "That Injun is bluffin'."

"I won't say you're wrong," said Lance, "but the fact still remains, we don't know for certain."

Turley's thoughts were probing deeper into the matter, for his question strayed slightly from the immediate topic, as he asked Lance, "Do you really think that the chief believes you will leave in the morning with his two braves to carry out the deal?"

The question was an effective one. Although they knew that come morning there would be no such trip, and whatever took place after that yet to be seen, they'd given the matter no thought, at least not by Dawson or Drum who gazed at Turley obvious with surprise.

The scout inhaled deeply before answering, then replied. "No."

"Then he knows we're stalling for time?" It was a question rather than a statement made by Drum.

"I'm sure of it now," came the reply.

"But you weren't in the beginning?"

"Not quite, but I've been thinking about it since. I hardly think that the chief expected to be lucky enough to have a disarmed patrol at his disposal. His chances of getting Naomi are remote any way he tries. His main interest at the moment is to wipe out the patrol."

"What more of a chance does the buzzard want then he had tonight?" asked Dawson.

"For some reason he just isn't ready yet," replied Lance thoughtfully.

"He could have sent for reinforcements," offered Turley.

"He could have," agreed Lance, but his voice carried no enthusiasm.

Suddenly, a signal sounded, coming from the direction where the chief and his braves entered the timber. Far to the right of that point came another. Still another to the far left. The ashen faces of the men indicated that something was brewing. Minutes of watchful silence were broken by Lance easing the intense situation as he remarked, "They're letting us know that we are still surrounded just in case we get any ideas of moving out in any of those directions." The men accepted that without comment, least they bring forth another distasteful angle.

Lance turned toward the men of the patrol briefly, then said to Drum, "Better have Stenton bring up the men and we'll all stretch out at the foot of the mountain here. We're going to need all the rest we can get."

The scout's gesture was welcomed by all and carried out in spirited haste. Animals were tied to saplings; thereafter men hit the soft earth without invitations. Strange incidents had been in the limelight since the patrol had left the trail, and if a tally were taken at this point it would still reign at the top, for the flickering flames now danced about the faces of five white men, where just a short time ago they performed for the red man. Usually it was Dawson who aroused men out of silent thought, but on this occasion it was Drum who spoke, in low tones, saying, "This is the first time I sat at a campfire knowing that we're surrounded by hostile Indians."

"Mighty nice of the chief to give up this warm seat and let us lay around the warm fire without interference," remarked Dawson, "at least for the time being."

"It was mighty nice of the chief to let us camp right at the foot of the ravine, too," said Lance in tones, unvaried with suspicion.

"I didn't realize we were that close," remarked Drum with a hint of surprise.

"Can't see the outline from here," said Lance, "but if you went into the woods there a little ways you'd be able to."

Dawson stared into the burning embers while he slowly rolled his mouth full of tobacco from one side of his cheek to the other with the aid of his tongue. Whatever he was thinking came to a decisive conclusion as he remarked without mirth, "The chief wants us in the ravine."

"I agree," said Lance as he glanced at the scout.

"That leads up, once again, to the question, why?" put in Drum wearily.

Turley was quick to list the possibilities and Drum, for one, became an anxious listener. "With the Indians scattered all over the place since Cook's regiments came into the territory, there could be a bunch of them hiding up on top of the mountain."

Lance ruled out the possibility as he cut in, saying, "We agreed earlier this evening that White Cloud is in this area because of us."

"Could be that he's been here 'afore," said Dawson.

"Well then," continued Turley, "he could have braves stationed up in there somewhere. Once we go up, the rest will close in from the rear and they've got us."

"Gentlemen," said Lance thoughtfully, "we're going to ride right into that trap, if the captain agrees, of course."

The four men eyed him sharply and waited for an explanation, but the scout remained silent, deliberately waiting for Drum to answer. Dawson, probably impatient, or on the other hand, giving the captain a bit more time to come up with whatever ran through his mind, decided on a few words. "Wall, we walked into one trap and ended up like all went well at the peace treaty. We may as well go into another and maybe continue smoking the long stemmed pipe. We're going to go again into something sooner or later."

Turley glanced at the old scout and said, "Down here we'd be bucking the Indians, but up there . . . " He broke off without saying any more, as he glanced toward the mountain just as Dawson spoke.

"It won't be a band of Mexicans you lop-eared, prairie rabbit."

A mild grin appeared on the younger scout's lips, then faded slowly as Drum spoke. "No matter what direction we choose to try, we're going to have to fight our way out." Facing Lance now he asked, "Why do you prefer the ravine, especially assuming it another trap?"

"Because I don't think they have enough men up there to keep most of us from breaking through. If we are hit from the rear as assumed, our guns will keep the attackers at bay because they will have to ride in order to stay near us and they must ride through the ravine."

"What's going to keep them from scattering all over the place and hitting us from every side?" asked Drum.

The answer came in a theoretical form as the scout explained. "The mountains, as we've noticed in the daylight, are quite steep. A man can make his way up over the boulders and ledges but a horse can't. I assume that the ravine is cliff-like also, therefore, the pursuers would have to stick to the very narrows of the ravine."

"Should that be the case then we have a good chance to bust out of here," said Drum with a ray of hope.

"I'm going to give it a check and make sure," said Lance as he got to his knees.

"The moon is about due over the horizon," said Dawson. "You can get a better look then."

"I believe I can find out as it is," said the scout. "When that moon appears, we want to be ready to go."

"Want company?" The voice was Turley's.

"Too short a trip for two men," replied Lance as he placed his hand on the scout's shoulder, and then said, "but if I'm not back in five minutes, come a-lookin'."

He then glanced at the captain and asked, "Any message for the chief, just in case he's sitting at the foot of the ravine collecting a passage toll?"

"Yeah, tell him that we'll send him back east and pay for his education if he'll sign a peace treaty before sun up."

"Why go through all that trouble," said Stenton in a mild voice. "Lance here holds classes occasionally, right? I received my diploma not too long ago."

"If I remember correctly," cut in Dawson, "that diploma hung around your right eye for about a week."

"No, it was the left eye," corrected Stenton as he winked at Lance.

A shy smile creased the scout's lips as he got to his feet and in a crouching position. He hastily glanced at the four men then spun around and headed for his objective. The scout made his way to the foot of the ravine in short order. Looking skyward, the steep incline on both sides of the potential escape route bore out his theory. He pressed forward for about another fifty yards without too much difficulty and decided that his purpose had been achieved. He turned around cautiously and peered about, for it was his ears that were at work, trying to pick up a familiar sound that would betray the presence of the enemy. After a few long moments, there was no indication to that effect, whereupon he started to backtrack.

The waiting men peered into the darkness, anxiously waiting for the scout to appear in view. Drum tore off an upper portion of a weed and placed it between his lips. With the aid of his tongue, the green stem rolled from one side of his mouth to another. He spoke without disrupting the action saying, "I expected signaling before this."

"I did too, but not from up there," said Dawson.

The military man made no comment as he pondered over the old scout's remark briefly, and became aware that the chief wouldn't show his hand from the direction of the assumed trap.

Relief surged through the bodies of the men as Turley's voice came sharply, saying, "Here he comes."

The scout, crouching low, made his way to his original spot and threw himself to the ground. The eager Drum was ready with a question. "How does it look?"

"I went up the incline a short ways without much trouble. As far as I could see under the circumstances it's quite steep on both sides. They can't flank us on the sides because it's impossible for the animals to climb."

The scout said no more as he glanced at the men, waiting for comment. It was Drum who spoke as he stood there with his hand wrapped around his chin. The remark could have been made to himself after giving the matter a final thought, at least it seemed so as he said, "Then this is it."

"Unless you want to try something down here," said Lance.

"No, I'll chance the gap even though it favors the chief at this point."

"When do we start?" asked Dawson.

"After the moon bares down on the ravine," replied Lance. He looked skyward suddenly as the thought of a cloudy sky entered his mind but made no outward remark as the stars blinked down at him from the clear heavens above.

"Any plans until then?" asked Drum.

"Yeah, have Stenton take the men in deeper. Turley, you go along. Take the direction in which I went and advance about fifty to seventy yards and wait for us there. We'll be along shortly and the patrol will proceed as if bedding down for the night. Just mosey along, quiet as possible, and don't be in no rush. Stenton, brief the men and set them up for the break."

"Right," the acknowledgement was brief. He quickly glanced at Turley and asked, "Ready?"

"Ready," replied the scout.

As they watched the patrol disappear into the darkness, Dawson took out a plug of tobacco from his coat pocket and made the attempt to bite into it but refrained from doing so as he noticed Drum and Lance watching him. He extended his hand saying, "Join me, Captain?"

"No thanks," replied Drum with a shade of a grin on his lips.

"How about you Lance?"

The younger scout made no reply, but eyed him with a sly look.

"Fool boys," muttered Dawson as he bit off a large portion, then slid the remainder back to its hiding place.

It was a long ten minutes before Lance nodded to the others, then got lazily to his feet, casually peering about without moving his head.

"Peaceful night, ain't it?" drawled Dawson.

"Yeah, but I doubt that it'll outlast the night," replied Lance. "Let's mosey on up."

Upon reaching the patrol, they glanced out past the campfire below them for some sign of pursuit but nothing stirred. Lance then remarked in low tones. "We'll lay around here 'til we're ready to move out."

Dead silence blanketed the area. The once brightly burning campfire had the appearance of the forlorn and deserted. The quiet of the night was disturbed on occasion as a small explosion occurred, sending a spray of ashes flying through the air and at times causing an unburnt particle to re-ignite, resulting in a small flicker of flame. It appeared to be literally trying to attract the attention in its seeming-loneliness, but it was in vain, for those who had but a short time ago enjoyed its warmth were now busy mentally planning a strategy for survival while the enemy lurked in the not too far distant shadows, waiting for their carefully laid plans already in effect to succeed. If they did, the result would be a replica of Custer's last stand.

Last minute briefing in low tones was in progress as the moon appeared slowly over the mountaintop. Minutes later, all was ready for the expected night battle through the ravine. Rifles were gripped tightly in one hand. The other hand held the reins to their mounts. The order from up front was anxiously waited and was not long in coming, for Lance had already started before the whispering acknowledgement reached the rear of the line.

With the exception of hoofs beating against small pebbles and soft earth, the short trip to the foot of the ravine was made in near silence. At this point, the patrol halted after an order from the front and a visual check in all directions was being made. Moments of anxiety were rewarded with silence. No move by the enemy had been detected.

Drums voice appeared in a whisper. "Nothing seems amiss but I can feel them breathing down my neck."

"Darn if I can figure this one out," remarked Dawson as he peered past the trees toward the dimly lit campfire.

"The fuse is already lit," said Lance slowly, "no turning back now. We'll have to survive the blast. Ready, Captain?"

"Ready," came the quick reply, and the whispering campaign after orders to move forward took its course toward the back of the line.

The ravine became gradually steeper as they progressed forward. After ten minutes of rugged going in the semi-darkness, the incline began to steepen dramatically causing Lance to whisper sharply, "Halt the patrol, Captain."

"See something?" asked Drum with a voice more than tinted with anxiety after issuing the order.

"Not visually," answered the scout as he peered ahead with squinted eyes with a definite reluctance.

"I have an idea what lies ahead." The voice was Turley's.

In response, Lance said quickly, "We'll go up and have a look around, we may both be right."

The scouts made their way forward and were soon lost in the darkness. Moments later, the scouts stood again in semi-bewilderment for they more than faintly anticipated what now confronted them, approximately a ninety degree incline, a sheer cliff.

"How are you fixed for mountain climbing?" The voice was without mirth, the voice Lance's.

"I may make it," came the reply, "but I can't speak for the horse."

"Well," said Lance, "shall we go back and add to the captain's problems?"

Drum was silent as Lance explained the latest development. Once again the immediate area and its occupants appeared to have been cast aside by lady luck, thus leaving the morale of the patrol in the category of the forlorn. The military leader's voice seemed far away as he spoke, at the same time running a bare palm across his brow. "I have pictured a variety of situations we could have to cope with, but something like this escaped my mind completely."

"Captain," the voice was Lance's and it brought Drum out from under his thoughts. But whatever the scout was about to say went unsaid, at least for the time being, as a shrill blood curdling yell tore through the darkness from down the ravine.

Pulses quickened as the men turned sharply on orders to be ready for the expected ambush. Men pulled on reins and scampered about on the narrow ravine floor in disorderly fashion. A sharp order from Lance caused the commotion to halt suddenly and remain in their positions.

"The campfire," said Lance quickly as he pointed toward it in the near darkness but other eyes were already witnessing the scene. The enemies were stamping around in wild dismay as they proceeded to extinguish the remaining embers of the dying fire. Soon, only the eerie voice of the medicine man that chilled the patrol's spine came through the darkness below.

The voice belonged to Drum. The question directed at Lance. "Would you say that we were in for an immediate attack?"

"No," was the quick reply.

"How do you have them figured at this point?" asked Drum who's light sigh of relief when unnoticed.

The scout's eyes were still focused toward the site of the once burning campfire as he answered. "To say the least, they have us where they want us. Bottled up in a hole. If we're still here come daylight, I would say that Custer had a better chance. And he was wiped out."

"Then we'll have to go back down the ravine and fight our way out tonight after all," said Drum.

"We chose against that when we were out of the ravine," said Lance. "Now it would be disaster to try and get through that narrow gap at the bottom. They've got that well covered now and we'd be slaughtered in short order in this darkness."

Silence befell the group as thoughts groped for some possibility that may have been overlooked in regard to a chance for survival, something less sinister than those already mentioned.

Turley's voice was soft and low as he placed a hand on Dawson's shoulder and asked, "How is your blade, fellow? Real sharp like?"

"Why, what's on your mind, you fool boy?"

"You may have to commit suicide," said the younger scout with a tint of mirth. The old scout made no comment, for he knew that there was more to be said and the voice appeared again before much hesitation.

"These cliffs are steep and high. You'll never make it over the top." Turley's casual remark was a hint for a way out of the ravine and he suspected that Lance was already planning along those lines. He deliberately cut Dawson short of any comment by facing Lance and pushing the issue. "I take it for granted that you may be ahead of me."

"Yes I am," said Lance. "As a matter of fact I have the plans completed mentally. All it needs is the captain's signature."

Drum's tone of voice was that of mild disappointment as he said, "Once again inexperience places me to the rear of the class."

At this point, Dawson cut in. "Move over, Captain, I'm afraid that I don't quite follow these coots myself."

Drum's tone of voice appeared a bit more cheerful as he remarked, "However, that can be overshadowed by the new surge of hope that lingers with me now. What idea have you boys been toying with?"

Lance replied quickly and to the point. "We'll gather our needs, leave the horses behind and climb out of the ravine. I'm almost sure that our move will create little resistance. They'll never expect us to leave behind the animals."

There was a lull of silence then Lance asked, "Well, Captain, what do you think?"

"I think one day we will all face the firing squad. Treason is a kin to this act. Seriously, I don't think that your plan includes escaping on foot. Perhaps I'm just hoping."

"You're groping in the dark, Captain. Should I go on?"

"Please do," came the eager reply.

The scout continued. "Once we're out over the top, we'll make a wide circle in order to keep any noise from reaching the enemy and finally end up at the foot of the mountain and not too far from the enemy. Out there we have a chance, come what may."

"I'm for it all the way," said Drum without any hesitation. "Let's get started with the first step."

The military leader's quick decision could be based on the fact that though he had a few important questions concerning the plan, his concern at the moment was to get his men out of the death trap since the unexpected opportunity was unveiled by the scout.

Lance's suggestion to move the animals up to the foot of the cliff was now in progress. Upon reaching their destination, proceeding orders were being carried out with speed and enthusiasm. Reins were being knotted around sapplings, rifles pulled out of sheaths, and ammo transferred from saddlebag to pockets. Shortly a form appeared from out of the near darkness and stopped within a few feet of Drum. It was Stenton, his voice a near whisper as he spoke, "The men are ready, Captain."

Drum quickly called to Lance, who with Dawson and Turley was looking up for a likeable route of escape. Upon reaching the side of the military leader, the latter asked, "Are you ready?"

"All set," was the reply.

He then addressed Stenton quickly, saying, "Have the men stay close to each other and we're going to make the climb single file."

"Right," whispered Stenton, as he already started toward the rear.

"Dawson, you and Turley back up the rear and keep a sharp lookout. And by the way, join me once we get on top in some cool mountain water. I'm buying."

"Now that's real white of you son," said the old scout. "You can count on me, but I can't say as much for this young one here. Don't think he's got enough in 'em to make the climb."

Any intended comment was cut short as Turley started to the rear, at the same time remarking, "Let's go, Dad, and bring some rope with you."

Lance made his way up the steep incline slowly. Saplings and shrubbery were a tremendous aid, in addition to the hope of escape, in making the treacherous climb. Progress was being made without mishap, at least up to the point where the vanguard started to ascend. A sharp tug on Turley's pants caused the latter to halt for a moment and he turned, looking down at Dawson below him.

"What did you want with the rope?"

"I thought it would be easier to drag you up over than to have you hanging on my pant leg," replied Turley whose light grin was obliterated by the darkness.

"You fool critter, you'll be up on my shoulder 'afore we get to the top. Now move along lively or I'll crawl right over you."

As Turley started, his foot loosened a clump of sod, which caught the old scout right on the mouth. The undesirable oath uttered in near silence smashed all records previously held by the old scout. He spat out the dirt that had entered his mouth, along with the tobacco and continued with a barrage of threats that was forthcoming sometime in the future in retaliation, which in turn widened the younger scout's grin.

The next fifteen minutes went without incident. Up front, the leaders went over the top of the incline and proceeded to help the others as they crawled over the rim. Last but not least, Dawson appeared into view, and with the aid of four outstretched arms, shot up over like a Bronco jumping a four-foot fence. Upon being released, he spat several times in quick succession, causing Lance to ask, "Eat some dirt on the way up, Will?"

"More 'en my share, thanks to this fool Apache here. I'm for stringing him up right here and now."

"For some reason I have the feeling that I have failed to win his friendship," said Turley, whose wide smile vanished suddenly as the forlorn cry of a lobo wolf chilled the spines of those within hearing distance.

Lance got quickly to his feet and then said, "Let's get on down the rest of the way and pick a likeable spot. If we're lucky, we'll get a few hours rest before daybreak."

The patrol was soon underway again, marching along the side of the mountain. Lance suddenly veered sharply to the right and headed downward at a very slow pace. The march in this direction was short and a sigh of relief swept over the men as the scout halted the march and made it known that their destination for the night had been reached.

"How far would you say we are from the foot of the mountain?" asked Drum as he stretched out on the ground.

"About thirty feet from where the terrain drops sharply to the bottom," replied Lance. "Come daylight, we'll have a good view from up here."

"Do you think they'll find us gone before then?"

"No, I don't," replied the scout.

"And when they do?" the voice was Dawson's.

"Your guess is as good as mine, Will," said Lance. "However, the Sioux will make the first move. We'll take it from there."

Thoughts of tomorrow disappeared slowly as the sleepless eyes stared up at the stars where familiar faces and more pleasant trails appeared, leading the way to home and then finally slumber. Hours before dawn, the moon still high in the sky found the men of the patrol suddenly wide eyed and cursing under their breaths as the call of the lobo wolves shattered the peaceful silence of the night. They stirred about, restlessly turning from one side to the other and hoping that the next call would be the last, but it was in vain.

The captain and the scouts were in sitting positions and waited in silence for the blood curdling calls to die off while their thoughts ran amuck concerning the situation.

Dawson was the first to speak as he uttered one word: "Indians."

"They're on to us then," remarked Drum reluctantly.

"I don't think so," said Lance. "There are only two voices making the calls and they're both near the foot of the ravine where the red men are staked out."

"They're up to something," said Drum.

"Yeah," agreed Lance. "For one thing they want to keep us awake. Another they hope to get us in a state of panic which would add greatly to their advantage."

"I agree with you, Son," said Dawson, "and I hope we're right. I'd hate to hear some Injun answer a call from atop of us here somewhere."

The uncanny possibility paved the way to silence with the exception of a brief comment by Turley, who edged closer to the old scout saying, "It's a good thing for you, we have no rope. You would be strung up higher than a church steeple for that remark."

"Fool critter," muttered Dawson as he lay back on his blanket.

The first sign of dawn had already vanished, for now it was quite obvious as the dim light appeared on the eastern horizon. A restless form turned from one side to another, then suddenly bolted to a sitting position. A moment before, he opened his eyes briefly and noticed that the darkness began to give away to the beams of ole sol. His next action was to turn quickly in surprise to the rear from which a voice asked, "Have a bad dream, Captain?"

Drum recognized Lance more from the voice than from appearance, as the scout sat with his back against a tree in the still darkened mountain background.

"No, it just occurred to me that it would be quite embarrassing if our neighbors came by and found us in bed. I notice you are wide awake. Force of habit, or are you up to listen to the song of the morning bird?"

"Thought I'd take in the early morning sights since sleep refused to stay with me," replied Lance.

"I assume that you neither saw nor heard any activity up to now," said Drum rather slowly as if he needed a bit of time to ready himself for some unpleasant assumption on the scout's part, or a possible fact that could be forthcoming under the circumstances.

"Not a thing, Captain," was the reply. "However, I can't say as much once they find out that the patrol has vanished."

"You're right there son," said a voice from nearby. "They are going to carry on down there like a bunch of old women at a wake." The speaker was Dawson, who now cast his blanket aside with the intention of getting up, but he froze as did Drum, who was about to say something after managing to say, "Will, I think that . . . " as several braves split the quiet of the morning with screams and continuous yells as they seemingly ran toward the bottom of the ravine.

"Well, gentlemen," said Dawson quickly. "The wake has started. They've discovered our absence."

The patrol was aroused quickly and alerted to the point of immediate action. Roving eyes searched the area where the campfire warmed the night before, but no movement was detected. Drum's voice was prompted by the touch of impatience after visualizing the red man's next move. "I would say that White Cloud will send trackers up over the ravine to find out where we've come."

"I think that'll be their next move," agreed Lance.

"If they follow the trail long enough, our backtrack will be a give-away that the patrol is still in the vicinity," said Drum. "Under those circumstances they'll see to it that we don't stand a chance getting to our mounts."

Suddenly, yelling and whooping filled the air as the red man began to appear into full view near the dead campfire. Minutes went by as the men watched in silence for a definite countermove but none was indicated. The enemy seemed to be in no hurry as they continued the noisy ritual.

Drum's uneasiness was apparent as he spoke. "They may have sent out the trackers and are now waiting for their return."

"Not light enough to do any effective tracking, Captain," said Lance. "Time is no major factor since they know we're afoot."

"Seems to me," said Drum, "that they would be concerned about the distance we would have covered by now."

"They're not," said Lance. "First of all, they don't know whether we are actually trying to escape on foot or still lingering in the vicinity. The move will be made once they are convinced one way or another."

Dawson, whose brow had been wrinkled in thought for quite a while, cut in with a question. "Suppose the trackers follow a short ways and tell White Cloud that the patrol is heading towards the river. Then I assume that the chief will gather his band, ride the foot of the mountain range to a spot where his horses can climb over, attempt to contact the patrol with the aid of trackers that had been previously sent up to follow from the rear."

"It won't take long for those braves to find out that they've been tricked and give the alarm before White Cloud rides out of the vicinity," cut in Turley quickly.

"But we have been assigned to eliminate those that tend to give away our position up there," continued the scout as he felt the point of his blade in his hand. "Am I right Lance?"

Before the scout could answer, Drum's voice chimed in, well-tinted with anger as he caught sight of the action below. "They brought our mounts out of the ravine."

The men watched the animals being hustled out into the open with grave concern, for any attempt on the part of the red man to rid the area of the military mounts would hasten the already unpleasant situation closer to a disastrous one.

A brave appeared with a coil of rope and began slipping it through the reins. In short order he tugged on the rope and led the forward moving animals a short distance and tied the ends around a large tree.

"Had me worried for a minute," confessed Drum as he wiped away the sudden appearance of perspiration.

"They won't take them far, at least not right away, as long as our whereabouts remain a question. Captain, Turley and I will go on up to the forward part of the trail. You and Will sit tight here with the men. Should we need to be notified because of a sudden move on the part of the Sioux, send Will up fast. Otherwise, we'll wait them out and move accordingly. I'll take along three of the men and post them at intervals. That way we will be able to communicate much faster if need be. With your approval, we'll be on our way."

Drum gazed at the two scouts briefly, perhaps in admiration, and decidedly refrained from intending comment, then said, "Be seeing you, gentlemen. Good luck."

Lance flipped his hand in a farewell gesture, then started the upward climb with Turley close at his heels. From their perch atop the mountain, the scouts gazed down into the valley below, keeping an eye on the exposed enemy whose wails and cries seemed to grow louder as the daylight neared its full strength. Turley was first to speak, his remark tinted with impatience as he said, "I'm beginning to wonder if those red skins are going to bother looking for us."

"I hardly think that the war dance down there is a practice session," said Lance. "They'll show their hand before long."

"You may be right," agreed Turley as he quickly pointed toward several braves that suddenly broke away from a group that were huddled a short distance from the dancers.

"That could be the scouting party," said Lance with a hint of anxiety. "Let's hightail it to where the trail doubles back. If they don't come out that far, then they are convinced that we are on our way to the river, and that they'll report back."

"And if they come out all the way?" questioned Turley.

"We'll discuss that while we're waiting for them back there. Come on."

At the telltale part of the trail where the double back occurred, the grim reaper waited patiently for those who would betray the secret of the horseless patrol. The leaves that fluttered lightly in the soft breeze were the only visible things in action. The rest of Mother Nature's beings were at a stand still, as if aware of the tense situation that actually existed. Well concealed in the thick of laurel, with piercing eyes geared for immediate detection, the two scouts awaited the potential informers.

After several minutes of silence, Turley shot a question at Lance, jarring him out of his thoughts. "How many are you expecting, Captain?"

"One or two," was the reply.

Turley frowned, indicating the fact that he had a larger number in mind. After a moment or two, he spoke again. "How do you plan on meeting the boys this morning?"

Lance was about to reply, but hesitated, as his eyes caught the movement of the scout's hand, which sported a knife that was slowly being dragged back and forth on the leg of his pants as if polishing it for inspection. He asked instead, "You going to slice some bacon this morning?"

The scout shook his head in the negative, and then added, "Hide."

Lance's expression changed as his eye caught movement in the distance, and after closer observation, he said, "Just keep that thing handy, fella, the hide out there is on the move and coming toward us."

Turley peered in the direction briefly, and then uttered, "Two of them."

"They must have eaten energy food this morning," said Lance. "Got up here mighty fast. Unfortunately, we're going to relieve them of all that pep. Since the opposition is light we need no battle plans. You steal on back here a little ways. Wait a minute." Instructions halted as the Indian party stopped suddenly.

"They stopping for lunch?" Turley's remark didn't match the soberness of his face but a light smile appeared on his lips as Lance replied.

"I doubt it. Didn't see them carrying a blanket."

Nothing more was said as they watched the enemy in silence. It appeared to them that the discussion concerned the braves' next moves. Impatience got no chance to put in an appearance, for the conference was abruptly over and the Indians' strategy put into motion. One of them backtracked and headed for the Indian camp the other proceeded to follow the trail.

"Now get back here a little ways," said Lance as he kept his eyes on the swiftly moving enemy. "We're going to have to end this fellow's career as a scout."

Moments later, they were in position for battle. Two steel blades were out of their sheaths, ready to cut through the cool morning air, slicing their way toward their target. The target was quickly closing in, unaware of the nearness of the enemy, unaware that his chances of ever becoming a chief and wearing a full head dress grew fainter with each forward step.

For a long moment, Lance looked beyond the enemy in search for a sign of the other brave, then focused his eyes back on the target, satisfied that the other had disappeared completely. He then snapped his head back for a quick look at Turley's position and got a wink from the latter, indicating readiness. As Lance resumed his former position, a bewildered expression befell his face and his eyes danced about in all directions, trying to spot the fast moving brave who, a few moments before, was in clear view. There was no sign of the Indian. He had suddenly vanished. In the rear, Turley was craning his neck, trying to pick up some sign of the brave and was quickly overcome by impatience as he called out in a loud whisper.

"Where in the hell is that Injun. I lost him."

Lance replied with a quick motion of his hand and the puzzled Turley soon scrambled to his side and asked, "What happened?"

"I don't know. We take our eyes off him for a second and he disappears."

"Maybe he stumbled and fell."

"He would have been up by now."

"Could he have caught some sign of us?"

"I doubt it but I won't say no."

"The fall could have been deliberate."

"Could be," agreed Lance. "Laying there in wait for the unforeseen enemy to make a move, should there be some nearby that may have spotted him is an old trick."

"We going to wait him out?"

"We'll give it a little time but let's keep our eyes covering the area just in case he plans to sneak ahead close to the ground for a while."

A full five minutes went by without incident. Lance took a deep breath and sighed heavily as if he had held his breath during that time. Baring his teeth as if in display could have indicated uncertainty concerning the matter. The scout finally spoke with a tint of disgust. "Damn if I don't think he's taking a nap."

"Should I tip-toe over and wake him up," said Turley.

"That remark isn't as funny as you may think," said Lance. "We're both going to where we seen him last. We can't afford to lose this boy. He's concealed somewhere around those large rocks and fallen trees. I'll circle around to the right of that spot. You circle round the left. Use your rifle only as a last resort. If he wants to play hide and seek, let's accommodate him. Ready?"

"Ready," came the reply.

Lance made a move, then glanced over his shoulder and asked, "Any questions?"

"No questions, Captain."

"See you later."

"That's a promise," said Turley as he moved out to the left. The scouts advanced slowly and in a crouching position. After a progress of about fifteen yards, Lance looked toward Turley, who caught his eye and returned the glance without any indication. With the conclusion of the silent message, the scout motioned lightly with his hand and they proceeded with the task. Although their eyes favored the spot of the expected enemy hideout, nevertheless, quick glances in other directions were directed for the possible unexpected.

They stole along almost noiselessly although they were quite tense and alert. The presence of the lone brave would hardly quicken the pulse under the circumstances, but they were keenly conscious of the consequences should the enemy send out a signal. A short time later, tension soared upward as the scouts came in line with the boulders and with a halt signal from Lance, began to close in toward the suspected hideout. Two pairs of eyes searched behind fallen trees, in and around uprooted tree trunks, anywhere else a body could be concealed. At the same time they were ready for the sudden attack by the enemy who they surely were prepared to quarrel with, should the opportunity arise.

The two scouts, though quite a distance apart, met each others' eyes warily. Lance, whose crouching body was as tense as the string of a pulled back bow and arrow, stood up slowly upon the realization that they may have lost their target. Turley, still crouching, pushed through a thick bushel of laurel growth to peer around a bit more, hoping to find a clue as to the location of their suddenly missing Indian target.

In a blink of an eye, Lance noticed that the tree branches high above Turley's head began to rustle and crack, and suddenly their previous singular target, the lone red man, launched himself out of the tree above and onto Blade Turley's back. Turley quickly crumpled to the ground. The more seasoned scout ran toward his friend; in any other circumstance, Turley might have been able to throw the enemy off his back in a flash. But the surprise, in addition to Turley's unfortunate crouching position prior to the attack, startled him, which made his struggle with the Indian that much more difficult.

No words were exchanged in that heated moment. Lance, being quick on his feet and in his thinking, threw his body toward the quarreling pair, but not before his knife was drawn and bared at an angle that would surely slice through whoever was unfortunate enough to meet its tip. The timing could not have been more precise, for the instant Turley turned, his body covered by the Indian whose bare back was exposed, Lance's knife slid into the red man's flesh as if it found its home.

The brave let out a strangled howl just as a little spray of blood splattered from his mouth and onto the back of Turley's sweaty neck. The scout, now holding the weight of a dead red man draped across his back, winced and looked up at Lance, who stood above him, catching his breath. Upon their eyes meeting, Lance lifted a finger to his mouth to motion for silence. Immediately Turley realized why: this brave was only one of the pair that left camp. They had to find and catch the other one, or else the threat of exposure was far more possible than before.

Lance turned around quickly at the sound of a twig cracking. His breathing had steadied and so had Turley's, and the dead red man's chest lay flat and steady, as he had already left this plane to take his forever-journey to the happy hunting grounds in the sky. The able-bodied scout's eyes narrowed to a point, and he held his breath to aid his hearing. There was an Indian nearby, Lance could feel it. He could sense the red man close by, but couldn't see his target. He let out his breath slowly and drew in another one, as silent as can be. His whole body was tensed, waiting for a sign of his attacker, but he dared not make the first move without indication of the location the brave might reside.

That's when Lance caught the sight of—and not the sound of—the enemy. It was rather unusual for the soldiers of the wild to be spotted by such means, but these were extraordinary and certainly unplanned circumstances. The rustling of leaves behind a smattering of bushes less than thirty feet from the pair of scouts gave the Indian soldier away, especially, Lance noted, since no other wind moved through the path; nothing else would have caught those bushes but the suspicious red man.

Inside a ten-second window, Lance heard the sharp snap of a bow releasing an arrow through the brush. There was nothing he could do but duck. He closed his eyes hard enough to produce a bright party of stars behind his eyelids, stars that on another occasion would have reminded him of the night sky on a moonless patrol. But Lance bracing himself for meeting his maker was not necessary. Having not felt a pinch of pain, the scout opened his eyes and looked around, only to notice the arrow, complete with its painted and carved tail, sticking out of the ground directly in between where the pursuer had to have been perched, and Lance himself.

Lance looked at the arrow, then back up to the thicket of bushes, and back at the earth. He was speechless. Never in his whole career of scouting and Indian relations did he ever experience an arrow from a red man miss its mark by that much. He swallowed hard and let out the breath he had been holding, his whole body relaxing just a mite.

Turley bit back a chuckle and cleared his throat. "Ain't no Indian anymore, Captain. Looks like we're the ones who been rescued this time." He nodded his head in the direction of the original hiding place of the brave. Crawling through the thicket was a familiar face, one that had seen and experienced many of the precarious moments the two scouts had lived through as of late: Stenton.

"You all right?" Stenton's voice was even, but the look on his face betrayed his attempt at mild manners. His brow was creased deeper than Lance had ever seen it, even on occasions when he had taught him a lesson in class. In addition to the furrow on his face, Stenton's hands were covered in fresh blood.

"Are we all right? You're the one who looks like he's about to bleed out," Lance remarked, acknowledging the blood.

"First time I ever had to kill a man with my bare hands." Stenton's voice shook now, though he swallowed hard and made every effort not to reveal just how shaken up he was. "I'm no good with throwin' knives, not like this here Turley is. So when I came to check on you, I was sneakin' up, tryin' to keep quiet since I didn't know what happened to you. You been gone longer than Drum thought you should. And I seen that Indian back there with his bow and arrow trained on something and I figured it couldn't be a deer, not with the ruckus I heard just a minute earlier. So, I came up from behind. He must not have heard me, 'cause I just opened up his throat like . . . " His voice trailed off as he took his handkerchief out of his pocket and tried to clean his hands.

Turley, attempting to help the younger soldier wrap his mind around the difficult situation he just came through, added a little humor. "Just think of it as you doing him a favor. Had I seen him first, I'd have strung him up by his ankles and taught him a lesson far worse than the ones Lance here taught you back at the fort."

Stenton let out a nervous chuckle. "I believe that, Turley. Winsor here took it easy on me, as far as I recall." He smiled at Lance, who looked at him laughingly.

At this, Turley let out a laugh and a sigh simultaneously. "Help your old friend up, would you? I think I may need to see a doctor when we get through with this here mission." He held out his hands, and Stenton and Lance helped heave him to his feet.

Turley stood and made every effort in his power to straighten out his back, but he was hunched over in such a way that he'd be riding back to camp sidesaddle, and mighty slowly, at that.

"Luckily for you," cut in Lance as he watched his friend struggle to get upright, "I witnessed you getting thrown to the ground from way up in that tree. At least you have me who can vouch for the fact. If I hadn't seen it happen with my own eyes, I bet Dawson would have a field day with you bein' all bent over and crooked like this. Might suggest we send you to a home where you could get around-the-clock care." Turley rolled his eyes and laughed a small, hardy laugh, though he thought twice of it when it caused him pain. His back cramped up and his face, too, contorted in ways that Lance hadn't seen just yet and hoped he'd never have to again, for it appeared that his friend may have permanently injured the part of his body most responsible for long scouting journeys into the wilderness.

Lance and Stenton each took one of Turley's arms and wrapped it over their shoulders, nearly carrying him out of the bushes. The walk was much shorter on the return than it had been on the way there, and upon seeing the patrol sitting concealed as best as they could be under the circumstances, Lance let a smile of relief and happiness spread across his face.

"Captain," he started, unable to control his joy, "I can't say there's been a time when I was happier to see you. We're reporting from our mission, sir. All intact, though one of us is most likely not going to be doing much scouting in the near future." He nodded to Turley, who sat bent over on a boulder that appeared to have been made perfectly in size and shape for this occasion.

"I'm all right, Captain," remarked Turley, who at this point was feeling a mixture of back pain and embarrassment. "Worst part of all of this is that I'm taken out of duty, sir. Couldn't do much scoutin' from this position now, I'm afraid."

Drum turned to face Lance and Turley, and paused, for he had another person to ask questions of first. "Stenton."

"Yes, sir."

"How is it you came upon helping the scouts? I thought you were merely checking to see where they were, and the orders I gave you were not to interfere unless absolutely necessary."

"Sir, you're correct. But it was absolutely necessary."

Drum said nothing, but his raised eyebrows spoke the volumes his voice did not.

"Captain, we knew nothing of Stenton's presence until the arrow that was meant for my heart met its end in the clay earth about ten feet from where I stood, utterly helpless to the potential threat of bow and brave. Stenton spotted the enemy and took him out before he took me out."

"I see," answered Drum. "And where were you, Turley, at the time of this attack?"

Turley took in a breath and winced again. He held out a hand to gesture that he needed a moment to catch his breath, and then he spoke. "I had already been injured, Sir. I was attacked by a brave who, if I hadn't known better, had flown into a tree to drop on me from up high. We wrestled until Lance here came up from behind and introduced him to the sharp end of his knife. That's when the arrow split the earth and we saw Stenton here climb out through the brush. Happiest change of plans I'd ever had."

Drum nodded, seemingly understanding the situation enough to trust that the aspect of the journey that sat on the scouts' shoulders had been completed. "Gentlemen, our horses."

"But what about White Cloud? Can he have gotten that far by now?" asked Lance curiously.

"They are far enough down to the river now that we should have no problem retrieving our horses and heading out. Stenton, I'll need to have you do double duty and make sure to bring back Turley here's mount."

"Yes, sir," came the reply.

The captain called out to his troops and, single file, they started toward the mouth of the meadow, which sat in the small valley that housed the hidden horses. Lance, volunteering to stay with Turley, kept him company with nothing more than his presence, for he understood that at the moment, the other scout's pride was as equally bruised as his posture.

The morning was turning golden and quite warm by the time the patrol returned with the horses, though the thick branches high above only revealed scattered sunshine. A breeze gently blew through the forest floor every few minutes, cooling the sweaty brows of the animals and men alike. It took four men to hoist and prop Turley up into a position on his horse that was comfortable to him. As it turned out, that position was in fact sitting side-saddle, with three blankets wadded up in a ball and propped in front of his crooked frame, for added support.

Lance knew the pain would be almost more than Turley could bear, and he knew that they had at least three or four more hours of riding before they got back to Fort Laramie. He wondered if his friend would be alright with the regular motion of the patrol moving forward.

The scout lifted his head toward his friend, who sat upon his saddle, leaning on the balled blankets, just waiting for the patrol to begin their return to the Fort. "Hi, Soldier. I know it isn't much, but I wondered if you and me could ride side by side, and you could tell me about some of your travels. You know, to keep your mind occupied."

Turley nodded and laughed. "Oh, I'll be alright, Captain. This here's nothing that can't be fixed. But I do appreciate your offer and would like nothing more than your company. Come to think of it though, it might be best if you did the talkin', instead of me." He smiled at his friend, and Lance nodded in agreement, understanding that the other scout might find talking a mite painful, given the circumstances.

Lance collected his mount from the rear of the patrol and met Turley, who hadn't moved a stitch. "Who'd have thought Blade Turley to be quiet on the last stretch home," he chuckled and smiled laughingly.

Turley's eyes watered as his animal jolted forward a mere inch without warning. Perhaps it was the excitement building with the patrol gathering together, headed back toward the fort, for there was no sign of anything unusual in the vicinity. The injured scout blinked back the tears that threatened to spill over on to his blanket-support. He inhaled and exhaled quickly, letting his cheeks fill up with air as he let the breath out. "You may or may not know this," he said to Lance, pausing to take another breath in and slowly let it out. "But there couldn't have been anything else that would have made this journey any better at this time, Captain. I appreciate the gesture; it will surely make the time pass quicker with you tellin' me stories along the way."

Lance lowered his head, tipping his hat to the other. "I know you would do the same for me. There are certain things you learn about your friends when the situation presents itself to vulnerability, especially out in the wild. You, Blade Turley, are a true soldier." Lance said, trailing off to create an affect.

Turley didn't have a chance to respond, for in that quiet moment, all the men had mounted their animals —all but Lance—and Drum made the hand signal to fall in line and head down the trail toward the Fort. In order to ride as close to his friend as possible during the journey, Lance sprung up from his statue-like pose and nearly leaped onto his animal, securing the saddle and reins only after the mount was in motion. He caught up with Turley, who was undoubtedly feeling the effects of the regular bounce of the ride, though he showed no signs that anything was amiss. The scout rode alongside his friend on the trail for an hour without incident before the entire party was pulled to a halt at once.

Stenton rode back to the pair of scouts from the front of the trail. "Blood. On the trail. Small amounts at first, but then it becomes heavy, and it looks real fresh. Captain Drum wants you to scout ahead, Winsor. I'll stay here with Turley."

Lance nodded without questioning, though the blood on the trail, fresh and heavy, could mean a few things. It wasn't likely to be a tracked animal, for deer and elk hardly made their appearances at well-travelled trails such as the one they were on. In addition to this fact, if Drum thought it were animal blood, there'd be no use in scouting ahead. *He must be certain its human blood,* he thought as he dismounted and hurried ahead.

When he met up with Drum and his mount, the captain didn't speak any words to confirm or deny his suspicions, though he motioned with his hands to where the evidence lay on the trail and where he thought it might lead. Not much in this world, besides an ambush or first kiss, caused Lance's heartbeat to flutter out of nerves, but for some reason, his heart knocked inside his chest like a panicked, caged animal. He noted the physical sensation with curiosity, wondering what he understood primally that his conscious mind did not yet visualize. Perhaps it was the mere fact that he was, once again, scouting alone, which was something he had not had to do since meeting Turley just a few short weeks ago.

As the scout crept silently along the well-worn path, he thought back on his meeting Turley. His memories, though peppered with intense danger and extravagant adventures, as well as a little jealousy if he was being honest with himself, were nothing but fond. He hoped the memories would continue, that he would have the chance to make more of them with his friends, just under less strenuous circumstances.

The trail of blood that Lance was following turned from what one might describe as a light trickle into a steady stream. It went up ahead, thicker and darker, and then suddenly, the blood stopped. Heart pounding, head swirling, and curiosity piqued, the faithful scout paused to listen for any sound that might betray the source, but none came. Once, he heard the decidedly accidental shuffle of a horse far behind him on the trail, but nothing from ahead, so he pressed on. Where the trail's blood turned to the right and off the beaten path, Lance turned off the trail to follow it.

His discovery, which he found once he peeked around an ancient elm tree, was laying on a pile of dead bush. It was a human, indeed. An Indian one, with a full headdress on that would signify authority: a chief. As Lance approached, he noticed six arrows sticking out of the chief's body; the most noticeable one clear through his neck and out the other end. Remarkably, he still looked chiefly, but upon closer examination, through the smeared blood and tattered attire, Lance could see exactly who he was. The scout realized in that moment that if there was a god, it existed here and now, and for him. The dead chief laying before him was none other than White Cloud himself.

Lance never thought he would be in such a lighthearted mood after seeing so much death up so close, but seeing this body changed his whole future along the Little Big Horn. In a flash, he went from wondering whether or not he would ever live in peace with his friends and his wife, or have the opportunity for a normal life of any kind, to having all of his problems solved in one fell swoop. He dropped to his knees to get a closer look and noticed that the arrows—all six of them—had the markings of the Sioux tribe that once belonged to Big Bear.

"Deer Foot!" he exclaimed in a hushed voice. He didn't know if there were any other Sioux around that may pose a threat, though his instinct told him the answer was in the negative. Deer Foot, he mused. He got his revenge. Finally. And now we can live in peace. If I ever see that young brave again, I owe him a debt. He gave me back my chance at a happy life, he thought as he pushed up to a standing position and backed away. Lance turned and made his way back to the patrol in a low, quiet crawl, for he wanted to avoid drawing any more attention to himself in the event there were others of White Cloud's tribe nearby.

When Drum saw the scout approach, his previously slack face drew in an expression of worry, though it was only due to the present activity. Lance skidded to a stop at the head of the patrol, knowing he had the best news he could ever convey to the captain, though he suddenly realized that it might not be as much of a triumph for Drum as it was for him.

"Captain. It's White Cloud," Lance remarked through ragged, cheery breaths.

Drum perked up and looked around in a panicky moment. "White Cloud?"

"Yes, that's his blood. He's dead. Off the trail up ahead, less than a minute's walk from here. Deer Foot killed him."

"How do you know it was Deer Foot?" Drum remarked, looking more and more relaxed and eager.

"It was his father's tribe's arrows. They paint them with a certain color at the tips so they can identify them. Trust me, Captain. It was Deer Foot. And I have never been more happy that an Indian was dead than I am right now."

Drum smiled and turned to his patrol. "Gentlemen," he said, catching as many ears as the vicinity would permit. "We have much to celebrate. Hang on to your reins as long as you can. I reckon we'll only be on trail another two or three hours. We'll be there by sundown for sure. And when we get to the Fort and get all cleaned up, meet in the center square. Much to celebrate, much to celebrate."

At that, Lance turned and walked back to Turley, who, despite the dull aching in his back, was in a cheerful mood as well. "It's a good day, my friend," remarked Turley just as Lance was saddled up and ready.

Lance responded in kind. "It's a good day, indeed, my friend. A good day, indeed."

XXIX

The early afternoon air was sticky and hot, for ole sol himself was making a starring appearance and quite obviously edged out any chance for a breeze that would relieve the patrols' sweaty brows. The terrain was all too familiar to them now, as they were but a mere handful of miles away from their desired destination. There hadn't been a place in the last several hours that could provide a watering rest for the animals and their riders, but that didn't matter. Soon they would enter through the gates of Fort Laramie, the place of refuge and rest in such uncertain times.

Lance looked over at Turley, whose face could not conceal his discomfort, but which was also mixed with an expression of excitement. The more seasoned scout looked forward, keeping his thoughts to himself in this moment, as he was considering the best time to tell Turley of his resignation but was clear that this moment was not the most effective one. The other, having developed a loyalty to Lance Winsor, might possibly deny the fact, or chuckle and laugh as if Lance were telling a tall tale. This time, though, the choice was made up in the Indian scout's mind: he was through with scouting. His wife, the only woman who ever gave him hope for happiness, was waiting for him now, and there was no amount of convincing in the world that would sway him away from his new mission.

The mounts at the front of the patrol began making noises of excitement and recognition; *they must see the gates of Laramie,*

Lance mused to himself. He smiled knowingly and looked at his friend, whose previously mixed expression was now one of pure happiness. *In just a short while,* Lance thought to himself, *all this danger business will be over. I wonder how Turley plans on going forward? I should ask him about that later, but not here, not now, Winsor. Not with the ears of the Captain so close as to possibly overhear. No, I will give him some space and let him tell me what his plans are,* he concluded.

Up ahead, the fort stood tall and strong, as it was the solitary structure along this stretch of former Indian Territory. As if the gates themselves spoke, they commanded from the patrol an overwhelming relief, for the hours in the not so distant past were hours that they would soon have to recount but would all much rather forget.

As the patrol approached the fort, the gates swung wide to allow the patrol through, whose width narrowed like a funnel to fit inside the gate. Something beyond Turley caught Lance's eye, something that drew him toward it but that he would not presently attend to: the glistening waters of the Laramie River. In that small moment, Lance imagined his ranch along the Little Big Horn with Naomi. He imagined his friends, Dawson and Turley, coming along with him to start their new lives and work the land, living out their days in the peace of the wild and with the protection of a not-far-off settlement. Lance wanted to remember this moment, the last moment in the frontier as a scout, for just beyond the walls of Fort Laramie was his next biggest challenge: handing in his resignation to General Terry and telling his friends of the news.

When the last of the men on their animals passed through the oversized gate, the guards on duty went into action and swiftly closed and locked them. Turley looked at Lance with his eyebrows raised in surprise. "Is it just me, Captain," he remarked, adjusting his sitting position to look at the scout more squarely. "Or are these security measures a little more on the extreme than they were when we left last time?"

Lance shook his head in the affirmative. "It's not you. Something must have happened to cause the general to reinforce the gates. I'll see about asking him when I see him next. Listen, Turley—" the scout's words cut off quickly as he noticed a fair-haired girl with clear blue eyes running toward the now-dismounting patrol.

"I am so glad to see you. You had me worried sick!" Helene caught her breath just as she halted in front of the scout, who dismounted upon her approach. She threw her arms around his shoulders in an embrace that said far more than her words did, and Lance knew in that moment that she was unaware of how much he knew about how she had betrayed him.

He drew away from her, her arms still entangled around his shoulders, her face telling a story of genuine sadness and concern. She looked older now than she had the last time he had seen her, with new crease lines appearing in her brow and around her mouth. *She must have been frowning a great deal, Winsor, and I bet you were the reason for it,* Lance thought to himself.

"Hello, Helene," came the reply. He stood back a step and looked at the young woman questioningly, not revealing the contempt he held for her in his heart, the contempt he felt for this woman who so coldheartedly made every effort to destroy his new wife's freedom.

At Lance's puzzling look, Helene matched his in kind. She tilted her head at him, like the way a dog would who was unsure of the words coming out of its master's mouth. The crease in her brow revealed itself again, further confirming to Lance that she was desperate for him to receive her welcome home as if she were his.

"I'd like to talk to you, if you don't mind, Helene. But first I have some other business to attend to in General Terry's quarters." At this, the unsuspecting woman gave no indication that anything else was amiss, other than perhaps needing to wait for their reunion until a bit later.

She nodded at Lance, reaching out her hand to grab his in a gesture that she had hoped would confirm or deny his affection. In that moment, however, the scout turned to his animal to retrieve his canteen and did not take her hand in return. *Maybe he just didn't see it,* she thought to herself, taking her hand back and adjusting her hair and blouse so as to appear preoccupied with another matter.

"I'll be waiting, Lance Winsor. I told you I would. I am just so relieved to see you alive . . ." Her voice trailed off with a tint of weariness and her eyes met the ground with her silence. The soldier nodded at her comment as if to acknowledge that he understood her feelings, though he could not understand how this woman could be so unaware of his knowledge of the truth. He turned on his heel towards Terry's quarters and also nodded to Turley, who at that moment was receiving aid from four servicemen who were in the process of lifting him off his horse and setting him down on the hard packed dirt that served as the fort's floor.

Lance met Terry's guard with a relaxed posture and a face that revealed nothing of the news he was on the verge of delivering. The guard, being aware of Lance's status in the army, as well as his successful missions, let a small smile cross his face as he nodded and went into the interior of the general's quarters. When he returned, he held back the heavy canvas that served as the door to the threshold, whereupon the scout entered and found the general pacing inside along the far wall.

"Winsor, Winsor. You and the men have returned. I am relieved to hear it, and also, terribly disappointed to hear about Custer," he remarked, his voice gruff and stern as if he were retelling details that did not involve the death of his friend and fellow leader.

"Sir," came the scout's unsteady reply, as he bowed his head momentarily to acknowledge his own disappointment in the loss of the patrol of which General Custer was the leader. "It is a day that, for all of us, is both joyful and sorrowful, as you just said yourself."

General Terry said nothing in response to this comment, for it appeared he was lost in a thought. His face bore the resemblance of concentration and focus, though he stared off into the air just beyond the scout, focusing on something that was only there in his imagination. After a moment of silence between the two loyal servicemen, one of whom was in charge of the expansion of the current military forces in this area, General Terry motioned for Lance to sit down.

"I fear, Winsor, you have some news for me that you had to deliver by yourself, otherwise you would have come with others in your patrol. Is it intelligence or new information that we can use to our advantage in our advancement?" The general's eyes were big with curiosity as he looked at the scout questioningly, waiting for the answer to his question.

"No, well, yes and no, Sir," replied Lance. He leaned forward in his chair, showing attentiveness and concern. "Sir, White Cloud is dead, and there is reason to believe that he met his end from the revenge of Deer Foot, the son of Chief Big Bear, who White Cloud slaughtered mercilessly not too long ago."

At this, the general sat up straighter and leaned his head in with more tension. "What is your reason to believe this? You're confirming that White Cloud is dead, and that you believe Deer Foot killed him?"

"Yes, Sir. Arrows with the markings of Deer Foot's Sioux tribe were stuck in White Cloud's body when I came upon it along the trail not more than a few hours ride from here. Six arrows, to be exact. He appears to have been the only target, and there were no more bodies nearby when we came upon him, Sir."

General Terry nodded with pensiveness. Though a smile did not appear even to crease his stern and hard-focused mouth, it was visible to the scout that the general's composure relaxed just a little, revealing a sense of relief that was there but hardly noticeable. "Good, good. This is excellent intelligence." The general looked across his table at Lance, who sat with a look on his face that could be conceived of as nothing other than anxiousness.

"Sir, there's something else," Lance answered, knowingly filling the silence that the general and he shared but was his responsibility to fill. "I am officially turning in my resignation as scout, Sir. I'm retiring from the military." The scout sat back in his seat, a weight as heavy as iron lifted from his chest, and he waited for the reply that he was sure was to be angry, disappointed, and perhaps even an attempt to convince him that his decision was not a sound one.

"I had a feeling, Winsor," came the reply. The scout looked up at the general with surprise, his face not able to conceal his emotions. The general went on, smiling lightly and adding, "You have done an excellent job scouting for us, young man. I can't say that I am happy to see you go, but I am certainly disappointed in the most understanding way possible."

Lance nodded, slightly unsure of how else to respond. He had expected such a conflict and now that there was none, he was left with nothing prepared but the truth. "I plan on going downriver with my new wife, Naomi."

General Terry's eyes widened at the sound of the Indian woman's name. "Your *wife?* You married that Apache girl, did you? When did you have time for that while you were in battle most of the time?" The general let out a chuckle and leaned back in his chair, seemingly even more relaxed now than Lance had ever seen him. *Maybe this is easier to discuss for him than matters regarding the expansion,* Lance mused to himself as he gathered his thoughts on how to proceed further in the conversation.

The scout smiled and spoke laughingly next. "It is surprising what can be done in one night of rest at camp in between Indian battles, Sir." He looked at the general amusingly and watched as the other began to laugh loudly at his response.

"I see, I see," came the reply. "Well, I'm sure you two will be very happy. When do you plan your departure? Is she up at Bacon's camp still? My men heard about her unfortunate run-in with the Sioux captors outside the fort, as well as her retrieval from them. I suspect you will have to meet her up there before long?" He reached across his desk and opened up a tin box that was decorated with aged scratches and time, pulling out an already-rolled cigarette. He stuck a match and put the cigarette to his lips just as Lance leaned forward to stand up.

"Yes, Sir. She is at Bacon's camp. I plan to head out there tomorrow, after a good night's rest and saying my goodbyes to Drum and the patrol." The scout stood, a look of gratitude on his face before remarking, "I appreciate your kind words, General. You are doing excellent work here, and I do hope we see one another again in the future, just under different circumstances." Lance's mouth, serious at first, creased up in a smile that revealed just how happy he truly was.

"Winsor, the feeling is mutual," remarked the general as he stood and met the scout's eyes evenly. "You're the best scout we have ever had, and I hope to one day use your scouting as an example for all scouts. Best of luck to you, young man." He reached across his table, which was covered in maps of all sizes, and shook Lance's hand. He bowed his head at Lance as if to dismiss him and blew a puff of cigarette smoke above his own head to keep the air clear. Lance turned on his heel to leave the general's quarters when the guardsman pulled back the canvas.

"General, two other servicemen are here to see you, Sir."

General Terry's face bore a surprised look, with his eyebrows raising just the amount one would anticipate from a man who has seen the darkest parts of life.

"Send them in. I was just finished with Winsor, here," came the general's reply. Lance moved to step aside and let the new visitors pass by him on his way out, when he was halted by his own surprise. There were not many things that would have undone his composure any further than the sight that presented itself before him: Will Dawson and Blade Turley entering General Terry's quarters right in front of him.

Dawson removed his hat, as did Turley, albeit the latter was moving a little slower than his normal manner of walking. "General," said the old scout, nodding his head out of respect, as Turley followed suit.

"Might I stay for this, General?" asked Lance, as he worked to conceal the smile that tried to spread across his face, for he understood in this very moment that his two friends had the same idea about the end of their scouting careers as he had.

The general looked at the two new occupants in the room with a questioning look. Upon first glance, they both hesitated, for the news they were about to deliver was also in the negative for the leader of the westward advancement, and both Dawson and Turley knew that they stood a chance of upsetting the general very much. On the other hand, however, it appeared to them that for the moment, the general had taken Lance's news in a friendly manner, though they had only assumption to go on for the reason for the scout's private meeting with General Terry.

In response to the general's question, Turley looked up at him, then casually looked over at Lance, hoping for a brief moment of visual support, which he received in the manner of a slight nod of the head. This gave Turley the final push he needed. "General, both Dawson and I have come to relay to you the very news that Lance Winsor has delivered to you."

Will Dawson, seasoned scout and old-timer, stood silently next to a solid wood chair that only moments before Lance had sat in, discussing his future with the general. The old man shifted his weight from one foot to the other, and lifted his hand up to his beard, touching it nervously. It was clear to Lance that if his old friend weren't in the company of his superior, he would have spit his tobacco juice out onto the ground, a gesture that Lance understood was one way he kept his nerves at ease.

The general's expression was one of mild annoyance, but his voice did not reveal a single tint of such a feeling. He inhaled deeply before speaking, and then made his reply. "Gentlemen, I understand the pressures of the frontier. I understand them firsthand. Turley, it is a disappointment to me that I would lose your services so soon after I acquired them, but I also understand that when a man makes up his mind, it is made." Terry lifted his cigarette to his mouth once more before continuing to speak, and in that small moment, Turley relaxed visibly. The hardest part for him was over.

"Will Dawson, on the other hand . . ." the general started, and then trailed off for a moment before gathering his thoughts. "Will, you and I have been friends for longer than I remember. I am sad to see you go but am honored you stayed in our company this long. You've earned your retirement, old soldier." He moved around his drawing table and outstretched his free hand to Dawson, who took it quietly and looked the general square in the eye.

"Thank you for everything, General. It has been an honor scoutin' under your leadership, Sir." The two veteran soldiers, one in the leadership role and the other a lifetime of scouting and fighting, looked at each other in a brief moment that communicated mutual respect, for they had fought side by side for many years.

The general's non-verbal response was in the form of a polite arm wave, which prevented any further discussion of their retiring from scouting, whereupon they were dismissed out into the light of day. Just as they reached the outside and were past the heavy canvas, Dawson and Turley both stopped short, the latter of which was standing taller than he had earlier in the day when his injury was newest. Turley took one look at Lance's face and his own matched what his thoughts concluded. "Can you believe we did it? We all just quit scoutin'." He looked at his two friends, waiting for a reply, which came from the younger scout first.

Lance replied, laughingly. "I had no idea you two were plannin' on that. Could have told me, huh? So what . . . you both comin' with me? I'm headed to Bacon's tomorrow morning, and I hope not to ever have to scout for this here regiment ever again. I'm ready for that ranch down by the river," he said, his face beaming with the relief and excitement he felt at the prospect of having the opportunity he had dreamed of so often in recent weeks.

Dawson, whose weathered face also bore the resemblance of relief, cut in to respond to the laughing Lance Winsor's remark and plans to go downriver. "You two young coots have another thing comin' if you think you can survive that blan Injun country without your old friend, Will Dawson, over here." The old scout spit a stream of tobacco out of his mouth toward the hard packed dirt, and when it struck, a spray of dust rose above the earth as if in contemptuous response.

The three men made their way out from under the eave of the general's quarters and headed toward their own temporary quarters, where they would be able to get cleaned up and ready for an afternoon of celebrating the fact that most of them had returned safely. As they made their way through the center of the courtyard,

Lance caught Helene's eyes from where she stood at the opposite edge.

"Excuse me, fellas. I have a brief conversation to attend to. I won't be long; see you in a minute," he remarked as he broke away from their stride and headed toward Helene.

"You came back for me," she half-whispered at the scout upon his approach.

"That's not exactly right, Helene," he remarked at her, taking off his hat with his right hand and placing his other hand on his head as if the gesture would help stir up the right words from his mind. "I . . . " he began, stuck momentarily for how to frame his statement. He wanted not to be unkind, but by the same respect, he felt she deserved to know the truth–what he knew the truth to be–and that was a harsh reality. "I know everything, Helene," he finally decided upon, letting the words hang in the air for a few moments, letting the awkward silence do its job.

The young woman looked at Lance this time with surprise, as though she were unsure of how to respond. Almost immediately, she composed herself, drawing in a long breath and blinking back the emotions that could at any moment leak from her eyes like waterfalls. "About what, Lance? Everything about how I've loved you since the first day I met you and would do anything to be your wife?"

Her forwardness caught Lance by surprise. Even in his most desperate moments, never did he dare relay such vulnerable information to a person he cared for so deeply if he was unsure of their response. The scout cleared his throat and switched his hat from one hand to the other. "No. I know that you had Naomi captured so that she was no longer an obstacle to me, Helene."

"Naomi? You mean the Indian girl? But Lance, she is unimportant to our happi–" but Lance cut her off.

"That 'Indian girl' is now my wife, Helene. I was able to rescue her from the Sioux renegades that you handed her over to. I hope I am clear, because I am only going to say this once. Your actions were low, and not only did you try to destroy my happiness, but you almost destroyed many lives in the process. I am through with you, Helene.

There is nothing you can do or say that will change my mind. And unless you want your reputation to be tarnished by the truth of your actions, I suggest you leave me and my new wife to live out our days without your intrusion." Lance met her eyes with a serious stare, wanting to make sure his words made the impact he had intended them to.

Helene stuttered a few sounds that did not turn into words. After the scout was satisfied that she understood his meaning, he replaced his hat on his head and turned to leave, but not before he heard the fair-haired girl cry out, "I'm so sorry, Lance," before her words were caught up in her teary sobbing.

The next morning came swifter than the former scouts had anticipated. Perhaps it was the unfamiliar experience of sleeping indoors without the sound of Mother Nature keeping them company, or perhaps it was the silence that existed when no immediate threat of Indian ambush laid in the unseen darkness; but whatever it was that helped the scouts sleep so soundly that night was the very thing that also prevented them from rising with the sun, as they all had become so accustomed to. In fact, the sound sleep that Turley encountered was precisely what he needed to stretch out and fix his injury from the day before, which, it turns out, was merely a strained muscle.

After a much-savored pot of strong coffee, courtesy of Mrs. Tuffs, the three men gathered their few belongings, tidied up their cabin, and departed for the last time. Under other circumstances, they would surely revisit this cabin again, for it was the quarters designated to scouts upon their return from a mission. However, with their new decision to move on from this particular career path, they would never sleep in this dwelling again.

Dawson reached into his coat pocket and pulled out a plug of tobacco. He offered it right, and then left, to both Lance and Turley, though both men refused the offer with a look of polite distaste on their faces. The older gentleman laughed the men off, biting a piece from the section and replacing the larger piece in his coat. "Don't know what yer missin', I tell ya, fool boys," he muttered as they made their way toward the front gate of the fort.

As the men mounted their animals and made sure they said their farewells, the three of them began their journey up to the Bacons' camp, where they were sure to collect Lance's wife and begin their lives down on the ranch. Once they were on the trail and far enough away from the fort to inspire a need for conversation, Dawson led his mount toward Turley.

"Son, I have a serious question for you," came the first comment, which sounded light and polite, though Turley eyed the old man warily.

"I can't say you'll get a serious answer from me, but I know you are planning on asking anyway, so go ahead," replied the other. Lance followed behind the pair, close enough to hear the conversation but not close enough to appear as though he were minding their business.

The old man led his animal just a nose ahead of Turley's, enough so that he had to turn his body around slightly in the saddle to face the other. "I know you young'uns don't like advice from those of us with leathery skin and years in the wild, but I plan on tellin' ya my thoughts, even if you toss it all to the wind. It's you and that young lady up at Bacon's camp. What was her name?" Dawson's eyes turned down toward the passing ground as he searched his memory.

Turley's face reddened at the mention of the young woman, even though he hadn't even spoken her name aloud. "Mary Lou, old man," he said in response, aiding his friend in his memory loss.

"Right, Mary Lou. What do you plan to do with her?"

"Do? I don't plan on doing anything with her without her father's permission."

The old man slapped his knee in excitement and shot out a stream of tobacco at the bushes alongside the trail. "In all my years of scoutin', I don't think I ever laid ma' eyes on a lady who was as smitten as that young lady thar," he chuckled amusingly.

Turley smiled out of the side of his mouth in a way that almost resembled a person who was not positive he was happy. He looked out of the corner of his eye at the old scout, gauging his excitement, ready to respond with an equally sly comment in return, but to his best judgment, Dawson was being direct with him.

“For the first time since I met you, old man, I think I agree with you,” Turley said as the full smile appeared on his face. “I plan on asking Bacon for Mary Lou’s hand when we arrive. No time to waste, right, fella?” No more words were exchanged between the two, and Lance was sure that this break from bantering would be brief, mildly speaking.

XXX

It was a full day of traveling along the prairie, through forest and up and down several ridges, before the trio of former soldiers ascended the last stretch of mountain near Bacon's camp. At the top of the ridge, they paused to survey the goings on below, taking note of ole sol's position hovering over the edge of the western ridge, streaking the remainder of the sky with hues only found in vibrant sunsets. The scene was a classic picture, with dusk setting in, a campfire at the center of the settlement and busy people preparing for the evening's activities. No doubt there had not been word that the three former scouts were on their way and would be making an appearance, so they were careful not to take advantage of the element of surprise.

"What do you think? Should we just head down ridge side by side? Think we'll be welcome?" spoke Turley with a tint of amusement in his voice.

"Darn fool critter, you are, boy. If there were ever a place we were always welcome, it's this here camp. Now get down that ridge and let's get us a welcome party started. Go on, now. Go!" The old man shouted at Turley, who fought his laughter back in response to the seemingly serious expression on the other's face.

Lance, remaining silent until this moment, let out a loud chuckle and added, "I don't know what's got you so riled up to get down there. I'm the one with the wife in camp."

Turley looked at his friend, who was disguising his humorous expression with raised eyebrows and a forced straight line in his mouth. "Not for long, there, Captain," remarked Turley.

Dawson urged his mount forward and nodded ahead. "Wall, now. If you behave yourselves, you young coots, you both are in for a treat with the women folk." The old scout turned to Turley and spoke directly to him, his former tone of seriousness returning to him, if only for this one moment. "Don't you forget, Lance here ain't a captain anymore, ya hear?" Without waiting for the other to respond, Dawson urged his animal forward into a full gallop, leaving the other two scouts with no other option than to follow behind in a small cloud of dust, chuckling hardily as they rode on.

The settlers below hardly noticed the approaching men; they went about their business tending the fire, boiling water, cooking the nightly meal, and completing chores without taking notice. All but one woman, that is.

The Indian woman stood in her small home, which was adjacent to the Bacon residence at the center of camp. She had just sighed heavily, thinking about her husband and with a twinge of wonder if she would ever see him again, she looked up and out the open flap of canvas to see the approaching horsemen. Her heart leaped in her chest and began to beat so hard that she wasn't sure she would be able to calm herself down. As fast as her little feet could take her in a ladylike fashion, Naomi made her way out of her home and found a path toward her husband. She made no secret of her excitement upon the return of her husband—alive and well, at that. Her little feet raced through camp, dodging several barrels and three blocks of stacked-up firewood, and weaving around two full tents before she skidded to a halt at the sight of the already growing crowd. Wanting to make contact with her beloved scout sooner than later, and figuring the roundabout fashion would be the most effective option, Naomi found her way around the gathering settlers so she could surprise her husband from behind.

Most certainly, upon Mrs. Bacon's call that Winsor, Turley, and Dawson had returned to camp, the business of the evening shifted in the blink of an eye to the business of welcoming the three scouts. The men dismounted from their animals and led them to the nearby trough for watering, securing them to the posts before greeting the oncoming welcomers.

Lance happily shook hands with the men who approached him, slapping him on the back as a gesture of gratitude for the work he and the others completed in their defense against the Sioux. Worriedly, and perhaps with a slight amount of anxious anticipation, the former scout looked up and past the welcoming party, and a trace of disappointment spread across his face at the visible absence of his new wife, even though he was still happy to be welcomed so warmly.

Various other women approached only to a certain distance, nodding and waving and smiling, equally as grateful as the men in the welcoming party, but exceptionally more modest. As the crowd thinned out, Lance looked around even more nervously for Naomi, but his eyes were unable to locate his wife, whose honey colored hair and brown eyes were forever seared in his memory.

To his surprise, he heard her voice from behind him.

"Hello," came the familiar voice.

Lance spun around quickly, almost losing his balance in his excitement. He rushed forward, his whole body bouncing as he swept his wife up into his arms and spun her around in an embrace that would make any woman swoon. A rare sight, the Apache woman smiled and pure joy appeared on her face. And then as Lance spun her, the smile quickly gave way to a small laugh, whereupon Lance stopped spinning abruptly and set her down.

She tucked the hair that had come loose in their embrace back behind her ears and smoothed out her dress. "Is everything ok?" she said, her joyful expression threatening to turn into worry. She could hardly contain her excitement, but she had learned a certain amount of female modesty in the last week while Lance had been gone.

"Yes! Yes. I . . . I just have never heard you laugh before, and I wanted to see what your face looked like when that happened." The scout reached up and touched her chin with his thumb and forefinger, softly tracing the outline of her mouth. Naomi lifted her hand to his, cupping her face in his hand and walking into his arms.

Lance held her there for a moment before speaking, and he did so with much more certainty than he ever had up to the moment. "Naomi, I will never leave you again. Do you understand me? I am finished with the military. We can go build our home now."

She leaned away from him to look into his eyes, which told the truth of how he felt about leaving and how sorry he was that he had to leave in the first place. Never had Lance been so inspired to live fully before this very moment. He looked deeply into her eyes, searching for the right words to say to ease the confusion and happiness that spread across her face as the next thought approached her mind. "What about White Cloud?" she asked questioningly.

The scout smiled reassuringly at his wife and touched the long braid that hung down her back. He let his fingers dwell on the thickness of her hair, understanding another aspect of being in the presence of his wife. His voice shook at the start of his next sentence but then evened out with confidence as he spoke. "White Cloud is dead. Deer Foot killed him. And before you ask if I'm sure, I am. I saw his body with my own eyes. We don't have to worry about him anymore," he said.

Naomi exhaled heavily, letting out weeks worth of tension she had been carrying in her mind without being fully aware of it. Her whole body relaxed into her husband's arms, and her words would have been lost as a murmur in his chest if he had not had such keen hearing. "Thank you for coming back. For everything. I am so happy to be your wife."

Lance held her there in that embrace for several moments longer, letting his breathing fall in tune with hers, letting their heartbeats return to their own rhythmic pattern. He drew in a long breath, inhaling the scent of her hair and her skin before speaking again. "I plan on doing everything in my power, for the rest of my life, to make sure you'll always be happy to be my wife." He kissed the top of her head and held the hand of his bride, whom he'd fought so hard for and who had found a place in her heart for him, leading her away from the crowd for a long overdue, sweet twilight walk.

Around the campfire that evening, Naomi and Lance sat on a fallen log that served as a bench and stared at the fire, speaking only occasionally about their plans to go downriver and make their home. There had been some talk of the pair bringing with them a few other more adventurous settlers, though that matter had not been decided upon as of yet.

Lance had not paid too much attention to his two friends since their arrival at the Bacon camp just a few short hours ago, but across the fire, he noticed Turley and Bacon engaged in a civil conversation, far enough away so that they would not be overheard by any straying ears. *Wonder what that's all about,* Lance mused to himself. Bacon thrust his hand out toward the other in a gesture of acceptance of whatever deal had been made, and in response, Turley shook it with firm certainty. Just as Lance thought it wise to perhaps detach himself from his current sitting position and engage himself in their deal making, the pair rejoined the talking and laughing residents of Bacon's camp.

Mary Lou sat several feet away from the Winsors at the fire, talking with her mother and another one of the older settler women, when Lance saw him approaching the young woman rapidly. *This is it,* Lance thought to himself. *Turley is finally going to settle down, and with Mary Lou. Well, I'll be . . .* Lance's thoughts were a mixture of memories of the time when he thought Turley might actually love Naomi and the excitement of the future for the scout who would, if all went as planned, be settling downriver with Lance and Naomi.

In the very moment that his feet planted in front of Mary Lou, the crowd of visitors went strangely silent, as if they had all been waiting for this one occasion. Turley held out his hand to Mary Lou, who looked from her mother to Turley and back and then took his hand nervously. She swallowed hard and visibly, as though it suddenly became a motion she had to remind her throat to do.

"Mary Lou?"

"Ye . . . Yes?" the poor girl muttered, her heart thumping wildly in her chest and her palms sweating from nerves.

"You know I think you're the prettiest thing in this land, and I couldn't help but stare the first time I met you. In fact, I think I catch myself staring still, even when I don't mean to," the retired scout said with a smile on his face, but one that was still cautious and ready to prove himself.

"And there's not a single girl in this here whole frontier who was able to steal my heart and take my sights off of Saint Louie," he said, stealing a look at Lance, who winked in response.

Turley continued his speech, taking Mary Lou's other hand, too, and holding them both up to his chest, as if he were asking her to join him in his excitement. "I would like nothing more than to make you my wife, if you'll have me," he finished, the silence of the night only letting through the sound of the crackling fire and the bated breath of the unintended audience.

What felt like eternity to Turley was only a mere few seconds, but in an instant, the young woman stammered, "Yes! Yes, I will!" and threw her arms around his neck in an enthusiastic embrace that even surprised the new groom-to-be. "Let's do it tomorrow! So we can go downriver with Lance and Naomi," she added, her excitement making the settlers clap and hoot with joy for the newly engaged couple.

At that, Turley laughed and nodded in the affirmative. "I don't think Lance here will have too much of a problem with that, now, will you, Winsor?"

"No problem at all, Turley, just as long as you two don't get into any trouble," said Lance, jokingly. He winked at his friend once more and then smiled down at Naomi, whose face also bore the mask of a happy woman in love. And as the settlers congratulated the pair and the fire died down, Lance, Naomi, and Turley walked Mary Lou back to her cabin.

"Soon we'll be saying goodbye and going to our own little home, isn't that right?" said Mary Lou to Turley with a bright and shining smile on her face.

At first, Turley could only smile in response to her comment, but after a moment of walking, he looked down at his almost-wife and said happily, "Soon is right. Very soon." With that, he leaned down and kissed the back of her hand and sent her inside for the rest of the evening.

The next day proved to be busier than the scouts thought. With any other wedding, such as Lance and Naomi's, the preparations that were to be made would no doubt reflect the generosity of the Bacon camp, and nothing less was to be expected. However, when the subject of the wedding was Bacon's daughter, well, the celebration and activity was at an all-time high.

As the day wore on and the men did what they were asked to, Turley expressed his nervousness to Lance only once, and it was a mild confession at that. "Any chance you think she'll decide no at the last minute?" he remarked questioningly at his friend as he paced his cabin.

"With all this going on? If she decided otherwise at this last minute, I'd say it would be better for you both, since she would likely not be in her right mind," the other reminded Turley, who paused his pacing to look at his friend. He nodded in agreement, took three deep breaths, and the nerves were never seen again.

The wedding went off without a hitch. Mary Lou's dress was no doubt the most elegant dress any settler wore to a wedding up until that point on the frontier. She composed herself in such a way that Turley fell in love with her all over again, and by the time the evening was over and the party-goers were making their way to their respective homes, Turley and his new wife stood at the edge of the campfire in a peaceful embrace, looking up at the dark sky that was dotted with flecks of unreachable stars. "We get to look at this together every night," Mary Lou said to her new husband. In response, the other pulled his wife into him in a more meaningful embrace, reaffirming that he, too, was happy they were to spend the rest of their lives together.

The next few days were busied with preparations, for both pairs of lovebirds made the firm decision to move downriver together and build their lives along the Little Big Horn. When it came time for them to depart, Lance and Turley met Dawson by the watering trough where he combed the mane of his trusted animal.

"Hey, old fella. You've been awfully distant there as we prepare to go downriver," said the former lead scout as he looked his friend in the eye.

Dawson stroked his beard and set the animal's comb down on the edge of the trough. He leaned up against the horse's post and took in a deep breath, seemingly searching for the right way to put his next thought. After he exhaled, a long and bellowing one, he looked at Turley and addressed him first.

"Blade . . . do ya mind if I call ya that? No? Good. Anyhow, I been thinkin' and there's nothin' I'd like more than to watch you two fool boys build ma' house down on the river, but the truth is, I'm nicer 'an that." The old man spit a stream of tobacco straight down at the ground, nearly missing his beard by a literal hair. Turley laughed at the whole scene, but it was a bittersweet laugh, for he knew what his old friend was saying.

"Old critter. You don't mind if I call ya that, do ya? Good? Ok, old critter. I understand that what you're sayin' is that you're stayin' here with the Bacons. Am I right?" He leaned in to his friend and noticed that Lance took a step in to speak rather quietly to their old friend.

"We'll miss you, Will. Best darn scoutin' party there ever was, us three. Promise you'll come down for a visit?" cut in Lance as he stuck out his hand to shake Will Dawson's.

"If I didn't know any better, I'd say there was a smile climbing up his face. But that beard makes it near impossible to tell exactly what's happening under there," cut in Turley before Dawson could answer Lance's request.

"Darn fool boy. You'll figure out what's under this here beard when my blood runs cold. But 'afore that, you can keep on wishin'. As for you," the old man turned to Lance. "I don't like makin' promises I don't know I can keep, so I'll promise you one thing: I'll try."

"Good enough, old friend. Good enough."

The farewell party was just as big of a sendoff as the welcoming party, although this time it came complete with two wagons full of supplies, a horse for each rider, and tearful goodbyes instead of excited hellos. Ole sol had only begun to rise, and the sky went from dark gray to light gray as the minutes wore on.

Mary Lou wept and hugged each of her friends, as well as her mother and a few other older women who had shown her affection in the past. Naomi, too, made her rounds of farewells and hugs, though the Apache woman's tears were dry, as she felt nothing but excitement to start her new life with Lance Winsor. The Bacon camp had proven to be the most welcoming group of settlers in her experience as a native in the western frontier, but that didn't change the fact that she carried with her a feeling of uncertainty when she was alone with them. She smiled warmly, a newly practiced facial expression, and said her thank yous to everyone for their kindness and hospitality.

As Bacon shook Lance's hand first, and then Turley's, he stopped and looked at them both seriously, adopting a sudden tone of concern. "If you ever need anything, and I mean *anything at all,* we won't be too far west of here. Less than ten miles. And don't let too much time pass without a visit, will you? Mrs. Bacon will be sick if she goes too long without seeing Mary Lou," the wagon master said to the both of them, his seriousness staying firm on his face. In unison, the pair of scouts agreed, nodding and expressing in the affirmative that they would do as they were asked.

At that, Mrs. Bacon gripped the sleeve of her husband's shirt, burying her face in his arm in an attempt to conceal her sobbing. Mary Lou walked in a ladylike fashion over to her mother so as not to excite her any further and pulled her from her father into a gentle embrace. "There, there, Mama. It's gonna be alright. I'll just be downriver, and you and Papa can come visit anytime you like. Just a few hours away, ok? And we'll come visit, too." The grown woman comforted her mother as if the roles were reversed, but this was to be expected. Mary Lou was embarking on a new journey that filled her with excitement that her mother did not have. The tearful Mrs. Bacon collected herself and took a deep breath inward.

"You're right, darlin'. I'll see you real soon. You just be safe, ok? Don't let them darn Ind—" she looked around to make sure she could speak freely, but lowered her voice to a whisper. " . . . just make sure you be safe, ok?" She pulled her daughter into one last quick embrace and then let her go just as quickly, backing up into a line with the farewell bidders.

Will Dawson stood away in the distance, nodding at the pair of his favorite scouts as they made eye contact with him across the dusty plain. He raised a hand up to his eyes as if to pinch something clean from them, though neither Lance nor Turley made any mention of it. Dawson had always been the most thoughtful of the three of them, so it came as no surprise that he was experiencing an increase in mistiness in his eyes on this occasion.

The riders and their animals mounted and pulled away from camp, hearing the shouts of farewell grow fainter and fainter with each passing gallop. After a short time, all that was left of the Bacon camp were the small outlines of people, far enough to cast a faint image of their true nature but not close enough to know them at all. With the only sound left as the rustling wind, the trotting of hooves and the quiet thoughtfulness of their breathing, some excitement mixed with deeper emotions, it was evident that their new lives had begun.

At the foot of the hill that crawled up and out of the valley where the camp rested, Lance paused for a brief moment to reach into his saddlebag to pull out his canteen and wet his whistle with a sip of water. He loosened the top and lifted the container to his lips when he felt something extra wrapped around the leather-encased container. The former scout kept his mount heading forward, his wife and company just ahead in his line of vision, whereupon he commenced the inspection of the external addition to his canteen.

Wrapped around the object was a leather cord, worn with age, oil, and time in a three-part braid. The cord was wrapped around the neck of the water container, and a small piece of parchment hung off the very end of the cord. On it were the inscribed words:

may these three cords
remind us of the days we spent givin
and savin, lovin, and sayin goodbye
one cord for each of us
separate, but always the strongest when we's together
may we never forget
and also
you young coots
better make sure to
take care of them women folk
-Will

Lance swallowed his feelings down in his throat with a painful effort, and when he looked up at Turley, who had turned around just in time to watch a salty tear escape the scout's eye, the morning sol cast a dusty glow about the four mounts and their riders. As quickly as the tear fell, it was wiped away, but the other made no mention of it. In fact, he slowed his mount to catch up with Lance's and leaned in to take a look at the parchment that his friend gripped tighter than he should.

Turley also felt the swell in his chest after reading the note and turned away to catch his breath and blame the mistiness on the rising sunlight. The note wasn't a final goodbye to the pair, no. It was merely an expression of the sentiments that their old friend held dearly, for the dangers they experienced and the happinesses as well created in them a bond that was unshakable, to speak mildly. Neither scout spoke of the memento in that instance, but as if in timed unison, they both rode up to the animal beneath their respective wives, leaned in, and gifted them with gentle kisses that expressed their true feelings of love.

And so it went that these four young people rode out of the valley on their horses with hope and excitement, and set out across the wilderness that led down toward the Little Big Horn River, where their dreams of starting a life together were finally coming true. As the pines swayed in the morning breeze, reminding them of Mother Nature's grace on the mountain ahead, the wind showed the way to the trail that the wagons and settlers would take to head downriver. The trail, now lit up with the golden rays of the earliest morning light, cast a delicate welcome path that surely let the riders understand that their new life and new path were in the right direction. Lance and Naomi, Turley and Mary Lou, and their futures as the first pioneers along the powerful river, would finally have their wish, and there was no amount of scouting that could have foreseen this most fortunate conclusion.

THE END

About The Author

Fred J. Bognar, known lovingly by his nieces and nephews as Uncle Fifi, lived the life of a humble renaissance man. Born in 1914, his careers included serving in the Navy Air Force during World War II from 1943-1945 and being a skilled tool- and die-maker for Kurtis Wright, where he retired after many years of loyal service.

In addition to the wide scope of skill in his professional life, Uncle Fifi had many recreational inclinations. He was passionate about theater and possessed an absolute love for music—for playing it, writing it, and recording it. That love was shared with his nieces and nephews, whose fond memories of their time together are treasured today. Uncle Fifi and his dear wife, Mary, who was truly his perfect match, spent their lives embracing the things that brought them joy, which included regular trips to Pocono Downs in Pennsylvania to watch the horses race. He is described by his family as a "brilliant man of few words," and his humility and excitement for his hobbies were the perfect mixture to keep him motivated to enjoy life while remaining out of the spotlight.

Beneath this list of his lifelong hobbies, however, lay the undercurrent of a deeper passion, one that he would throw himself into for most of his adult life until he was no longer physically able to: writing. Uncle Fifi's life's work, *The Cry of the Whippoorwill*, published posthumously, was his intellectual and creative outpouring for a great many years. For as long as he could, he dedicated himself to the quality, characters, and epic journey within the story, and as a result, he created a masterpiece that will be enjoyed for generations to come.

He is survived by his loving wife, and his memory and legacy will continue to live on in this work and in the hearts of those who knew and loved him best.

www.ingramcontent.com/pod-product-compliance
Lightning Source LLC
LaVergne TN
LVHW040824090826
845145LV00001BA/53

* 9 7 8 0 6 1 5 8 9 8 1 4 8 *